The Collected Shorter Supernatural & Weird Fiction of Algernon Blackwood Volume 3

ALGERNON BLACKWOOD

The Collected Shorter Supernatural & Weird Fiction of Algernon Blackwood Volume 3

Eighteen Short Stories & One Novella of the Strange and Unusual Including 'The Transfer', 'Entrance and Exit', 'The Eccentricity of Simon Parnacute' and 'The Temptation of the Clay'

Algernon Blackwood

LEONAUR

The Collected Shorter Supernatural & Weird Fiction of
Algernon Blackwood
Volume 3
Eighteen Short Stories & One Novella of the Strange and Unusual Including 'The
Transfer', 'Entrance and Exit', 'The Eccentricity of Simon Parnacute' and '
The Temptation of the Clay'
by Algernon Blackwood

Leonaur is an imprint of Oakpast Ltd

Copyright in this form © 2023 Oakpast Ltd

ISBN: 978-1-916535-14-5 (hardcover)
ISBN: 978-1-916535-15-2 (softcover)

http://www.leonaur.com

Contents

A Bit of Wood

He found himself in Meran with some cousins who had various slight ailments, but, being rich and imaginative, had gone to a sanatorium to be cured. But for its sanatoria, Meran might be a cheerful place; their ubiquity reminds a healthy man too often that the air is really good. Being well enough himself, except for a few mental worries, he went to a *gasthaus* in the neighbourhood. In the sanatorium his cousins complained bitterly of the food, the ignorant "sisters," the inattentive doctors, and the idiotic regulations generally—which proves that people should not go to a sanatorium unless they are really ill. However, they paid heavily for being there, so felt that something was being accomplished, and were annoyed when he called each day for tea, and told them cheerfully how much better they looked—which proved, again, that their ailments were slight and quite curable by the local doctor at home. With one of the ailing cousins, a rich and pretty girl, he believed himself in love.

It was a three weeks' business, and he spent his mornings walking in the surrounding hills, his mind reflective, analytical, and ambitious, as with a man in love. He thought of thousands of things. He mooned. Once, for instance, he paused beside a rivulet to watch the buttercups dip, and asked himself, "Will she be like this when we're married—so anxious to be well that she thinks fearfully all the time of getting ill?" For if so, he felt he would be bored. He knew himself accurately enough to realise that he never could stand *that*. Yet money was a wonderful thing to have, and he, already thirty-five, had little enough!

"Am I influenced by her money, then?" he asked himself . . . and so went on to ask and wonder about many things besides, for he was of a reflective temperament and his father had been a minor poet. And doubt crept in. He felt a chill. He was not much of a man, perhaps, thin-blooded and unsuccessful, rather a dreamer, too, into the bargain.

He had £100 a year of his own and a position in a Philanthropic Institution (due to influence) with a nominal salary attached. He meant to keep the latter after marriage. He would work just the same. Nobody should ever say *that* of him——!

And as he sat on the fallen tree beside the rivulet, idly knocking stones into the rushing water with his stick, he reflected upon those banal truisms that epitomise two-thirds of life. The way little unimportant things can change a person's whole existence was the one his thought just now had fastened on. His cousin's chill and headache, for instance, caught at a gloomy picnic on the Campagna three weeks before, had led to her going into a sanatorium and being advised that her heart was weak, that she had a tendency to asthma, that gout was in her system, and that a treatment of X-rays, radium, sun-baths and light baths, violet rays, no meat, complete rest, with big daily fees to experts with European reputations, were imperative.

"From that chill, sitting a moment too long in the shadow of a forgotten Patrician's tomb," he reflected, "has come all this"—"all this" including his doubt as to whether it was herself or her money that he loved, whether he could stand living with her always, whether he need *really* keep his work on after marriage, in a word, his entire life and future, and her own as well—"all from that tiny chill three weeks ago!" And he knocked with his stick a little piece of sawn-off board that lay beside the rushing water.

Upon that bit of wood his mind, his mood, then fastened itself. It was triangular, a piece of sawn-off wood, brown with age and ragged. Once it had been part of a triumphant, hopeful sapling on the mountains; then, when thirty years of age, the men had cut it down; the rest of it stood somewhere now, at this very moment, in the walls of the house. This extra bit was cast away as useless; it served no purpose anywhere; it was slowly rotting in the sun. But each tap of the stick, he noticed, turned it sideways without sending it over the edge into the rushing water. It was obstinate. "It doesn't want to go in," he laughed, his father's little talent cropping out in him, "but, by Jove, it shall!" And he pushed it with his foot.

But again, it stopped, stuck end-ways against a stone. He then stooped, picked it up, and threw it in. It plopped and splashed, and went scurrying away downhill with the bubbling water. "Even that scrap of useless wood," he reflected, rising to continue his aimless walk, and still idly dreaming, "even that bit of rubbish may have a purpose, and may change the life of someone—somewhere!"—and then went strolling through the fragrant pine woods, crossing a dozen similar streams, and hitting scores of stones and scraps and fir cones as he went—till he finally reached his *gasthaus* an hour later, and found a note from *her*.

> We shall expect you about three o'clock. We thought of going for a drive. The others feel so much better.

It was a revealing touch—the way she put it on "the others." He made his mind up then and there—thus tiny things divide the course of life—that he could never be happy with such an "affected creature." He went for that drive, sat next to her consuming beauty, proposed to her passionately on the way back, was accepted before he could change his mind, and is now the father of several healthy children—and just as much afraid of getting ill, or of *their* getting ill, as she was fifteen years before. The female, of course, matures long, long before the male, he reflected, thinking the matter over in his study once . . .

And that scrap of wood he idly set in motion out of impulse also went its destined way upon the hurrying water that never dared to stop. Proud of its new-found motion, it bobbed down merrily, spinning and turning for a mile or so, dancing gaily over sunny meadows, brushing the dipping buttercups as it passed, through vineyards, woods, and under dusty roads in neat, cool gutters, and tumbling headlong over little waterfalls, until it neared the plain. And so, finally, it came to a wooden trough that led off some of the precious water to a sawmill where bare-armed men did practical and necessary things. At the parting of the ways its angles delayed it for a moment, undecided which way to take. It wobbled. And upon that moment's wobbling hung tragic issues—issues of life and death.

Unknowing (yet assuredly not unknown), it chose the trough. It swung light-heartedly into the tearing sluice. It whirled with the gush of water towards the wheel, banged, spun, trembled, caught fast in the side where the cogs just chanced to be—and abruptly stopped the wheel. At any other spot the pressure of the water must have smashed it into pulp, and the wheel have continued as before; but it was caught in the *one* place where the various tensions held it fast immovably. It stopped the wheel, and so the machinery of the entire mill. It jammed like iron. The particular angle at which the double-handed saw, held by two weary and perspiring men, had cut it off a year before just enabled it to fit and wedge itself with irresistible exactitude.

The pressure of the tearing water combined with the weight of the massive wheel to fix it tight and rigid. And in due course a workman—it was the foreman of the mill—came from his post inside to make investigations. He discovered the irritating item that caused the trouble. He put his weight in a certain way; he strained his hefty muscles; he swore—and the scrap of wood was easily dislodged. He fished the morsel out, and tossed it on the bank, and spat on it. The great wheel started with a mighty groan.

But it started a fraction of a second before he expected it would start. He overbalanced, clutching the revolving framework with a frantic effort, shouted, swore, leaped at nothing, and fell into the pouring flood. In an instant he was turned upside down, sucked under, drowned. He was engaged to be married, and had put by a thousand *kronen* in the *Tiroler Sparbank*. He was a sober and hard-working man....

There was a paragraph in the local paper two days later. The Englishman, asking the porter of his *gasthaus* for something to wrap up a present he was taking to his cousin in the sanatorium, used that very issue. As he folded its crumpled and recalcitrant sheets with sentimental care about the precious object his eye fell carelessly upon the paragraph. Being of an idle and reflective temperament, he stopped to read it—it was headed "*Unglücksfall*," and his poetic eye, inherited from his foolish, rhyming father, caught the pretty expression "*fliessandes Wasser*."

He read the first few lines. Some fellow, with a picturesque Tyrolese name, had been drowned beneath a mill-wheel; he was popular in the neighbourhood, it seemed; he had saved some money, and was just going to be married. It was very sad. "Our readers' sympathy" was with him.... And, being of a reflective temperament, the Englishman thought for a moment, while he went on wrapping up the parcel. He wondered if the man had really loved the girl, whether she, too, had money, and whether they would have had lots of children and been happy ever afterwards. And then he hurried out towards the sanatorium. "I shall be late," he reflected. "Such little, unimportant things delay one...!"

Dream Trespass

The little feathers of the dusk were drifting through the autumn leaves when we came so unexpectedly upon the inn that was not marked upon our big-scaled map. And most opportunely, for Ducommun, my friend, was clearly overtired. An irritability foreign to his placid temperament had made the last few hours' trudge a little difficult, and I felt we had reached that narrow frontier which lies between non-success and failure.

"Another five miles to the inn we chose this morning," I told him; "but we'll soon manage it at a steady pace."

And he groaned, "I'm done! I simply couldn't do it."

He sank down upon the bit of broken wall to rest, while the darkness visibly increased, and the wind blew damp and chill across the marshes on our left. But behind the petulance of his tone, due to exhaustion solely, lay something else as well, something that had been accumulating for days. For our walking tour had not turned out quite to measure, distances always under-calculated; the inns, moreover, bad; the people surly and inhospitable; even the weather cross.

And Ducommun's disappointment had in a sense been double, so that I felt keen sympathy with him. For this was the country where his ancestors once reigned as proprietors, grand *seigneurs*, and the rest; he had always longed to visit it; and secretly in his imagination had cherished a reconstructed picture in which he himself would somehow play some high, distinguished *rôle* his proud blood entitled him to, clerk today in a mere insurance office, but descendant of romantic, ancient stock, he knew the history of the period intimately; the holiday had been carefully, lovingly planned; and—the unpleasantness of the inhabitants had shattered his dream thus fostered and so keenly anticipated.

The breaking-point had been reached. Was not this inn we hoped to reach by dark a portion of the very *château*—he had established it from musty records enough-where once his family dwelt in old-time splendour? And had he not indulged all manner of delightful secret dreaming in advance?. . . .

It was here, then, returning from a little private reconnoitring on my own account, that I reported my brave discovery of an unexpected half-way house, and found him almost asleep upon the stones, unwilling to believe the short a half-mile I promised. Only another nest of robbery and insolence," he laughed sourly, "and, anyhow, not the inn we counted on." He dragged after me in silence, eyeing askance the tumbled, ivy-covered shanty that stood beside the roadway, yet gladly going in ahead of me to rest his weary limbs, and troubling himself no whit with bargaining that he divined might be once more unpleasant.

Yet the inn proved a surprise in another way—it was entirely delightful. There was glowing fire of peat in a biggish hall, the *patron* and his wife were all smiles and pleasure, welcoming us with an old-fashioned dignity that made bargaining impossible, and in ten minutes we felt as much at home as if we had arrived at a country house where we had been long expected.

"So few care to stop here now," the old woman told us, with a gracious gesture that was courtly rather than deferential, "we stand no longer upon the old high road," and showed in a hundred nameless ways that all they had was entirely at our disposal.

Till even Ducommun melted and turned soft: "Only in France could this happen," he whispered with a touch of pride, as though claiming that this fragrance of gentle life, now fast disappearing from the world, still lingered in the land of his descent and in his own blood too. He patted the huge, rough deer-hound that seemed to fill the little room where we awaited supper, and the friendly creature, bounding with a kind of subdued affection, added another touch of welcome. His face and manners were evidence of kind treatment; he was proud of his owners and of his owners' guests. I thought of well-loved pets in our English country houses.

"This beast," I laughed, "has surely lived with gentlemen." And Ducommun took the compliment to himself with personal satisfaction.

It is difficult to tell afterwards with accuracy the countless little touches that made the picture all so gentle—they were so delicately suggested, painted in silently with such deft spiritual discretion. It stands out in my memory, set in some strange, high light, as the most enchanting experience of many a walking tour; and yet, about it all, like a veil of wonder that evades description, an atmosphere of something at the same time—I use the best available word—truly singular. This touch of something remote, indefinite, unique, began to steal over me from the very first, bringing with it an incalculable, queer charm. It lulled like a drug all possible suspicions. And in my friend—detail of the picture nearest to my heart, that is—it first betrayed itself, with a degree of surprise, moreover, not entirely removed from shock.

For as he passed before me underneath that low-browed porch, quite undeniably he-altered. This indefinable change clothed his entire presentment to my eyes; to tired eyes, I freely grant, as also that it was dusk, and that the transforming magic of the peat fire was behind him. Yet, eschewing paragraphs of vain description, I may put a portion of it crudely thus, perhaps: that his lankiness turned suddenly all grace; the atmosphere of the London office stool, as of the clerk a-holidaying, vanished; and that the way he bowed his head to enter the dark-beamed lintel of the door was courtly and high bred, instinct with native elegance, and in the real sense aristocratic.

It came with an instant and complete conviction. It was wonderful to see; and it gave me a moment's curious enchantment. All that I divined and loved in the man, usually somewhat buried, came forth upon the surface. A note of explanation followed readily enough, half explanation at any rate—that houses alter people because, like dressing-up with women and children, they furnish a new setting to the general appearance, and the points one is accustomed to undergo a readjustment. Yet with him this subtle alteration did not pass; it not only clung to him during the entire evening, but most curiously increased. He maintained, indeed, his silence the whole time, but it was a happy, dreaming silence holding the charm of real companionship, his disappointment gone as completely as the memory of our former cheerless inns and ill-conditioned people.

I cannot pretend, though, that I really watched him carefully, since an attack from another quarter divided my attention equally, and the charm of the daughter of the house, in whose eyes, it seemed to me, lay all the quiet sadness of the country we had walked through—*triste, morne*, forsaken land—claimed a great part of my observant sympathy. The old people left us entirely to her care, and the way she looked after us, divining our wants before we ventured to express them, was more suggestive of the perfect hostess than merely of someone who would take payment for all that she supplied.

The question of money, indeed, did not once intrude, though I cannot say whence came my impression that this hospitality was, in fact, offered without the least idea of remuneration in silver and gold. That it did come, I can swear; also, that behind it lay no suggestion of stiff prices to be demanded at the last moment on the plea that terms had not been settled in advance. We were made welcome like expected guests, and my heart leaped to encounter this spirit of old-fashioned courtesy that the greed of modern life has everywhere destroyed.

"Tomorrow or the next day, when you are rested," said the maiden softly, sitting beside us after supper and tending the fire, "I will take you through the *Allée des tilleuls* towards the river, and show you where the fishing is so good."

For it seemed natural that she should sit and chat with us, and only afterwards I remembered sharply that the river was a good five miles from where we housed, across marshes that could boast no trees at all, *tilleuls* least of all, and of avenues not a vestige anywhere.

"We'll start," Ducommun answered promptly, taking my breath a little, "in the dawn"; and presently then made signs to go to bed.

She brought the candles, lit them for us with a spill of paper from the peat, and handed one to each, a little smile of yearning in her deep, soft eyes that I remember to this day.

"You will sleep long and well," she said half shyly, accompanying us to the foot of the stairs. "I made and aired the beds with my own hands."

And the last I saw of her, as we turned the landing corner overhead, was her graceful figure against the darkness, with the candle light falling upon the coiled masses of her dark-brown hair. She gazed up after us with those large grey eyes that seemed to me so full of yearning, and yet so sad, so patient, so curiously resigned. . . .

Ducommun pulled me almost roughly by the "Come," he said with sudden energy, and as though everything was settled. "We have an early start, remember!"

I moved unwillingly; it was all so strange and dreamlike, the beauty of the girl so enchanting, the change in himself so utterly perplexing.

"It's like staying with friends in a country house," I murmured, lingering in a moment of bewilderment by his door. "Old family retainers almost, proud and delighted to put one up, eh?"

And his answer was so wholly unexpected that I waited, staring blankly into his altered eyes:

"I only hope we shall get away all right," he muttered. "I mean, that is—get off."

Evidently his former mood had flashed a moment back.

"You feel tired?" I suggested sympathetically, "so do I."

"Dog-tired, yes," he answered shortly, then added in a slow, suggestive whisper—"And I feel cold, too—extraordinarily cold."

The significant, cautious way he said it made me start. But before I could prate of chills and remedies, he quickly shut the door upon me, leaving those last words ringing in my brain—"cold, extraordinarily cold." And an inkling stole over me of what he meant; uninvited and unwelcome it came, then passed at once, leaving a vague uneasiness behind. For the cold he spoke of surely was not bodily cold. About my own heart, too, moved some strange touch of chill. Cold sought an entrance. But it was not common cold. Rather it was in the mind and thoughts, and settled down upon the spirit. In describing his own sensations, he had also described my own; for something at the very heart of me seemed turning numb. . . .

I got quickly into bed. The night was still and windless, but, though I was tired, sleep held long away. Uneasiness continued to affect me. I lay, listening to the blood hurrying along the thin walls of my veins, singing and murmuring, and, when at length I dropped off, two vivid pictures haunted me into unconsciousness—his face in the doorway as he made that last remark, and the face of the girl as she had peered up so yearningly at him over the shaded candle.

Then—at once, it seemed—I was wide awake again, aware, however, that an interval had passed, but aware also of another thing that was incredible, and somehow dreadful, namely, that while I slept, the house had undergone a change. It caught me, shivering in my bed, utterly unprepared, as though unfair advantage had been taken of me while I lay unconscious. This startling idea of external alteration made me shudder. How I so instantly divined it lies beyond all explanation. I somehow realised that, while the room I woke in was the same as before, the building of which it formed a little member had known in the darkness some transmuting, substituting change that had turned it otherwise.

My terror I also cannot explain, nor why, almost immediately, instead of increasing, it subtly shifted into that numbness I have already mentioned—a curious, deep bemusement of the spirit that robbed it of really acute distress. It seemed as if only a part of me—the wakened part—knew what was going on, and that some other part remained in sleep and ignorance.

For the house was now enormous. It *had* experienced this weird transformation. The roof, I somehow knew, rose soaring through the darkness; the walls ran over acres; it had towers, wings, and battlements, broad balconies, and magnificent windows. It had grown both dignified and ancient . . . and had swallowed up our little inn as comfortably as a palace includes a single bedroom. The blackness about me of course concealed it, but I *felt* the yawning corridors, the gape of lofty halls, high ceilings, spacious chambers, till I seemed lost in the being of some stately building that extended itself with imposing majesty upon the night.

Then came the instinct—more, perhaps, driving impulse than a mere suggestion—to go out and see. See what? I asked myself, as I made my way towards the window gropingly, unwilling or afraid to strike a light. And the answer, utterly without explanation, came hard and sharp like this—

"To catch them on the lawn."

And the curious phrase I knew was right, for the surroundings had changed equally with the house. I drew aside the curtain and peered out upon a lawn that a few hours ago had been a surely a rather desolate, plain roadway, and beyond it into spacious gardens, bounded by park-like timber, where before had been but dreary, half-cultivated fields.

Through a risen mist the light of the moon shone faintly, and everywhere my sight confirmed the singular impression of extension I have mentioned, for away to the left another mass of masonry that was like the wing of some great mansion rose dimly through the air, and beneath my very eyes a projecting balcony obscured pathways and beds of flowers. Next, where a gleam of moonlight caught it, I saw the broad, slow bend of river edging the lawn through clumps of willows. Even the river had come close. And while I stared, striving to force from so much illusion a single fact that might explain, a little tree upon the lawn just underneath moved slightly nearer, and I saw it was a human figure—a figure that I recognised.

Wrapped in some long, loose garment, the daughter of the house stood there in an attitude of waiting. And the waiting was at once explained, for another figure—this time the figure of a man that seemed to me both strange and familiar at the same time—emerged from the shadows of the house to join her. She slipped into his arms. Then came a sound of horses neighing in their stalls, and the couple moved away with sudden swiftness silently as ghosts, disappearing in the mist while three minutes later I heard the crunch of hoofs on gravel, dying rapidly away into the distance of the night.

And here a sudden, wild reaction, not easy of analysis, rushed over me, as if that other part of me that had not waked now came sharply to the rescue, set free from the inhibition of some drug. I felt anger, disgust, resentment, and a wave of indignation that somehow, I was being tricked. Impulsively—there seemed no time for judgment or reflection—I crossed the landing, now so oddly deep and lofty, and, without knocking, ran headlong into my friend's room. The bed, I saw at once, was empty, the sheets not even lain in. The furniture was in disorder, garments strewn about the floor, signs of precipitate flight in all directions. And Ducommun, of course, was gone.

What happened next confuses me when I try to think of it, for my only recollection is of hurrying distractedly to and fro between his bedroom and my own. There was a rush and scuttling in the darkness, and then I blundered heavily against walls or furniture or both, and the darkness rose up over my mind with a smothering thick curtain that blinded everything and I came to my senses in the open road, my friend standing over me, enormous in the dusk, and the bit of broken wall where he had rested while I reconnoitred, just behind us. The moon was rising, the air was damp and chill, and he was shouting in my ear, "I thought you were never coming back again. I'm rested now. We'd better hurry on and do those beastly five miles to the inn."

We started, walking so briskly that we reached it in something over seventy minutes, and passing on the way no single vestige of a house nor of any kind of building. I was the silent one, but when Ducommun talked it was only to curse the desolate, sad country, and wonder why his forbears had ever chosen such a wilderness to live in. And when at length we put up at this inn which he made out was a part of his original family estate, he spent the evening poring over maps and papers, by means of which he admitted finally his calculations were all wrong. "The house itself," he said, "must have stood farther back along the road we came by. The river, you see," pointing to the dirty old chart, "has changed its course a bit since then. Its older bed lay much nearer to the *château*, flanking the garden lawn below the park." And he pointed again to the place with a finger that obviously now held office pens.

Entrance and Exit

These three—the old physicist, the girl, and the young Anglican parson who was engaged to her—stood by the window of the country house. The blinds were not yet drawn. They could see the dark clump of pines in the field, with crests silhouetted against the pale wintry sky of the February afternoon. Snow, freshly fallen, lay upon lawn and hill. A big moon was already lighting up.

"Yes, that's the wood," the old man said, "and it was this very day fifty years ago—February 13—the man disappeared from its shadows; swept in this extraordinary, incredible fashion into invisibility—*into some other place*. Can you wonder the grove is haunted?" A strange impressiveness of manner belied the laugh following the words.

"Oh, please tell us," the girl whispered; "we're all alone now." Curiosity triumphed; yet a vague alarm betrayed itself in the questioning glance she cast for protection at her younger companion, whose fine face, on the other hand, wore an expression that was grave and singularly rapt. He was listening keenly.

"As though Nature," the physicist went on, half to himself, "here and there concealed vacuums, gaps, holes in space (his mind was always speculative; more than speculative, some said), through which a man might drop into invisibility—a new direction, in fact, at right angles to three known ones—'higher space,' as Bolyai, Gauss, and Hinton might call it; and what you, with your mystical turn"—looking toward the young priest—"might consider a spiritual change of condition, into a region where space and time do not exist, and where all dimensions are possible—because they are *one*."

"But, *please*, the story," the girl begged, not understanding these dark sayings, "although I'm not sure that Arthur ought to hear it. He's much too interested in such queer things as it is!" Smiling, yet uneasy, she stood closer to his side, as though her body might protect his soul.

"Very briefly, then, you shall hear what I remember of this haunting, for I was barely ten years old at the time. It was evening—clear and cold like this, with snow and moonlight—when someone reported to my father that a peculiar sound, variously described as crying, singing, wailing, was being heard in the grove. He paid no attention until my sister heard it too, and was frightened. Then he sent a groom to investigate.

"Though the night was brilliant the man took a lantern. We watched from this very window till we lost his figure against the trees, and the lantern stopped swinging suddenly, as if he had put it down. It remained motionless. We waited half an hour, and then my father, curiously excited, I remember, went out quickly, and I, utterly terrified, went after him. We followed his tracks, which came to an end beside the lantern, the last step being a stride almost impossible for a man to have made. All around the snow was unbroken by a single mark, but the man himself had vanished. Then we heard him calling for help—above, behind, beyond us; from all directions at once, yet from none, came the sound of his voice; but though we called back he made no answer, and gradually his cries grew fainter and fainter, as if going into tremendous distance, and at last died away altogether."

"And the man himself?" asked both listeners.

"Never returned—from that day to this has never been seen....At intervals for weeks and months afterwards reports came in that he was still heard crying, always crying for help. With time, even these reports ceased—for most of us," he added under his breath; "and that is all I know. A mere outline, as you see."

The girl did not quite like the story, for the old man's manner made it too convincing. She was half disappointed, half frightened.

"See! there are the others coming home," she exclaimed, with a note of relief, pointing to a group of figures moving over the snow near the pine trees. "Now we can think of tea!" She crossed the room to busy herself with the friendly tray as the servant approached to fasten the shutters. The young priest, however, deeply interested, talked on with their host, though in a voice almost too low for her to hear. Only the final sentences reached her, making her uneasy—absurdly so, she thought—till afterwards.

"—for matter, as we know, interpenetrates matter," she heard, "and two objects may conceivably occupy the same space. The odd thing really is that one should hear, but not see; that air-waves should bring the voice, yet ether-waves fail to bring the picture."

And then the older man: "—as if certain places in Nature, yes, invited the change—places where these extraordinary forces stir from the earth as from the surface of a living Being with organs—places like islands, mountain-tops, pine-woods, especially pines isolated from their kind. You know the queer results of digging absolutely virgin soil, of course—and that theory of the earth's being *alive*—"The voice dropped again.

"States of mind also helping the forces of the place," she caught the priest's reply in part; "such as conditions induced by music, by intense listening, by certain moments in the Mass even—by ecstasy or—"

"I say, what do you think?" cried a girl's voice, as the others came in with welcome chatter and odours of tweeds and open fields. "As we passed your old haunted pinewood, we heard such a queer noise. Like someone wailing or crying. Caesar howled and ran; and Harry refused to go in and investigate. He positively funked it!" They all' laughed.

"More like a rabbit in a trap than a person crying," explained Harry, a blush kindly concealing his startling pallor. "I wanted my tea too much to bother about an old rabbit."

It was some time after tea when the girl became aware that the priest had disappeared, and putting two and two together, ran in alarm to her host's study. Quite easily, from the hastily opened shutters, they saw his figure moving across the snow. The moon was very bright over the world, yet he carried a lantern that shone pale yellow against the white brilliance.

"Oh, for God's sake, quick!" she cried, pale with fear. "Quick! or we're too late! Arthur's simply wild about such things. Oh, I might have known—I might have guessed. And this is the very night. I'm terrified!"

By the time he had found his overcoat and slipped round the house with her from the back door, the lantern, they saw, was already swinging close to the pinewood. The night was still as ice, bitterly cold. Breathlessly they ran, following the tracks. Half-way his steps diverged, and were plainly visible in the virgin snow by themselves. They heard the whispering of the branches ahead of them, for pines cry even when no airs stir. "Follow me close," said the old man sternly. The lantern, he already saw lay upon the ground unattended; no human figure was anywhere visible.

"See! The steps come to an end here," he whispered, stooping down as soon as they reached the lantern. The tracks, hitherto so regular, showed an odd wavering—the snow curiously disturbed. Quite suddenly they stopped. The final step was a very long one—a stride, almost immense, "as though he was pushed forward from behind," muttered the old man, too low to be overheard, "or sucked forward from in front—as in a fall."

The girl would have dashed forward but for his strong restraining grasp. She clutched him, uttering a sudden dreadful cry. "Hark! I hear his voice!" she almost sobbed. They stood still to listen. A mystery that was more than the mystery of night closed about their hearts—a mystery that is beyond life and death, that only great awe and terror can summon from the deeps of the soul. Out of the heart of the trees, fifty feet away, issued a crying voice, half wailing, half singing, very faint.

"Help! Help!" it sounded through the still night; "for the love of God, pray for me!"

The melancholy rustling of the pines followed; and then again, the singular crying voice shot past above their heads, now in front of them, now once more behind. It sounded everywhere. It grew fainter and fainter, fading away, it seemed, into distance that somehow was appalling. The grove, however, was empty of all but the sighing wind; the snow unbroken by any tread. The moon threw inky shadows; the cold bit; it was a terror of ice and death and this awful singing cry. . . .

"But why *pray?*" screamed the girl, distracted, frantic with her bewildered terror. "Why *pray?* Let us do something to help—do something . . .!" She swung round in a circle, nearly falling to the ground. Suddenly she perceived that the old man had dropped to his knees in the snow beside her and was—praying.

"Because the forces of prayer, of thought, of the will to help, alone can reach and succour him where he now is," was all the answer she got. And a moment later both figures were kneeling in the snow, praying, so to speak, their very heart's life out. . . .

The search may be imagined—the steps taken by police, friends, newspapers, by the whole country in fact. . . . But the most curious part of this queer "Higher Space" adventure is the end of it—at least, the "end" so far as at present known. For after three weeks, when the winds of March were a-roar about the land, there crept over the fields towards the house the small dark figure of a man. He was thin, pallid as a ghost, worn and fearfully emaciated, but upon his face and in his eyes were traces of an astonishing radiance—a glory unlike anything ever seen. . . . It may, of course, have been deliberate, or it may have been a genuine loss of memory only; none could say—least of all the girl whom his return snatched from the gates of death; but, at any rate, what had come to pass during the interval of his amazing disappearance he has never yet been able to reveal.

"And you must never ask me," he would say to her—and repeat even after his complete and speedy restoration to bodily health—"for I simply cannot tell. I know no language, you see, that could express it. I was near you all the time. But I was also—elsewhere and otherwise."

Perspective

1

The amount of duty and pleasure combined in Alpine summer chaplaincies of a month each just suited the Rev. Phillip Ambleside. He was still young enough to climb—carefully; and genuine enough to enjoy seeing the crowd of holidaymakers, having a good time. As a rule, he was on the Entertainment Committee that organised the tennis, dances, and gymkhanas. During the week one would hardly have guessed his calling. On Sundays he appeared a bronzed, lean, vigorous figure in the pulpit of the hot little wooden church, and people liked to see him. His sermons, never over ten minutes, were the same four every year: one for each Sunday of the month; and when he passed on to another month's duty in the next place, he repeated them.

The surroundings suggested them obviously: Beauty, Rest, Power, Majesty; and they were more like little confidential talks than sermons. Moreover, incidents from the life of the place—the escape of a tourist, the accident to a guide, and what not, usually came ready to hand to point a moral. One summer, however, there occurred a singular adventure that he has never yet been able to introduce into a sermon. Only in private conversation with souls as full of faith as himself does he ever mention it. And the short recital always begins with a sentence more or less as follows—

". . . . Talking of the wondrous ways of God, and the little understanding of the children of men, I am always struck by the huge machinery He sometimes adopts to accomplish such delicate and apparently insignificant ends. I remember once when I was doing summer 'duty' in a Swiss resort high up among the mountains of the Valais . . ."

And then follows the curious occurrence I was once privileged to hear, and have obtained permission to re-tell, duly disguised.

In the particular mountain village where he was taking a month's duty at the time, his church was full every Sunday, so full indeed that twice a week he held afternoon services for those who cared to worship more quietly. And to these little ceremonies, beloved of his own heart, came two persons regularly who attracted his attention in spite of himself. They sat together at the back; shared the same books, although there was no necessity to do so; courted the shadowy corners of the pews: in a word, they came to worship one another, not to worship God.

But the clergyman took a broad view. Courtships fostered in the holy atmosphere of the sacred building were more likely to be true than those fanned to flame in the feverish surroundings of the dance-room. And true love is ever an offering to God. He knew the couple, too. The man, quiet, earnest, well over forty; the girl, young, dashing, spirited, leader in mischief, hard to believe sincere, flirting with more than one. In spite of the careful concealment with which she covered their proceedings, choosing the deserted afternoon service rather than the glare of the garden or ballroom for their talks, the couple were marked.

The difference in their ages, characters, and appearance singled them out, as much as the general knowledge that she was rich, vain, flighty, while he was poor, strenuous, living a life of practical charity in London, that precluded gaiety or pleasure, so called.

"What *can* she see in that dull man twice her age?" the elder women said to one another—the answer generally being that it probably amused the girl to turn him so easily round her little finger.

"What a chance for her fortune to be well spent," reflected one or two. While the men, when they said anything at all, contented themselves with: "Pretty hard hit, isn't he? A fine fellow though! Hope he gets her!"

It is always somewhat pathetic to see a man of real value fall before the conquering beauty of an ordinary young girl of the world. The clergyman, however, with an eye for spiritual values, even deeply hidden, divined that beneath her lightness and love for conquest's sake there lay the desire for something more real. And he guessed, though at first the wish may have been father to the thought only, that it was the elder man's fine zeal and power that attracted the butterfly in spite of herself towards a life that was more worth living. Hers, after all, he felt, was a soul worth "saving"; and this middle-aged man, perhaps, was the force God brought into her life to provide her with the opportunity of escape—could she but seize it.

So far Ambleside's story runs along ordinary lines enough. One sees his man and girl without further detail. From this point, however, it slips into a stride where the sense of proportion seems somehow lost, or else "man's little understanding" is too close to the thing to obtain the proper perspective. If anyone but this devout and clear-headed clergyman told the tale, one might say "Fancy," "Delusion," or any other description that seemed suitable.

But to hear him tell it, with that air of conviction and truth, in those short, abrupt, even jerky sentences, that left so much to the imagination, and with that pallor of the skin that threw into such vivid contrast the fire burning in his far-seeing blue eyes—to sit close to him and hear the story grow in that tense low voice, was to know beyond all question that he spoke of something real and actual, in the same sense that a train or St. Paul's Cathedral are real and actual.

What he saw, he really saw: though the sight may have been of a kind unfamiliar to the majority. He was used as a real pawn in a real game. The girl's life and soul were rescued, so to speak, by the marriage brought about, and her forces of mind and spirit lifted bodily for what they were worth into the scheme that God had ordained for them from the beginning of the world. Only—the machinery brought to bear upon the end in view seemed so prodigious, so extraordinary, so unnecessary. . . . One thinks of the sentence with which Ambleside always began his tale. One wonders. But no one who heard the tale ever asked questions at its close. There was absolutely nothing to say.

Even to the smallest details the affair seemed thought out and planned, for that particular Tuesday Ambleside started without the guide-porter who usually carried his telescope, camera, and lunch. He went off at six a.m., with merely an ice-axe and a small knapsack containing food and Shetland vest for the summit.

It was one of those days towards the end of August when some quality in the atmosphere—usually sign of approaching rain—brings the mountains uncannily close, yet, at the same time, sets out every detail of pinnacle, precipice, and ridge with a terror of size and grandeur that makes one realize their true and gigantic scale. They press up close, yet at the same time stand away in the depths of the sky like unattainable masses in some dream world. This mingling of proximity and distance has a confusing effect upon the eye.

When Ambleside toiled up the zigzags without actually looking beyond, he felt that the towering massif of the Valais Alps all about him loomed very close; but when he stopped for breath and raised his eyes steadily into their detail, he felt that their distance was too great

27

to be conquered by any little two-legged being like himself merely taking steps.

And as he rose out of the valley into the clearer strata of air this effect increased. The whole scale of the chain of Alps about him seemed raised to an immeasurably higher power than he had ever known. He felt like an insect crawling over the craters of the moon. The prodigious splendours of the scenery all round oppressed him more than ever before with his own futile littleness, yet at the same time made him conscious of the grandeur of his soul before the God who had set him and his kind above all this chaos of tumbled planet.

He thought of the mountains as part of the "garment of God," and of nature as expressing some portion of the Deity not intended to be expressed by man—all part of His purpose, alive with His informing will. This glory of the inanimate Alps linked on to some stranger glory in himself that interpreted for him, as in a mystical revelation, God's thundering message and purpose known in the great forms and moods of nature. Closely in touch with the spirit of the mountains he was; glad to be alone.

This, in a sentence, expresses his mood: that the mountains accepted him. Forces in his deepest being that were akin to the life of the planet on which he made his tiny track rose up and triumphed. Over the treacherous Pas d'Iliez, where he usually felt giddy and unsafe, he felt this morning only exhilaration. The gulf yawning at his feet touched him with its splendour, not its terror.

Thus, feeling inclined to shout and run, he eventually reached the desolate valley of rock and shale that lies, unrelieved by a single blade of grass, between the glacier-covered slopes that shut it in impassably on three sides. The bed of this valley lies some 7,000 feet above the sea. The peaks and ridges that rear about it reach 12,000 feet. Here, being a good climber, he rested for the first time at the end of two hours' steady ascent. The air nipped. The loneliness and desolation were very impressive.

Beyond him hung the glaciers like immense thick blankets of blue-white upon the steep slopes, dropping from time to time lumps of ice into the shale-strewn valley below. For the sun shining in a cloudless sky was fierce. The clergyman, before attacking the long snow-field that began at his very feet, took out his blue spectacles and disentangled the cord. He ate some chocolate, and took the dried prunes from his knapsack, knowing that thirst would soon be upon him, and that ice-water was not for drinking.

28

"What a mite I am, to be sure, amid all this appalling wilderness!" he exclaimed; "and how splendid to be able to hold my own!"

And then it was, just as he stood up to arrange the glasses on his forehead, ready to pull down at a moment's notice, that he became aware of something that was strange—unaccustomed. Through the giant splendours of the scorching August day, across all this stupendous Scenery of desolation and loneliness, something fine as a needle, delicate as a hair, had begun picking at his mind. The idea came to him that he was no longer alone. Like a man who hears his name called out of darkness he turned instinctively to find the speaker; almost as though someone had been calling to him for a considerable time, and he had only just had his attention drawn to it. He looked keenly up and down the immense, deserted valley.

In every direction, however, he saw nothing but miles of rock, dazzling snow-fields, dark precipices, and endless peaks cutting the blue sky overhead with teeth that gleamed like burnished steel. It was desolation everywhere. The gentle wind that fanned his cheek made no sound against the stones. There was neither tree nor grass for it to rustle through. No bird's wing whirred the air; and the far-off falling of a hundred cascades was of too regular and monotonous a character to have taken on the quality of a voice or the rhythm of uttered words. He examined, so far as he could, the enormous sides of mountain about him, and the great soaring ridges.

It was just possible some climber in distress had spied him out, and shouted down upon him from the heights. But he searched in vain. There was no moving human figure. The sound, if sound it had been, was not repeated; only he was no longer alone, as before. That, at least, was certain. . . . He nibbled more chocolate, put a couple of sour prunes into his mouth to suck, arranged the blue snow-glass over his eyes, and started on again for a steady pull up to the next ridge.

And as he rose the scale of the surrounding mountains rose appallingly with him. The true distance of the peaks proclaimed itself; the tremendous reaches that from below appeared telescoped up into a little space opened up and stretched themselves. The hour grew into two. It was considerably after twelve before he reached the *arête* where he had promised himself lunch. And all the way, without ceasing, the idea that he was being accompanied remained insistent in his mind. It troubled and perplexed him. Perhaps it frightened him a little, too. More than once it came close enough to make him pause and consider whether he should continue or turn back.

For the curious part of it was that this idea exercised a direct and deliberate effect upon him. By a hundred little details that seemed to be spontaneous until he examined them, it kept suggesting somehow that he should change his route. Something in his consciousness grew that had not been there before. He thought of a bird bringing tiny morsels of grass and twig until a nest formed. In this way the steady stream of thoughts from somewhere outside himself came nesting in his brain until at length they acquired the consistency of an impression, next of a distinct desire, lastly, the momentum of a definite intention. They acted upon his volition, stirring softly among the roots of his will. Before he realized how it had quite come about, he *had changed his mind.*

"Instead of going on to the top as I intended," he said to himself, as he sat on the dizzy ledge munching hard-boiled eggs and sugar sandwiches, "I shall strike off to the left and find my way back into the valley again. That, I think, would be—nicer!"

He had no real reason; he invented none.

And the moment he said it there was a sense of pressure removed, a consciousness of relief, the knowledge, in a word, that he was following a route that it was desired he should follow.

To a man, of course, whose habit it was to seek often the will of a personal Deity he worshipped, there was nothing very out of the way in all this, although he never remembered to have felt any guidance so distinctly and forcibly indicated before. The feeling that he was being "guided" now became a certainty, and in order to follow instructions as well as possible he made his will of no account and opened himself to receive the slightest token this other Directing Agency might care to vouchsafe.

After lunch, therefore, he struck out a diagonal course across a steep snow-slope that would eventually bring him down again to the valley a little nearer its head. And before he had gone a hundred yards he ran into the track of another climber. The marks were a couple of days old, perhaps, for in their hollows lay little heaps of fine snow-dust, freshly blown. Judging by the size there had been two men. He noted the trace of the ice-axe and the occasional streak of the trailing rope. The men had made straight for the valley far below. Here and there they had glissaded. Here and there, too, they had also tumbled gloriously, for the snow was tossed about by their floundering. Yet there was no danger; no precipices intervened; the snow sloped without a break right down into the shale below.

"I'll follow their example," said the Rev. Phillip Ambleside. He strapped on the extra leather seat he carried for sliding and sat down. A moment later he was rushing at high speed over the hard surface. There were hollows of softer snow, however, which stopped him from time to time, drifts as it were into which he plunged, and from which he emerged, wet and shivering. Then he stood up and leaned on his axe, trying to glissade on his feet. For this, however, the surface was not smooth enough. The result was he tumbled, rolled, slid, sat down, and took immense gliding strides. It was very exhilarating. He revelled in it.

But all the while he kept his eyes sharply about him, for in his heart he felt that he was obeying that guiding Influence so strongly impressed upon him—the Power that had persuaded him to change his route, and was now leading him to Some particular point with some particular purpose. Now, too, for the first time a vague sense of calamity touched him. Once introduced, it grew.

Soon it amounted to a positive foreboding, a presentiment of disaster almost. He could not avoid the idea that he was being led by supernatural means to the scene of some catastrophe where he was to prove of use—a rescue, an arrival in the nick of time to save someone. He actually looked about him already for—yes, for the body. And through his sub-conscious mind, with the force of habit, ran the magnificent use he could make of it all in a future sermon.

Yet nothing came. The tracks of the other men stretched clear and unbroken into the valley of rocks below. He traced the wavering thin line the whole way down.

"It's nothing to do with *these* men, at any rate," he said to himself, as he sat down for the final slide that should take him to the bottom of the slope. "No accident could possibly have happened here. The snow's too soft, and there are no rocks to fall over or—"

The sentence, or the thought, remained unfinished, for the mouth of the Rev. Phillip was stopped temporarily with wet snow as he lost his balance and rushed sideways with an undignified plunge into a drifted hollow. His eyes were blinded, his feet twisted, the skin of his back drenched and icy. He rose spluttering and gasping. Luckily his axe had a leather loop, or he would have lost it; as it was, his slouch hat was already a hundred feet below, sliding and turning like a top on its way to the bottom, followed by the snow-goggles.

And in the act of brushing himself free of snow the truth came to him. It was as though a hand had struck him on the back and pointed—as though a voice had uttered the five words: "*This is the place. Look!*"

Swiftly, searchingly, keenly he looked, and saw— nothing; nothing, at least, that explained the impression of disaster that had possessed him. There was no body certainly, nor any sign of an accident; no place, indeed, where an accident could possibly have come about. He dug quickly in the loose snow with his axe, but the snow was barely two feet deep in this particular hollow, and all round it was a hard surface of smoothly and tightly-packed stuff that was almost ice. Nothing bigger than a cat could have lain buried there!

"This is the place! Look well!" the words seemed to ring in his ears.

Yet the more he looked and saw nothing, the more strongly beat this message upon his brain. This was the place where he was to come, where he was to fulfil some purpose, to find something, do something, accomplish the end intended by the Will that had so carefully guided him all day. The feeling was positive; not to be denied. It was, at the same time, distressingly vast—mighty.

Fixing himself securely against his axe, he stood and stared. The sun beat back into his face from the glittering snow on all sides. Tremendous black precipices towered not far behind him; to his left rolled the frozen mass of the huge glacier, its pinnacles of tottering ice catching the afternoon sun; to his right stretched into bewildering distance the interminable and desolate reaches of shale and moraine till the eye rested upon summits of a dozen peaks that literally swam in the sky where white clouds streamed westwards.

There was no sound but falling water, no sign of humanity except the single track of those other climbers, no indication of any disturbance upon the vast face of nature that spread all about him, immense, still, terrific.

Then, piercing the monotony of the falling water, a faint sound of fluttering, heard for the first time, reached his ear. He turned as at the sound of a pistol-shot in the direction whence it came—but again saw nothing. The sound ceased. From the slope below came a breath of icy wind that made him shiver, and with it, he fancied, came the faint hissing noise of his sliding hat and spectacles. This, perhaps, was the sound he had heard as "fluttering."

At length after prolonged and vain searching, the clergyman decided there was nothing for him to do but continue his journey, for the sun was getting low, and he had a long way to go before dusk could be regarded with equanimity. He felt exhausted, wearied, impatient too if the truth were told, yet ashamed of his impatience.

"If this is all *real*," he argued under his breath, "why isn't it made clear what I'm to do?"

And immediately upon the heels of the thought came again that faint and curious sound of something fluttering.

Now, there can be no question that he understood perfectly well that this sound of fluttering had a direct connection with the whole purpose of the day—that it was the clue to his presence in this particular spot, and that he had been forced to halt here by means of his fall in order that he might investigate something or other on this very spot. He knew it; he felt it. But he was too impatient, too cold, too weary to spend any further time over it all. Alarm, too, was plucking uneasily at his reins.

So, this time he affected to ignore the sound. Leaning back on his axe he threw his body into position for sliding down to the bottom of the slope. In another second he would have started—when something that froze him into the immobility of a terror worse than death arrested him with a power beyond anything he had ever known before in his life—a Power that seemed to carry behind it the pressure of the entire universe.

There, close beside him in this mountain wilderness, had risen up suddenly a Face—close as the handle of the ice-axe he so tightly grasped, yet at the same time so far away, so immense, so stupendous in scale that he has never understood to this day how it was he could have perceived that it was a Face. Yet a face it undoubtedly was, a living face; and its eyes—its regard, at any rate, for eyes he divined rather than saw—were focussed upon some object that lay at his very feet.

Clammy with fear, his heart thumping dreadfully, he dropped back upon the snow. Without looking at any particular detail he became aware that the entire world of giant scenery about him was involved in the building up of this appalling Countenance, whose gaze was directed upon a tiny point immediately before him—the point, he now perceived, whence proceeded that familiar little sound of fluttering.

Words obviously fail him when he attempts to describe the terror of this Visage that rose about him through the day. Pallid and immense, it seemed to stretch itself against the wastes of grey rock, with entire slopes of snow upon the cheeks, ridged and furrowed by precipice and cliff, with torn clouds of flying hair that streaked the blue, and the expanse of glaciers for the splendid brows. Across it the dark line of two moraines tilted for eyebrows, and the massive columns of compressed *strata* embedded in the whole structure of the mountain chain bulged for the muscles of the awful neck.... Moreover, the shoulders upon which it all rested—the vast framework of body that he divined below—the dizzy drop in space where such fearful limbs must seek their resting-place—!

His mind went reeling. The titanic proportions of this Countenance of splendour threatened in some horrible way to overwhelm his life. Its calmness, its iron immobility, its remorseless fixity of mien petrified him. The thought that he had dared to question it, to put himself in opposition to its purpose, even to be impatient with it—this turned all his soul within him soft and dead with a kind of ultimate terror that bereft him of any clear memory, perhaps momentarily, too, of consciousness.

The clergyman *thinks* he fainted. Exactly what happened, probably, he never knew nor realised. All that he can say in attempting to describe it is that he found his own eyes caught up and carried away in the gigantic stream of vision that this Face of Mountains poured upon the ground—caught up and directed upon a tiny little white object that fluttered in the wind at his very feet.

He saw what the Face was looking at and wished him to look at. It made him see what it saw.

For there, in front of him, unnoticed hitherto, lay a scrap of paper half embedded in the snow. Automatically he stooped and picked it up. It was an envelope bearing the printed inscription of an hotel in the village. It was sealed. On the outside in a fine handwriting, he read the Christian name of a man. Opening the corner, he saw inside a small lock of dark-coloured hair. And this was all ....

Then it was just at this moment that the snow where his feet rested gave way, and he started off at full speed to slide to the bottom of the slope, where he only just stopped himself in time to prevent shooting with a violent collision into a mass of shale and loose stones.

In less than thirty seconds it had all happened ... and the swift descent and tumble had shaken him back as it were into a normal state of mind. But the oppression that had burdened him all day was gone. The mountains looked as usual. An indescribable sense of relief came over him. He felt a free agent once more—no longer guided, pushed, directed. He had fulfilled the purpose.

Putting the little envelope in his inside pocket he picked up his slouch hat and snow-goggles, ate some chocolate and dried prunes, and started off at a brisk pace for his return journey of three hours to the village and—dinner. And the whole way home the grandeur of that face, with its splendid pallor, and its expression of majesty, haunted him with indescribable sensations. With it, however, all the time ran the accompanying thought: "What a tremendous business for so small a result! All that vast manoeuvring, all that terror of the imagination, and all that complex pressure upon my insignificant spirit merely in the end to find a wisp of girl's hair in an envelope evidently fallen from the pocket of some careless climber!"

The more the Rev. Phillip Ambleside thought about it, the more bewildered he felt. He was uncommonly glad, however, to get in before dark. The memory of that Mountain Countenance was no agreeable companion for the forest paths and lonely slopes through which his way led in the dusk.

2

That same night it so happened, before he was able to take any steps to trace the owner of the little envelope, there was a Bal de Têtes at the principal hotel. Although the clergyman was on the Entertainment Committee which organised the simple gaieties of the place, he held that honorary position only as a personal compliment to himself; he did not at a rule take an active part in the detail, nor did he as a general rule attend the balls.

This particular night, however, he strolled down to the hotel, and after a little conversation with one or two friends in the hall he made his way to a secluded corner of the glass gallery where the dancers sat out between times, and lit his pipe for a quiet smoke. From behind the shelter of a large sham palm he was able to see all he wanted of the ballroom, to hear the music, and to take in the pleasant sight of all the people enjoying themselves. And the sight did him good. He liked to see it. A number were in costume, which added to the picturesqueness of the scene.

Perhaps he sat more in the shadows than he knew, or perhaps the dancers who came to "sit out" near him in the gallery did not realise how their voices carried. Several couples, as the evening advanced, came so close to him that, had he wished, he could have overheard easily every word they uttered. He did not wish, however. His mind was busy with thoughts of its own. That haunting scene of desolation in the mountains obsessed him still; and about ten o'clock, his pipe being finished, he was on the point of getting up to leave, when two dancers came and sat down immediately behind him and began to talk in such very distinct tones that it was impossible to avoid hearing every single word they uttered.

The clergyman pushed his chair aside to make room to go, when, in doing so, he threw a passing glance at the couple—and instantly recognized them. The girl, a Carmen, and a very becoming Carmen, was the one who frequented his afternoon services, and the man, who wore simple evening dress and was not in costume at all, was the middle-aged Englishman who had been at her heels like a slave all the summer. They were absorbed in one another, and evidently unaware of his presence.

To say that he hesitated would not be true. Some force beyond himself simply took him by the shoulders and pushed him back into the chair. Against his own will—for Mr. Ambleside was no eavesdropper—he remained there deliberately to listen.

In telling the story he tells it just like this, making no excuses for conduct that was certainly dishonourable. He declares he could not help himself; the instinct was too imperious to be disobeyed. Again, as in the afternoon, he understood that he was merely being used as a pawn in the game, a game of great importance to some Intelligence that saw through to the distant end.

The man was quiet, but tremendously in earnest, with the kind of steady manner that no woman likes unless she finds it in her to respond with a similar sincerity. Under the bronze his skin showed pale a little. He began to speak the instant they sat down; and in his voice was passion.

"I want you, and I want your money, and I want your life and soul—everything," he said, evidently continuing a conversation; "your youth and energy, your talents, your will, all that is you and yours—*all*." His voice was pitched very low, yet without tremor. He was playing the whole stake, as a strong man of middle age plays it when he is utterly in earnest. "For my scheme, for *our* scheme, for God's scheme I want you; and no one else but you will do. I want you to awake, and change your life, and be your true, fine self. We can make a success, you and I, a success for ourselves and for others. I shall never give you up until—until you give yourself to the world, or"—his voice dropped very low—"to another."

The clergyman waited breathlessly for the answer. The man's words vibrated with such suppressed fire that only a serious reply could be forthcoming. But for a space Carmen merely toyed with her fan, the little red spangled fan that swung from a single finger. Behind the black domino her eyes sparkled, but the expression of her face was hidden.

"The difference in age is nothing," he continued almost sternly. "For me, you are *the* woman, and for you I will prove that I am *the* man. I see clean through to the great soul hidden in you. I can bring it out. I can make you *real*—a soul of value in the big order of God's purposes. What can these boys ever be, or do, for you? I've got a big, useful, practical scheme that can use you, just as it can use me. And my great unselfish love has picked you out of the whole world as the one woman necessary. Will you come to me?"

Still the girl was silent. She tapped him on the knee two or three times, would-be playfully, with the tip of her fan. Her head was bent down a little.

"And I'm strong," he went on earnestly; "I'm a man. The power in me recognises and calls to the power in you. Let me hold you and mould you, and let's take the fine, high life together. Drop this life of child's play you've been leading. Come to me; my arms are hungry for you! But I want you for a higher purpose than my own happiness—though I swear I can make you happy as no woman in this world has ever before been happy. And without you," he added more softly after a slight pause, "this splendid scheme of mine, of ours, can come to nothing. For I cannot do it alone—and there is only one *You* in the world. Answer me now. It was tonight, remember, you promised. I leave tomorrow, and London days lie far ahead. Give me your answer to go back with."

It was a curious way to make love. The reverend gentleman thought he had never heard anything quite like it. An ordinarily frivolous girl, of course, would have been impatient long ago. But the fine passion of the man broke everywhere through his rather lame words, and set something in the air about them aflame. The violins sounded thin and trashy compared to the rhythm of this earnest voice; all the glitter of the ball-room seemed cheap—the costume of Carmen absurdly incongruous.

Mr. Ambleside slipped back somehow into the key of the afternoon when Cosmic Powers had held direct communion with his soul. He understood that he was meant to listen. Something big was in progress, something important in a high sense. He did listen—to every word. It was Carmen speaking now; but her voice marred the picture. It was thin, trifling, even affected.

"It's very flattering," she simpered, "but—don't you see—it means the end of all my fun and enjoyment in life. You're so fearfully in earnest. You'd exhaust me in the first week!" She cocked her pretty head on one side, holding the fan against her cheek. Something, nevertheless, belied the lightness of her words, the listener felt.

"But I'll teach you a different kind of happiness," replied the man eagerly, "so that you'll never again want this passing excitement, this 'unrest which men miscall delight.' Give me your answer—now. I see it in your eyes. Let me go away tomorrow with this great new happiness in my heart." He leaned forward. "Let your real self speak out once for all!" He took her fan away and she made no resistance. She clasped her hands in her lap, still looking at him mischievously through her mask.

"Let's wait till we meet later in town," she sighed at length prettily, coaxingly. "I shall be able to enjoy myself here then for the rest of the summer first—I feel so young for such a programme."

But the man cut her short.

"*Now*," he said, holding her steadily with his eyes. "You said that to me a year ago, remember. I have waited ever since. It is your youth I want."

The girl played with him for another ten minutes, while the clergyman listened, wondering greatly at the other's patience. Clearly, she delighted to feel his great love beating up against the citadel she meant in the end to yield. The lighter side of her was vastly interested and amused by it; but all the time the deeper part was ready with its answer. It was only that the "child" in her wanted to enjoy itself a little longer before it capitulated for ever to the strength that should take her captive, and lead her by sharp ways of sacrifice to the high *rôle* she was meant to fill.

It would all have vexed and wearied Mr. Ambleside exceedingly, but for this singular feeling that it was part of some much larger scheme of which he might never know the whole perhaps, but in which he was playing his little part with a secret thrill. Through the tawdry glitter of that scented ballroom he saw again that terrible white-lipped Face, and felt the measure of this great purpose rolling past him—immense, remorseless—which, for all its splendour, could include even so small a thing as this vain and silly girl. The tide of it rose about him with a flood of power. He glanced at the small black domino of the Carmen opposite him . . . he saw the little flashing eyes, the pert lips and mouth—thinking with something like a shudder of

38

that other countenance in the hollow of whose eyes hid tempests, yet which could look down upon a tiny fluttering paper, because that paper was an item of importance in its great scheme of which both beginning and end were nevertheless veiled. . . .

His thoughts must have wandered for a time. The conversation, at any rate, had meanwhile taken a singular turn. The girl was on her feet, the man facing her.

"Then what is this test of yours?" he was saying, half serious, half laughing—"this test which you say will prove how much I care?"

The girl put back between her lips the small red rose that was part of the Carmen costume. Either it was that the stalk made her lisp a little, or else that a sudden rush of the violins in the waltz drowned her words. The Reverend Phillip, standing there trembling—he never quite understood why he should have awaited her answer so nervously—only caught the second half of her phrase.

". . . that I gave you in this very room six weeks ago, and that you promised to carry about with you always?" he heard the end of her sentence, in a voice that for the first time that evening was serious; "because, if you've kept your word in a small thing like that, I can trust you to keep it in bigger things. It was a part of myself, you know, that little bit of hair!" She laughed deliciously in his face, raising herself on tiptoe with her hands behind her back. "You said so yourself, didn't you? You promised it should never, *never* leave you."

The man made a curiously sudden gesture as though a pain beyond his control passed through him. His hands were on the back of a chair. The chair squeaked audibly along the polished floor beneath a violent momentary pressure. He looked straight into his companion's eyes, but made no immediate reply.

Carmen's gaze behind the black mask became hard. With a truly feminine idiocy she was obviously playing this whim as a serious move in the game.

"For if you have lost *that*," she continued, her face flushing beneath the paint, "how can you expect to keep the rest of me, the important part of me?" She spoke as though she believed that he, too, was half-playing—that the next minute he would put his hand into his pocket and produce it. His delay, his awkwardness, above all his silence, angered her. For the surface of her self-contradictory character was obviously—minx.

After a pause that seemed interminable the man spoke, and for the first time his deep voice shook a little.

"This time tomorrow night you shall have it," he said.

"But you're leaving, you said, in the morning!" The tone was piqued and shrill.

"I shall stay another day—on purpose." A pause followed.

"Then you really have lost it—envelope and all—with your name in *my* writing on the outside, and my hair for all to recognise who find it—and to sneer."

Her eyes flashed as she said it. The girl was disappointed, incensed, furious. It was all silly enough, of course, and utterly out of proportion. But how silly and childish real life is apt to be at such moments, only those who have reached middle age and have observed closely can know. At the time, to the clergyman who stood there listening and observing, it seemed genuinely poignant, even tragic.

"Until the day before yesterday it had never left me for a single instant," he said at length. "I was in the mountains—glissading with your brother. It fell out of my pocket with a lot of other papers. I lost it on the upper snow slopes of the Dents Blenches—"

The rest of his words were drowned by an inrush of people, for the band was beginning a two-step and couples were sorting themselves and seeking their partners. A Frenchman, dressed as Napoleon, came up to claim his dance. Carmen was swept away. Scornfully, angrily, with concentrated resentment in her voice and manner, she turned upon her heel and from the lips that bit the stalk of the small red rose came the significant words—

"And with it you have also lost—*me!*"

She was gone. Perhaps the Reverend Phillip Ambleside only imagined the tears in her voice. He never knew, and had no time to think, for he found himself looking straight into the eyes of the lover, thus absurdly rejected, and who now became aware of his close presence for the first time. Even then the absurdity of the whole situation did not wholly reveal itself. It came later with reflection. At the moment he felt that it was all like a vivid and singular dream in which the values and proportions were oddly exaggerated, yet in which the sense of tragedy was distressingly real. His heart went out to the faithful and patient man who was being so trifled with, yet who might be in danger of losing by virtue of his very simplicity what was to be of real value in his life—and scheme.

"It's *my* move now," was the thought in his mind as he took a step forward.

The other, embarrassed and annoyed to discover that the whole scene had probably been overheard, made an awkward movement to withdraw, but before he could do so, the clergyman approached him. Only one step was necessary. He moved up from behind a palm, and drawing his hand from an inner pocket, he handed across to him a white envelope bearing the printed name of the hotel and a neat inscription in feminine writing just below it.

"I found this on the snow slopes of the Dents Blanches this afternoon," he said courteously. The other stared him steadily in the face—his colour coming and going quickly. "Take it to her and say that after all it was you—you, who were applying the test—that you wished to see if for so small a thing she was ready to reject so true a love. And, pray, pardon this interference which—er—chance has placed in my power. The matter, I need hardly say, is entirely between yourself and me."

The man took the paper awkwardly, a soft smile of gratitude and comprehension dawning in his eyes. He began to stammer a few words, but the clergyman did not stay to listen. He bowed politely and left him.

He went out of the hotel into the night, and a wind from the surrounding snow slopes brushed his face with its touch of great spaces. He looked up and saw the crowding stars, brilliant as in winter. The mountains in this faint light seemed incredibly close. Slowly he walked up the village street to his rooms in the *châlet* by the church. And suddenly the true proportion of normal things in this little life returned to him, and with it a sharp realisation of the triviality of the scene he had been forced to witness—and of the horrible grandeur of the means by which he had been dragged, by the scruff of his priestly neck as it were, so awkwardly into the middle of it all: merely to provide a scrap of evidence the loss of which threatened to bring about a foolish estrangement, and might conceivably have prevented a marriage of apparently insignificant importance.

He felt as though the machinery of the entire solar system had been employed to help a pair of ants carry a pine-needle too heavy for them to the top of the nest.

And then a moment's reflection brought to him another thought. For who could say what the result of this marriage might be? Who could say that from just the exact combination of those two forces—the earnest man, and the lighter girl—a son might not be born who should shake the world and lead some cherished purpose of Deity to completion? For, truly, of the threads which weave into the pattern of life and out again, men see but the tiny section immediately beneath their eyes. The majority focus their gaze upon some detail—thus losing the view of the whole. The beginning and the end are for ever hidden; and what appears insignificant and out of proportion when caught alone at close quarters, may reveal all the splendour of the Eternal Purpose when surveyed with the proper perspective—of the Infinite. The Reverend Phillip Ambleside felt as if for a moment he had been lifted to a height whence he had caught perhaps a glimpse of these larger horizons.

With his faith vastly strengthened, but his nerves considerably shaken, the clergyman went to bed and slept the sleep of a just man who has done his duty by chance as it were. He had helped forward a purpose of which he really understood nothing, but which, he somehow felt, was bigger than anything with which he had so far been connected in his life. Some day—his faith whispered it next morning while he was preparing his sermon—he would see the matter with proper perspective, and would understand.

The Deferred Appointment

The little "Photographic Studio" in the side-street beyond Shepherd's Bush had done no business all day, for the light had been uninviting to even the vainest sitter, and the murky sky that foreboded snow had hung over London without a break since dawn. Pedestrians went hurrying and shivering along the pavements disappearing into the gloom of countless ugly little houses the moment they passed beyond the glare of the big electric standards that lit the thundering motor-buses in the main street. The first flakes of snow, indeed, were already falling slowly, as though they shrank from settling in the grime. The wind moaned and sang dismally, catching the ears and lifting the shabby coat-tails of Mr. Mortimer Jenkyn, "Photographic Artist," as he stood outside and put the shutters up with his own cold hands in despair of further trade. It was five minutes to six.

With a lingering glance at the enlarged portrait of a fat man in masonic regalia who was the pride and glory of his windowfront, he fixed the last hook of the shutter, and turned to go indoors. There was developing and framing to be done upstairs, not very remunerative work, but better, at any rate, than waiting in an empty studio for customers who did not come—wasting the heat of two oil-stoves into the bargain. And it was then, in the act of closing the street-door behind him, that he saw a man standing in the shadows of the narrow passage, staring fixedly into his face.

Mr. Jenkyn admits that he jumped. The man was so very close, yet he had not seen him come in; and in the eyes was such a curiously sad and appealing expression. He had already sent his assistant home, and there was no other occupant of the little two-storey house. The man must have slipped past him from the dark street while his back was turned. Who in the world could he be, and what could he want? Was he beggar, customer, or rogue?

"Good evening," Mr. Jenkyn said, washing his hands, but using only half the oily politeness of tone with which he favoured sitters. He was just going to add "sir," feeling it wiser to be on the safe side, when the stranger shifted his position so that the light fell directly upon his face, and Mr. Jenkyn was aware that he—recognised him. Unless he was greatly mistaken, it was the second-hand bookseller in the main street.

"Ah, it's you, Mr. Wilson!" he stammered, making half a question of it, as though not quite convinced. "Pardon me; I did not quite catch your face—er—I was just shutting up." The other bowed his head in reply. "Won't you come in? Do, please."

Mr. Jenkyn led the way. He wondered what was the matter. The visitor was not among his customers; indeed, he could hardly claim to know him, having only seen him occasionally when calling at the shop for slight purchases of paper and what not. The man, he now realised, looked fearfully ill and wasted, his face pale and haggard. It upset him rather, this sudden, abrupt call. He felt sorry, pained. He felt uneasy.

Into the studio they passed, the visitor going first as though he knew the way, Mr. Jenkyn noticing through his flurry that he was in his "Sunday best." Evidently, he had come with a definite purpose. It was odd. Still without speaking, he moved straight across the room and posed himself in front of the dingy back-ground of painted trees, facing the camera. The studio was brightly lit. He seated himself in the faded armchair, crossed his legs, drew up the little round table with the artificial roses upon it in a tall, thin vase, and struck an attitude.

He meant to be photographed. His eyes, staring straight into the lens, draped as it was with the black velvet curtain, seemed, however, to take no account of the Photographic Artist. But Mr. Jenkyn, standing still beside the door, felt a cold air playing over his face that was not merely the winter cold from the street. He felt his hair rise. A slight shiver ran down his back. In that pale, drawn face, and in those staring eyes across the room that gazed so fixedly into the draped camera, he read the signature of illness that no longer knows hope. It was Death that he saw.

In a flash the impression came and went—less than a second. The whole business, indeed, had not occupied two minutes. Mr. Jenkyn pulled himself together with a strong effort, dismissed his foolish obsession, and came sharply to practical considerations. "Forgive me," he said, a trifle thickly, confusedly, "but I—er—did not quite realise. You desire to sit for your portrait, of course. I've had such a busy day, and—'ardly looked for a customer so late." The clock, as he spoke, struck six. But he did not notice the sound. Through his mind ran another reflection: "A man shouldn't 'ave his picture taken when he's ill and next door to dying. Lord! He'll want a lot of touching-up and finishin', too!"

He began discussing the size, price, and length—the usual rigmarole of his "profession," and the other, sitting there, still vouchsafed no comment or reply. He simply made the impression of a man in a great hurry, who wished to finish a disagreeable business without unnecessary talk. Many men, reflected the photographer, were the same; being photographed was worse to them than going to the dentist. Mr. Jenkyn filled the pauses with his professional running talk and patter, while the sitter, fixed and motionless, kept his first position and stared at the camera.

The photographer rather prided himself upon his ability to make sitters look bright and pleasant; but this man was hopeless. It was only afterwards Mr. Jenkyn recalled the singular fact that he never once touched him—that, in fact, something connected possibly with his frail appearance of deadly illness had prevented his going close to arrange the details of the hastily assumed pose.

"It must be a flashlight, of course, Mr. Wilson," he said, fidgeting at length with the camera-stand, shifting it slightly nearer; while the other moved his head gently yet impatiently in agreement. Mr. Jenkyn longed to suggest his coming another time when he looked better, to speak with sympathy of his illness; to say something, in fact, that might establish a personal relation. But his tongue in this respect seemed utterly tied. It was just this personal relation which seemed impossible to approach—absolutely and peremptorily impossible. There seemed a barrier between the two. He could only chatter the usual professional commonplaces. To tell the truth, Mr. Jenkyn thinks he felt a little dazed the whole time— not quite his usual self. And, meanwhile, his uneasiness oddly increased. He hurried. He, too, wanted the matter done with and his visitor gone.

At length everything was ready, only the flashlight waiting to be turned on, when, stooping, he covered his head with the velvet cloth and peered through the lens—at no one! When he says "at no one," however, he qualifies it thus: "There was a quick flash of brilliant white light and a face in the middle of it—my gracious Heaven! But such a face—'im, yet not 'im like a sudden rushing glory of a face! It shot off like lightning out of the camera's field of vision. It left me blinded, I assure you, 'alf blinded, and that's a fac'. It was sheer dazzling!"

It seems Mr. Jenkyn remained entangled a moment in the cloth, eyes closed, breath coming in gasps, for when he got clear and straightened up again, staring once more at his customer over the top of the camera, he stared for the second time at—no one. And the cap that he held in his left hand he clapped feverishly over the uncovered lens. Mr. Jenkyn staggered . . . looked hurriedly round the empty studio, then ran, knocking a chair over as he went, into the passage. The hall was deserted, the front door closed. His visitor had disappeared "almost as though he hadn't never been there at all"—thus he described it to himself in a terrified whisper. And again, he felt the hair rise on his scalp; his skin crawled a little, and something put back the ice against his spine.

After a moment he returned to the studio and somewhat feverishly examined it. There stood the chair against the dingy background of trees; and there, close beside it, was the round table with the flower vase. Less than a minute ago Mr. Thomas Wilson, looking like death, had been sitting in that very chair. "It wasn't *all* a sort of dreamin', then," ran through his disordered and frightened mind. "I did see something . . .!" He remembered vaguely stories he had read in the newspapers, stories of queer warnings that saved people from disasters, apparitions, faces seen in dream, and so forth. "Maybe," he thought with confusion, "something's going to 'appen to *me!*"

Further than that he could not get for some little time, as he stood there staring about him, almost expecting that Mr. Wilson might reappear as strangely as he had disappeared. He went over the whole scene again and again, reconstructing it in minutest detail. And only then for the first time, did he plainly realise two things which somehow or other he had not thought strange before, but now thought very strange. For his visitor, he remembered, had not uttered a single word, nor had he, Mr. Jenkyn, once touched his person. . . . And, thereupon, without more ado, he put on his hat and coat and went round to the little shop in the main street to buy some ink and stationery, which he did not in the least require.

The shop seemed all as usual, though Mr. Wilson himself was not visible behind the littered desk. A tall gentleman was talking in low tones to the partner. Mr. Jenkyn bowed as he went in, then stood examining a case of cheap stylographic pens, waiting for the others to finish. It was impossible to avoid overhearing. Besides, the little shop had distinguished customers sometimes, he had heard, and this evidently was one of them. He only understood part of the conversation, but he remembers all of it. "Singular, yes, these last words of dying men," the tall man was saying, "very singular. You remember Newman's: 'More light,' wasn't it?" The bookseller nodded. "Fine," he said, "fine, that!"

There was a pause. Mr. Jenkyn stooped lower over the pens. "This, too, was fine in its way," the gentleman added, straightening up to go; "the old promise, you see, unfulfilled but not forgotten. Cropped up suddenly out of the delirium. Curious, very curious! A good, conscientious man to the last. In all the twenty years I've known him he never broke his word. . .

A motor-bus drowned a sentence, and then was heard in the bookseller's voice, as he moved towards the door: ". . .You see, he was halfway down the stairs before they found him, always repeating the same thing, 'I promised the wife, I promised the wife.' And it was a job. I'm told, getting him back again . . . he struggled so. That's what finished him so quick, I suppose. Fifteen minutes later he was gone, and his last words were always the same, 'I promised the wife'. . ."

The tall man was gone, and Mr. Jenkyn forgot about his purchases. "When did it 'appen?" he heard himself asking in a voice he hardly recognised as his own. And the reply roared and thundered in his ears as he went down the street a minute later to his house: "Close on six o'clock—a few minutes before the hour. Been ill for weeks, yes. Caught him out of bed with high fever on his way to your place, Mr. Jenkyn, calling at the top of his voice that he'd forgotten to see you about his picture being taken. Yes, very sad, very sad indeed."

But Mr. Jenkyn did not return to his studio. He left the light burning there all night. He went to the little room where he slept out, and next day gave the plate to be developed by his assistant. "Defective plate, sir," was the report in due course; "shows nothing but a flash of light—uncommonly brilliant."

"Make a print of it all the same," was the reply. Six months later, when he examined the plate and print, Mr. Jenkyn found that the singular streaks of light had disappeared from both. The uncommon brilliance had faded out completely as though it had never been there.

The Eccentricity of Simon Parnacute

1

It was one of those mornings in early spring when even the London streets run beauty. The day, passing through the sky with clouds of flying hair, touched every one with the magic of its own irresponsible gaiety, as it alternated between laughter and the tears of sudden showers.

In the parks the trees, faintly clothed with gauze, were busying themselves shyly with the thoughts of coming leaves. The air held a certain sharpness, but the sun swam through the dazzling blue spaces with bursts of almost summer heat; and a wind, straight from the haunted south, laid its soft persuasion upon all, bringing visions too fair to last—long thoughts of youth, of cowslip-meadows, white sails, waves on yellow sand, and other pictures innumerable and enchanting.

So potent, indeed, was this spell of awakening spring that even Simon Parnacute, retired Professor of Political Economy—elderly, thin-faced, and ruminating in his big skull those large questions that concern the polity of nations—formed no exception to the general rule. For, as he slowly made his way down the street that led from his apartment to the Little Park, he was fully aware that this magic of the spring was in his own blood too, and that the dust which had accumulated with the years upon the surface of his soul was being stirred by one of the softest breezes he had ever felt in the whole course of his arduous and tutorial career.

And—it so happened—just as he reached the foot of the street where the houses fell away towards the open park, the sun rushed out into one of the sudden blue spaces of the sky, and drenched him in a wave of delicious heat that for all the world was like the heat of July.

Professor Parnacute, once lecturer, now merely ponderer, was an exact thinker, dealing carefully with the facts of life as he saw them. He was a good man and a true. He dealt in large emotions, becoming for one who studied nations rather than individuals, and of all diplomacies of the heart he was rudely ignorant. He lived always at the centre of the circle—his own circle—and eccentricity was a thing to him utterly abhorrent. Convention ruled him, body, soul and mind. To know a disordered thought, or an unwonted emotion, troubled him as much as to see a picture crooked on a wall, or a man's collar projecting beyond his overcoat. Eccentricity was the symptom of a disease.

Thus, as he reached the foot of the street and felt the sun and wind upon his withered cheeks, this unexpected call of the spring came to him sharply as something altogether out of place and illegitimate—symptom of an irregular condition of mind that must be instantly repressed. And it was just here, while the crowd jostled and delayed him, that there smote upon his ear the song incarnate of the very spring whose spell he was in the act of relegating to its proper place in his personal economy: he heard the entrancing *singing of a bird!*

Transfixed with wonder and delight, he stood for a whole minute and listened. Then, slowly turning, he found himself staring straight into the small beseeching eyes of a—thrush; a thrush in a cage that hung upon the outside wall of a bird-fancier's shop behind him.

Perhaps he would not have lingered more than these few seconds, however, had not the crowd held him momentarily prisoner in a spot immediately opposite the shop, where his head, too, was exactly on a level with the hanging cage. Thus, he was perforce obliged to stand, and watch, and listen; and, as he did so, the bird's rapturous and appealing song played upon the feelings already awakened by the spring, urging them upwards and outwards to a point that grew perilously moving.

Both sound and sight caught and held him spellbound.

The bird, once well-favoured perhaps, he perceived was now thin and bedraggled, its feathers disarrayed by continual flitting along its perch, and by endless fluttering of wings and body against the bars of its narrow cage. There was not room to open both wings properly; it frequently dashed itself against the sides of its wooden prison; and all the force of its vain and passionate desire for freedom shone in the two small and glittering eyes which gazed beseechingly through the bars at the passers-by.

It looked broken and worn with the ceaseless renewal of the futile struggle. Hopping along the bar, cocking its dainty little head on one side, and looking straight into the professor's eyes, it managed (by some inarticulate magic known only to the eyes of creatures in prison) to spell out the message of its pain—the poignant longing for the freedom of the open sky, the lift of the great winds, the glory of the sun upon its lustreless feathers.

Now it so chanced that this combined onslaught of sight and sound caught the elderly professor along the line of least resistance—the line of an untried, and therefore unexhausted, sensation. Here, apparently, was an emotion hitherto unrealised, and so not yet regulated away into atrophy.

For, with an intuition as singular as it was searching, he suddenly understood something of the passion of the wild Caged Things of the world, and realised in a flash of passing vision something of their unutterable pain.

In one swift moment of genuine mystical sympathy he *felt with* their peculiar quality of unsatisfied longing exactly as though it were his own; the longing, not only of captive birds and animals, but of anguished men and women, trapped by circumstance, confined by weakness, cabined by character and temperament, all yearning for a freedom they knew not how to reach—caged by the smallness of their desires, by the impotence of their wills, by the pettiness of their souls—caged in bodies from which death alone could finally bring release.

Something of all this found its way into the elderly professor's heart as he stood watching the pantomime of the captive thrush—the Caged Thing;—and, after a moment's hesitation that represented a vast amount of condensed feeling, he deliberately entered the low doorway of the shop and inquired the price of the bird.

"The thrush—er—singing in the small cage," he stammered.

"One *and* six only, sir," replied the coarse, red-faced man who owned the shop, looking up from a rabbit that he was pushing with clumsy fingers into a box; "only one shilling and sixpence,"—and then went on with copious remarks upon thrushes in general and the superior qualities of this one in particular. "Been 'ere four months and sings just lovely," he added, by way of climax.

"Thank you," said Parnacute quietly, trying to persuade himself that he did not feel mortified by his impulsive and eccentric action; "then I will purchase the bird—at once—er—if you please."

"Couldn't go far wrong, sir," said the man, shoving the rabbit to one side, and going outside to fetch the thrush.

"No, I shall not require the cage, but—er—you may put him in a cardboard box perhaps, so that I can carry him easily."

51

He referred to the bird as "him," though at any other time he would have said "it," and the change, noted surreptitiously as it were, added to his general sense of confusion. It was too late, however, to alter his mind, and after watching the man force the bird with gross hands into a cardboard box, he gathered up the noose of string with which it was tied and walked with as much dignity and self-respect as he could muster out of the shop.

But the moment he got into the street with this living parcel under his arm—he both heard and felt the scuttling of the bird's feet—the realisation that he had been guilty of what he considered an outrageous act of eccentricity almost overwhelmed him. For he had succumbed in most regrettable fashion to a momentary impulse, and had bought the bird in order to release it!

"Dear me!" he thought, "how ever could I have allowed myself to do so eccentric and impulsive a thing!"

And, but for the fact that it would merely have accentuated his eccentricity, he would then and there have returned to the shop and given back the bird.

That, however, being now clearly impossible, he crossed the road and entered the Little Park by the first iron gateway he could find. He walked down the gravel path, fumbling with the string. In another minute the bird would have been out, when he chanced to glance round in order to make sure he was unobserved and saw against the shrubbery on his left—a policeman.

This, he felt, was most vexatious, for he had hoped to complete the transaction unseen. Straightening himself up, he nervously fastened the string again, and walked on slowly as though nothing had happened, searching for a more secluded spot where he should be entirely free from observation.

Professor Parnacute now became aware that his vexation—primarily caused by his act of impulse, and increased by the fact that he was observed—had become somewhat acute. It was extraordinary, he reflected, how policemen had this way of suddenly outlining themselves in the least appropriate—the least necessary—places. There was no reason why a policeman should have been standing against that innocent shrubbery, where there was nothing to do, no one to watch. At almost any other point in the Little Park he might have served some possibly useful purpose, and yet, forsooth, he must select the one spot where he was not wanted—where his presence, indeed, was positively objectionable.

The policeman, meanwhile, watched him steadily as he retreated with the obnoxious parcel. He carried it upside down now without knowing it. He felt as though he had been detected in a crime. He watched the policeman, too, out of the corner of his eye, longing to be done with the whole business.

"That policeman is a tremendous fellow," he thought to himself. "I have never seen a constable so large, so stalwart. He must be *the* policeman of the district"—whatever that might mean—"a veritable wall and tower of defence." The helmet made him think of a battering ram, and the buttons on his overcoat of the muzzles of guns.

He moved away round the corner with as much innocence as he could assume, as though he were carrying a package of books or some new article of apparel.

It is, no doubt, the duty of every alert constable to observe as acutely as possible the course of events passing before his eyes, yet this particular Bobby seemed far more interested than the circumstances warranted in Parnacute's cardboard box. He kept his gaze remorselessly upon it. Perhaps, thought the professor, he heard the scutterings of the frightened bird within. Perhaps he thought it was a cat going to be drowned in the ornamental water. Perhaps—oh, dreadful ideal—he thought it was a baby!

The suspicions of an intelligent policeman, however, being past finding out, Simon Parnacute wisely ignored them, and just then passed round a corner where he was screened from this persistent observer by a dense growth of rhododendron bushes.

Seizing the opportune moment, and acting with a prompt decision born of the dread of the reappearing policeman, he cut the string, opened the lid of the box, and an instant later had the intense satisfaction of seeing the imprisoned thrush hop upon the cardboard edge and then fly with a beautiful curving dip and a whirr of wings off into the open sky. It turned once as it flew, and its bright brown eye looked at him. Then it was gone, lost in the sunshine that blazed over the shrubberies and beckoned it out over their waving tops across the river.

The prisoner was free. For the space of a whole minute, the professor stood still, conscious of a sense of genuine relief. That sound of wings, that racing sweep of the little quivering body escaping into limitless freedom, that penetrating look of gratitude from the wee brown eyes—these stirred in him again the same prodigious emotion he had experienced for the first time that afternoon outside the bird-fancier's shop. The release of the "caged creature" provided him with a kind of vicarious experience of freedom and delight such as he had never before known in his whole life. It almost seemed as though he had escaped himself—out of his "circle."

Then, as he faced about, with the empty box dangling in his hand, the first thing he saw, coming slowly down the path towards him with measured tread, was—the big policeman.

Something very stern, something very forbidding, hung like an atmosphere of warning about this guardian of the law in a blue uniform. It brought him back sharply to the rigid facts of life, and the soft beauty of the spring day vanished and left him untouched. He accepted the reminder that life is earnest, and that eccentricities are invitations to disaster. Sooner or later the policeman is bound to make his appearance.

However, this particular constable, of course, passed him without word or gesture, and as soon as he came to one of the little wire baskets provided for the purpose, the professor dropped his box into it, and then made his way slowly and thoughtfully back to his apartment and his luncheon.

But the eccentricity of which he had been guilty circled and circled in his mind, reminding him with merciless insistence of a foolish act he should not have committed, and plaguing him with remorseless little stabs for having indulged in an impulsive and irregular proceeding.

For, to him, the inevitableness of life came as a fact to which he was resigned, rather than as a force to be appropriated for the ends of his own soul; and the sight of the happy bird escaping into sky and sunshine, with the figure of the inflexible and stern-lipped policeman in the background, made a deep impression upon him that would sooner or later be certain to bear fruit.

"Dear me," thought the Professor of Political Economy, giving mental expression to this sentiment, "I shall pay for this in the long run! Without question I shall pay for it!"

2

If it may be taken that there is no Chance, playing tricksy-wise behind the scenes of existence, but that all events falling into the lives of men are the calculated results of adequate causes, then Mr. Simon Parnacute, late Professor of Political Economy in C— College, certainly did pay for his spring aberration, in the sense that he caught a violent chill which brought him to bed and speedily developed into pneumonia.

It was the evening of the sixth day, and he lay weary and feverish in his bedroom on the top floor of the building which held his little self-contained apartment. The nurse was downstairs having her tea. A shaded lamp stood beside the bed, and through the window—the blinds being not yet drawn —he saw the sea of roofs and chimney-pots, and the stream of wires, sharply outlined against a sunset sky of gold and pink. High and thin above the dusk floated long strips of coloured cloud, and the first stars twinkled through the April vapours that gathered with the approach of night.

Presently the door opened and someone came in softly half-way across the room, and then stopped. The professor turned wearily and saw that the maid stood there and was trying to speak. She seemed flustered, he noticed, and her face was rather white.

"What's the matter *now*, Emily?" he asked feebly, yet irritably.

"Please, professor—there's a gentleman—" there she stuck.

"Someone to see me? The doctor again already?" queried the patient, wondering in a vague, absent way why the girl should seem so startled.

As he spoke there was a sound of footsteps on the landing outside—heavy footsteps.

"But please, professor, sir, it's not the doctor," the maid faltered, "only I couldn't get his name, and I couldn't stop him, an' he said you expected him— and I think he looks like—"

The approaching footsteps frightened the girl so much that she could not find words to complete her description. They were just outside the door now.

"—like a perliceman!" she finished with a rush, backing towards the door as though she feared the professor would leap from his bed to demolish her.

"A *policeman!*" gasped Mr. Parnacute, unable to believe his ears. "A policeman, Emily! In my apartment?"

And before the sick man could find words to express his particular annoyance that any stranger (above all a constable) should intrude at such a time, the door was pushed wide open, the girl had vanished with a flutter of skirts, and the tall figure of a man and stood in full view upon the threshold, and stared steadily across the room at the occupant of the bed on the other side.

It was indeed a policeman, and a very large policeman. Moreover, it was *the* policeman.

The instant the professor recognised the familiar form of the man from the park his anger, for some quite unaccountable reason, vanished almost entirely; the sharp vexation he had felt a moment before died away; and, sinking back exhausted among the pillows, he only found breath to ask him to close the door and come in. The fact was, astonishment had used up the small store of energy at his disposal, and for the moment he could think of nothing else to do.

The policeman closed the door quietly and moved forward towards the centre of the room, so that the circle of light from the shaded lamp at the head of the bed reached his figure but fell just short of his face.

The invalid sat up in bed again and stared. As nothing seemed to happen, he recovered his scattered wits a little.

"You are the policeman from the park, unless I mistake?" he asked feebly, with mingled pomposity and resentment.

The big man bowed in acknowledgment and removed his helmet, holding it before him in his hand. His face was peculiarly bright, almost as though it reflected the glow of a bull's-eye lantern concealed somewhere about his huge person.

"I thought I recognised you," went on the professor, exasperated a little by the other's self-possession. "Are you perhaps aware that I am ill—too ill to see strangers, and that to force your way up in this fashion!" He left the sentence unfinished for lack of suitable expletives.

"You are certainly ill," replied the constable, speaking for the first time; "but then—I am *not* a stranger." His voice was wonderfully pitched and modulated for a policeman.

"Then, by what right, pray, do you dare to intrude upon me at such a time?" snapped the other, ignoring the latter statement.

"My duty, sir," the man replied, with a rather wonderful dignity, "knows nothing of time or place."

Professor Parnacute looked at him a little more closely as he stood there helmet in hand. He was something more, he gathered, than an ordinary constable; an inspector perhaps. He examined him carefully; but he understood nothing about differences in uniform, of bands or stars upon sleeve and collar.

"If you are here in the prosecution of your duty, then," exclaimed the man of careful mind, searching feverishly for some possible delinquency on the part of his small staff of servants, "pray be seated and state your business; but as briefly as possible. My throat pains me, and my strength is low." He spoke with less acerbity. The dignity of the visitor began to impress him in some vague fashion he did not understand.

The big figure in blue bowed again, but made no sign of advance.

"You come from X—— Station, I presume?" Parnacute added, mentioning the police station round the corner. He sank deeper into his pillows, conscious that his strength was becoming exhausted.

"From Headquarters—I come," replied the colossus in a deep voice. The professor had only the vaguest idea what Headquarters meant, yet the phrase conveyed an importance that somehow was not lost upon him. Meanwhile his impatience grew with his exhaustion.

"I must request you, officer, to state your business with dispatch," he said tartly, "or to come again when I am better able to attend to you. Next week, no doubt—"

"There is no time *but* the present," returned the other, with an odd choice of words that escaped the notice of his perplexed hearer, as he produced from a capacious pocket in the tail of his overcoat a notebook bound with some shining metal like gold.

"Your name is Parnacute?" he asked, consulting the book.

"Yes," answered the other, with the resignation of exhaustion.

"*Simon* Parnacute?"

"Of course, yes."

"And on the third of April last," he went on, looking keenly over the top of the note-book at the sick man, "you, Simon Parnacute, entered the shop of Theodore Spinks in the Lower P—— Road, and purchased from him a certain living creature?"

"Yes," answered the professor, beginning to feel hot at the discovery of his folly.

"A bird?"

"A bird."

"A thrush?"

"A thrush."

"A singing thrush?"

"Oh yes, it was a singing thrush, if you *must* know."

"In money you paid for this thrush the sum of one shilling *and* six pennies?" He emphasised the "and" just as the bird-fancier had done.

"One and six, yes."

"But in true value," said the policeman, speaking with grave emphasis, "it cost you a great deal more?"

"Perhaps." He winced internally at the memory. He was so astonished, too, that the visit had to do with himself and not with some of his servants.

"You paid for it with your heart?" insisted the other.

The professor made no reply. He started. He almost writhed under the sheets.

"Am I right?" asked the policeman.

"That is the fact, I suppose," he said in a low voice, sorely puzzled by the catechism.

"You carried this bird away in a cardboard box to E— Gardens by the river, and there you gave it freedom and watched it fly away?"

"Your statement is correct, I think, in every particular. But really— this absurd cross-examination, my good man—!"

"And your motive in so doing," continued the policeman, his voice quite drowning the invalid's feeble tones, "was the unselfish one of releasing an imprisoned and tortured creature?"

Simon Parnacute looked up with the greatest possible surprise.

"I think—well, well!—perhaps it was," he murmured apologetically. "The extraordinary singing—it *was* extraordinary, you know, and the sight of the little thing beating its wings pained me."

The big policeman put away his note-book suddenly, and moved closer to the bed so that his face entered the circle of lamplight.

"In that case," he cried, "*you are my man!*"

"I am your man!" exclaimed the professor, with an uncontrollable start.

"The man I want," repeated the other, smiling.

His voice had suddenly grown soft and wonderful, like the ringing of a silver gong, and into his face had come an expression of wistful tenderness that made it positively beautiful. It shone. Never before, out of a picture, had he seen such a look upon a human countenance, or heard such tones issue from the lips of a human being. He thought, swiftly and confusedly, of a woman, of *the* woman he had never found—of a dream, an enchantment as of music or vision upon the senses.

"Wants me!" he thought with alarm. "What have I done now? What new eccentricity have I been guilty of?"

Strange, bewildering ideas crowded into his mind, blurred in outline, preposterous in character. A sensation of cold caught at his fever and overmastered it, bathing him in perspiration, making him tremble, yet not with fear. A new and curious delight had begun to pluck at his heart-strings.

Then an extravagant suspicion crossed his brain, yet a suspicion not wholly unwarranted.

"Who are you?" he asked sharply, looking up. "Are you really only a policeman?"

"The man drew himself up so that he appeared, if possible, even huger than before.

"I am a World-Policeman," he answered, "a guardian, perhaps, rather than a detective."

"Heavens above!" cried the professor, thinking of madness and the crimes committed in madness.

"Yes," he went on in those calm, musical tones that before long began to have a reassuring effect upon his listener, "and it is my duty, among many others, to keep an eye upon eccentric people; to lock them up when necessary, and when their sentences have expired, to release them. Also," he added impressively, "as in your case, to let them out of their cages without pain—when they've earned it."

"Gracious goodness me!" exclaimed Parnacute, unaccustomed to the use of expletives, but unable to think of anything else to say.

"And sometimes to see that their cages do not destroy them—and that they do not beat themselves to death against the bars," he went on, smiling quite wonderfully. "Our duties are varied and numerous. I am one of a large force."

The man learned in political economy felt as though his head were spinning. He thought of calling for help. Indeed, he had already made a motion with his hand towards the bell when a gesture on the part of his strange visitor restrained him.

"Then why do you want *me*, if I may ask?" he faltered instead.

"To mark you down; and when the time comes to let you out of your cage easily, comfortably, without pain. That's one reward for your kindness to the bird."

The professor's fears had now quite disappeared. The policeman seemed perfectly harmless after all.

"It's *very* kind of you," he said feebly, drawing his arm back beneath the bedclothes. "Only—er—I was not aware, exactly, that I lived in a cage."

He looked up resignedly into the man's face.

"You only realise that when you get out," he replied. "They're all like that. The bird didn't quite understand what was wrong; it only knew that it felt miserable. Same with you. You feel unhappy in that body of yours, and in that little careful mind you regulate so nicely; but, for the life of you, you don't quite know what it is that's wrong.

You want space, freedom, a taste of liberty. You want to fly, that's what you want!" he cried, raising his voice.

"I—want—to—fly?" gasped the invalid.

"Oh," smiling again, "we World-Policemen have thousands of cases just like yours. Our field is a large one, a very large one indeed."

He stepped into the light more fully and turned sideways.

"Here's my badge, if you care to see it," he said proudly.

He stooped a little so that the professor's beady eyes could easily focus themselves upon the collar of his overcoat. There, just like the lettering upon the collar of an ordinary London policeman, only in bright gold instead of silver, shone the constellation of the Pleiades. Then he turned and showed the other side, and Parnacute saw the constellation of Orion slanting upwards, as he had often seen it tilting across the sky at night.

"Those are my badges," he repeated proudly, straightening himself up again and moving back into the shadow.

"And very fine they are, too," said the professor, his increasing ex-haustion suggesting no better observation. But with the sight of those starry figures had come to him a strange whiff of the open skies, space, and wind—the winds of the world.

"So that when the time comes," the World-Policeman resumed, "you may have confidence. I will let you out without pain or fear just as you let out the bird. And, meanwhile, you may as well realise that you live in a cage just as cramped and shut away from light and freedom as the thrush did."

"Thank you; I will certainly try," whispered Parnacute, almost fainting with fatigue.

There followed a pause, during which the policeman put on his helmet, tightened his belt, and then began to search vigorously for something in his coat-tail pockets.

"And now," ventured the sick man, feeling half fearful, half happy, though without knowing exactly why, "is there anything more I can do for you, Mr. World-Policeman?" He was conscious that his words were peculiar yet he could not help it. They seemed to slip out of their own accord.

"There's nothing more you can do for *me*, sir, thank you," answered the man in his most silvery tones. "But there's something more I can do for *you!* And that is to give you a preliminary taste of freedom, so that you may realise you do live in a cage, and be less confused and puzzled when you come to make the final Escape."

Parnacute caught his breath sharply—staring open-mouthed.

With a single stride the policeman covered the space between himself and the bed. Before the withered, fever-stricken little professor could utter a word or a cry, he had caught up the wasted body out of the bed, shaken the bedclothes off him like paper from a parcel, and slung him without ceremony across his gigantic shoulders. Then he crossed the room, and producing the key from his coat-tail pocket, he put it straight into the solid wall of the room. He turned it, and the entire side of the house opened like a door.

For one second Simon Parnacute looked back and saw the lamp, and the fire, and the bed. And in the bed, he saw his own body lying motionless in profound slumber.

Then, as the policeman balanced, hovering upon the giddy edge, he looked outward and saw the network of street-lamps far below, and heard the deep roar of the city smite upon his ears like the thunder of a sea.

The next moment the man stepped out into space, and he saw that they were rising up swiftly towards the dark vault of sky, where stars twinkled down upon them between streaks of thin flying clouds.

3

Once outside, floating in the night, the policeman gave his shoulder a mighty jerk and tossed his small burden into free space. "Jump away!" he cried. "You're quite safe."

The professor dropped like a bullet towards the pavement; then suddenly began to rise again, like a balloon. All traces of fever or bodily discomfort had left him utterly. He felt light as air, and strong as lightning. "Now, where shall we go to?" The voice sounded above him. Simon Parnacute was no flyer. He had never indulged in those strange flying-dreams that form a weird pleasure in the sleep-lives of many people. He was terrified beyond belief until he found that he did not crash against the earth, and that he had within him the power to regulate his movements, to rise or sink at will.

Then, of course, the wildest fury of delight and freedom he had ever known flashed all over him and burned in his brain like an intoxication. "The big cities, or the stars?" asked the World-Policeman.

"No, no," he cried, "the country—the open country. And other lands." For Simon Parnacute had never travelled. Incredible as it may seem, the professor had never in his life been farther out of England than in a sailingboat at Southend. His body had travelled even less than his imagination. With this suddenly increased capacity for motion, the desire to race about and see became a passion. "Woods, Mountains, Seas, Deserts. Anything but houses and people !" he shouted, rising upwards to his companion without the smallest effort. An intense longing to see the desolate, unfrequented regions of the earth seized him and tore its way out into words strangely unlike his normal and measured mode of speech.

All his life he had paced to and fro in a formal little garden with the most precise paths imaginable. Now he wanted a trackless world. The reaction was terrific. The desire of the Arab for the desert, of the gipsy for the open heaths, the "desire of the snipe for the wilderness"—the longing of the eternal wanderer—possessed his soul and found vent in words. It was just as though the passion of the released thrush were reproducing itself in him and becoming articulate. "I am haunted by the faces of the world's forgotten places," he cried aloud impetuously. "Beaches lying in the moonlight, all forsaken in the moonlight—"

His utterance, like the bird's, had become lyrical. "Can this be what the thrush felt?" he wondered.

"Let's be off then," the policeman called back. "There's no time but the present, remember."

He rushed through space like a huge projectile. He made a faint whistling noise as he went. Parnacute followed suit. The lightest desire, he found, gave him instantly the ease and speed of thought. The policeman had taken off his helmet, overcoat and belt, and dropped them down somewhere into a London street. He now appeared as a mere blue outline of a man, scarcely discernible against the dark sky —an outline filled with air. The professor glanced down at himself and saw that he, too, was a mere outline of a man—a pallid outline filled with the purple air of night. "Now then," sang out this "Bobby-of-the-World."

Side by side they shot up with a wild rush, and the lights of London, town and suburbs, flashed away beneath them in streaming lines and patches. In a second darkness filled the huge gap, pouring behind them like a mighty wave. Other streams and patches of light succeeded quickly, blurred and faint, like lamps of railway stations from a night express, as other towns dropped past them in a series and were swallowed up in the gulf behind. A cool salt air smote their faces, and Parnacute heard the soft crashing of waves as they crossed the Channel, and swept on over the fields and forests of France, glimmering below like the squares of a mighty chess-board.

Like toys, village after village shot by, smelling of peat-smoke, cattle, and the faint windiness of coming spring. Sometimes they passed below the clouds and lost the stars, sometimes above them and lost the world; sometimes over forests roaring like the sea, sometimes above vast plains still and silent as the grave; but always Parnacute saw the constellations of Orion and Pleiades shining on the coat-collar of the soaring policeman, their little patterns picked out as with tiny electric lamps. Below them lay the huge map of the earth, raised, scarred, darkly coloured, and breathing—a map alive. Then came the Jura, soft and purple, carpeted with forests, rolling below them like a dream, and they looked down into slumbering valleys and heard far below the tumbling of water and the singing of countless streams.

"Glory, glory!" cried the professor. "And do the birds know *this?*"

"Not the imprisoned ones," was the reply.

And presently they whipped across large gleaming bodies of water as the lakes of Switzerland approached. Then, entering the zones of icy atmosphere, they looked down and saw white towers and pinnacles of silver, and the forms of scarred and mighty glaciers that rose and fell among the fields of eternal snow, folding upon the mountains in vast procession.

"I think—I'm frightened," gasped Parnacute, clutching at his companion, but seizing only the frigid air.

The policeman shouted with laughter.

"This is nothing—compared to Mars or the moon," he cried, soaring till the Alps looked like a patch of snowdrops shining in a Surrey garden. "You'll soon get accustomed to it." The Professor of Political Economy rose after him. But presently they sank again in an immense curving sweep and touched the tops of the highest mountains with their toes. This sent them instantly aloft again, bounding with the impetus of rockets, and so they careered on through the perfumed, pathless night till they came to Italy and left the Alps behind them like the shadowy wall of another world that had silently moved up close to them through space.

"Mother of Mountains!" shouted the delighted man of colleges. "And did the thrush know this too?"

"It has you to thank, if so," the policeman answered.

"And I have you to thank."

"No—yourself," replied his flying guide.

And then the desert! They had crossed the scented Mediterranean and reached the zones of sand. It rose in clouds and sheets as a mighty

63

wind stirred across the leagues of loneliness that stretched below them into blue distance. It whirled about them and stung their faces.

"Thin ropes of sand which crumble ere they bind!" cried the professor with a peal of laughter, not knowing what he said in the delirium of his pleasure.

The hot smell of the sand excited him; the knowledge that for hundreds of miles he could not see a house or a human being thrilled him dizzily with the incalculable delight of freedom. The splendour of the night, mystical and incommunicable, overcame him. He rose, laughing wildly, shaking the sand from his hair, and taking gigantic curves into the starry space about him. He remembered vividly the sight of those bedraggled wings in the little cramped cage—and then looked down and realised that here the winds sank exhausted from the very weariness of too much space. Oh, that he could tear away the bars of every cage the world had ever known—set free all captive creatures—restore to all wild, winged life the liberty of open spaces that is theirs by right!

He cried again to the stars and winds and deserts, but his words found no intelligible expression, for their passion was too great to be confined in any known medium. The World-Policeman alone understood, perhaps, for he flew down in circles round the little professor and laughed and laughed and laughed.

And it seemed as if tremendous figures formed themselves out of the sky to listen, and bent down to lift him with a single sweep of their immense arms from the earth to the heavens. Such was the torrential power and delight of escape in him, that he almost felt as if he could skim the icy abysses of Death itself—without being ever caught. . . .

The colossal shapes of Egypt, terrible and monstrous, passed far below in huge and shadowy procession, and the desolate Lybian Mountains drew him hovering over their wastes of stone. . . .

And this was only a beginning ! Asia, India, and the Southern Seas all lay within reach. All could be visited in turn. The interstellar spaces, the far planets, and the white moon were yet to know! "We must be thinking of turning soon," he heard the voice of his companion, and then remembered how his own body, hot and feverish, lay in that stuffy little room at the other end of Europe. It was indeed caged—the withered body in the room, and himself in the withered body—doubly caged. He laughed and shuddered. The wind swept through him, licking him clean.

He rose again in the ecstasy of free flight, following the lead of the policeman on the homeward journey, and the mountains below became a purple line on the map. In a series of great sweeps they rested on the top of the Pyramid, and then upon the forehead of the Sphinx, and so onwards, touching the earth at intervals, till they heard once more the waves upon the coast-line, and soared aloft again across the sea, racing through Spain and over the Pyrenees. The thin blue outline of the policeman kept ever at his side.

"From all the far blue hills of heaven these winds of freedom blow!" he shouted into space, following it with a peal of laughter that made his guide circle round and round him, chuckling as he flew. A curious, silvery chuckle it was—yet it sounded as though it came to him through a much greater distance than before. It came, as it were, through barriers. . . .

The picture of the bird-fancier's shop came again vividly before him. He saw the beseeching and frightened little eyes; heard the ceaseless pattering of the imprisoned feet, wings beating against the bars, and soft furry bodies pushing vainly to get out. He saw the red face of Theodore Spinks, the proprietor, gloating over the scene of captive life that gave him the means to live—the means to enjoy his own little measure of freedom. He saw the sea-gull drooping in its corner, and the owl, its eyes filled with the dust of the street, its feathered ears twitching;—and then he thought again of the caged human beings of the world—men, women and children, and a pain, like the pain of a whole universe, burned in his soul and set his heart aflame with yearning . . . to set them all instantly free.

And, unable to find words to give expression to what he felt, he found relief again in his strange, impetuous singing.

Simon Parnacute, Professor of Political Economy, sang in mid-heaven. But this was the last vivid memory he knew. It all began to fade a little after that. It changed swiftly like a dream when the body nears the point of waking. He tried to seize and hold it, to delay the moment when it must end; but the power was beyond him. He felt heavy and tired, and flew closer to the ground; the intervals between the curves of flight grew smaller and smaller, the impetus weaker and weaker as he became every moment more dense and stupid.

His progress across the fields of the south of England, as he made his way almost laboriously homewards, became rather a series of long, low leaps than actual flight. More and more often he found himself obliged to touch the earth to acquire the necessary momentum. The big policeman seemed suddenly to have quite melted away into the blue of night.

Then he heard a door open in the sky over his head. A star came down rather too close and half blinded his eyes. Instinctively he called for help to his friend, the World-Policeman.

"It's time for your soup now," was the only answer he got. And it did not seem the right answer, or the right voice either. A terror of being permanently lost came over him, and he cried out again louder than before.

"And the medicine first," dropped the thin, shrill voice out of endless space.

It was not the policeman's voice at all. He knew now, and understood. A sensation of weariness, of sickening disgust and boredom came over him. He looked up. The sky had turned white; he saw curtains and walls and a bright lamp with a red shade. This was the star that had nearly blinded him—a lamp merely, in a sick-room And, standing at the farther end of the room, he saw the figure of the nurse in cap and apron.

Below him lay his body in the bed. His sensation of disgust and boredom became a positive horror. But he sank down exhausted into it—into his cage.

"Take this soup, sir, after the medicine, and then perhaps you'll get another bit of sleep," the nurse was saying with gentle authority, bending over him.

4

The progress of Professor Parnacute towards recovery was slow and tedious, for the illness had been severe and it left him with a dangerously weak heart. And at night he still had the delights of the flying dreams. Only, by this time, he had learned to fly alone. His phantom friend, the big World-Policeman, no longer accompanied him.

And his chief occupation during these weary hours of convalescence was curious and, the nurse considered, not very suitable for an invalid: for he spent the time with endless calculations, poring over the list of his few investments, and adding up times without number the total of his savings of nearly forty years. The bed was strewn with papers and documents; pencils were always getting lost among the clothes; and each time the nurse collected the paraphernalia and put them aside, he would wait till she was out of the room, and then crawl over to the table and carry them all back into bed with him.

Then, finally, she gave up fighting with him, and acquiesced, for his restlessness increased and he could not sleep unless his beloved half-sheets and pencils lay strewn upon the counterpane within instant reach.

Even to the least observant it was clear that the professor was hatching the preliminary details of a profound plot.

And his very first visitor, as soon as he was permitted to see anybody, was a gentleman with parchment skin and hard, dry, peeping eyes who came by special request—a solicitor, from the firm of Messrs. Costa & Delay.

"I will ascertain the price of the shop and stock-in-trade and inform you of the result at the earliest opportunity, Professor Parnacute," said the man of law in his gritty, professional voice, as he at length took his departure and left the sick-room with the expressionless face of one to whom the eccentricities of human nature could never be new or surprising.

"Thank you; I shall be most anxious to hear," replied the other, turning in his long easy-chair to save his papers, and at the same time to defend himself against the chiding of the good-natured nurse.

"I knew I should have to pay for it," he murmured, thinking of his original sin; "but I hope,"—here he again consulted his pencilled figures—"I think I can manage it—just. Though with Consols so low—" He fell to musing again. "Still, I can always sublet the shop, of course, as they suggest," he concluded with a sigh, turning to appeal to the bewildered nurse and finding for the first time that she had gone out of the room.

He fell to pondering deeply. Presently the "list enclosed" by the solicitors caught his eye among the pillows, and he began listlessly to examine it. It was typewritten and covered several sheets of foolscap. It was split up into divisions headed as "Lot 1, Lot 2, Lot 3," and so on. He began to read slowly half aloud to himself; then with increasing excitement—

50 Linnets, guaranteed not straight from the fields; *all caged.*
10 fierce singing Linnets.
10 grand cock Throstles, *just on song.*
5 Pear-Tree Goldfinches, with deep, square blazes, well buttoned and mooned.
4 Devonshire Woodlarks, guaranteed full song; *caged three months.*

The professor sat up and gripped the paper tightly. His face wore a pained, intent expression. A convulsive movement of his fingers, automatic perhaps, crumpled the sheet and nearly tore it across. He went on reading, shedding rugs and pillows as though they oppressed him. His breath came a little faster.

5 cock Blackbirds, full plumage, *lovely songsters.*
1 Song-Thrush, show-cage and hamper; *splendid whistler,* picked bird.
1 beautiful, large upstanding singing Skylark; *sings all day; been caged positively five months.*

Simon Parnacute uttered a curious little cry. It was deep down in his throat. He was conscious of a burning desire to be rich—a millionaire; powerful —an autocratic monarch. After a pause he brought back his attention with an effort to the type-written page and the consideration of further "Lots"

3 cock Skylarks; can hear them 200 yards off when singing.

"*Two hundred yards off when singing,*" muttered the professor into his one remaining pillow.

He read on, kicking his feet, somewhat viciously for a sick man, against the wicker rest at the end of the lounge chair. "1 special, select, singing cock Skylark; gauranteed caged three months; sings his wild note." He suddenly dashed the list aside. The whole chair creaked and groaned with the violence of his movement. He kicked three times running at the wicker foot-rest, and evidently rejoiced that it was still stiff enough to make it worth while to kick again—harder.

"Oh, that I had all the money in the world !" he cried to himself, letting his eyes wander to the window and the clear blue spaces between the clouds; "all the money in the world !" he repeated with growing excitement. He saw one of London's sea-gulls circling high, high up. He watched it for some minutes, till it sailed against a dazzling bit of white cloud and was lost to view.

"*Sings his wild note—guaranteed caged three months—can be heard two hundred yards off.*" The phrases burned in his brain like consuming flames.

And so the list went on. He was glancing over the last page when his eye fell suddenly upon an item that described a lot of—

8 Linnets caged four months; raving with song.

He dropped the list, rose with difficulty from his chair and paced the room, muttering to himself "raving with song, raving with song, raving with song." His hollow cheeks were flushed, his eyes aglow.

"Caged, caged, caged," he repeated under his breath, while his thoughts travelled to that racing flight across Europe, over seas and mountains.

"Sings his wild note!" He heard again the whistling wind about his ears as he flew through the zones of heated air above the desert sands.

"Raving with song!" He remembered the passion of his own cry—that strange lyrical outburst of his heart when the magic of freedom caught him, and he had soared at will through the unchartered regions of the night.

And then he saw once more the blinking owl, its eyes blinded by the dust of the London street, its feathery ears twitching as it heard the wind sighing past the open doorway of the dingy shop.

And again the thrush looked into his face and poured out the rapture of its spring song.

And half-an-hour later he was so exhausted by the unwonted emotion and exercise that the nurse herself was obliged to write at his dictation the letter he sent in reply to the solicitors, Messrs. Costa & Delay in Southampton Row.

But the letter was posted that night and the professor, still mumbling to himself about "having to pay for it," went to bed with the first hour of the darkness, and plunged straight into another of his delightful flying dreams almost the very moment his eyes had closed.

5

". . . Thus, all the animals have been disposed of according to your instructions," ran the final letter from the solicitors, "and we beg to append list of items so allotted, together with country addresses to which they have been sent. We think you may feel assured that they are now in homes where they will be well cared for.

"We still retain the following animals against your further instructions—

2 Zonure Lizards,

1 Angulated Tortoise,

2 Mealy Rosellas,

2 Scaly-breasted Lorikeets.

"With regard to these we should advise. . . .

"The caged birds, meanwhile, which you intend the children shall release, are being cared for satisfactorily; and the premises will be ready for taking over as from June 1. . . ."

And, with the assistance of the nurse, he then began to issue a steady stream of letters to the parents of children he knew in the country, carefully noting and tabulating the replies, and making out little white labels inscribed in plain lettering with the words "Lot 1," "Lot 2," and so on, precisely as though he were in the animal business himself, and were getting ready for a sale.

But the sale which took place a fortnight later on June 1 was no ordinary sale.

It was a brilliant hot day when Simon Parnacute, still worn and shaky from his recent illness, made his way towards the shop of the "retired " birdfancier. The sale of the premises and stock-in-trade, and the high price obtained, had made quite a stir in the "Fancy," but of that the professor was sublimely ignorant as he crossed the street in front of a truculent motor-omnibus and stood before the dingy three-storey red-brick house.

He produced the key sent to him by Messrs. Costa & Delay, and opened the door. It was cool after the glare of the burning street, and delightfully silent. He remembered the chorus of crying birds that had greeted his last appearance. The silence now was eloquent.

"Good, good," he said to himself, with a quiet smile, as he noticed the temporary counter built across the front room for cloaks and par-cels, "very good indeed." Then he went upstairs, climbing painfully, for he was still easily exhausted. There was hardly a stick of furniture in the house, nor an inch of carpet on the floor and stairs, but the rooms had been swept and scrubbed; everything was fresh and scrupulously clean, and the tenant to whom he was to sub-let could have no fault to find on that score.

In the first-floor rooms he saw with pleasure the flowers arranged about the boards as he had directed. The air was sweet and perfumed. The windows at the back—the sills deep with jars of roses—opened upon a small bit of green garden, and Parnacute looked out and saw the blue sky and the clouds floating lazily across it.

"Good, very good," he exclaimed again, sitting down on the stairs a moment to recover his breath. The excitement and the heat of the day tired him. And, as he sat, he put his hand to his ear and listened attentively. A sound of birds singing reached him faintly from the up-per part of the house.

"Ah !" he said, drawing a deep breath, and colour coming into his cheeks. "Ah! Now I hear them."

The sound of singing came nearer, as on a passing wind. He climbed laboriously to the top floor, and then, after resting again, scrambled up a ladder through an open skylight on to the roof. The moment he put his perspiring face above the tiles a wild chorus of singing birds greeted him with a sound like a whole countryside in spring.

"If only my friend, the park policeman, could see this," he said aloud, with a delighted chuckle, "and hear it!" He sought a precarious resting-place upon the butt of a chimney-stack, mopping his forehead.

All around him the sea of London roofs and chimneys rolled away in a black sea, but here, like an oasis in a desert, was a roof of limited extent, and not very high compared to others, converted into a perfect garden. Flowers—but why describe them, when he himself did not even know the names? It was enough that his orders had been carried out to his entire satisfaction, and that this little roof was a world of living colour, moving in the wind, scenting the air, welcoming the sunshine.

Everywhere among the pots and boxes of flowers stood the cages. And in the cages the thrushes and blackbirds, the larks and linnets, poured their hearts out with a chorus of song that was more exquisite, he thought, than anything he had ever heard. And there in the corner by the big chimney, carefully shaded from the glare, stood the large cage containing the owls.

"I can almost believe they have guessed my purpose after all," exclaimed the professor.

For a long time he sat there, leaning against the chimney, oblivious of a blackened collar, listening to the singing, and feasting his eyes upon the garden of flowers all about him. Then the sound of a bell ringing downstairs roused him suddenly into action, and he climbed with difficulty down again to the hall door.

"Here they come," he thought, greatly excited. "Dear me, I do trust I shall not make any mistakes."

He felt in his pocket for his note-book, and then opened the door into the street.

"Oh, it's only you !" he exclaimed, as his nurse came in with her arms full of parcels.

"Only me," she laughed, "but I've brought the lemonade and the biscuits. The others will be here now any minute. It's after three. There's just time to arrange the glasses and plates. We must expect about fifty according to the letters you got. And mind you don't get over-tired."

71

"Oh, I'm all right!" he answered.

She ran upstairs. Before her steps had sounded once on the floor above, a carriage-and-pair stopped at the door, and a footman came up smartly and asked if Professor Parnacute was at home.

"Indeed I am," answered the old man, blushing and laughing at the same time, and then going down himself to the carriage to welcome the little girl and boy who got out. He bowed stiffly and awkwardly to the pretty lady in the victoria, who thanked him for his kindness with a speech he did not hear properly, and then led his callers into the house. They were very shy at first, and hardly knew what to make of it all, but once inside, the boy's sense of adventure was stirred by the sight of the empty shop, and the counter, and the strange array of flowers upon the floor.

He remembered the letter his father had read out from Professor Parnacute a week ago.

"My Lot is No. 7, isn't it, Mr. Professor?" he cried. "I let out a cage of linnets, and get a guinea-pig and a mealy-something-or-other as a present, don't I?" Mr. Parnacute, shaky and beaming, consulted his note-book hurriedly, and replied that this was "perfectly correct."

"Master Edwin Burton," he read out; "to release—Lot 7. To take away—one guinea-pig, and one mealy rosella."

"I'm Lot 8, please," piped the voice of the little girl, standing with wide-open eyes beside him.

"Oh, are you, my dear?" said he: "yes, yes, I believe you are." He fumbled anew with the notebook.

"Here it is," he added, reading aloud again—"Miss Angelina Burton;" he peered closely in the gloom to decipher the writing; "To release—Lot 8— that's woodlarks, my dear, you know. To take away —one angulated tortoise. Quite correct, yes; quite correct."

He called to the nurse upstairs to show the children their presents hidden away in boxes among the flowers —their rosella and tortoise—and then went again to the door to receive his other guests, who now began to arrive in a steady stream. To the number of twenty or thirty they came, and not one of them appeared to be much over twelve. And the majority of them left their elders at the door and came in unattended.

The marshalling of this array of youngsters among the birds and flowers was a matter of some difficulty, but here the nurse came to the professor's assistance with energy and experience, so that his strength was economised and the children were arranged without danger to anyone.

And upon that little roof the sight was certainly a unique one. There they all stood, an extraordinary patchwork of colour for the tiles of South-West London—the bright frocks of the girls, the plumage of the birds, the blues and yellows and scarlets of the flowers; while the singing and voices sent up a chorus that brought numerous surprised faces to the windows of the higher buildings about them, and made people stop in the street below and ask themselves with startled faces where in the world these sounds came from this still June afternoon!

"Now!" cried Simon Parnacute, when all lots and owners had been placed carefully side by side. "The moment I give the word of command, open your cages and let the prisoners escape! And point in the direction of the park."

The children stooped and picked up their cages. The voices and the singing in a hundred busy little throats ceased. A hush fell upon the roof and upon the strange gathering. The sun poured blazingly down over everything, and the professor's face streamed.

"One," he cried, his voice tremulous with excitement, "two, three—and away!" There was a rattling sound of opening doors and wire bars—and then a sudden burst of half-suppressed, long-drawn "Ahhhhs." At once there followed a rush of fluttering feathers, a rapid vibration of the air, and the small host of prisoners shot out like a cloud into the air, and a moment later with a great whirring of wings had disappeared over the walls beyond the forest of chimneys and were lost to view. Blackbirds, thrushes, linnets and finches were gone in a twinkling, so that the eye could hardly follow them.

Only the sea-gulls, puzzled by their sudden freedom, with wings still stiff after their cramped quarters, lingered on the edge of the roof for a few minutes, and looked about them in a dazed fashion, until they, too, realised their liberty and sailed off into the open sky to search for splendours of the sea.

A second hush, deeper even than the first, fell over all for a moment, and then the children with one accord burst into screams of delight and explanation, shouting, for all who cared to listen, the details of how their birds, respectively, had flown; where they had gone; what they thought and looked like; and a hundred other details as to where they would build their nests and the number of eggs they would lay.

And then came the descent for the presents and refreshment. One by one they approached the professor, holding out the tickets with the number of their "lot" and the description of animal they were to receive and find a home for. The few accompanied by elders came first.

"The owls, I think?" said the pink-faced clergyman who had chaperoned other children besides his own, picking his way across the roof as the crowd tapered off down the skylight.

"Two owls," he repeated, with a smile. "In the windy towers of my belfry under the Mendips, I hope——"

"Oh, the very thing, the very place," replied Parnacute, with pleasure, remembering his correspondent. For, of course, the owls had not been released with the other birds.

"And for my little girl you thought, perhaps, a lorikeet——"

"A scaly-breasted lorikeet, papa," she interrupted, with a degree of excitement too intense for smiles, and pronouncing the name as she had learned it—in a single word; "*and* a lizard." They moved off towards the trapdoor, the owl cage under the clergyman's arm.

They would receive the lorikeet and lizard downstairs from the nurse on presenting their ticket.

"And remember," added Parnacute slyly, addressing the child, "to comb their feathered trousers with a very fine comb!"

The clergyman turned a moment at the skylight as he helped the owls and children to squeeze through.

"I shall have something to say about this in my sermon next Sunday," he said. He smiled as his head disappeared.

"Oh, but, my dear sir——" cried the professor, tripping over a flower-pot in his pleasure and embarrassment, and just reaching the skylight in time to add, "And, remember, there are cakes and lemonade on the floor below!"

The animals had all been provided with happy homes; the last cab had driven away, and the nurse had gone to find the flower-man. Parnacute had strewn the roof with food, and with moss and hair-material for nesting, in case any of the birds returned. He stood alone and watched the sunset pour its gold over the myriad houses—the cages of the men and women of London town.

He felt exhausted; the sky was soothing and pleasant to behold. . . .

He sat down to rest, conscious of a great weakness now that the excitement was over and the reaction had begun to set in. Probably he had exerted himself unduly.

His mind reverted to his first impulsive eccentricity of two months before.

"I knew I should pay for it," he murmured, with a smile, "and I have. But it was worth it." He stopped abruptly and caught his breath a moment. He was thoroughly over-tired; the excitement of it all had been too much for him. He must get home as quickly as possible to rest.

The nurse would be back any minute now.

A sound of wings rapidly beating the air passed overhead, and he looked up and saw a flight of pigeons wheeling by. He fancied, too, that he just caught the notes of a thrush singing far away in the park at the end of the street. He recalled the phrases of that dreadfully haunting list. "Wild singing note," "Can be heard two hundred yards off," "Raving with song." A momentary spasm passed through his frame. Far up in the air the sea-gulls still circled, making their way with all the splendour of real freedom to the sea.

"Tonight," he thought, "they will roost on the marshes, or perched upon the lonely cliffs. Good, good, *very* good!"

He got up, stiffly and with difficulty, to watch the pigeons better, and to hear the thrush, and, as he did so, the bell rang downstairs to admit the nurse and the flower-man.

"Odd," he thought; "I gave her the key!"

He made his way towards the skylight, picking his way with uncertain tread between the flower-boxes; but before he could reach it a head and shoulders suddenly appeared above the opening.

"Odd," he thought again, "that she should have come up so quickly—" But he did not complete the thought. It was not the nurse at all. A very different figure followed the emerging head and shoulders, and there in front of him on the roof stood—a policeman.

It was *the* policeman.

"Oh," said Parnacute quietly, "it's *you!*" A wild tumult of yearning and happiness caught at his heart and made it impossible to think of anything else to say.

The big blue figure smiled his shining smile.

"One more flight, sir," said the silvery, ringing voice respectfully, "and the last." The pigeons wheeled past overhead with a sharp whirring of wings. Both men looked up significantly at their vanishing outline over the roofs. A deep silence fell between them.

Parnacute was aware that he was smiling and contented. "I am quite ready, I think," he said in a low tone. "You promised—"

"Yes," returned the other in the voice that was like the ringing of a silver gong, "I promised—without pain."

The Policeman moved softly over to him; he made no sound; the constellations of Orion and the Pleiades shone on his coat-collar. There was another whirring rush as the pigeons swept again overhead and wheeled abruptly, but this time there was no one on the roof to watch them go, and it seemed that their flying wedge, as they flashed away, was larger and darker than before. . . .

And when the nurse returned with the man for the boxes, they came up to the roof and found the body of Simon Parnacute, late Professor of Political Economy, lying face upwards among the flowers. The human cage was empty. Someone had opened the door.

The Kit-Bag

When the words 'Not Guilty' sounded through the crowded courtroom that dark December afternoon, Arthur Wilbraham, the great criminal KC, and leader for the triumphant defence, was represented by his junior; but Johnson, his private secretary, carried the verdict across to his chambers like lightning.

'It's what we expected, I think,' said the barrister, without emotion; 'and, personally, I am glad the case is over.' There was no particular sign of pleasure that his defence of John Turk, the murderer, on a plea of insanity, had been successful, for no doubt he felt, as everybody who had watched the case felt, that no man had ever better deserved the gallows.

'I'm glad too,' said Johnson. He had sat in the court for ten days watching the face of the man who had carried out with callous detail one of the most brutal and cold-blooded murders of recent years.

The counsel glanced up at his secretary. They were more than employer and employed; for family and other reasons, they were friends. 'Ah, I remember; yes,' he said with a kind smile, 'and you want to get away for Christmas? You're going to skate and ski in the Alps, aren't you? If I was your age, I'd come with you.'

Johnson laughed shortly. He was a young man of twenty-six, with a delicate face like a girl's. 'I can catch the morning boat now,' he said; 'but that's not the reason I'm glad the trial is over. I'm glad it's over because I've seen the last of that man's dreadful face. It positively haunted me. That white skin, with the black hair brushed low over the forehead, is a thing I shall never forget, and the description of the way the dismembered body was crammed and packed with lime into that—'

'Don't dwell on it, my dear fellow,' interrupted the other, looking at him curiously out of his keen eyes, 'don't think about it. Such pictures have a trick of coming back when one least wants them.' He paused a moment. 'Now go,' he added presently, 'and enjoy your holiday. I shall want all your energy for my Parliamentary work when you get back. And don't break your neck skiing.'

Johnson shook hands and took his leave. At the door he turned suddenly.

'I knew there was something I wanted to ask you,' he said. 'Would you mind lending me one of your kit-bags? It's too late to get one tonight, and I leave in the morning before the shops are open.'

'Of course; I'll send Henry over with it to your rooms. You shall have it the moment I get home.'

'I promise to take great care of it,' said Johnson gratefully, delighted to think that within thirty hours he would be nearing the brilliant sunshine of the high Alps in winter. He thought of that criminal court was like an evil dream in his mind.

He dined at his club and went on to Bloomsbury, where he occupied the top floor in one of those old, gaunt houses in which the rooms are large and lofty. The floor below his own was vacant and unfurnished, and below that were other lodgers whom he did not know. It was cheerless, and he looked forward heartily to a change. The night was even more cheerless: it was miserable, and few people were about. A cold, sleety rain was driving down the streets before the keenest east wind he had ever felt. It howled dismally among the big, gloomy houses of the great squares, and when he reached his rooms he heard it whistling and shouting over the world of black roofs beyond his windows.

In the hall he met his landlady, shading a candle from the draughts with her thin hand. 'This come by a man from Mr Wilbr'im's, sir.'

She pointed to what was evidently the kit-bag, and Johnson thanked her and took it upstairs with him. 'I shall be going abroad in the morning for ten days, Mrs Monks,' he said. 'I'll leave an address for letters.'

'And I hope you'll 'ave a merry Christmas, sir,' she said, in a raucous, wheezy voice that suggested spirits, 'and better weather than this.'

'I hope so too,' replied her lodger, shuddering a little as the wind went roaring down the street outside.

When he got upstairs, he heard the sleet volleying against the window panes. He put his kettle on to make a cup of hot coffee, and then set about putting a few things in order for his absence. 'And now I must pack—such as my packing is,' he laughed to himself, and set to work at once.

He liked the packing, for it brought the snow mountains so vividly before him, and made him forget the unpleasant scenes of the past ten days. Besides, it was not elaborate in nature. His friend had lent him the very thing—a stout canvas kit-bag, sack-shaped, with holes round the neck for the brass bar and padlock. It was a bit shapeless, true, and not much to look at, but its capacity was unlimited, and there was no need to pack carefully. He shoved in his waterproof coat, his fur cap and gloves, his skates and climbing boots, his sweaters, snow-boots, and ear-caps; and then on the top of these he piled his woollen shirts and underwear, his thick socks, *puttees*, and knickerbockers. The dress suit came next, in case the hotel people dressed for dinner, and then, thinking of the best way to pack his white shirts, he paused a moment to reflect. 'That's the worst of these kit-bags,' he mused vaguely, standing in the centre of the sitting-room, where he had come to fetch some string.

It was after ten o'clock. A furious gust of wind rattled the windows as though to hurry him up, and he thought with pity of the poor Londoners whose Christmas would be spent in such a climate, whilst he was skimming over snowy slopes in bright sunshine, and dancing in the evening with rosy-checked girls—Ah! that reminded him; he must put in his dancing-pumps and evening socks. He crossed over from his sitting-room to the cupboard on the landing where he kept his linen.

And as he did so he heard someone coming softly up the stairs.

He stood still a moment on the landing to listen. It was Mrs Monks's step, he thought; she must he coming up with the last post. But then the steps ceased suddenly, and he heard no more. They were at least two flights down, and he came to the conclusion they were too heavy to be those of his bibulous landlady. No doubt they belonged to a late lodger who had mistaken his floor. He went into his bedroom and packed his pumps and dress-shirts as best he could.

The kit-bag by this time was two-thirds full, and stood upright on its own base like a sack of flour. For the first time he noticed that it was old and dirty, the canvas faded and worn, and that it had obviously been subjected to rather rough treatment. It was not a very nice bag to have sent him—certainly not a new one, or one that his chief valued. He gave the matter a passing thought, and went on with his packing. Once or twice, however, he caught himself wondering who it could have been wandering down below, for Mrs Monks had not come up with letters, and the floor was empty and unfurnished. From time to time, moreover, he was almost certain he heard a soft tread of someone padding about over the bare boards—cautiously, stealthily, as silently as possible—and, further, that the sounds had been lately coming distinctly nearer.

For the first time in his life, he began to feel a little creepy. Then, as though to emphasise this feeling, an odd thing happened: as he left the bedroom, having, just packed his recalcitrant white shirts, he noticed that the top of the kit-bag lopped over towards him with an extraordinary resemblance to a human face. The canvas fell into a fold like a nose and forehead, and the brass rings for the padlock just filled the position of the eyes. A shadow—or was it a travel stain? for he could not tell exactly—looked like hair. It gave him rather a turn, for it was so absurdly, so outrageously, like the face of John Turk the murderer.

He laughed, and went into the front room, where the light was stronger.

'That horrid case has got on my mind,' he thought; 'I shall be glad of a change of scene and air.' In the sitting-room, however, he was not pleased to hear again that stealthy tread upon the stairs, and to realise that it was much closer than before, as well as unmistakably real. And this time he got up and went out to see who it could be creeping about on the upper staircase at so late an hour.

But the sound ceased; there was no one visible on the stairs. He went to the floor below, not without trepidation, and turned on the electric light to make sure that no one was hiding in the empty rooms of the unoccupied suite. There was not a stick of furniture large enough to hide a dog. Then he called over the banisters to Mrs Monks, but there was no answer, and his voice echoed down into the dark vault of the house, and was lost in the roar of the gale that howled outside. Everyone was in bed and asleep—everyone except himself and the owner of this soft and stealthy tread.

'My absurd imagination, I suppose,' he thought. 'It must have been the wind after all, although—it seemed so *very* real and close, I thought.' He went back to his packing. It was by this time getting on towards midnight. He drank his coffee up and lit another pipe—the last before turning in.

It is difficult to say exactly at what point fear begins, when the causes of that fear are not plainly before the eyes. Impressions gather on the surface of the mind, film by film, as ice gathers upon the surface of still water, but often so lightly that they claim no definite recognition from the consciousness. Then a point is reached where the accumulated impressions become a definite emotion, and the mind realises that something has happened. With something of a start, Johnson suddenly recognised that he felt nervous—oddly nervous; also, that for some time past the causes of this feeling had been gathering slowly in his mind, but that he had only just reached the point where he was forced to acknowledge them.

It was a singular and curious malaise that had come over him, and he hardly knew what to make of it. He felt as though he were doing something that was strongly objected to by another person, another person, moreover, who had some right to object. It was a most disturbing and disagreeable feeling, not unlike the persistent promptings of conscience: almost, in fact, as if he were doing something he knew to be wrong. Yet, though he searched vigorously and honestly in his mind, he could nowhere lay his finger upon the secret of this growing uneasiness, and it perplexed him. More, it distressed and frightened him.

'Pure nerves, I suppose,' he said aloud with a forced laugh. 'Mountain air will cure all that! Ah,' he added, still speaking to himself, 'and that reminds me—my snow-glasses.'

He was standing by the door of the bedroom during this brief soliloquy, and as he passed quickly towards the sitting-room to fetch them from the cupboard he saw out of the corner of his eye the indistinct outline of a figure standing on the stairs, a few feet from the top. It was someone in a stooping position, with one hand on the banisters, and the face peering up towards the landing. And at the same moment he heard a shuffling footstep. The person who had been creeping about below all this time had at last come up to his own floor. Who in the world could it be? And what in the name of Heaven did he want?

Johnson caught his breath sharply and stood stock still. Then, after a few seconds' hesitation, he found his courage, and turned to investigate. The stairs, he saw to his utter amazement, were empty; there was no one. He felt a series of cold shivers run over him, and something about the muscles of his legs gave a little and grew weak. For the space of several minutes, he peered steadily into the shadows that congregated about the top of the staircase where he had seen the figure, and then he walked fast—almost ran, in fact—into the light of the front room; but hardly had he passed inside the doorway when he heard someone come up the stairs behind him with a quick bound and go swiftly into his bedroom. It was a heavy, but at the same time a stealthy footstep—the tread of somebody who did not wish to be seen. And it was at this precise moment that the nervousness he had hitherto experienced leaped the boundary line, and entered the state of fear, almost of acute, unreasoning fear. Before it turned into terror there was a further boundary to cross, and beyond that again lay the region of pure horror. Johnson's position was an unenviable one.

'By Jove! That was someone on the stairs, then,' he muttered, his flesh crawling all over; 'and whoever it was has now gone into my bedroom.' His delicate, pale face turned absolutely white, and for some minutes he hardly knew what to think or do. Then he realised intuitively that delay only set a premium upon fear; and he crossed the landing boldly and went straight into the other room, where, a few seconds before, the steps had disappeared.

'Who's there? Is that you, Mrs Monks?' he called aloud, as he went, and heard the first half of his words echo down the empty stairs, while the second half fell dead against the curtains in a room that apparently held no other human figure than his own.

'Who's there?' he called again, in a voice unnecessarily loud and that only just held firm. 'What do you want here?'

The curtains swayed very slightly, and, as he saw it, his heart felt as if it almost missed a beat; yet he dashed forward and drew them aside with a rush. A window, streaming with rain, was all that met his gaze. He continued his search, but in vain; the cupboards held nothing but rows of clothes, hanging motionless; and under the bed there was no sign of anyone hiding. He stepped backwards into the middle of the room, and, as he did so, something all but tripped him up. Turning with a sudden spring of alarm he saw—the kit-bag.

'Odd!' he thought. 'That's not where I left it!' A few moments before it had surely been on his right, between the bed and the bath; he did not remember having moved it. It was very curious. What in the world was the matter with everything? Were all his senses gone queer? A terrific gust of wind tore at the windows, dashing the sleet against the glass with the force of small gunshot, and then fled away howling dismally over the waste of Bloomsbury roofs. A sudden vision of the Channel next day rose in his mind and recalled him sharply to realities.

'There's no one here at any rate; that's quite clear!' he exclaimed aloud. Yet at the time he uttered them he knew perfectly well that his words were not true and that he did not believe them himself. He felt exactly as though someone was hiding close about him, watching all his movements, trying to hinder his packing in some way. 'And two of my senses,' he added, keeping up the pretence, 'have played me the most absurd tricks: the steps I heard and the figure I saw were both entirely imaginary.'

He went back to the front room, poked the fire into a blaze, and sat down before it to think. What impressed him more than anything else was the fact that the kit-bag was no longer where he had left at. It had been dragged nearer to the door.

What happened afterwards that night happened, of course, to a man already excited by fear, and was perceived by a man that had not the full and proper control, therefore, of the senses. Outwardly, Johnson remained calm and master of himself to the end, pretending to the very last that everything he witnessed had a natural explanation, or was merely delusions of his tired nerves. But inwardly, in his very heart, he knew all along that someone had been hiding downstairs in the empty suite when he came in, that this person had watched his opportunity and then stealthily made his way up to the bedroom, and that all he saw and heard afterwards, from the moving of the kit-bag to—well, to the other things this story has to tell—were caused directly by the presence of this invisible person.

And it was here, just when he most desired to keep his mind and thoughts controlled, that the vivid pictures received day after day upon the mental plates exposed in the courtroom of the Old Bailey, came strongly to light and developed themselves in the dark room of his inner vision. Unpleasant, haunting memories have a way of coming to life again just when the mind least desires them—in the silent watches of the night, on sleepless pillows, during the lonely hours spent by sick and dying beds. And so now, in the same way, Johnson saw nothing but the dreadful face of John Turk, the murderer, lowering at him from every corner of his mental field of vision; the white skin, the evil eyes, and the fringe of black hair low over the forehead. All the pictures of those ten days in court crowded back into his mind unbidden, and very vivid.

'This is all rubbish and nerves,' he exclaimed at length, springing with sudden energy from his chair. 'I shall finish my packing and go to bed. I'm overwrought, overtired. No doubt, at this rate I shall hear steps and things all night!'

But his face was deadly white all the same. He snatched up his field-glasses and walked across to the bedroom, humming a music-hall song as he went—a trifle too loud to be natural; and the instant he crossed the threshold and stood within the room something turned cold about his heart, and he felt that every hair on his head stood up.

The kit-bag lay close in front of him, several feet nearer to the door than he had left it, and just over its crumpled top he saw a head and face slowly sinking down out of sight as though someone were crouching behind it to hide, and at the same moment a sound like a long-drawn sigh was distinctly audible in the still air about him between the gusts of the storm outside.

Johnson had more courage and willpower than the girlish indecision of his face indicated; but at first such a wave of terror came over him that for some seconds he could do nothing but stand and stare. A violent trembling ran down his back and legs, and he was conscious of a foolish, almost a hysterical, impulse to scream aloud. That sigh seemed in his very ear, and the air still quivered with it. It was unmistakably a human sigh.

'Who's there?' he said at length, finding his voice; but thought he meant to speak with loud decision, the tones came out instead in a faint whisper, for he had partly lost the control of his tongue and lips.

He stepped forward, so that he could see all round and over the kit-bag. Of course, there was nothing there, nothing but the faded carpet and the bulging canvas sides. He put out his hands and threw open the mouth of the sack where it had fallen over, being only three parts full, and then he saw for the first time that round the inside, some six inches from the top, there ran a broad smear of dull crimson. It was an old and faded blood stain. He uttered a scream, and drew back his hands as if they had been burnt. At the same moment the kit-bag gave a faint, but unmistakable, lurch forward towards the door.

Johnson collapsed backwards, searching with his hands for the support of something solid, and the door, being further behind him than he realised, received his weight just in time to prevent his falling, and shut to with a resounding bang. At the same moment the swinging of his left arm accidentally touched the electric switch, and the light in the room went out.

It was an awkward and disagreeable predicament, and if Johnson had not been possessed of real pluck, he might have done all manner of foolish things. As it was, however, he pulled himself together, and groped furiously for the little brass knob to turn the light on again. But the rapid closing of the door had set the coats hanging on it a-swinging, and his fingers became entangled in a confusion of sleeves and pockets, so that it was some moments before he found the switch. And in those few moments of bewilderment and terror two things happened that sent him beyond recall over the boundary into the region of genuine horror—he distinctly heard the kit-bag shuffling heavily across the floor in jerks, and close in front of his face sounded once again the sigh of a human being.

In his anguished efforts to find the brass button on the wall he nearly scraped the nails from his fingers, but even then, in those frenzied moments of alarm—so swift and alert are the impressions of a man keyed-up by a vivid emotion—he had time to realise that he dreaded the return of the light, and that it might be better for him to stay hidden in the merciful screen of darkness. It was but the impulse of a moment, however, and before he had time to act upon it, he had yielded automatically to the original desire, and the room was flooded again with light.

But the second instinct had been right. It would have been better for him to have stayed in the shelter of the kind darkness. For there, close before him, bending over the half-packed kit-bag, clear as life in the merciless glare of the electric light, stood the figure of John Turk, the murderer. Not three feet from him the man stood, the fringe of black hair marked plainly against the pallor of the forehead, the whole horrible presentment of the scoundrel, as vivid as he had seen him day after day in the Old Bailey, when he stood there in the dock, cynical and callous, under the very shadow of the gallows.

In a flash Johnson realised what it all meant: the dirty and much-used bag; the smear of crimson within the top; the dreadful stretched condition of the bulging sides. He remembered how the victim's body had been stuffed into a canvas bag for burial, the ghastly, dismembered fragments forced with lime into this very bag; and the bag itself produced as evidence—it all came back to him as clear as day.

Very softly and stealthily his hand groped behind him for the handle of the door, but before he could actually turn it the very thing that he most of all dreaded came about, and John Turk lifted his devil's face and looked at him. At the same moment that heavy sigh passed through the air of the room, formulated somehow into words: It's my bag. And I want it.'

Johnson just remembered clawing the door open, and then falling in a heap upon the floor of the landing, as he tried frantically to make his way into the front room.

He remained unconscious for a long time, and it was still dark when he opened his eyes and realised that he was lying, stiff and bruised, on the cold boards. Then the memory of what he had seen rushed back into his mind, and he promptly fainted again. When he woke the second time the wintry dawn was just beginning to peep in at the windows, painting the stairs a cheerless, dismal grey, and he managed to crawl into the front room, and cover himself with an overcoat in the armchair, where at length he fell asleep.

A great clamour woke him. He recognised Mrs Monks's voice, loud and voluble.

'What! You ain't been to bed, sir! Are you ill, or has anything 'appened? And there's an urgent gentleman to see you, though it ain't seven o'clock yet, and—'

'Who is it?' he stammered. 'I'm all right, thanks. Fell asleep in my chair, I suppose.'

'Someone from Mr Wilb'rim's, and he says he ought to see you quick before you go abroad, and I told him—'

'Show him up, please, at once,' said Johnson, whose head was whirling, and his mind was still full of dreadful visions.

Mr Wilbraham's man came in with many apologies, and explained briefly and quickly that an absurd mistake had been made, and that the wrong kit-bag had been sent over the night before.

'Henry somehow got hold of the one that came over from the courtroom, and Mr Wilbraham only discovered it when he saw his own lying in his room, and asked why it had not gone to you,' the man said.

'Oh!' said Johnson stupidly.

'And he must have brought you the one from the murder case instead, sir, I'm afraid,' the man continued, without the ghost of an expression on his face. 'The one John Turk packed the dead body in. Mr Wilbraham's awful upset about it, sir, and told me to come over first thing this morning with the right one, as you were leaving by the boat.'

He pointed to a clean-looking kit-bag on the floor, which he had just brought. 'And I was to bring the other one back, sir,' he added casually.

For some minutes Johnson could not find his voice. At last, he pointed in the direction of his bedroom. 'Perhaps you would kindly unpack it for me. Just empty the things out on the floor.'

The man disappeared into the other room, and was gone for five minutes. Johnson heard the shifting to and fro of the bag, and the rattle of the skates and boots being unpacked.

'Thank you, sir,' the man said, returning with the bag folded over his arm. 'And can I do anything more to help you, sir?'

'What is it?' asked Johnson, seeing that he still had something he wished to say.

The man shuffled and looked mysterious. 'Beg pardon, sir, but knowing your interest in the Turk case, I thought you'd maybe like to know what's happened—'

'Yes.'

'John Turk killed hisself last night with poison immediately on getting his release, and he left a note for Mr Wilbraham saying as he'd be much obliged if they'd have him put away, same as the woman he murdered, in the old kit-bag.'

'What time—did he do it?' asked Johnson.

'Ten o'clock last night, sir, the warder says.'

The Man Who Played Upon the Leaf

Where the Jura pine-woods push the fringe of their purple cloak down the slopes till the vineyards stop them lest they should troop into the lake of Neuchâtel, you may find the village where lived the Man Who Played upon the Leaf.

My first sight of him was genuinely prophetic— that spring evening in the garden *café* of the little mountain *auberge*. But before I saw him, I heard him, and ever afterwards the sound and the sight have remained inseparable in my mind.

Jean Grospierre and Louis Favre were giving me confused instructions—the *vin rouge* of Neuchâtel is heady, you know—as to the best route up the *Tête-de-Rang*, when a thin, wailing music, that at first, I took to be rising wind, made itself heard suddenly among the apple trees at the end of the garden, and riveted my attention with a thrill of I know not what.

Favre's description of the bridle path over Mont Racine died away; then Grospierre's eyes wandered as he, too, stopped to listen; and at the same moment a mongrel dog of indescribably forlorn appearance came whining about our table under the walnut tree.

"It's Perret 'Comment-va,' the man who plays on the leaf," said Favre.

"And his cursed dog," added Grospierre, with a shrug of disgust. And, after a pause, they fell again to quarrelling about my complicated path up the *Tête-de-Rang*.

I turned from them in the direction of the sound. The dusk was falling. Through the trees I saw the vineyards sloping down a mile or two to the dark blue lake with its distant-shadowed shore and the white line of misty Alps in the sky beyond. Behind us the forests rose in folded purple ridges to the heights of Boudry and La Tourne, soft and thick like carpets of cloud. There was no one about in the cabaret. I heard a horse's hoofs in the village street, a rattle of pans from the kitchen, and the soft roar of a train climbing the mountain railway through gathering darkness towards France—and, singing through it all, like a thread of silver through a dream, this sweet and windy music.

But at first there was nothing to be seen. The Man Who Played on the Leaf was not visible, though I stared hard at the place whence the sound apparently proceeded. The effect, for a moment, was almost ghostly.

Then, down there among the shadows of fruit trees and small pines, something moved, and I became aware with a start that the little *sapin* I had been looking at all the time was really not a tree, but a man—hatless, with dark face, loose hair, and wearing a *pélerine* over his shoulders. How he had produced this singularly vivid impression and taken upon himself the outline and image of a tree is utterly beyond me to describe. It was, doubtless, some swift suggestion in my own imagination that deceived me. . . . Yet he was thin, small, straight, and his flying hair and spreading *pèlerine* somehow pictured themselves in the network of dusk and background into the semblance, I suppose, of branches.

I merely record my impression with the truest available words—also my instant persuasion that this first view of the man was, after all, significant and prophetic: his dominant characteristics presented themselves to me symbolically. I saw the man first as a tree; I heard his music first as wind.

Then, as he came slowly towards us, it was clear that he produced the sound by blowing upon a leaf held to his lips between tightly closed hands. And at his heel followed the mongrel dog.

"The inseparables" sneered Grospierre, who did not appreciate the interruption. He glanced contemptuously at the man and the dog, his face and manner, it seemed to me, conveying a merest trace, however, of superstitious fear. "The tune your father taught you, *hein?*" he added, with a cruel allusion I did not at the moment understand.

"Hush!" Favre said; "he plays thunderingly well all the same!" His glass had not been emptied quite so often, and in his eyes as he listened there was a touch of something that was between respect and wonder.

"The music of the devil," Grospierre muttered as he turned with the gesture of surly impatience to the wine and the rye bread. "It makes me dream at night. *Ooua!*"

The man, paying no attention to the gibes, came closer, continuing his leaf-music, and as I watched and listened the thrill that had first stirred in me grew curiously. To look at, he was perhaps forty, perhaps fifty; worn, thin, broken; and something seizingly pathetic in his appearance told its little wordless story into the air. The stamp of the outcast was mercilessly upon him. But the eyes were dark and fine. They proclaimed the possession of something that was neither worn nor broken, something that was proud to be outcast, and welcomed it.

"He's cracky, you know," explained Favre, "and half blind. He lives in that hut on the edge of the forest"—pointing with his thumb toward Côtendard—"and plays on the leaf for what he can earn."

We listened for five minutes perhaps while this singular being stood there in the dusk and piped his weird tunes; and if imagination had influenced my first sight of him it certainly had nothing to do with what I now heard. For it was unmistakable; the man played, not mere tunes and melodies, but the clean, strong, elemental sounds of Nature—especially the crying voices of wind. It was the raw material, if you like, of what the masters have used here and there —Wagner, and so forth—but by him heard closely and wonderfully, and produced with marvellous accuracy. It was now the notes of birds or the tinkle and rustle of sounds heard in groves and copses, and now the murmur of those airs that lose their way on summer noons among the tree tops; and then, quite incredibly, just as the man came closer and the volume increased, it grew to the crying of bigger winds and the whispering rush of rain among tossed branches. . .

How he produced it passed my comprehension, but I think he somehow mingled his own voice with the actual notes of the vibrating edge of the leaf; perhaps, too, that the strange passion shaking behind it all in the depths of the bewildered spirit poured out and reached my mind by ways unknown and incalculable. I must have momentarily lost myself in the soft magic of it, for I remember coming back with a start to notice that the man had stopped, and that his melancholy face was turned to me with a smile of comprehension and sympathy that passed again almost before I had time to recognise it, and certainly before I had time to reply. And this time I am ready to admit that it was my own imagination, singularly stirred, that translated his smile into the words that no one else heard—

"I was playing for you—because you understand."

Favre was standing up and I saw him give the man the half loaf of coarse bread that was on the table, offering also his own partly-emptied wine-glass. "I haven't the *sou* today," he was saying, "but if you're hungry, *mon brave*—" And the man, refusing the wine, took the bread with an air of dignity that precluded all suggestion of patronage or favour, and ought to have made Favre feel proud that he had offered it.

"And that for his son!" laughed the stupid Grospierre, tossing a cheese-rind to the dog, "or for his forest god!"

The music was about me like a net that still held my words and thoughts in a delicate bondage—which is my only explanation for not silencing the coarse guide in the way he deserved; but a few minutes later, when the men had gone into the inn, I crossed to the end of the garden, and there, where the perfumes of orchard and forest deliciously mingled, I came upon the man sitting on the grass beneath an apple-tree. The dog, wagging its tail, was at his feet, as he fed it with the best and largest portions of the bread. For himself, it seemed, he kept nothing but the crust, and—what I could hardly believe, had I not actually witnessed it—the cur, though clearly hungry, had to be coaxed with smiles and kind words to eat what it realised in some dear dog-fashion was needed even more by its master.

A pair of outcasts they looked indeed, sharing dry bread in the back garden of the village inn; but in the soft, discerning eyes of that mangy creature there was an expression that raised it, for me at least, far beyond the ranks of common curdom; and in the eyes of the man, half-witted and pariah as he undoubtedly was, a look that set him somewhere in a lonely place where he heard the still, small voices of the world and moved with the elemental tides of life that are never outcast and that include the farthest suns.

He took the *franc* I offered; and, closer, I perceived that his eyes, for all their moments of fugitive brilliance, were indeed half sightless, and that perhaps he saw only well enough to know men as trees walking. In the village some said he saw better than most, that he saw in the dark, possibly even into the peopled regions beyond this world, and there were reasons— uncanny reasons—to explain the belief. I only know, at any rate, that from this first moment of our meeting he never failed to recognise me at a considerable distance, and to be aware of my whereabouts even in the woods at night; and the best explanation I ever heard, though of course unscientific, was Louis Favre's whispered communication that "he sees with the whole surface of his skin!"

He took the *franc* with the same air of grandeur that he took the bread, as though he conferred a favour, yet was grateful. The beauty of that gesture has often come back to me since with a sense of wonder for the sweet nobility that I afterwards understood inspired it. At the time, however, he merely looked up at me with the remark, "*C'est pour le Dieu—merci!"*

"He did not say *'le bon Dieu,'* as everyone else did.

And though I had meant to get into conversation with him, I found no words quickly enough, for he at once stood up and began to play again on his leaf; and while he played his thanks and gratitude, or the thanks and gratitude of his God, that shaggy mongrel dog stopped eating and sat up beside him to listen, as everyone else. Both fixed their eyes upon me as the sounds of wind and birds and forest poured softly and wonderfully about my ears . . . So that, when it was over and I went down the quiet street to my *pension*, I was aware that some tiny sense of bewilderment had crept into the profounder regions of my consciousness and faintly disturbed my normal conviction that I belonged to the common world of men as of old. Some aspect of the village, especially of the human occupants in it, had secretly changed for me.

Those pearly spaces of sky, where the bats flew over the red roofs, seemed more alive, more exquisite than before; the smells of the open stables where the cows stood munching, more fragrant than usual of sweet animal life that included myself delightfully, keenly; the last chatterings of the sparrows under the eaves of my own *pension* more intimate and personal. . . .

Almost as if those strands of elemental music the man played on his leaf had for the moment made me free of the life of the earth, as distinct from the life of men. . . .

I can only suggest this, and leave the rest to the care of the imaginative reader; for it is impossible to say along what inner byways of fancy I reached the conclusion that when the man spoke of "the God," and not "the *good* God," he intended to convey his sense of some great woodland personality—some Spirit of the Forests whom he knew and loved and worshipped, and whom, he was intuitively aware, I also knew and loved and worshipped.

★★★★★★★★★★★★

During the next few weeks, I came to learn more about this poor, half-witted man. In the village he was known as Perret *"Comment-va,"* the Man Who Plays on the Leaf; but when the people wished to be more explicit, they described him as the man "without parents and without God." The origin of *"Comment-va"* I never discovered, but the other titles were easily explained—he was illegitimate and outcast. The mother had been a wandering Italian girl and the father a loose-living *bûcheron*, who was, it seems, a standing disgrace to the community. I think the villagers were not conscious of their severity; the older generation of farmers and *vignerons* had pity, but the younger ones and those of his own age were certainly guilty, if not of deliberate cruelty, at least of a harsh neglect and the utter withholding of sympathy. It was like the thoughtless cruelty of children, due to small unwisdom, and to that absence of charity which is based on ignorance.

They could not in the least understand this crazy, picturesque being who wandered day and night in the forests and spoke openly, though never quite intelligibly, of worshipping another God than their own anthropomorphic deity. People looked askance at him because he was queer; a few feared him; one or two I found later—all women— felt vaguely that there was something in him rather wonderful, they hardly knew what, that lifted him beyond the reach of village taunts and sneers. But from all he was remote, alien, solitary—an outcast and a pariah.

It so happened that I was very busy at the time, seeking the seclusion of the place for my work, and rarely going out until the day was failing; and so, it was, I suppose, that my sight of the man was always associated with a gentle dusk, long shadows and slanting rays of sun-light. Every time I saw that thin, straight, yet broken figure, every time the music of the leaf reached me, there came too, the inexplicable thrill of secret wonder and delight that had first accompanied his presence, and with it the subtle suggestion of a haunted woodland life, beautiful with new values. To this day I see that sad, dark face moving about the street, touched with melancholy, yet with the singular light of an inner glory that sometimes lit flames in the poor eyes.

Perhaps—the fancy entered my thoughts sometimes when I passed him—those who are half out of their minds, as the saying goes, are at the same time half in another region whose penetrating loveliness has so bewildered and amazed them that they no longer can play their dull part in our commonplace world; and certainly, for me this man's presence never failed to convey an awareness of some hidden and se-cret beauty that he knew apart from the ordinary haunts and pursuits of men.

Often, I followed him up into the woods—in spite of the menac-ing growls of the dog, who invariably showed his teeth lest I should approach too close—with a great longing to know what he did there and how he spent his time wandering in the great forests, sometimes, I was assured, staying out entire nights or remaining away for days together. For in these Jura forests that cover the mountains from

Neuchâtel to Yverdon, and stretch thickly up to the very frontiers of France, you may walk for days without finding a farm or meeting more than an occasional *bûcheron*. And at length, after weeks of failure, and by some process of sympathy he apparently communicated in turn to the dog, it came about that I was—*accepted*. I was allowed to follow at a distance, to listen and, if I could, to watch.

I make use of the conditional, because once in the forest this man had the power of concealing himself in the same way that certain animals and insects conceal themselves by choosing places instinctively where the colour of their surroundings merge into their outlines and obliterate them. So long as he moved all was well; but the moment he stopped and a chance dell or cluster of trees intervened I lost sight of him, and more than once passed within a foot of his presence without knowing it, though the dog was plainly there at his feet.

And the instant I turned at the sound of the leaf, there he was, leaning against some dark tree-stem, part of a shadow perhaps, growing like a forest-thing out of the thick moss that hid his feet, or merging with extraordinary intimacy into the fronds of some drooping pine bough! Moreover, this concealment was never intentional, it seems, but instinctive. The life to which he belonged took him close to its heart, draping about the starved and wasted shoulders the cloak of kindly sympathy which the world of men denied him.

And, while I took my place some little way off upon a fallen stem, and the dog sat looking up into his face with its eyes of yearning and affection, Perret "*Comment-va*" would take a leaf from the nearest ivy, raise it between tightly pressed palms to his lips and begin that magic sound that seemed to rise out of the forest-voices themselves rather than to be a thing apart.

★★★★★★★★★★★★

It was a late evening towards the end of May when I first secured this privilege at close quarters, and the memory of it lives in me still with the fragrance and wonder of some incredible dream. The forest just there was scented with wild lilies of the valley which carpeted the more open spaces with their white bells and big, green leaves; patches of violets and pale anemone twinkled down the mossy stairways of every glade; and through slim openings among the pine-stems I saw the shadowed blues of the lake beyond and the far line of the high Alps, soft and cloud-like in the sky.

Already the woods were drawing the dusk out of the earth to cloak themselves for sleep, and in the east a rising moon stared close over the ground between the big trees, dropping trails of faint and yellowish silver along the moss. Distant cow-bells, and an occasional murmur of village voices, reached the ear. But a deep hush lay over all that mighty slope of mountain forest, and even the footsteps of ourselves and the dog had come to rest.

Then, as sounds heard in a dream, a breeze stirred the topmost branches of the pines, filtering down to us as from the wings of birds. It brought new odours of sky and sun-kissed branches with it. A moment later it lost itself in the darkening aisles of forest beyond; and out of the stillness that followed, I heard the strange music of the leaf rising about us with its extraordinary power of suggestion.

And, turning to see the face of the player more closely, I saw that it had marvellously changed, had become young, unlined, soft with joy. The spirit of the immense woods possessed him, and he was at peace. . . .

While he played, too, he swayed a little to and fro, just as a slender *sapin* sways in wind, and a revelation came to me of that strange beauty of combined sound and movement—trees bending while they sing, branches trembling and a-whisper, children that laugh while they dance. And, oh, the crying, plaintive notes of that leaf, and the profound sense of elemental primitive sound that they woke in the penetralia of the imagination, subtly linking simplicity to grandeur! Terribly yet sweetly penetrating, how they searched the heart through, and troubled the very sources of life!

Often and often since have I wondered what it was in that singular music that made me *know* the distant Alps listened in their sky-spaces, and that the purple slopes of Boudry and Mont Racine bore it along the spires of their woods as though giant harp-strings stretched to the far summits of Chasseral and the arid wastes of *Tête de Rang*.

In the music this outcast played upon the leaf there was something of a wild, mad beauty that plunged like a knife to the home of tears, and at the same time sang out beyond them—something coldly elemental, close to the naked heart of life. The truth, doubtless, was that his strains, making articulate the sounds of Nature, touched deep, primitive yearnings that for many are buried beyond recall. And between the airs, even between the bars, there fell deep weeping silences when the sounds merged themselves into the sigh of wind or the murmur of falling water, just as the strange player merged his body into the form and colour of the trees about him.

And when at last he ceased, I went close to him, hardly knowing what it was I wanted so much to ask or say. He straightened up at my approach. The melancholy dropped its veil upon his face instantly.

"But that was beautiful—unearthly!" I faltered. "You never have played like that in the village—"

And for a second his eyes lit up as he pointed to the dark spaces of forest behind us:

"In there," he said softly, "there is light!"

"You hear true music in these woods," I ventured, hoping to draw him out; "this music you play—this exquisite singing of winds and trees—"

He looked at me with a puzzled expression and I knew, of course, that I had blundered with my banal words. Then, before I could explain or alter, there floated to us through the trees a sound of church bells from villages far away; and instantly, as he heard, his face grew dark, as though he understood in some vague fashion that it was a symbol of the faith of those parents who had wronged him, and of the people who continually made him suffer. Something of this, I feel sure, passed through his tortured mind, for he looked menacingly about him, and the dog, who caught the shadow of all his moods, began to growl angrily.

"My music," he said, with a sudden abruptness that was almost fierce, "is for my God."

"Your God of the Forests?" I said, with a real sympathy that I believe reached him.

"*Pour sûr! Pour sûr!* I play it all over the world"—he looked about him down the slopes of villages and vineyards—"and for those who understand—those who belong—to come."

He was, I felt sure, going to say more, perhaps to unbosom himself to me a little; and I might have learned something of the ritual this self-appointed priest of Pan followed in his forest temples—when, the sound of the bells swelled suddenly on the wind, and he turned with an angry gesture and made to go. Their insolence, penetrating even to the privacy of his secret woods, was too much for him.

"And you find many?" I asked.

Perret "*Comment-va*" shrugged his shoulders and smiled pityingly.

"*Moi. Puis le chien—puis maintenant—vous!*"

He was gone the same minute, as if the branches stretched out dark arms to draw him away among them, . . . and on my way back to the village, by the growing light of the moon, I heard far away in that deep world of a million trees the echoes of a weird, sweet music, as this unwitting votary of Pan piped and fluted to his mighty God upon an ivy leaf.

And the last thing I actually saw was the mongrel cur turning back from the edge of the forest to look at me for a moment of hesitation. He thought it was time now that I should join the little band of worshippers and follow them to the haunted spots of worship.

"*Moi—puis le chien—puis maintenant—vous!*"

****

From that moment of speech, a kind of unexpressed intimacy between us came into being, and whenever we passed one another in the street he would give me a swift, happy look, and jerk his head significantly towards the forests. The feeling that, perhaps, in his curious lonely existence I counted for something important made me very careful with him. From time to time, I gave him a few *francs*, and regularly twice a week when I knew he was away, I used to steal unobserved to his hut on the edge of the forest and put parcels of food inside the door—*salamé*, cheese, bread; and on one or two occasions when I had been extravagant with my own tea, pieces of plum-cake— what the Colombier baker called *plume-cak'!*

He never acknowledged these little gifts, and I sometimes wondered to what use he put them, for though the dog remained well favoured, so far as any cur can be so, he himself seemed to waste away more rapidly than ever. I found, too, that he did receive help from the village—official help-but that after the night when he was caught on the church steps with an oil can, kindling-wood and a box of matches, this help was reduced by half, and the threat made to discontinue it altogether. Yet I feel sure there was no inherent maliciousness in the Man who Played upon the Leaf, and that his hatred of an "alien" faith was akin to the mistaken zeal that in other days could send poor sinners to the stake for the ultimate safety of their souls.

Two things, moreover, helped to foster the tender belief I had in his innate goodness: first, that all the children of the village loved him and were unafraid, to the point of playing with him and pulling him about as though he were a big dog; and, secondly, that his devotion for the mongrel hound, his equal and fellow-worshipper, went to the length of genuine self-sacrifice. I could never forget how he fed it with the best of the bread, when his own face was pinched and drawn with hunger; and on other occasions I saw many similar proofs of his unselfish affection. His love for that mongrel, never uttered, in my presence at least, perhaps unrecognised as love even by himself, must surely have risen in some form of music or incense to sweeten the very halls of heaven.

In the woods I came across him anywhere and everywhere, sometimes so unexpectedly that it occurred to me he must have followed me stealthily for long distances. And once, in that very lonely stretch above the mountain railway, towards Montmollin, where the trees are spaced apart with an effect of cathedral aisles and Gothic arches, he caught me suddenly and did something that for a moment caused me a thrill of genuine alarm.

Wild lilies of the valley grow very thickly thereabouts, and the ground falls into a natural hollow that shuts it off from the rest of the forest with a peculiar and delightful sense of privacy; and when I came across it for the first time I stopped with a sudden feeling of quite bewildering enchantment—with a kind of childish awe that caught my breath as though I had slipped through some fairy door or blundered out of the ordinary world into a place of holy ground where solemn and beautiful things were the order of the day.

I waited a moment and looked about me. It was utterly still. The haze of the day had given place to an evening clarity of atmosphere that gave the world an appearance of having just received its finishing touches of pristine beauty. The scent of the lilies was overpoweringly sweet. But the whole first impression—before I had time to argue it away—was that I stood before some mighty chancel steps on the eve of a secret festival of importance, and that all was prepared and decorated with a view to the coming ceremony. The hush was the most delicate and profound imaginable—almost forbidding. I was a rude disturber.

Then, without any sound of approaching footsteps, my hat was lifted from my head, and when I turned with a sudden start of alarm, there before me stood Perret "*Comment-va*," the Man Who Played upon the Leaf.

An extraordinary air of dignity hung about him. His face was stern, yet rapt; something in his eyes genuinely impressive; and his whole appearance produced the instant impression—it touched me with a fleeting sense of awe-that here I had come upon him in the very act—had surprised this poor, broken being in some dramatic moment when his soul sought to find its own peculiar region, and to transform itself into loveliness through some process of outward worship.

He handed the hat back to me without a word, and I understood that I had unwittingly blundered into the secret place of his strange cult, some shrine, as it were, haunted doubly by his faith and imagination, perhaps even into his very Holy of Holies. His own head, as usual, was bared. I could no more have covered myself again than I could have put my hat on in Communion service of my own church.

"But—this wonderful place—this peace, this silence!" I murmured, with the best manner of apology for the intrusion I could muster on the instant. "May I stay a little with you, perhaps—and see?"

And his face passed almost immediately, when he realised that I understood, into that soft and happy expression the woods invariably drew out upon it—the look of the soul, complete and healed.

"Hush!" he whispered, his face solemn with the mystery of the listening trees; "*Vous êtes un peu en retard—mais pourtant. . . .*"

And lifting the leaf to his lips he played a soft and whirring music that had for its undercurrent the sounds of running water and singing wind mingled exquisitely together. It was half chant, half song, solemn enough for the dead, yet with a strain of soaring joy in it that made me think of children and a perfect faith. The music *blessed* me, and the leagues of forest, listening, poured about us all their healing forces.

I swear it would not have greatly surprised me to see the shaggy flanks of Pan himself disappearing behind the moss-grown boulders that lay about the hollows, or to have caught the flutter of white limbs as the nymphs stepped to the measure of his tune through the mosaic of slanting sunshine and shadow beyond.

Instead, I saw only that picturesque madman playing upon his ivy leaf, and at his feet the faithful dog staring up without blinking into his face, from time to time turning to make sure that I listened and understood.

★★★★★★★★★★★★

But the desolate places drew him most, and no distance seemed too great either for himself or his dog.

In this part of the Jura there is scenery of a sombre and impressive grandeur that, in its way, is quite as majestic as the revelation of far bigger mountains. The general appearance of soft blue pine woods is deceptive. The Boudry cliffs, slashed here and there with inaccessible *couloirs*, are undeniably grand, and in the sweep of the *Creux du Van* precipices there is a splendid terror quite as solemn as that of the Matterhorn itself. The shadows of its smooth, circular walls deny the sun all day, and the winds, caught within the 700ft. sides of its huge amphitheatre, as in the hollow of some awful cup, boom and roar with the crying of lost thunders.

I often met him in these lonely fastnesses, wearing that half-bewildered, half-happy look of the wandering child; and one day in particular, when I risked my neck scrambling up the most easterly of the Boudry *couloirs*, I learned afterwards that he had spent the whole time—four hours and more—on the little *Champ de Trémont* at the bottom, watching me with his dog till I arrived in safety at the top. His fellow-worshippers were few, he explained, and worth keeping; though it was ever inexplicable to me how his poor damaged eyes performed the marvels of sight they did.

And another time, at night, when, I admit, no sane man should have been abroad, and I had lost my way coming home from a climb along the torn and precipitous ledges of La Tourne, I heard his leaf thinly piercing the storm, always in front of me yet never overtaken, a sure though invisible guide. The cliffs on that descent are sudden and treacherous. The torrent of the Areuse, swollen with the melting snows, thundered ominously far below; and the forests swung their vast wet cloaks about them with torrents of blinding rain and clouds of darkness—yet all fragrant with warm wind as a virgin world answering to its first spring tempest. There he was, the outcast with his leaf, playing to his God amid all these crashings and bellowings. . . .

In the night, too, when skies were quiet and stars a-gleam, or in the still watches before the dawn, I would sometimes wake with the sound of clustered branches combing faint music from the gently-rising wind, and figure to myself that strange, lost creature wandering with his dog and leaf, his *pélerine*, his flying hair, his sweet, rapt expression of an inner glory, out there among the world of swaying trees he loved so well. And then my first soft view of the man would come back to me when I had seen him in the dusk as a tree; as though by some queer optical freak my outer and my inner vision had mingled so that I perceived both his broken body and his soul of magic.

For the mysterious singing of the leaf, heard in such moments from my window while the world slept, expressed absolutely the inmost cry of that lonely and singular spirit, damaged in the eyes of the village beyond repair, but in the sight of the wood-gods he so devoutly worshipped, made whole with their own peculiar loveliness and fashioned after the image of elemental things.

★★★★★★★★★★★

The spring wonder was melting into the peace of the long summer days when the end came. The vineyards had begun to dress themselves in green, and the forest in those soft blues when individual trees lose their outline in the general body of the mountain. The lake was indistinguishable from the sky; the Jura peaks and ridges gone a-soaring into misty distances; the white Alps withdrawn into inaccessible and remote solitudes of heaven. I was making reluctant preparations for leaving—dark London already in my thoughts—when the news came. I forget who first put it into actual words. It had been about the village all the morning, and something of it was in every face as I went down the street.

But the moment I came out and saw the dog on my doorstep, looking up at me with puzzled and beseeching eyes, I knew that something untoward had happened; and when he bit at my boots and caught my trousers in his teeth, pulling me in the direction of the forest, a sudden sense of poignant bereavement shot through my heart that I found it hard to explain, and that must seem incredible to those who have never known how potent may be the conviction of a sudden intuition.

I followed the forlorn creature whither it led, but before a hundred yards lay behind us, I had learned the facts from half-a-dozen mouths. That morning, very early, before the countryside was awake, the first mountain train, swiftly descending the steep incline below Chambrelien, had caught Perret "Comment-va" just where the Mont Racine *sentier* crosses the line on the way to his best-beloved woods, and in one swift second had swept him into eternity. The spot was in the direct line he always took to that special woodland shrine—his Holy Place.

And the manner of his death was characteristic of what I had divined in the man from the beginning; for he had given up his life to save his dog—this mongrel and faithful creature that now tugged so piteously at my trousers. Details, too, were not lacking; the engine-driver had not failed to tell the story at the next station, and the news had travelled up the mountain-side in the way that all such news travels—swiftly. Moreover, the woman who lived at the hut beside the crossing, and lowered the wooden barriers at the approach of all trains, had witnessed the whole sad scene from the beginning.

And it is soon told. Neither she nor the engine-driver knew exactly how the dog got caught in the rails, but both saw that it *was* caught, and both saw plainly how the figure of the half-witted wanderer, hatless as usual and with cape flying, moved deliberately across the line to release it. It all happened in a moment. The man could only have saved himself by leaving the dog to its fate. The shrieking whistle had as little effect upon him as the powerful breaks had upon the engine in those few available moments. Yet, in the fraction of a second before the engine caught them, the dog somehow leapt free, and the soul of the Man Who Played upon the Leaf passed into the presence of his God—singing.

As soon as it realised that I followed willingly, the beastie left me and trotted on ahead, turning every few minutes to make sure that I was coming. But I guessed our destination without difficulty. We passed the Pontarlier railway first, then climbed for half-an-hour and crossed the mountain line about a mile above the scene of the disaster, and so eventually entered the region of the forest, still quivering with innumerable flowers, where in the shaded heart of trees we approached the spot of lilies that I knew—the place where a few weeks before the devout worshipper had lifted the hat from my head because the earth whereon, I stood was holy ground.

We stood in the pillared gateway of his Holy of Holies. The cool airs, perfumed beyond belief, stole out of the forest to meet us on the very threshold, for the trees here grew so thickly that only patches of the summer blaze found an entrance. And this time I did not wait on the out-skirts, but followed my four-footed guide to a group of mossy boulders that stood in the very centre of the hollow.

And there, as the dog raised its eyes to mine, soft with the pain of its great unanswerable question, I saw in a cleft of the grey rock the ashes of many hundred fires; and, placed about them in careful array, an assortment of the sacrifices he had offered, doubtless in sharp personal deprivation, to his deity:—bits of mouldy bread, half-loaves, untouched portions of cheese, *salamé* with the skin uncut—most of it exactly as I had left it in his hut; and last of all, wrapped in the original white paper, the piece of Colombier *plume-cak'*, and a row of ten silver *francs* round the edge. . . .

I learned afterwards, too, that among the almost unrecognisable remains on the railway, untouched by the devouring terror of the iron, they had found a hand—tightly clasping in its dead fingers a crumpled ivy leaf. . . . My efforts to find a home for the dog delayed my departure, I remember, several days; but in the autumn when I returned it was only to hear that the creature had refused to stay with anyone, and finally had escaped into the forest and deliberately starved itself to death. They found its skeleton, Louis Favre told me, in a rocky hollow on the lower slopes of Mont Racine in the direction of Montmollin. But Louis Favre did not know, as I knew, that this hollow had received other sacrifices as well, and was consecrated ground.

And somewhere, if you search well the Jura slopes between Champ du Moulin, where Jean-Jacques Rousseau had his temporary house, and Côtendard where he visited Lord Wemyss when "Milord Maréchal Keith" was Governor of the Principality of Neuchâtel under Frederic II, King of Prussia—if you look well these haunted slopes, somewhere between the vineyards and the gleaming limestone heights, you shall find the forest glade where lie the bleached bones of the mongrel dog, and the little village cemetery that holds the remains of the Man Who Played upon the Leaf to the honour of the Great God Pan.

The Price of Wiggins's Orgy

1

It happened to be a Saturday when Samuel Wiggins drew the first cash sum on account of his small legacy—some twenty pounds, ten in gold and ten in notes. It felt in his pocket like a bottled-up prolongation of life. Never before had he seen so many dreams within practical reach. It produced in him a kind of high and elusive exaltation of the spirit. From time to time, he put his hand down to make the notes crackle and let his fingers play through the running sovereigns as children play through sand.

For twenty years he had been secretary to a philanthropist interested in feeding—feeding the poor. Soup kitchens had been the keynote of those twenty years, the distribution of victuals his sole objective. And now he had his reward—a legacy of £100 a year for the balance of his days.

To him it was riches. He wore a shortish frockcoat, a low, spreading collar, a black made-up tie, and boots with elastic sides. On this particular day he wore also a new pair of rather bright yellow leather gloves. He was unmarried, over forty, bald, plump in the body, and possessed of a simple and emotional heart almost childlike. His brown eyes shone in a face that was wrinkled and dusty—all his dreams driven inwards by the long years of uninspired toil for another.

For the first time in his life, released from the dingy purlieus of soup kitchens and the like, he wandered towards evening among the gay and lighted streets of the "West End"—Piccadilly Circus where the flaming lamps positively hurt the eyes, and Leicester Square. It was bewildering and delightful, this freedom. It went to his head. Yet he ought to have known better.

"I'm going to dine at a restaurant tonight, by Jove," he said to himself, thinking of the gloomy boarding-house where he usually sat between a missionary and a typewriter. He fingered his money. "I'm going to celebrate my legacy. I've earned it." The thought of a motor-car flashed absurdly through his mind; it was followed by another: a holiday in Spain, Italy, Hungary—one of those sunny countries where music was cheap, in the open air, and of the romantic kind he loved. These thoughts show the kind of exaltation that possessed him.

"It's nearly, though not quite, £2 a week," he repeated to himself for the fiftieth time, reflecting upon his legacy. "I simply can't believe it!"

After indecision that threatened to be endless, he turned at length through the swinging glass doors of a big and rather gorgeous restaurant. Only once before in his life had he dined at a big London restaurant—a Railway Hotel. Passing with some hesitation through the gaudy *café* where a number of foreigners sat drinking at little marble tables, he entered the main dining-room, long, lofty, and already thronged. Here the light and noise and movement dazed him considerably, and for the life of him he could not decide upon a table. The people all looked so prosperous and important; the waiters so like gentlemen in evening dress—the kind that came to the philanthropist's table. The roar of voices, eating, knives and forks, rose about him and filled him with a certain dismay. It was all rather overwhelming.

"I should have liked a smaller place better," he murmured, "but still—" And again he fingered his money to gain confidence.

The choice of a table was intimidating, for he was absurdly retiring, was Wiggins; more at home with papers and the reports of philanthropic societies; his holidays spent in a boarding-house at Worthing with his sister and her invalid husband. Then relief came in the form of a sub-head waiter who, spying his helplessness, inquired with a bland grandeur of manner if he "looked perhaps for someone?"

"Oh, a table, thanks, only a table—"

The man, washing his hands in mid-air, swept down the crowded aisles and found one without the least difficulty. It emerged from nowhere so easily that Wiggins felt he had been a fool not to discover it alone. He wondered if he ought to tip the man half-a-crown now or later, but, before he could decide, another occupied his place, bland and smiling, with black eyes and plush-like hair, bending low before him and holding out a large pink programme.

He examined it, feeling that he ought to order dishes with outlandish names just to show that he knew his way about. Before he could steady his eye upon a single line, however, a third waiter, very youthful, suggested in broken English that Wiggins should leave his

106

hat, coat and umbrella elsewhere. This he did willingly, though without grace or dispatch, for the yellow gloves stuck ridiculously to his hands. Then he sat down and turned to the menu again.

It was a very ordinary restaurant really, in spite of the vast height of the gilded ceiling, the scale of its sham magnificence and the excessive glitter of its hundred lights. The menu, disguised by various expensive and *recherché* dishes (which when ordered were invariably found to be "off"), was even more ordinary than the hall. But to the dazed Wiggins the words looked like a series of death-sentences printed in different languages, but all meaning the same thing: *order me—or die!* That waiter standing over him was the executioner. Unless he speedily ordered something really worth the proprietor's while to provide, the head waiter would be summoned and he, Wiggins, would be beheaded. Those stars against certain cheap dishes meant that they could only be ordered by privileged persons, and those crosses—

"This is *vairy* nice this sevening, sir," said the waiter, suddenly bending and pointing with a dirty finger to a dish that Wiggins found buried in a list uncommonly like "Voluntary Subscriptions" in his reports. It was entitled "Lancashire Hot-Pot . . . 2/0"—two shillings, not two pounds, as he first imagined. He leaped at it.

"Yes, thanks; that'll do, then—for tonight," he said, and the waiter ambled away indifferently, looking all round the room in search of sympathy.

By degrees, however, the other recovered his self-possession, and realised that to spend his legacy on mere Hot-Pot was to admit he knew not the values of life. He called the plush-headed waiter back and with a rush of words ordered some oysters, soup, a fried sole, and half a partridge to follow.

"Then ze 'Ot-Pot, sir?" queried the man, with respect.

"I'll see about that later."

For he was already wondering what he should drink, knowing nothing of wines and vintages. At luncheon with the philanthropist, he sometimes had a glass of sherry; at Worthing with his sister, he drank beer. But now he wanted something really good, something generous that would help him to celebrate. He would have ordered champagne as a conciliation to the waiter, now positively obsequious, but someone had told him once that there was not enough champagne in the world to go round, and that hotels and restaurants were supplied with "something rather bad." Burgundy, he felt, would be more the thing—rich, sunny, full-bodied.

He studied the wine-card till his head swam. A waiter, while he was thus engaged, sidled up and watched him from an angle. Wiggins, looking up distractedly at the same moment, caught his eye. Whew It was the Head Waiter himself, a man of quite infinite presence, who at once bowed himself forward, and with a gentle but commanding manner drew his attention to the wines he could "especially recommend." Something in the man's face struck him momentarily as familiar—vaguely familiar—then passed.

Now Wiggins, as has been said, did not know one wine from another; but the spirit of his foolish pose fairly had him by the throat at last, and each time this condescending individual indicated a new vintage he shook his head knowingly and shrugged his shoulders with the air of a connoisseur. This pantomime continued for several minutes.

"Something *really* good, you know," he mumbled after a while, determined to justify himself in the eyes of this high official who was taking such pains. "A rare wine—er—with body in it." Then he added, with a sudden impulse of confidence, "It's Saturday night, remember!" And he smiled knowingly, making a gesture that a man of the world was meant to understand.

Why he should have said this remains a mystery. Perhaps it was a semi-apologetic reference to the supposed habit of men to indulge themselves on a Saturday because they need not rise early to work next day. Perhaps it was meant in some way to excuse all the trouble he was giving. In any case, there can be no question that the manner of the Head Waiter instantly changed in a subtle way difficult to describe, and from mere official politeness passed into deferential attention. He bowed slightly. He increased his distance by an inch or two. Wiggins, noticing it and slightly bewildered, repeated his remark, for want of something to say more than anything else. "It's Saturday night, of course," he repeated, murmuring, yet putting more meaning into the words than they could reasonably hold.

"As *Monsieur* says," the man replied, with a marked respect in his tone not there before; "and we —close early."

"Of course," said the other, gaining confidence pleasantly, "you close early."

He had quite forgotten the fact, even if he ever knew it, but he spoke with decision. Glancing up from the wine-list, he caught the man's eye; then instantly lowered his gaze, for the Head Waiter was staring at him in a fixed and curious manner that seemed unnecessary.

And once again that passing touch of familiarity appeared upon the features and was gone.

"*Monsieur* is here for the first time, if I may ask?" came next.

"Er—yes, I am," he replied, thinking all this attention a trifle excessive.

"Ah, *pardon*, of course, I understand," the Head Waiter added softly. "A new—a recent member, then—"

A little non-plussed, a little puzzled, Wiggins agreed with a nod of the head. He did not know that head waiters referred to customers as "members." For an instant it occurred to him that possibly he was being mistaken for somebody else. It was really—but at that moment the oysters arrived. The Head Waiter said something in rapid Italian to his subordinate—something that obviously increased that plush-headed person's desire to please—bent over with his best manner to murmur, "And I will get *Monsieur* the wine he will like, the right kind of wine!"—and was gone.

It was a new and delightful sensation. Wiggins, feeling proud, pleased and important under the effect of this excellent service and attention, turned to his oysters. The wine would come presently. And, meanwhile, the music had begun. . . .

2

He began to enjoy himself thoroughly, and the wine—still, fragrant, soft—soon ran in his veins and drove out the last vestige of his absurd shyness. Behind the palm trees, somewhere out of sight, the orchestra played soothingly, and if the selections were somewhat bizarre it made no difference to him. He drank in the sound just as he drank in the wine—eagerly. Both fed the consciousness that he was enjoying himself, and the Danse Macabre gave him as much pleasure as did the Bohème, the Strauss Waltz, or Donizetti. Everything—wine, music, food, people–served to intensify his interest *in himself.*

He examined his face in the big mirrors and realized what a dog he was and what a good time he was having. He watched the other customers, finding them splendid and distinguished. The whole place was really fine—he would come again and again, always ordering the same wine, for it was certainly an unusual wine, as the Head Waiter had called it, "the right kind." The price of it he never asked, for in his pocket lay the price of a whole case. His hand slipped down to finger the sovereigns—hot and slippery now—and the notes, somewhat moist and crumpled. . . . The needles of the big staring clock meanwhile swung onwards. . . .

Thus, aided by the tactful and occasional superintendence of the Head Waiter from a distance, the evening passed along in a happy rush of pleasurable emotion. The half-partridge had vanished, and Wiggins toyed now with a wonderful-looking "sweet"— the most expensive he could find. He did not eat much of it, but liked to see it on his plate. The wine helped things enormously. He had ordered another half-bottle some time ago, delighted to find that it exhilarated without confusing him. And everyone else in the place was enjoying himself in the same way. He was thrilled to discover this.

Only one thing jarred a little. A very big man, with a round, clean-shaven face inclined to fatness, stared at him more than he cared about from a table in the corner diagonally across the room. He had only come in half-an-hour ago. His face was somehow or other dog-like— something between a boarhound and a pup, Wiggins thought. Each time he looked up the fellow's large and rather fierce eyes were fixed upon him, then lingeringly withdrawn. It was unpleasant to be stared at in this way by an offensive physiognomy.

But most of the time he was too full of personal visions conjured up by the wine to trouble long about external matters. His head was simply brimming over with thoughts and ideas—about himself, about soup-kitchens, feeding the poor, the change of life effected by the legacy, and a thousand other details. Once or twice, however, in sharp, clear moments when the tide of alcohol ebbed a little, other questions assailed him: Why should the Head Waiter have become so obsequious and attentive? What was it in his face that seemed familiar? What was there about the remark "It's Saturday evening" to change his manner? And—what was it about the dinner, the restaurant and the music that seemed just a little out of the ordinary?

Or was he merely thinking nonsense? And was it his imagination that this man stared so oddly? The alcohol rushed deliciously in his veins.

The vague uneasiness, however, was a passing matter, for the orchestra was tearing madly through a Csardas, and his thoughts and feelings were swept away in the wild rhythm. He drank his bottle out and ordered another. Was it the second or the third? He could not remember. Counting always made his head ache. He did not care anyhow. "Let 'er go! I'm enjoying myself I've got a fat legacy—money lying in the bank—money I haven't earned!" The carefulness of years was destroyed in as many minutes. "That music's simply spiffing!"

Then he glanced up and caught the clean-shaven face bearing down upon him across the shimmering room like the muzzle of a moving gun. He tried to meet it, but found he could not focus it properly. The same moment he saw that he was mistaken; the man was merely staring at him. Two faces swam and wobbled into one. This movement, and the appearance of coming towards him, were both illusions produced by the alcohol. He drank another glass quickly to steady his vision—and then another. . . .

"I'll call for my bill. Itshtime to go. . . . . .!" he murmured aloud later, with a very deep sigh. He looked about him for the waiter, who instantly appeared—with coffee and liqueurs, however.

"Dear me, yes. Qui' forgot I or'ered those," he observed offhand, smiling in the man's face, willing and anxious to say a lot of things, but not quite certain what.

"My bill," was what he said finally, "mush b'off!"

The waiter laughed pleasantly, but very politely, in reply. Wiggins, repeated his remark about his bill.

"Oh, that will be all right, sir," returned the man, as though no such thing as payment was ever heard of in *this* restaurant. It was rather confusing. Wiggins laughed to himself, drank his liqueur and forgot about everything except the ballet music of Délibes the strings were sprinkling in a silver shower about the hall. His mind ran after them through the glittering air.

"Just fancy if I could catch 'em and take 'em home in a bunch," he said to himself, immensely pleased. He was enjoying himself hugely by now.

And then, suddenly, he became aware that the place was rapidly thinning, lights being lowered, goodnights being said, and that everybody seemed—drunk.

"P'rapsh they've all got legacies!" he thought, flushing with excitement.

He rose unsteadily to his feet and was delighted to find that *he* was not in the least—drunk. He at once respected himself.

"Itsh really 'sgusting that fellows can't stop when they've had 'nough!" he murmured, making his way with steps that required great determination towards the door, and remembering before he got halfway that he had not paid his bill. Turning in a half-circle that brought an unnecessary quantity of the room round with him, he made his way back, lost his way, fumbled about in the increasing gloom, and found himself face to face with the—Head Waiter. The unexpected meeting braced him astonishingly. The dignity of the man had curiously increased.

"I'm looking for my bill," observed Wiggins thickly, wondering for the twentieth time of whom the man's face reminded him; "you haven't seen it about anywhere, I shuppose?" He sat down with more dignity than he could have supposed possible and produced a £5 note from his pocket, the lining of the pocket coming out with it like a dirty glove.

Most of the guests had gone out by this time, and the big hall was very dark. Two lights only remained, and these, reflected from mirror to mirror, made its proportions seem vast and unreal. They flew from place to place, too, distressingly—these lights.

"Half-a-crown will settle that, sir," replied the man, with a respectful bow.

"Nonshense!" replied the other. "Why, I ordered Lancashire hotch-potch, grilled shole, a-a bird or something of the kind, and the wine—"

"I beg your pardon, sir, but—if you will permit me to say so—the others will soon be here now, and— as there will be a specially large attendance, perhaps you would like to make sure of your place." He pocketed the half-crown with a bow, pointed to the far, dim corner of the room, and stepped aside a little to make space for Wiggins to pass.

And Wiggins did pass—though it is not quite clear how he managed to dodge the flying tables. With deep sighs, hot, confused and puzzled, but too obfuscated to understand what it was all about, he obeyed the directions, at the same time wondering uneasily how it was he had forgotten what was a-foot. He wandered towards the end of the hall with the uncertainty of a butterfly that makes many feints before it settles. . . . At a vast distance off the Head Waiter was moving to close the main doors, utterly oblivious now of his existence. He felt glad of that. Something about that fellow was disagreeable—downright nasty.

This suddenly came over him with a flood of conviction. The man was more than peculiar: he was sinister. . . . The air smelt horribly of cooked food, tobacco smoke, breathing crowds, scented women and the rest. Whiffs of it, hot and foetid, brought him a little to his senses. . . . Then suddenly he noticed that the big man with the face that was dark and smooth like the muzzle of a cannon, was watching him keenly from a table on the other side where an electric light still burned.

"By George! There he is again, that feller! Wonder whatsh he's smiling at me for. Looking for'sh bill too, p'raps— Now, in a Soup Kishen nothing of the kind—"

He bowed in return, smiling insolently, holding steady by a chair to do so. He shoved and tumbled his way on into the shadows, half-mingling with the throng passing out into the street. Then, making a sharp turn back into the room unobserved, he took a few uncertain steps and collapsed silently and helplessly upon a chair that was hidden behind a big palm-tree in a dark corner.

And the last thing he remembered as he sank, boneless, like soft hay, into that corner was that the sham palm-tree bowed towards him, then ran off into the ceiling, and from that elevation, which in no way diminished its size, bowed to him yet again. . . .

It was just after his eyes closed that the door in the gilt panelling at the end of the room softly opened and a woman entered on tiptoe. She was followed by other women and several girls; these, again, from time to time, by men, all dressed in black, all silent, and all ushered by the majestic Head Waiter to their places. The big man with the face like a gun-muzzle superintended. And each individual, on entering, was held there at the secret doorway until a certain sentence had passed his lips. Evidently a password: "It is Saturday night," said the one being admitted, "and we close early," replied the Head Waiter and the big man. And then the door was closed until the next soft tapping came.

But Wiggins, plunged in the stupor of the first sleep, knew none of all this. His frock-coat was bunched about his neck, his black tie under his ear, his feet resting higher than his head. He looked like a collapsed air-ship in a hedge, and he snored heavily.

3

It was about an hour later when he opened his eyes, climbed pain-fully and heavily to his feet, staggered back against the wall utterly be-wildered—and stared. At the far end of the great hall, its loftiness now dim, was a group of people. The big mirrors on all sides reflected them with the effect of increasing their numbers indefinitely. They stood and sat upon an improvised platform. The electric lights, shaded with black, dropped a pale glitter upon their faces. They were systematically grouped, the big man in the centre, the Head Waiter at a small table just behind him. The former was speaking in low, measured tones.

In his dark and distant corner Wiggins first of all seized the *carafe* and quenched his feverish thirst. Next, he advanced slowly and with the utmost caution to a point nearer the group where he could hear what was being said. He was still a good deal confused in mind, and had no idea what the hour was or what he had been doing in the meantime. There were some twenty or thirty people, he saw, of both sexes, well dressed, many of them distinguished in appearance, and all wearing black; even their gloves were black; some of the women, too, wore black veils— very thick. But in all the faces without exception there was something—was it about the lips and mouths?—that was peculiar and—repellent.

Obviously, this was a meeting of some kind. Some society had hired the hall for a private gathering. Wiggins, understanding this, began to feel awkward. He did not wish to intrude; he had no right to listen; yet to make himself known was to betray that he was still very considerably intoxicated. The problem presented itself in these simple terms to his dazed intelligence. He was also aware of another fact: about these black-robed people there was something which made him secretly and horribly—afraid.

The big man with the smooth face like a gun-muzzle sat down after a softly-uttered speech, and the group, instead of applauding with their hands, waved black handkerchiefs. The fluttering sound of them trickled along the wastes of hall towards the concealed eavesdropper. Then the Head Waiter rose to introduce the next speaker, and the instant Wiggins saw him he understood what it was in his face that was familiar. For the false beard no longer adorned his lips, the wig that altered the shape of his forehead and the appearance of his eyes had been removed, and the likeness he bore to the philanthropist, Wiggins's late employer, was too remarkable to be ignored. Wiggins just repressed a cry, but a low gasp apparently did escape him, for several members of the group turned their heads in his direction and stared.

The Head Waiter, meanwhile, saved him from immediate discovery by beginning to speak. The words were plainly audible, and the resemblance of the voice to that other voice he knew now to be stopped with dust, was one of the most dreadful experiences he had ever known. Each word, each trick of expression came as a new and separate shock.

". . . and the learned Doctor will say a few words upon the rationale of our subject," he concluded, turning with a graceful bow to make room for a distinguished-looking old gentleman who advanced shambling from the back of the improvised platform.

What Wiggins then heard—in somewhat disjointed sentences owing to the buzzing in his ears—was at first apparently meaningless. Yet it was freighted, he knew, with a creeping and sensational horror that would fully reveal itself the instant he discovered the clue. The old clever-faced scoundrel was saying vile things. He knew it. But the key to the puzzle being missing, he could not quite guess what it was all about. The Doctor, gravely and with balanced phrases, seemed to be speaking of the fads of the day with regard to food and feeding. He ridiculed vegetarianism, and all the other *isms*. He said that one and all were based upon ignorance and fallacy, declaring that the time had at last come in the history of the race when a rational system of feeding was a paramount necessity.

The physical and psychical conditions of the times demanded it, and the Soul of man could never be emancipated until it was adopted. He himself was proud to be one of the founders of their audacious and secret Society, revolutionary and pioneer in the best sense, to which so many of the medical fraternity now belonged, and so many of the brave women too, who were in the van of the feminist movements of the times. He said a great deal in this vein. Wiggins, listening in growing amazement and uneasiness, waited for the clue to it all.

In conclusion, the speaker referred solemnly to the fact that there was a stream of force in their Society which laid them open to the melancholy charge of being called "hysterical." "But after all," he cried, with rising enthusiasm and in accents that rang down the hall, "a Society without hysteria is a dull Society, just as a woman without hysteria is a dull woman. Neither the Society nor the woman need yield to the tendency; but that it is present potentially infers the faculty, so delicious in the eyes of all sane men—the faculty of running to extremes. It is a sign of life, and of very vivid life. It is not for nothing, dear friends, that we are named the—"

But the buzzing in Wiggins's ears was so loud at this moment that he missed the name. It sounded to him something between "Can-I-believes" and "Camels," but for the life of him he could not overtake the actual word. The Doctor had uttered it, moreover, in a lowered voice—a suddenly lowered voice. . . . When the noise in his ears had passed he heard the speaker bring his address to an end in these words: ". . . and I will now ask the secretaries to make their reports from their various sections, after which, I understand"—his tone grew suddenly thick and clouded—"we are to be regaled with a collation—a sacramental collation—of the usual kind. . . ." His voice hushed away

115

to nothing. His mouth was working most curiously. A wave of excitement unquestionably ran over the faces of the others. Their mouths also worked oddly. Dark and sombre things were afoot in that hall.

Wiggins crouched a little lower behind the edge of the overhanging table-cloth and listened. He was perspiring now, but there were touches of icy horror fingering about in the neighbourhood of his heart. His mental and physical discomfort were very great, for the conviction that he was about to witness some dreadful scene—black as the garments of the participants in it—grew rapidly within him. He devised endless plans for escape, only to reject them the instant they were formed. There was no escape possible. He had to wait till the end.

A charming young woman was on her feet, addressing the audience in silvery tones; sweet and comely she was, her beauty only marred by that singular leer that visited the lips and mouths of all of them. The flesh of his back began to crawl as he listened. He would have given his whole year's legacy to be out of it, for behind that voice of silver and sweetness there crowded even to her lips the rush of something that was unutterable—loathsome. Wiggins felt it. The uncertainty as to its exact nature only added to his horror and distress.

". . . . so, this question of supply, my friends," she was saying, "is becoming more and more difficult. It resolves itself into a question of ways and means."

She looked round upon her audience with a touch of nervous apprehension before she continued. "In my particular sphere of operations—West Kensington—I have regretfully to report that the suspicions and activity of the police, the foolish, old-fashioned police, have now rendered my monthly contributions no longer possible. There have been too many disappearances of late—" She paused, casting her eyes down. Wiggins felt his hair rise, drawn by a shivery wind. The words "contributions" and "disappearances" brought with them something quite freezing.

". . . . As you know," the girl resumed, "it is to the doctors that we must look chiefly for our steadier supplies, and unfortunately in my sphere of operations we have but one doctor who is a member. . . . I do not like to—to resign my position, but I must ask for lenient consideration of my failure"—her voice sank lower still—". . . my failure to furnish tonight the materials—" She began to stammer and hesitate dreadfully; her voice shook; an ashen pallor spread to her very lips. ". . . the elements for our customary feast—"

A movement of disapproval ran over the audience like a wave; murmurs of dissent and resentment were heard. As the girl paled more perceptibly the singular beauty of her face stood out with an effect of almost shining against that dark background of shadows and black garments. In spite of himself, and forgetting caution for the moment, Wiggins peeped over the edge of the table to see her better. She was a lady, he saw, high-bred and spirited. That pallor, and the timidity it bespoke, was but evidence of a highly sensitive nature facing a situation of peculiar difficulty—and danger.

He read in her attitude, in the poise of that slim figure standing there before disapproval and possible disaster, the bearing and proud courage of a type that would face execution with calmness and dignity. Wiggins was amazed that this thought should flash through him so vividly —from nowhere. Born of the feverish aftermath of alcohol, perhaps—yet born inevitably, too, of this situation before his eyes.

With a thrill he realised that the girl was speaking again, her voice steady, but faint with the gravity of her awful position.

"....and I ask for that justice in consideration of my failure which— the difficulties of the position demand. I have had to choose between that bold and ill-considered action which might have betrayed us all to the authorities, and—the risk of providing nothing for tonight."

She sat down. Wiggins understood that it was a question of life and death. The air about him turned icy. He felt the perspiration trickling on several different parts of his body at once.

An old lady rose instantly to reply; her face was stern and dreadful, although the signature of breeding and culture was plainly there in the delicate lines about the nostrils and forehead. Her mien held something implacable. She was dressed in black silk that rustled, and she was certainly well over sixty; but what made Wiggins squirm there in his narrow hiding-place was the extraordinary resemblance she bore to Mrs. Sturgis, the superintendent of one of his late employer's soup kitchens. It was all diabolically grotesque. She glanced round upon the group of members, who clearly regarded her as a leader. The machinery of the whole dreadful scene then moved quicker.

"Then are we to understand from the West Kensington secretary," she began in firm, even tones, "that for tonight there is—nothing?" The young girl bowed her head without rising from her chair.

"I beg to move, then, Mr. Chairman," continued the terrible old lady in iron accents, "that the customary procedure be followed, and that a Committee of Three be appointed to carry it into immediate effect." The words fell like bomb-shells into the deserted spaces of the hall.

"I second the motion," was heard in a man's voice. "Those in favour of the motion will show their hands," announced the big chairman with the cleanshaven face.

Several score of black-gloved hands waved in the air, with the effect of plumes upon a jolting hearse.

"And those who oppose it?"

No single hand was raised. An appalling hush fell upon the group.

"I appoint Signor Carnamorte as chairman of the sub-committee, with power to choose his associates," said the big man. And the "Head Waiter" bowed his acceptance of the duty imposed upon him. There was at once then a sign of hurried movement, and the figure of the young girl was lost momentarily to view as several members surged round her. The next instant they fell away and she stood clear, her hands bound. Her voice, soft as before but very faint, was audible through the hush.

"I claim the privilege belonging to the female members of the Society," she said calmly; "the right to find, if possible, a substitute."

"Granted," answered the chairman gravely. "The customary ten minutes will be allowed you in which to do so. Meanwhile, the preparations must proceed in the usual way."

With a dread that ate all other emotions, Wiggins watched keenly from his concealment, and the preparations that he saw in progress, though simple enough in themselves, filled him with a sense of ultimate horror that was freezing. The Committee of Three were very busy with something at the back of the improvised platform, something that was heavy and, on being touched, emitted a metallic and sonorous ring.

As in the strangling terror and heat of nightmare the full meaning of events is often kept concealed until the climax, so Wiggins knew that this simple sound portended something that would only be revealed to him later—something appalling as Satan—sinister as the grave. That ring of metal was the Gong of Death. He heard it in his own heart, and the shock was so great that he could not prevent an actual physical movement. His jerking leg drove sharply against a chair. The chair—squeaked.

The sound pierced the deep silence of the big hall with so shrill a note that of course everybody heard it. Wiggins, expecting to have the whole crew of these black-robed people about his ears, held his breath in an agony of suspense. All those pairs of eyes, he felt, were searching the spot where he lay so thinly hidden by the table-cloth. But no steps came towards him. A voice, however, spoke: the voice of the girl: she had heard the sound and had divined its cause.

"Loosen my bonds," she cried, "for there is someone yonder among the shadows. I have found a substitute! And—I swear to Heaven—*he is plump!*"

The sentence was so extraordinary, that Wiggins felt a spring of secret merriment touched somewhere deep within him, and a gush of uncontrollable laughter came up in his throat so suddenly that before he could get his hand to his mouth, it rang down the long dim hall and betrayed him beyond all question of escape. Behind it lay the strange need of violent expression. He had to do something.

The life of this slender and exquisite girl was in danger. And the nightmare strain of the whole scene, the hints and innuendoes of a dark purpose, the implacable nature of the decree that threatened so fair a life—all resulted in a pressure that was too much for him. Had he not laughed, he would certainly have shrieked aloud. And the next minute he did shriek aloud. The screams followed his laughter with a dreadful clamour, and at the same instant he staggered noisily to his feet and rose into full view from behind the table. Everybody then saw him.

Across the length of that dimly-lighted hall he faced the group of people in all their hideous reality, and what he saw cleared from his fuddled brain the last fumes of the alcohol. The white visage of each member seemed already close upon him. He saw the glimmering pallor of their skins against the black clothes, the eyes ashine, the mouths working, fingers pointing at him. There was the Head Waiter, more than ever like the dead philanthropist whose life had been spent in feeding others; there the odious smooth face of the big chairman; there the stern-lipped old lady who demanded the sentence of death.

The whole silent crew of them stared darkly at him, and in front of them, like some fair lily growing amid decay, stood the girl with the proud and pallid face, calm and self-controlled. Immediately beyond her, a little to one side, Wiggins next perceived the huge iron cauldron, already swinging from its mighty tripod, waiting to receive her into its capacious jaws. Beneath it gleamed and flickered the flames from a dozen spirit-lamps.

"My substitute!" rang out her clear voice. "My substitute! Unloose my hands! And seize him before he can escape!"

"He cannot escape!" cried a dozen angry voices.

"In darkness!" thundered the chairman, and at the same moment every light was extinguished from the switch-board—every light but one. The bulb immediately behind him in the wall was left burning.

And the crew were upon him, coming swiftly and stealthily down the empty aisles between the tables. He saw their forms advance and shift by the gleam of the lamps beneath the awful cauldron. With the advance came, too, the sound of rushing, eager breathing. He imagined, though he could not see, those evil mouths a-working. And at this moment the subconscious part of him that had kept the secret all this time, suddenly revealed in letters of flame the name of the Society which fifteen minutes before he had failed to catch. The subconscious self, that supreme stage manager, that arch conspirator, rose and struck him in the face as it were out of the darkness, so that he understood, with a shock of nauseous terror, the terrible nature of the net in which he was caught.

For this Secret Society, meeting for their awful rites in a great public restaurant of mid-London, were maniacs of a rare and singular description—vilely mad on one point but sane on all the rest. They were *Cannibals!*

★★★★★★★★★★★★

Never before had he run with such speed, agility and recklessness; never before had he guessed that he could leap tables, clear chairs with the flying manner of a hurdle race, and dodge palms and flower-pots as an athlete of twenty dodges collisions in the football field. But in each dark corner where he sought a temporary refuge, the electric light on the wall above immediately sprang into brilliance, one of the crew having remained by the switchboard to control this diabolically ingenious method of keeping him ever in sight.

For a long time, however, he evaded his crowding and clumsy pursuers. It was a vile and ghastly chase. His flying frock-coat streamed out behind him, and he felt the elastic side of his worn boots split under the unusual strain of the twisting, turning ankles as he leaped and ran. His pursuers, it seemed, sought to prolong the hunt on purpose. The passion of the chase was in their blood. Round and round that hall, up and down, over tables and under chairs, behind screens, shaking the handles of doors—all immovable, past gleaming dish-covers on the wheeled joint-tables, taking cover by swing doors, curtains, palms, everything and anything, Wiggins flew for his life from the pursuing forces of a horrible death.

And at last they caught him. Breathless and exhausted, he collapsed backwards against the wall in a dark corner. But the light instantly flashed out above him. He lay in full view, and in another second the advancing horde—he saw their eyes and mouths so close—would be upon him, when something utterly unexpected happened: his head in falling struck against a hard projecting substance and—a bell rang sharply out. It was a telephone!

How he ever managed to get the receiver to his lips, or why the answering exchange came so swiftly he does not pretend to know. He had just time to shout, "Help! help! Send police X. . . Restaurant! Murder! Cannibals!" when he was seized violently by the collar, his arms and legs grasped by a dozen pairs of hands, and a struggle began that he knew from the start must prove hopeless.

The fact that help might be on the way, however, gave him courage. Wiggins smashed right and left, screamed, kicked, bit and butted. His frock coat was ripped from his back with a whistling tear of cloth and lining, and he found himself free at the edge of a group that clawed and beat everywhere about him. The dim light was now in his favour. He shot down the hall again like a hare, leaping tables on the way, and flinging dish-covers, *carafes*, menus at the pursuing crowd as fast as he could lay hands upon them.

Then came a veritable pandemonium of smashed glass and crockery, while a grip of iron caught his arms behind and pinioned them beyond all possibility of moving. Turning quickly, he found himself looking straight into the eyes of a big blue policeman, the door into the street open beside him. The crowd became at once inextricably mixed up and jumbled together. The chairman, and the girl who was to have been eaten, melted into a single person. The philanthropist and the old lady slid into each other. It was a horrible bit of confusion. He felt deadly sick and dizzy. Everything dropped away from his sight then, and darkness tore up round him from the carpet. He remembered nothing more for a long time.

★★★★★★★★★★

Perhaps the most vivid recollection of what occurred afterwards—he remembers it to this day, and his memory may be trusted, for he never touched wine again—was the weary smile of the magistrate, and the still more weary voice as he said in the court two days later—

"Forty shillings, and be bound over to keep the peace in two sureties for six months. And £5 to the proprietor of the restaurant to pay damages for the broken windows and crockery. Next case. . . . .!"

The Return

It was curious—that sense of dull uneasiness that came over him so suddenly, so stealthily at first, he scarcely noticed it, but with such marked increase after a time that he presently got up and left the theatre. His seat was on the gangway of the dress circle, and he slipped out awkwardly in the middle of what seemed to be the best and jolliest song of the piece. The full house was shaking with laughter; so infectious was the gaiety that even strangers turned to one another as much as to say: 'Now, isn't *that* funny—?'

It was curious, too, the way the feeling first got into him at all, here in the full swing of laughter, music, light-heartedness, for it came as a vague suggestion: 'I've forgotten something—something I meant to do—something of importance. What in the world was it, now?' And he thought hard, searching vainly through his mind; then dismissed it as the dancing caught his attention. It came back a little later again, during a passage of long-winded talk that bored him and set his attention free once more, but came more strongly this time, insisting on an answer. What could it have been that he had overlooked, left undone, omitted to see to? It went on nibbling at the subconscious part of him. Several times this happened, this dismissal and return, till at last the thing declared itself more plainly—and he felt bothered, troubled, distinctly uneasy.

He was wanted somewhere. There was somewhere else he ought to be. That describes it best, perhaps. Some engagement of moment had entirely slipped his memory—an engagement that involved another person, too. But where, what, with whom? And, at length, this vague uneasiness amounted to positive discomfort, so that he felt unable to enjoy the piece—and left abruptly. Like a man to whom comes suddenly the horrible idea that the match he lit his cigarette with and flung into the waste-paper basket on leaving was not really out—a sort of panic distress—he jumped into a taxi-cab and hurried to his flat: to find everything in order, of course; no smoke, no fire, no smell of burning.

But his evening was spoilt. He sat smoking in his armchair at home—this business man of forty, practical in mind, of character some called stolid—cursing himself for an imaginative fool. It was now too late to go back to the theatre; the club bored him; he spent an hour with the evening papers, dipping into books, sipping a long cool drink; doing odds and ends about the flat; 'I'll go to bed early for a change,' he laughed, but really all the time fighting yes, deliberately fighting this strange attack of uneasiness that so insidiously grew up-wards, outwards from the buried depths of him that sought so strenu-ously to deny it. It never occurred to him that he was ill. He was *not* ill. His health was thunderingly good. He was robust as a coal-heaver.

The flat was roomy, high up on the top floor, yet in a busy part of town, so that the roar of traffic mounted round it like a sea. Through the open windows came the fresh night air of June. He had never noticed before how sweet the London night air could be, and that not all the smoke and dust could smother a certain touch of wild fragrance that tinctured it with perfume—yes, almost perfume—as of the country. He swallowed a draught of it as he stood there, staring out across the tangled world of roofs and chimney-pots. He saw the procession of the clouds; he saw the stars; he saw the moonlight fall-ing in a shower of silver spears upon the slates and wires and steeples. And something in him quickened—something that had never stirred before.

He turned with a horrid start, for the uneasiness had of a sudden leaped within him like an animal. There was someone in the flat.

Instantly, with action, even this slight action, the fancy vanished; but, all the same, he switched on the electric lights and made a search. For it seemed to him that someone had crept up close behind him while he stood there watching the Night—someone, moreover, whose silent presence fingered with unerring touch both this new thing that had quickened in his heart *and* that sense of original deep uneasiness.

He was amazed at himself, angry; indignant that he could be thus foolishly upset over nothing, yet at the same time profoundly dis-tressed at this vehement growth of a new thing in his well-ordered personality. Growth? He dismissed the word the moment it occurred to him. But it had occurred to him. It stayed. While he searched the empty flat, the long passages, the gloomy bedroom at the end, the little hall where he kept his overcoats and golf sticks—it stayed. Growth! It was oddly disquieting. Growth, to him, involved—though he neither acknowledged nor recognised the truth perhaps—some kind of undesirable changeableness, instability, unbalance.

Yet, singular as it all was, he realised that the uneasiness and the sudden appreciation of Beauty that was so new to him had both entered by the same door into his being. When he came back to the front room, he noticed that he was perspiring. There were little drops of moisture on his forehead. And down his spine ran positively chills—little, faint quivers of cold. He was shivering.

He lit his big *meerschaum* pipe, and left the lights all burning. The feeling that there was something he had overlooked, forgotten, left undone, had vanished. Whatever the original cause of this absurd uneasiness might be—he called it absurd on purpose, because he now realised in the depths of him that it was really more vital than he cared about it—was much nearer to discovery than before. It dodged about just below the threshold of discovery. It was as close as that. Any moment he would know what it was: he would remember. Yes, he would *remember*. Meanwhile, he was in the right place. No desire to go elsewhere afflicted him, as in the theatre. Here was the place, here in the flat.

And then it was, with a kind of sudden burst and rush—it seemed to him the only way to phrase it—memory gave up her dead.

At first, he only caught her peeping round the corner at him, drawing aside a corner of an enormous curtain, as it were; striving for more complete entrance as though the mass of it were difficult to move. But he understood; he knew; he recognised. It was enough for that. An entrance into his being—heart, mind, soul—was being attempted, and the entrance, because of his stolid temperament, was difficult of accomplishment. There was effort, strain. Something in him had first to be opened up, widened, made soft and ready as by an operation, before full entrance could be effected. This much he grasped, though for the life of him he could not have put it into words. Also, he *knew* who it was that sought an entrance. Deliberately from himself he withheld the name. But he knew, as surely as though Straughan stood in the room and faced him with a knife, saying, 'Let me in, let me in. I wish you to know I'm here. I'm clearing a way . . .! You recall our promise . . .?'

He rose from his chair and went to the open window again, the strange fear slowly passing. The cool air fanned his cheeks. Beauty, till now, had scarcely ever brushed the surface of his soul. He had never troubled his head about it. It passed him by, indifferent; and he had

125

ever loathed the mouthy prating of it on others' lips. He was practical; beauty was for dreamers, for women, for men who had means and leisure. He had not exactly scorned it; rather it had never touched his life, to sweeten, cheer, uplift.

Artists for him were like monks—another sex almost, useless beings who never helped the world go round. He was for action always, work, activity, achievement—as he saw them. He remembered Straughan vaguely—Straughan, the ever impecunious, friend of his youth, always talking of colour, sound—mysterious, ineffective things. He even forgot what they had quarrelled about, if they *had* quarrelled at all even; or why they had gone apart all these years ago. And, certainly, he had forgotten any promise. Memory, as yet, only peeped round the corner of that huge curtain at him, tentatively, suggestively, yet—he was obliged to admit it—somewhat winningly. He was conscious of this gentle, sweet seductiveness that now replaced his fear.

And, as he stood now at the open window, peering over huge London, Beauty came close and smote him between the eyes. She came blindingly, with her train of stars and clouds and perfumes. Night, mysterious, myriad-eyed, and flaming across her sea of haunted shadows, invaded his heart and shook him with her immemorial wonder and delight. He found no words, of course, to clothe the new, unwonted sensations. He only knew that all his former dread, uneasiness, distress, and with them this idea of 'growth' that had seemed so repugnant to him, were merged, swept up, and gathered magnificently home into a wave of Beauty that enveloped him. 'See it . . . and understand,' ran a secret inner whisper across his mind. He saw. He understood. . . .

He went back and turned the lights out. Then he took his place again at that open window, drinking in the night. He saw a new world; a species of intoxication held him. He sighed . . . as his thoughts blundered for expression among words and sentences that knew him not. But the delight was there, the wonder, the mystery. He watched, with heart alternately tightening and expanding, the transfiguring play of moon and shadow over the sea of buildings. He saw the dance of the hurrying clouds, the open patches into outer space, the veiling and unveiling of that ancient silvery face; and he caught strange whispers of the hierophantic, sacerdotal Power that has echoed down the world since Time began and dropped strange magic phrases into every poet's heart since first 'God dawned on Chaos'—the Beauty of the Night. . . .

A long time passed—it may have been one hour, it may have been three—when at length he turned away and went slowly to his bedroom. A deep peace lay over him. Something quite new and blessed had crept into his life and thought. He could not quite understand it all. He only knew that it uplifted. There was no longer the least sign of affliction or distress. Even the inevitable reaction that, of course, set in could not destroy that.

And then, as he lay in bed, nearing the borderland of sleep, suddenly and without any obvious suggestion to bring it, he remembered another thing. He remembered the promise. Memory got past the big curtain for an instant, and showed her face. She looked into his eyes. It must have been a dozen years ago when Straughan and he had made that foolish, solemn promise that whoever died first should show himself, if possible, to the other.

He had utterly forgotten it—till now. But Straughan had not forgotten it. The letter came three weeks later, from India. That very evening Straughan had died—at nine o'clock. And he had come back—in the Beauty that he loved.

The Sea Fit

The sea that night sang rather than chanted; all along the far-running shore a rising tide dropped thick foam, and the waves, white-crested, came steadily in with the swing of a deliberate purpose. Overhead, in a cloudless sky, that ancient Enchantress, the full moon, watched their dance across the sheeted sands, guiding them carefully while she drew them up. For through that moonlight, through that roar of surf, there penetrated a singular note of earnestness and meaning almost as though these common processes of Nature were instinct with the flush of an unusual activity that sought audaciously to cross the borderland into some subtle degree of conscious life. A gauze of light vapour clung upon the surface of the sea, far out—a transparent carpet through which the rollers drove shorewards in a moving pattern.

In the low-roofed bungalow among the sand-dunes the three men sat. Foregathered for Easter, they spent the day fishing and sailing, and at night told yarns of the days when life was younger. It was fortunate that there were three—and later four—because in the mouths of several witnesses an extraordinary thing shall be established—when they agree. And although whisky stood upon the rough table made of planks nailed to barrels, it is childish to pretend that a few drinks invalidate evidence, for alcohol, up to a certain point, intensifies the consciousness, focusses the intellectual powers, sharpens observation; and two healthy men, certainly three, must have imbibed an absurd amount before they all see, or omit to see, the same things.

The other bungalows still awaited their summer occupants. Only the lonely tufted sand-dunes watched the sea, shaking their hair of coarse white grass to the winds. The men had the whole spit to themselves—with the wind, the spray, the flying gusts of sand, and that great Easter full moon. There was Major Reese of the Gunners and his half brother, Dr. Malcolm Reese, and Captain Erricson, their host,

129

all men whom the kaleidoscope of life had jostled together a decade ago in many adventures, then flung for years apart about the globe. There was also Erricson's body-servant, 'Sinbad,' sailor of big seas, and a man who had shared on many a ship all the lust of strange adventure that distinguished his great blonde-haired owner—an ideal servant and dog-faithful, divining his master's moods almost before they were born. On the present occasion, besides crew of the fishing-smack, he was cook, valet, and steward of the bungalow smoking-room as well.

'Big Erricson,' Norwegian by extraction, student by adoption, wanderer by blood, a Viking reincarnated if ever there was one, belonged to that type of primitive man in whom burns an inborn love and passion for the sea that amounts to positive worship—devouring tide, a lust and fever in the soul. 'All genuine votaries of the old sea-gods have it,' he used to say, by way of explaining his carelessness of worldly ambitions. 'We're never at our best away from salt water—never quite right. I've got it bang in the heart myself. I'd do a bit before the mast sooner than make a million on shore. Simply can't help it, you see, and never could! It's our gods calling us to worship.'

And he had never tried to 'help it,' which explains why he owned nothing in the world on land except this tumble-down, one-storey bungalow—more like a ship's cabin than anything else, to which he sometimes asked his bravest and most faithful friends—and a store of curious reading gathered in long, becalmed days at the ends of the world. Heart and mind, that is, carried a queer cargo. 'I'm sorry if you poor devils are uncomfortable in her. You must ask Sinbad for anything you want and don't see, remember.' As though Sinbad could have supplied comforts that were miles away, or converted a draughty wreck into a snug, taut, brand-new vessel.

Neither of the Reeses had cause for grumbling on the score of comfort, however, for they knew the keen joys of roughing it, and both weather and sport besides had been glorious. It was on another score this particular evening that they found cause for uneasiness, if not for actual grumbling. Erricson had one of his queer sea fits on— the doctor was responsible for the term—and was in the thick of it, plunging like a straining boat at anchor, talking in a way that made them both feel vaguely uncomfortable and distressed. Neither of them knew exactly perhaps why he should have felt this growing malaise, and each was secretly vexed with the other for confirming his own unholy instinct that something uncommon was astir. The loneliness of the sandspit and that melancholy singing of the sea before their very door may have had something to do with it, seeing that both were landsmen; for Imagination is ever Lord of the Lonely Places, and adventurous men remain children to the last. But, whatever it was that affected both men in different fashion, Malcolm Reese, the doctor, had not thought it necessary to mention to his brother that Sinbad had tugged his sleeve on entering and whispered in his ear significantly: 'Full moon, sir, please, and he's better without too much! These high spring tides get him all caught off his feet sometimes—clean sea-crazy'; and the man had contrived to let the doctor see the hilt of a small pistol he carried in his hip-pocket.

For Erricson had got upon his old subject: that the gods were not dead, but merely withdrawn, and that even a single true worshipper was enough to draw them down again into touch with the world, into the sphere of humanity, even into active and visible manifestation. He spoke of queer things he had seen in queerer places. He was serious, vehement, voluble; and the others had let it pour out unchecked, hoping thereby for its speedier exhaustion. They puffed their pipes in comparative silence, nodding from time to time, shrugging their shoulders, the soldier mystified and bewildered, the doctor alert and keenly watchful.

'And I like the old idea,' he had been saying, speaking of these departed pagan deities, 'that sacrifice and ritual feed their great beings, and that death is only the final sacrifice by which the worshipper becomes absorbed into them. The devout worshipper'—and there was a singular drive and power behind the words—'should go to his death singing, as to a wedding the wedding of his soul with the particular deity he has loved and served all his life.'

He swept his tow-coloured beard with one hand, turning his shaggy head towards the window, where the moonlight lay upon the procession of shaking waves. 'It's playing the whole game, I always think, man-fashion. . . . I remember once, some years ago, down there off the coast by Yucatan——'

And then, before they could interfere, he told an extraordinary tale of something he had seen years ago, but told it with such a horrid earnestness of conviction—for it was dreadful, though fine, this adventure—that his listeners shifted in their wicker chairs, struck matches unnecessarily, pulled at their long glasses, and exchanged glances that attempted a smile yet did not quite achieve it. For the tale had to do with sacrifice of human life and a rather haunting pagan ceremonial of the sea, and at its close the room had changed in some indefinable manner—was not exactly as it had been before perhaps—as though the savage earnestness of the language had introduced some new element that made it less cosy, less cheerful, even less warm. A secret lust in the man's heart, born of the sea, and of his intense admiration of the pagan gods called a light into his eye not altogether pleasant.

'They were great Powers, at any rate, those ancient fellows,' Erricson went on, refilling his huge pipe bowl; 'too great to disappear altogether, though today they may walk the earth in another manner. I swear they're still going it—especially the——' (he hesitated for a mere second) 'the old water Powers—the Sea Gods. Terrific beggars, every one of 'em.'

'Still move the tides and raise the winds, eh?' from the doctor.

Erricson spoke again after a moment's silence, with impressive dignity. 'And I like, too, the way they manage to keep their names before us,' he went on, with a curious eagerness that did not escape the doctor's observation, while it clearly puzzled the soldier. 'There's old Hu, the Druid God of justice, still alive in "Hue and Cry"; there's Typhon hammering his way against us in the typhoon; there's the mighty Hurakar, serpent god of the winds, you know, shouting to us in hurricane and ouragan; and there's——'

' Venus still at it as hard as ever,' interrupted the major, facetiously, though his brother did not laugh because of their host's almost sacred earnestness of manner and uncanny grimness of face. Exactly how he managed to introduce that element of gravity—of conviction—into such talk neither of his listeners quite understood, for in discussing the affair later they were unable to pitch upon any definite detail that betrayed it. Yet there it was, alive and haunting, even distressingly so. All day he had been silent and morose, but since dusk, with the turn of the tide, in fact, these queer sentences, half mystical, half unintelligible, had begun to pour from him, till now that cabin-like room among the sand-dunes fairly vibrated with the man's emotion.

And at last Major Reese, with blundering good intention, tried to shift the key from this portentous subject of sacrifice to something that might eventually lead towards comedy and laughter, and so relieve this growing pressure of melancholy and incredible things. The Viking fellow had just spoken of the possibility of the old gods manifesting themselves visibly, audibly, physically, and so the major caught him up and made light mention of spiritualism and the so-called ' materialisation seances,' where physical bodies were alleged to be built up out of the emanations of the medium and the sitters. This crude aspect of the Supernatural was the only possible link the soldier's mind could manage.

He caught his brother's eye too late, it seems, for Malcolm Reese realised by this time that something untoward was afoot, and no longer needed the memory of Sinbad's warning to keep him sharply on the look-out. It was not the first time he had seen Erricson 'caught' by the sea; but he had never known him quite so bad, nor seen his face so flushed and white alternately, nor his eyes so oddly shining. So that Major Reese's well-intentioned allusion only brought wind to fire.

The man of the sea, once Viking, roared with a rush of boisterous laughter at the comic suggestion, then dropped his voice to a sudden hard whisper, awfully earnest, awfully intense. Anyone must have started at the abrupt change and the life-and-death manner of the big man. His listeners undeniably both did.

' Bunkum!' he shouted, 'bunkum, and be damned to it all! There's only one real materialisation of these immense Outer Beings possible, and that's when the great embodied emotions, which are their sphere of action'—his words became wildly incoherent, painfully struggling to get out—'derived, you see, from their honest worshippers the world over—constituting their Bodies, in fact—come down into matter and get condensed, crystallised into form—to claim that final sacrifice I spoke about just now, and to which any man might feel himself proud and honoured to be summoned. . . . No dying in bed or fading out from old age, but to plunge full-blooded and alive into the great Body of the god who has deigned to descend and fetch you——'

The actual speech may have been even more rambling and incoherent than that. It came out in a torrent at white heat. Dr. Reese kicked his brother beneath the table, just in time. The soldier looked thoroughly uncomfortable and amazed, utterly at a loss to know how he had produced the storm. It rather frightened him.

'I know it because I've seen it,' went on the sea man, his mind and speech slightly more under control. 'Seen the ceremonies that brought these whopping old Nature gods down into form—seen 'em carry off a worshipper into themselves—seen that worshipper, too, go off singing and happy to his death, proud and honoured to be chosen.'

'Have you really—by George!' the major exclaimed. 'You tell us a queer thing, Erricson'; and it was then for the fifth time that Sinbad cautiously opened the door, peeped in and silently withdrew after giving a swiftly comprehensive glance round the room.

The night outside was windless and serene, only the growing

thunder of the tide near the full woke muffled echoes among the sand-dunes.

'Rites and ceremonies,' continued the other, his voice booming with a singular enthusiasm, but ignoring the interruption, 'are simply means of losing one's self by temporary ecstasy in the God of one's choice—the God one has worshipped all one's life—of being partially absorbed into his being. And sacrifice completes the process——'

'At death, you said?' asked Malcolm Reese, watching him keenly.

'Or voluntary,' was the reply that came flash-like. 'The devotee becomes wedded to his Deity goes bang into him, you see, by fire or water or air—as by a drop from a height—according to the nature of the particular God; at-one-ment, of course. A man's death that! Fine, you know!'

The man's inner soul was on fire now. He was talking at a fearful pace, his eyes alight, his voice turned somehow into a kind of sing-song that chimed well, singularly well, with the booming of waves outside, and from time to time he turned to the window to stare at the sea and the moon-blanched sands. And then a look of triumph would come into his face—that giant face framed by slow-moving wreaths of pipe smoke.

Sinbad entered for the sixth time without any obvious purpose, busied himself unnecessarily with the glasses and went out again, lingeringly. In the room he kept his eye hard upon his master. This time he contrived to push a chair and a heap of netting between him and the window. No one but Dr. Reese observed the manoeuvre. And he took the hint.

'The port-holes fit badly, Errison,' he laughed, but with a touch of authority. 'There's a five-knot breeze coming through the cracks worse than an old wreck!' And he moved up to secure the fastening better.

'The room is confoundedly cold,' Major Reese put in; 'has been for the last half-hour, too.' The soldier looked what he felt—cold—distressed—creepy. 'But there's no wind really, you know,' he added.

Captain Errison turned his great bearded visage from one to the other before he answered; there was a gleam of sudden suspicion in his blue eyes. 'The beggar's got that back door open again. If he's sent for anyone, as he did once before, I swear I'll drown him in fresh water for his impudence—or perhaps—can it be already that he expects?——'

He left the sentence incomplete and rang the bell, laughing with a boisterousness that was clearly feigned. 'Sinbad, what's this cold in the place? You've got the back door open. Not expecting anyone, are you——?'

'Everything's shut tight, Captain. There's a bit of a breeze coming up from the east. And the tide's drawing in at a raging pace——'

'We can all hear that. But are you expecting anyone? I asked,' repeated his master, suspiciously, yet still laughing. One might have said he was trying to give the idea that the man had some land flirtation on hand. They looked one another square in the eye for a moment, these two. It was the straight stare of equals who understood each other well.

'Someone—might be—on the way, as it were, Captain. Couldn't say for certain.'

The voice almost trembled. By a sharp twist of the eye, Sinbad managed to shoot a lightning and significant look at the doctor.

'But this cold—this freezing, damp cold in the place? Are you sure no one's come—by the back ways?' insisted the master. He whispered it. 'Across the dunes, for instance?' His voice conveyed awe and delight, both kept hard under.

'It's all over the house, Captain, already,' replied the man, and moved across to put more sea-logs on the blazing fire. Even the soldier noticed then that their language was tight with allusion of another kind. To relieve the growing tension and uneasiness in his own mind he took up the word 'house' and made fun of it.

'As though it were a mansion,' he observed, with a forced chuckle, 'instead of a mere sea-shell!'

Then, looking about him, he added: 'But, all the same, you know, there is a kind of fog getting into the room—from the sea, I suppose; coming up with the tide, or something, eh?' The air had certainly in the last twenty minutes turned thickish; it was not all tobacco smoke, and there was a moisture that began to precipitate on the objects in tiny, fine globules. The cold, too, fairly bit.

'I'll take a look round,' said Sinbad, significantly, and went out. Only the doctor perhaps noticed that the man shook, and was white down to the gills. He said nothing, but moved his chair nearer to the window and to his host. It was really a little bit beyond comprehension how the wild words of this old sea-dog in the full sway of his 'sea fit' had altered the very air of the room as well as the personal equations of its occupants, for an extraordinary atmosphere of enthusiasm that was almost splendour pulsed about him, yet vilely close to something that suggested terror!

Through the armour of every-day common sense that normally clothed the minds of these other two, had crept the faint wedges
of a mood that made them vaguely wonder whether the incredible
could perhaps sometimes—by way of bewildering exceptions—actually come to pass. The moods of their deepest life, that is to say, were
already affected. An inner, and thoroughly unwelcome, change was
in progress. And such psychic disturbances once started are hard to
arrest. In this case it was well on the way before either the Army or
Medicine had been willing to recognise the fact. There was something
coming coming—from the sand-dunes or the sea. And it was invited,
welcomed at any rate, by Erricson. His deep, volcanic enthusiasm and
belief provided the channel. In lesser degree they, too, were caught in
it. Moreover, it was terrific, irresistible.

And it was at this point—as the comparing of notes afterwards
established—that Father Norden came in, Norden, the big man's
nephew, having bicycled over from some point beyond Corfe Castle
and raced along the hard Studland sand in the moonlight, and then
hullood till a boat had ferried him across the narrow channel of Poole
Harbour. Sinbad simply brought him in without any preliminary
question or announcement. He could not resist the splendid night
and the spring air, explained Norden. He felt sure his uncle could 'find
a hammock' for him somewhere aft, as he put it. He did not add that
Sinbad had telegraphed for him just before sundown from the coast-
guard hut. Dr. Reese already knew him, but he was introduced to the
major. Norden was a member of the Society of Jesus, an ardent, not
clever, and unselfish soul.

Erricson greeted him with obviously mixed feelings, and with an
extraordinary sentence: 'It doesn't really matter,' he exclaimed, after a
few commonplaces of talk, ' for all religions are the same if you go
deep enough. All teach sacrifice, and, without exception, all seek final
union by absorption into their Deity.' And then, under his breath,
turning sideways to peer out of the window, he added a swift rush
of half-smothered words that only Dr. Reese caught: 'The Army, the
Church, the Medical Profession, and Labour—if they would only all
come! What a fine result, what a grand offering! Alone—I seem so
unworthy—insignificant . . .!'

But meanwhile young Norden was speaking before any one could
stop him, although the major did make one or two blundering attempts. For once the Jesuit's tact was at fault. He evidently hoped to
introduce a new mood—to shift the current already established by the

single force of his own personality. And he was not quite man enough to carry it off.

It was an error of judgment on his part. For the forces he found established in the room were too heavy to lift and alter, their impetus being already acquired. He did his best, anyhow. He began moving with the current—it was not the first sea fit he had combated in this extraordinary personality—then found, too late, that he was carried along with it himself like the rest of them.

'Odd—but couldn't find the bungalow at first,' he laughed, somewhat hardly. 'It's got a bit of sea-fog all to itself that hides it. I thought perhaps my pagan uncle——'

The doctor interrupted him hastily, with great energy. 'The fog does lie caught in these sand hollows—like steam in a cup, you know,' he put in. But the other, intent on his own procedure, missed the cue. '—— thought it was smoke at first, and that you were up to some heathen ceremony or other,' laughing in Erricson's face; 'sacrificing to the full moon or the sea, or the spirits of the desolate places that haunt sand-dunes, eh?'

No one spoke for a second, but Erricson's face turned quite radiant.

'My uncle's such a pagan, you know,' continued the priest, 'that as I flew along those deserted sands from Studland I almost expected to hear old Triton blow his wreathed horn ... or see fair Thetis's tinsel-slippered feet. . . .'

Erricson, suppressing violent gestures, highly excited, face happy as a boy's, was combing his great yellow beard with both hands, and the other two men had begun to speak at once, intent on stopping the flow of unwise allusion. Norden, swallowing a mouthful of cold soda-water, had put the glass down, spluttering over its bubbles, when the sound was first heard at the window. And in the back room the manservant ran, calling something aloud that sounded like 'It's coming, God save us, it's coming in . . .!' Though the major swears some name was mentioned that he afterwards forgot—Glaucus—Proteus—Pontus—or some such word.

The sound itself, however, was plain enough a kind of imperious tapping on the window-panes as of a multitude of objects. Blown sand it might have been or heavy spray or, as Norden suggested later, a great watersoaked branch of giant seaweed. Every one started up, but Erricson was first upon his feet, and had the window wide open in a twinkling. His voice roared forth over those moonlit sand-dunes and out towards the line of heavy surf ten yards below.

'All along the shore of the Ægean,' he bellowed, with a kind of hoarse triumph that shook the heart, 'that ancient cry once rang. But it was a lie, a thumping and audacious lie. And He is not the only one. Another still lives—and, by Poseidon, He comes! He knows His own and His own know Him—and His own shall go to meet Him . . .!'

That reference to the Ægean 'cry'! It was so wonderful. Everyone, of course, except the soldier, seized the allusion. It was a comprehensive, yet subtle, way of suggesting the idea. And meanwhile all spoke at once, shouted rather, for the Invasion was somehow—monstrous.

'Damn it—that's a bit too much. Something's caught my throat!' The major, like a man drowning, fought with the furniture in his amazement and dismay. Fighting was his first instinct, of course. 'Hurts so infernally—takes the breath,' he cried, by way of explaining the extraordinarily violent impetus that moved him, yet half ashamed of himself for seeing nothing he could strike. But Malcolm Reese struggled to get between his host and the open window, saying in tense voice something like 'Don't let him get out! Don't let him get out!' While the shouts of warning from Sinbad in the little cramped back offices added to the general confusion. Only Father Norden stood quiet watching—with a kind of admiring wonder the expression of magnificence that had flamed into the visage of Erricson.

'Hark, you fools! Hark!' boomed the Viking figure, standing erect and splendid.

And through that open window, along the fardrawn line of shore from Canford Cliffs to the chalk bluffs of Studland Bay, there certainly ran a sound that was no common roar of surf. It was articulate—a message from the sea—an announcement—a thunderous warning of approach. No mere surf breaking on sand could have compassed so deep and multitudinous a voice of dreadful roaring—far out over the entering tide, yet at the same time close in along the entire sweep of shore, shaking all the ocean, both depth and surface, with its deep vibrations. Into the bungalow chamber came—the *Sea*!

Out of the night, from the moonlit spaces where it had been steadily accumulating, into that little cabined room so full of humanity and tobacco smoke, came invisibly—the Power of the Sea. Invisible, yes, but mighty, pressed forward by the huge draw of the moon, softcoated with brine and moisture—the great Sea. And with it, into the minds of those three other men, leaped instantaneously, not to be denied, overwhelming suggestions of water-power, the tear and strain of thousand-mile currents, the irresistible pull and rush of tides, the suction of giant whirlpools—more, the massed and awful impetus of whole driven oceans. The air turned salt and briny, and a welter of seaweed clamped their very skins.

'Glaucus! I come to Thee, great God of the deep Waterways. . . . Father and Master!' Erricson cried aloud in a voice that most marvellously conveyed supreme joy.

The little bungalow trembled as from a blow at the foundations, and the same second the big man was through the window and running down the moonlit sands towards the foam.

'God in Heaven! Did you all see that?' shouted Major Reese, for the manner in which the great body slipped through the tiny window-frame was incredible. And then, first tottering with a sudden weakness, he recovered himself and rushed round by the door, followed by his brother. Sinbad, invisible, but not inaudible, was calling aloud from the passage at the back. Father Norden, slimmer than the others—well controlled, too—was through the little window before either of them reached the fringe of beach beyond the sand-dunes. They joined forces halfway down to the water's edge. The figure of Erricson, towering in the moonlight, flew before them, coasting rapidly along the wave-line.

No one of them said a word; they tore along side by side, Norden a trifle in advance. In front of them, head turned seawards, bounded Erricson in great flying leaps, singing as he ran, impossible to overtake.

Then, what they witnessed all three witnessed; the weird grandeur of it in the moonshine was too splendid to allow the smaller emotions of personal alarm, it seems. At any rate, the divergence of opinion afterwards was unaccountably insignificant. For, on a sudden, that heavy roaring sound far out at sea came close in with a swift plunge of speed, followed simultaneously—accompanied, rather—by a dark line that was no mere wave moving: enormously, up and across, between the sea and sky it swept close in to shore. The moonlight caught it for a second as it passed, in a cliff of her bright silver.

And Erricson slowed down, bowed his great head and shoulders, spread his arms out and . . .

And what? For no one of those amazed witnesses could swear exactly what then came to pass. Upon this impossibility of telling it in language they all three agreed. Only those eyeless dunes of sand that watched, only the white and silent moon overhead, only that long, curved beach of empty and deserted shore retain the complete

139

record, to be revealed some day perhaps when a later Science shall have learned to develop the photographs that Nature takes incessantly upon her secret plates. For Erricson's rough suit of tweed went out in ribbons across the air; his figure somehow turned dark like strips of tide-sucked seaweed; something enveloped and overcame him, half shrouding him from view.

He stood for one instant upright, his hair wild in the moonshine, towering, with arms again outstretched; then bent forward, turned, drew out most curiously sideways, uttering the singing sound of tumbling waters. The next instant, curving over like a falling wave, he swept along the glistening surface of the sands—and was gone. In fluid form, wave-like, his being slipped away into the Being of the Sea. A violent tumult convulsed the surface of the tide near in, but at once, and with amazing speed, passed careering away into the deeper water—far out. To his singular death, as to a wedding, Erricson had gone, singing, and well content.

'May God, who holds the sea and all its powers in the hollow of His mighty hand, take them both into Himself!' Norden was on his knees, praying fervently.

The body was never recovered . . . and the most curious thing of all was that the interior of the cabin, where they found Sinbad shaking with terror when they at length returned, was splashed and sprayed, almost soaked, with salt water. Up into the bigger dunes beside the bungalow, and far beyond the reach of normal tides, lay, too, a great streak and furrow as of a large invading wave, caking the dry sand. A hundred tufts of the coarse grass tussocks had been torn away.

The high tide that night, drawn by the Easter full moon, of course, was known to have been exceptional, for it fairly flooded Poole Harbour, flushing all the coves and bays towards the mouth of the Frome. And the natives up at Arne Bay and Wych always declare that the noise of the sea was heard far inland even up to the nine Barrows of the Purbeck Hills—triumphantly singing.

The Terror of the Twins

That the man's hopes had built upon a son to inherit his name and estates—a single son, that is—was to be expected; but no one could have foreseen the depth and bitterness of his disappointment, the cold, implacable fury, when there arrived instead—twins. For, though the elder legally must inherit, that other ran him so deadly close. A daughter would have been a more reasonable defeat. But twins! To miss his dream by so feeble a device

The complete frustration of a hope deeply cherished for years may easily result in strange fevers of the soul, but the violence of the father's hatred, existing as it did side by side with a love he could not deny, was something to set psychologists thinking. More than unnatural, it was positively uncanny. Being a man of rigid self-control, however, it operated inwardly, and doubtless along some morbid line of weakness little suspected even by those nearest to him, preying upon his thought to such dreadful extent that finally the mind gave way.

The suppressed rage and bitterness deprived him, so the family decided, of his reason, and he spent the last years of his life under restraint. He was possessed naturally of immense forces—of will, feeling, desire; his dynmamic value truly tremendous, driving through life like a great engine; and the intensity of this concentrated and buried hatred was guessed by. few. The twins themselves, however, knew it. They divined it, at least, for it operated ceaselessly against them side by side with the genuine soft love that occasionally sweetened it, to their great perplexity. They spoke of it only to each other, though.

"At twenty-one," Edward, the elder, would remark sometimes, unhappily. "we shall know more."

"Too much," Ernest would reply, with a rush of unreasoning terror the thought never failed to evoke—*in him.* "Things, father said, always happened—in life." And they paled perceptibly. For the hatred, thus compressed into a veritable bomb of psychic energy, had found at the last a singular expression in the cry of the father's distraught mind. On the occasion of their final visit to the asylum, preceding his death by a few hours only, very calmly, but with an intensity that drove the words into their hearts like points of burning metal, he had spoken. In the presence of the attendant, at the door of the dreadful padded cell, he said it: "You are not two, but *one*. I still regard you as one. And at the coming of age, by h——, you shall find it out!"

The lads perhaps had never fully divined that icy hatred which lay so well concealed against them, but that this final sentence was a curse, backed by all the man's terrific force, they quite well realised; and accordingly, almost unknown to each other, they had come to dread the day inexpressibly. On the morning of that twenty first birthday—their father gone these five years into the Unknown, yet still sometimes so strangely close to them—they shared the same biting, inner terror, just as they shared all other emotions of their life—intimately, without speech.

During the daytime they managed to keep it at a distance, but when the dusk fell about the old house, they knew the stealthy approach of a kind of panic sense. Their self-respect weakened swiftly . . . and they persuaded their old friend, and once tutor, the vicar, to sit up with them till midnight. . . . He had humoured them to that extent, willing to forgo his sleep, and at the same time more than a little interested in their singular belief—that before the day was out, before midnight struck, that is, the curse of that terrible man would somehow come into operation against them.

Festivities over and the guests departed, they sat up in the library, the room usually occupied by their father, and little used since. Mr. Curtice, a robust man of fifty-five, and a firm believer in spiritual principalities and powers, dark as well as good, affected (for their own good) to regard the youths' obsession with a kindly cynicism. "I do not think it likely for one moment," he said gravely, "that such a thing would be permitted. All spirits are in the hands of God, and the violent ones more especially."

To which Edward made the extraordinary reply: "Even if father does not come himself, he will—*send!*"

And Ernest agreed: "All this time he's been making preparations for this very day. We've both known it for a long time—by odd things that have happened, by our dreams, by nasty little dark hints of various kinds, and by these persistent attacks of terror that come from nowhere, especially of late. Haven't we, Edward?"

Edward assenting with a shudder: "Father has been at us of late with renewed violence. Tonight, it will be a regular assault upon our lives, or minds, or souls!"

"Strong personalities *may* possibly leave behind them forces that continue to act," observed Mr. Curtice with caution, while the brothers replied almost in the same breath: "That's exactly what we feel so curiously. Though—nothing has actually happened yet, you know, and it's a good many years now since—"

This was the way the twins spoke of it all. And it was their profound conviction that had touched their old friend's sense of duty. The experiment should justify itself—and cure them. Meanwhile none of the family knew. Everything was planned secretly.

The library was the quietest room in the house. It had shuttered bow-windows, thick carpets, heavy doors. Books lined the walls, and there was a capacious open fireplace of brick in which the wood-logs blazed and roared, for the autumn night was chilly. Round this the three of them were grouped, the clergyman reading aloud from the Book of Job in low tones: Edward and Ernest, in dinner-jackets, occupying deep leather armchairs, listening. They looked exactly what they were—Cambridge "undergrads," their faces pale against their dark hair, and alike as two peas.

A shaded lamp behind the clergyman threw the rest of the room into shadow. The reading voice was steady, even monotonous, but something in it betrayed an underlying anxiety, and although the eyes rarely left the printed page, they took in every movement of the young men opposite, and noted every change upon their faces. It was his aim to produce an unexciting atmosphere, yet to miss nothing; if anything did occur to see it from the very beginning. Not to be taken by surprise was his main idea. . . . And thus, upon this falsely peaceful scene, the minutes passed the hour of eleven and slipped rapidly along towards midnight.

The novel element in his account of this distressing and dreadful occurrence seems to be that what happened—happened without the slightest warning or preparation. There was no gradual presentment of any horror; no strange blast of cold air; no dwindling of heat or light; no shaking of windows or mysterious tapping upon furniture. Without preliminaries it fell with its black trappings of terror upon the scene.

The clergyman had been reading aloud for some considerable time, one or other of the twins—Ernest usually—making occasional remarks, which proved that his sense of dread was disappearing. As the time grew short and nothing happened, they grew more at their ease. Edward, indeed, actually nodded, dozed, and finally fell asleep. It was a few minutes before midnight. Ernest, slightly yawning, was stretching himself in the big chair. "Nothing's going to happen," he said aloud, in a pause. "Your good influence has prevented it." He even laughed now. "What superstitious asses we've been, sir; haven't we?"

Curtice, then, dropping his Bible, looked hard at him under the lamp. For in that second, even while the words sounded, there had come about a most abrupt and dreadful change; and so swiftly that the clergyman, in spite of himself, was taken utterly by surprise and had no time to think. There had swooped down upon the quiet library— so he puts it an immense hushing silence, so profound that the peace already reigning there seemed clamour by comparison; and out of this enveloping stillness there rose through the space about them a living and abominable Invasion—soft, motionless, terrific. It was as though vast engines, working at full speed and pressure, yet too swift and delicate to be appreciable to any definite sense, had suddenly dropped down upon them—from nowhere.

"It made me think," the vicar used to say afterwards, "of the *Mauretania* machinery compressed into a nutshell, yet losing none of its awful power."

". . . . haven't we" repeated Ernest, still laughing. And Curtice, making no audible reply, heard the true answer in his heart: "Because everything has *already happened*—even as you feared."

Yet, to the vicar's supreme astonishment, Ernest still noticed— nothing!

"Look," the boy added, "Eddy's sound asleep—sleeping like a pig. Doesn't say much for your reading, you know, sir!" And he laughed again—lightly, even foolishly. But that laughter jarred, for the clergyman understood now that the sleep of the elder twin was either feigned—or *unnatural*.

And while the easy words fell so lightly from his lips, the monstrous engines worked and pulsed against him and against his sleeping brother, all their huge energy concentrated down into points fine as Suggestion, delicate as Thought. The Invasion affected everything. The very objects in the room altered incredibly, revealing suddenly behind their normal exteriors, horrid little hearts of darkness. It was truly amazing, this vile metamorphosis. Books, chairs, pictures, all yielded up their pleasant aspect, and betrayed, as with silent mocking laughter, their inner soul of blackness—their *decay*. This is how Curtice tries to body forth in words what he actually witnessed. . . . And Ernest, yawning, talking lightly, half foolishly—still noticed nothing!

For all this, as described, came about in something like ten seconds; and with it swept into the clergyman's mind, like a blow, the memory of that sinister phrase used more than once by Edward: "If father doesn't come, he will certainly—*send*." And Curtice understood that he had done both—both sent and come himself. . . That violent mind, released from its spell of madness in the body, yet still retaining the old implacable hatred, was now directing the terrible, unseen assault. This silent room, so hushed and still, was charged to the brim. The horror of it, as he said later, "seemed to peel the very skin from my back." . . . And, while Ernest noticed nothing, Edward slept! . . . The soul of the clergyman, strong with the desire to help or save, yet realising that he was alone against a Legion, poured out in wordless prayer to his Deity. The clock just then, whirring before it struck, made itself audible.

"By Jove! It's all right, you see!" exclaimed Ernest, his voice oddly fainter and lower than before. "There's midnight—and nothing's happened. Bally nonsense, all of it!" His voice had dwindled curiously in volume. "I'll get the whisky and soda from the hall." His relief was great and his manner showed it. But in him somewhere was a singular change. His voice, manner, gestures, his very tread as he moved over the thick carpet toward the door, all showed it. He seemed less *real*, less alive, reduced somehow to littleness, the voice without timbre or quality, the appearance of him diminished in some fashion quite ghastly. His presence, if not actually shrivelled, was at least impaired. Ernest had suffered a singular and horrible *decrease*, . . .

The clock was still whirring before the strike. One heard the chain running up softly. Then the hammer fell upon the first stroke of midnight.

"I'm off," he laughed faintly from the door; "it's all been pure funk—on my part, at least . . .!" He passed out of sight into the hall. *The Power that throbbed so mightily about the room followed him out.* Almost at the same moment Edward woke up. But he woke with a tearing and indescribable cry of pain and anguish on his lips: "Oh, oh, oh! But it hurts! It hurts! I can't hold you: leave me. It's breaking me asunder—"

The clergyman had sprung to his feet, but in the same instant everything had become normal once more—the room as it was before, the horror gone. There was nothing he could do or say, for there was no longer anything to put right, to defend, or to attack. Edward was speaking; his voice, deep and full as it never had been before: "By Jove, how that sleep has refreshed me! I feel twice the chap I was before—twice the chap. I feel quite splendid. Your voice, sir, must have hypnotised me to sleep. . . ." He crossed the room with great vigour. "Where's—er—where's—Ernie, by the bye?" he asked casually, hesitating—almost searching—for the name. And a shadow as of a vanished memory crossed his face and was gone. The tone conveyed the most complete indifference where once the least word or movement of his twin had wakened solicitude, love. "Gone away, I suppose—gone to bed, I mean, of course."

Curtice has never been able to describe the dreadful conviction that overwhelmed him as he stood there staring, his heart in his mouth—the conviction, the positive certainty, that Edward had changed interiorly, had suffered an incredible accession to his existing personality. But he *knew* it as he watched. His mind, spirit, soul had most wonderfully increased. Something that hitherto the lad had known from the outside only, or by the magic of loving sympathy, had now passed, to be incorporated with his own being. And, being himself, it required no expression. Yet this visible increase was somehow terrible. Curtice shrank back from him. The instinct—he has never grasped the profound psychology of *that*, nor why it turned his soul dizzy with a kind of nausea—the instinct to strike him where he stood, passed, and a plaintive sound from the hall, stealing softly into the room between them, sent all that was left to him of self-possession into his feet. He turned and ran. Edward followed him—very leisurely.

They found Ernest, or what had been Ernest, crouching behind the table in the hall, weeping foolishly to himself. On his face lay blackness. The mouth was open, the jaw dropped; he dribbled hopelessly; and from the face had passed all signs of intelligence—of spirit.

For a few weeks he lingered on, regaining no sign of spiritual or mental life before the poor body, hopelessly disorganised, released what was left of him, from pure inertia—from complete and utter loss of vitality.

And the horrible thing—so the distressed family thought, at least—was that all those weeks Edward showed an indifference that was singularly brutal and complete. He rarely even went to visit him. I believe, too, it is true that he only once spoke of him by name; and that was when he said—

"Ernie? Oh, but Ernie is much better and happier where he is—!"

The Transfer

The child first began to cry in the early afternoon—about three o'clock, to be exact. I remember the hour, because I had been listening with secret relief to the sound of the departing carriage. Those wheels fading into distance down the gravel drive with Mrs. Frene, and her daughter Gladys to whom I was governess, meant for me some hours' welcome rest, and the June day was oppressively hot. Moreover, there was this excitement in the little country household that had told upon us all, but especially upon myself.

This excitement, running delicately behind all the events of the morning, was due to some mystery, and the mystery was of course kept concealed from the governess. I had exhausted myself with guessing and keeping on the watch. For some deep and unexplained anxiety possessed me, so that I kept thinking of my sister's dictum that I was really much too sensitive to make a good governess, and that I should have done far better as a professional clairvoyant.

Mr. Frene, senior, 'Uncle Frank,' was expected for an unusual visit from town about tea-time. That I knew. I also knew that his visit was concerned somehow with the future welfare of little Jamie, Gladys' seven-year-old brother. More than this, indeed, I never knew, and this missing link makes my story in a fashion incoherent—an important bit of the strange puzzle left out. I only gathered that the visit of Uncle Frank was of a condescending nature, that Jamie was told he must be upon his very best behaviour to make a good impression, and that Jamie, who had never seen his uncle, dreaded him horribly already in advance.

Then, trailing thinly through the dying crunch of the carriage wheels this sultry afternoon, I heard the curious little wail of the child's crying, with the effect, wholly unaccountable, that every nerve in my body shot its bolt electrically, bringing me to my feet with a tingling of unequivocal alarm. Positively, the water ran into my eyes. I recalled his white distress that morning when told that Uncle Frank was motoring down for tea and that he was to be 'very nice indeed' to him. It had gone into me like a knife. All through the day, indeed, had run this nightmare quality of terror and vision.

'The man with the 'normous face?' he had asked in a little voice of awe, and then gone speechless from the room in tears that no amount of soothing management could calm. That was all I saw; and what he meant by 'the 'normous face' gave me only a sense of vague presentiment. But it came as anti-climax somehow—a sudden revelation of the mystery and excitement that pulsed beneath the quiet of the stifling summer day. I feared for him. For of all that commonplace household I loved Jamie best, though professionally I had nothing to do with him. He was a high-strung, ultra-sensitive child, and it seemed to me that no one understood him, least of all his honest, tender-hearted parents; so that his little wailing voice brought me from my bed to the window in a moment like a call for help.

The haze of June lay over that big garden like a blanket; the wonderful flowers, which were Mr. Frene's delight, hung motionless; the lawns, so soft and thick, cushioned all other sounds; only the limes and huge clumps of guelder roses hummed with bees. Through this muted atmosphere of heat and haze the sound of the child's crying floated faintly to my ears—from a distance. Indeed, I wonder now that I heard it at all, for the next moment I saw him down beyond the garden, standing in his white sailor suit alone, two hundred yards away. He was down by the ugly patch where nothing grew—the Forbidden Corner.

A faintness then came over me at once, a faintness as of death, when I saw him there of all places—where he never was allowed to go, and where, moreover, he was usually too terrified to go. To see him standing solitary in that singular spot, above all to hear him crying there, bereft me momentarily of the power to act. Then, before I could recover my composure sufficiently to call him in, Mr. Frene came round the corner from the Lower Farm with the dogs, and, seeing his son, performed that office for me. In his loud, good-natured, hearty voice he called him, and Jamie turned and ran as though some spell had broken just in time—ran into the open arms of his fond but uncomprehending father, who carried him indoors on his shoulder, while asking 'what all this hubbub was about?' And, at their heels, the tail-less sheepdogs followed, barking loudly, and performing what Jamie called their 'Gravel Dance,' because they ploughed up the moist, rolled gravel with their feet.

I stepped back swiftly from the window lest I should be seen. Had I witnessed the saving of the child from fire or drowning the relief could hardly have been greater. Only Mr. Frene, I felt sure, would not say and do the right thing quite. He would protect the boy from his own vain imaginings, yet not with the explanation that could really heal. They disappeared behind the rose trees, making for the house. I saw no more till later, when Mr. Frene, senior, arrived.

★★★★★★★★★★★★

To describe the ugly patch as 'singular' is hard to justify, perhaps, yet some such word is what the entire family sought, though never—oh, never!—used. To Jamie and myself, though equally we never mentioned it, that treeless, flowerless spot was more than singular. It stood at the far end of the magnificent rose garden, a bald, sore place, where the black earth showed uglily in winter, almost like a piece of dangerous bog, and in summer baked and cracked with fissures where green lizards shot their fire in passing. In contrast to the rich luxuriance of the whole amazing garden it was like a glimpse of death amid life, a centre of disease that cried for healing lest it spread. But it never did spread. Behind it stood the thick wood of silver birches and, glimmering beyond, the orchard meadow, where the lambs played.

The gardeners had a very simple explanation of its barrenness— that the water all drained off it owing to the lie of the slopes immediately about it, holding no remnant to keep the soil alive. I cannot say. It was Jamie—Jamie who felt its spell and haunted it, who spent whole hours there, even while afraid, and for whom it was finally labelled 'strictly out of bounds' because it stimulated his already big imagination, not wisely but too darkly—it was Jamie who buried ogres there and heard it crying in an earthy voice, swore that it shook its surface sometimes while he watched it, and secretly gave it food in the form of birds or mice or rabbits he found dead upon his wanderings. And it was Jamie who put so extraordinarily into words the *feeling* that the horrid spot had given me from the moment I first saw it.

'It's bad, Miss Gould,' he told me.

'But, Jamie, nothing in Nature is bad—exactly; only different from the rest sometimes.'

'Miss Gould, if you please, then it's empty. It's not fed. It's dying because it can't get the food it wants.'

And when I stared into the little pale face where the eyes shone so dark and wonderful, seeking within myself for the right thing to say to him, he added, with an emphasis and conviction that made me

149

suddenly turn cold: 'Miss Gould'—he always used my name like this in all his sentences 'it's hungry, don't you see? But *I* know what would make it feel all right.'

Only the conviction of an earnest child, perhaps, could have made so outrageous a suggestion worth listening to for an instant; but for me, who felt that things an imaginative child believed were important, it came with a vast disquieting shock of reality. Jamie, in this exaggerated way, had caught at the edge of a shocking fact a hint of dark, undiscovered truth had leaped into that sensitive imagination. Why there lay horror in the words I cannot say, but I think some power of darkness trooped across the suggestion of that sentence at the end, 'I know what would make it feel all right.'

I remember that I shrank from asking explanation. Small groups of other words, veiled fortunately by his silence, gave life to an unspeakable possibility that hitherto had lain at the back of my own consciousness. The way it sprang to life proves, I think, that my mind already contained it. The blood rushed from my heart as I listened. I remember that my knees shook. Jamie's idea was—had been all along—my own as well.

And now, as I lay down on my bed and thought about it all, I understood why the coming of his uncle involved somehow an experience that wrapped terror at its heart. With a sense of nightmare certainty that left me too weak to resist the preposterous idea, too shocked, indeed, to argue or reason it away, this certainty came with its full, black blast of conviction; and the only way I can put it into words, since nightmare horror really is not properly tellable at all, seems this: that there was something missing in that dying patch of garden; something lacking that it ever searched for; something, once found and taken, that would turn it rich and living as the rest; more—that there was some living person who could do this for it. Mr. Frene, senior, in a word, 'Uncle Frank,' was this person who out of his abundant life could supply the lack—unwittingly.

For this connection between the dying, empty patch and the person of this vigorous, wealthy, and successful man had already lodged itself in my subconsciousness before I was aware of it. Clearly it must have lain there all along, though hidden. Jamie's words, his sudden pallor, his vibrating emotion of fearful anticipation had developed the plate, but it was his weeping alone there in the Forbidden Corner that had printed it. The photograph shone framed before me in the air. I hid my eyes. But for the redness—the charm of my face goes to pieces unless my eyes are clear I could have cried. Jamie's words that morning about the "'normous face' came back upon me like a battering-ram.

Mr. Frene, senior, had been so frequently the subject of conversation in the family since I came, I had so often heard him discussed, and had then read so much about him in the papers—his energy, his philanthropy, his success with everything he laid his hand to—that a picture of the man had grown complete within me. I knew him as he was—within; or, as my sister would have said—clairvoyantly. And the only time I saw him (when I took Gladys to a meeting where he was chairman, and later felt his atmosphere and presence while for a moment he patronisingly spoke with her) had justified the portrait I had drawn. The rest, you may say, was a woman's wild imagining; but I think rather it was that kind of divining intuition which women share with children. If souls could be made visible, I would stake my life upon the truth and accuracy of my portrait.

For this Mr. Frene was a man who drooped alone, but grew vital in a crowd—because he used their vitality. He was a supreme, unconscious artist in the science of taking the fruits of others' work and living—for his own advantage. He vampired, unknowingly no doubt, everyone with whom he came in contact; left them exhausted, tired, listless. Others fed him, so that while in a full room he shone, alone by himself and with no life to draw upon he languished and declined. In the man's immediate neighbourhood, you felt his presence draining you; he took your ideas, your strength, your very words, and later used them for his own benefit and aggrandisement.

Not evilly, of course; the man was good enough; but you felt that he was dangerous owing to the facile way he absorbed into himself all loose vitality that was to be had. His eyes and voice and presence devitalised you. Life, it seemed, not highly organised enough to resist, must shrink from his too near approach and hide away for fear of being appropriated, for fear, that is, of—death.

Jamie, unknowingly, put in the finishing touch to my unconscious portrait. The man carried about with him some silent, compelling trick of drawing out all your reserves—then swiftly pocketing them. At first you would be conscious of taut resistance; this would slowly shade off into weariness; the will would become flaccid; then you either moved away or yielded—agreed to all he said with a sense of weakness pressing ever closer upon the edges of collapse. With a male antagonist it might be different, but even then, the effort of resistance would generate force that *he* absorbed and not the other. He never gave out. Some instinct taught him how to protect himself from that. To human beings, I mean, he never gave out. This time it was a very different matter. He had no more chance than a fly before the wheels of a huge—what Jamie used to call—'attraction' engine.

So, this was how I saw him—a great human sponge, crammed and soaked with the life, or proceeds of life, absorbed from others—stolen. My idea of a human vampire was satisfied. He went about carrying these accumulations of the life of others. In this sense his 'life' was not really his own. For the same reason, I think, it was not so fully under his control as he imagined.

★★★★★★★★★★★★

And in another hour this man would be here. I went to the window. My eye wandered to the empty patch, dull black there amid the rich luxuriance of the garden flowers. It struck me as a hideous bit of emptiness yawning to be filled and nourished. The idea of Jamie playing round its bare edge was loathsome. I watched the big summer clouds above, the stillness of the afternoon, the haze. The silence of the overheated garden was oppressive. I had never felt a day so stifling, motionless. It lay there waiting. The household, too, was waiting—waiting for the coming of Mr. Frene from London in his big motorcar.

And I shall never forget the sensation of icy shrinking and distress with which I heard the rumble of the car. He had arrived. Tea was all ready on the lawn beneath the lime trees, and Mrs. Frene and Gladys, back from their drive, were sitting in wicker chairs. Mr. Frene, junior, was in the hall to meet his brother, but Jamie, as I learned afterwards, had shown such hysterical alarm, offered such bold resistance, that it had been deemed wiser to keep him in his room. Perhaps, after all, his presence might not be necessary.

The visit clearly had to do with something on the uglier side of life—money, settlements, or what not; I never knew exactly; only that his parents were anxious, and that Uncle Frank had to be propitiated. It does not matter. That has nothing to do with the affair. What has to do with it—or I should not be telling the story—is that Mrs. Frene sent for me to come down 'in my nice white dress, if I didn't mind,' and that I was terrified, yet pleased, because it meant that a pretty face would be considered a welcome addition to the visitor's landscape.

Also, most odd it was, I felt my presence was somehow inevitable, that in some way it was intended that I should witness what I did witness. And the instant I came upon the lawn—I hesitate to set it down, it sounds so foolish, disconnected—I could have sworn, as my

152

eyes met his, that a kind of sudden darkness came, taking the summer brilliance out of everything, and that it was caused by troops of small black horses that raced about us from his person—to attack.

After a first momentary approving glance he took no further notice of me. The tea and talk went smoothly; I helped to pass the plates and cups, filling in pauses with little under-talk to Gladys. Jamie was never mentioned. Outwardly all seemed well, but inwardly everything was awful—skirting the edge of things unspeakable, and so charged with danger that I could not keep my voice from trembling when I spoke.

I watched his hard, bleak face; I noticed how thin he was, and the curious, oily brightness of his steady eyes. They did not glitter, but they drew you with a sort of soft, creamy shine like Eastern eyes. And everything he said or did announced what I may dare to call the *suction* of his presence. His nature achieved this result automatically. He dominated us all, yet so gently that until it was accomplished no one noticed it.

Before five minutes had passed, however, I was aware of one thing only. My mind focussed exclusively upon it, and so vividly that I marvelled the others did not scream, or run, or do something violent to prevent it. And it was this: that, separated merely by some dozen yards or so, this man, vibrating with the acquired vitality of others, stood within easy reach of that spot of yawning emptiness, waiting and eager to be filled. Earth scented her prey.

These two active 'centres' were within fighting distance; he so thin, so hard, so keen, yet really spreading large with the loose 'surround' of others' life he had appropriated, so practised and triumphant; that other so patient, deep, with so mighty a draw of the whole earth behind it, and—ugh!—so obviously aware that its opportunity at last had come.

I saw it all as plainly as though I watched two great animals prepare for battle, both unconsciously; yet in some inexplicable way I saw it, of course, within me, and not externally. The conflict would be hideously unequal. Each side had already sent out emissaries, how long before I could not tell, for the first evidence *he* gave that something was going wrong with him was when his voice grew suddenly confused, he missed his words, and his lips trembled a moment and turned flabby.

The next second his face betrayed that singular and horrid change, growing somehow loose about the bones of the cheek, and larger, so that I remembered Jamie's miserable phrase. The emissaries of the two kingdoms, the human and the vegetable, had met, I make it out, in that very second. For the first time in his long career of battening on others, Mr. Frene found himself pitted against a vaster kingdom than he knew and, so finding, shook inwardly in that little part that was his definite actual self. He felt the huge disaster coming.

'Yes, John,' he was saying, in his drawling, self-congratulating voice, 'Sir George gave me that car—gave it to me as a present. Wasn't it char—?' and then broke off abruptly, stammered, drew breath, stood up, and looked uneasily about him. For a second there was a gaping pause. It was like the click which starts some huge machinery moving—that instant's pause before it actually starts. The whole thing, indeed, then went with the rapidity of machinery running down and beyond control. I thought of a giant dynamo working silently and invisible.

'What's that?' he cried, in a soft voice charged with alarm. 'What's that horrid place? And someone's crying there—who is it?'

He pointed to the empty patch. Then, before anyone could answer, he started across the lawn towards it, going every minute faster. Before anyone could move, he stood upon the edge. He leaned over—peering down into it.

It seemed a few hours passed, but really, they were seconds, for time is measured by the quality and not the quantity of sensations it contains. I saw it all with merciless, photographic detail, sharply etched amid the general confusion. Each side was intensely active, but only one side, the human, exerted *all* its force—in resistance. The other merely stretched out a feeler, as it were, from its vast, potential strength; no more was necessary. It was such a soft and easy victory.

Oh, it was rather pitiful! There was no bluster or great effort, on one side at least. Close by his side I witnessed it, for I, it seemed, alone had moved and followed him. No one else stirred, though Mrs. Frene clattered noisily with the cups, making some sudden impulsive gesture with her hands, and Gladys, I remember, gave a cry—it was like a little scream—'Oh, mother, it's the heat, isn't it?' Mr. Frene, her father, was speechless, pale as ashes.

But the instant I reached his side, it became clear what had drawn me there thus instinctively. Upon the other side, among the silver birches, stood little Jamie. He was watching. I experienced—for him—one of those moments that shake the heart; a liquid fear ran all over me, the more effective because unintelligible really. Yet I felt that if I could know all, and what lay actually behind, my fear would be more than justified; that the thing *was* awful, full of awe.

And then it happened—a truly wicked sight—like watching a universe in action, yet all contained within a small square foot of space. I think he understood vaguely that if someone could only take his place he might be saved, and that was why, discerning instinctively the easiest substitute within reach, he saw the child and called aloud to him across the empty patch, 'James, my boy, come here!'

His voice was like a thin report, but somehow flat and lifeless, as when a rifle misses fire, sharp, yet weak; it had no 'crack' in it. It was really supplication. And, with amazement, I heard my own ring out imperious and strong, though I was not conscious of saying it, 'Jamie, don't move. Stay where you are!' But Jamie, the little child, obeyed neither of us. Moving up nearer to the edge, he stood there—laughing! I heard that laughter, but could have sworn it did not come from him. The empty, yawning patch gave out that sound.

Mr. Frene turned sideways, throwing up his arms. I saw his hard, bleak face grow somehow wider, spread through the air, and downwards. A similar thing, I saw, was happening at the same time to his entire person, for it drew out into the atmosphere in a stream of movement. The face for a second made me think of those toys of green india-rubber that children pull. It grew enormous. But this was an external impression only. What actually happened, I clearly understood, was that all this vitality and life he had transferred from others to himself for years was now in turn being taken from him and transferred elsewhere.

One moment on the edge he wobbled horribly, then with that queer sideways motion, rapid yet ungainly, he stepped forward into the middle of the patch and fell heavily upon his face. His eyes, as he dropped, faded shockingly, and across the countenance was written plainly what I can only call an expression of destruction. He looked utterly destroyed. I caught a sound—from Jamie?—but this time not of laughter. It was like a gulp; it was deep and muffled and it dipped away into the earth. Again, I thought of a troop of small black horses galloping away down a subterranean passage beneath my feet—plunging into the depths their tramping growing fainter and fainter into buried distance. In my nostrils was a pungent smell of earth.

★★★★★★★★★★★★

And then—all passed. I came back into myself. Mr. Frene, junior, was lifting his brother's head from the lawn where he had fallen from the heat, close beside the tea-table. He had never really moved from

155

there. And Jamie, I learned afterwards, had been the whole time asleep upon his bed upstairs, worn out with his crying and unreasoning alarm. Gladys came running out with cold water, sponge and towel, brandy too—all kinds of things. 'Mother, it *was* the heat, wasn't it?' I heard her whisper, but I did not catch Mrs. Frene's reply. From her face it struck me that she was bordering on collapse herself. Then the butler followed, and they just picked him up and carried him into the house. He recovered even before the doctor came.

But the queer thing to me is that I was convinced the others all had seen what I saw, only that no one said a word about it; and to this day no one *has* said a word. And that was, perhaps, the most horrid part of all.

From that day to this I have scarcely heard a mention of Mr. Frene, senior. It seemed as if he dropped suddenly out of life. The papers never mentioned him. His activities ceased, as it were. His afterlife, at any rate, became singularly ineffective. Certainly, he achieved nothing worth public mention. But it may be only that, having left the employ of Mrs. Frene, there was no particular occasion for me to hear anything.

The afterlife of that empty patch of garden, however, was quite otherwise. Nothing, so far as I know, was done to it by gardeners, or in the way of draining it or bringing in new earth, but even before I left in the following summer it had changed. It lay untouched, full of great, luscious, driving weeds and creepers, very strong, full-fed, and bursting thick with life.

You May Telephone from Here

She sent the servant to bed at half-past ten, and sat up in the flat alone. "I'll let my cousin in," she explained; "she may be rather late." She read, knitted, began a letter, poked the fire, and examined her husband's photographs on the mantelpiece; but most of the time she looked about her nervously, sometimes going to the door to listen, sometimes lifting the corner of the blind to look out upon the lights of North Kensington struggling with the blackness. The fog was thicker than ever. A rumble of traffic feeling its way floated up to her from below.

But at last, the doorbell rang sharply, and she ran to let in the cousin who had promised to spend the two nights with her during her husband's absence in Paris. They kissed. Both began talking at once.

"I thought you were *never* coming, Sybil—!"

"The play was out late—and the fog's bad. I sent on my box this afternoon on purpose."

"It came safely; and your room's quite ready. I do hope you'll manage all right without a maid. Oh, I'm *so* glad you've come, though!"

"Foolish little country mouse!"

"Oh, it's not that so much, though I admit that London still terrifies me at night rather; but you know this is the first time he's been away—and I suppose—"

"I know, dear; I understand perfectly." The cousin was brisk and cheerful. "You feel lonely, of course." They kissed again. Just unhook me, will you?" she added, "and I'll get into my dressing-gown, and then we'll be cosy over the fire."

"I saw him off at Victoria at 8.45," said the little wife when the operation was over.

"Newhaven and Dieppe?"

"Yes. He gets to Paris at seven in the morning. He promised to telephone the first thing."

157

"You expensive little monkey!"

"Why?"

"It's ten shillings for three minutes, or something like that, and you have to go to the G.P.O. or the Mansion House or some such place, I believe."

"But I thought it was the usual long-distance thing direct here to the flat. He never told me all that."

"Probably you didn't give him the chance!"

They laughed, and went on chatting, with feet on the fender and skirts tucked up. The cousin lit her second cigarette. It was after midnight.

"I'm afraid I'm not the least bit sleepy," said the wife apologetically.

"Nor am I, dear. For once the play excited me." She began to describe it vigorously. Half-way through the recital the telephone sounded in the hall. It tinkled faintly, but gave no proper ring.

The other started. "There it is again! It's always doing that—ever since Harry put it in a week ago. I don't quite like it." She spoke in a hushed voice.

The cousin looked at her curiously. "Oh, you mustn't mind that," she laughed with a reassuring manner. "It's a little way they have when the line gets out of order. You're not used to playing the telephone game yet. You should call up the Exchange and complain. Always complain, you know, in this world if you want—"

"There it goes again," interrupted her friend nervously. "Oh, I do wish it would stop. It's so like someone standing out there in the hall and trying to talk—"

The cousin jumped up. They went into the hall together, and the experienced one briskly rang up the Exchange and asked if there was anybody trying to "get through." With fine indignation she complained that no one in the flat could sleep for the noise. After a brief conversation she turned, receiver in hand, to her companion.

"The operator says he's very sorry, but your line's a bit troublesome tonight for some reason. Got mixed, or something. He can't understand it. Advises you to leave the receiver unhooked till the morning. Then it can't possibly ring, you see!"

They left the receiver swinging, and went back to the fire.

"I'm sorry I'm such a timid donkey," the wife said, laughing a little; "but I'm not used to it yet. There was no telephone at the farm, you know." She turned with a sudden start, as though she heard the bell again. And tonight," she added in a lower voice, though with an obvious effort at self-control, "for some reason or other I feel uncomfortable, rather—excited, queer, I think."

"How? Queer?"

"I don't know exactly; almost as if there was someone else in the flat—someone besides ourselves and the servant, I mean."

The cousin moved abruptly. She switched on the electric lights in the wall beside her.

"Yes; but it's only imagination, *really*," she said with decision. "It's natural enough. It's the fog and the strangeness of London after the loneliness of your farm-life, and your husband being away, and—and all that. Once you analyse these queer feelings they always go—"

"Hark!" exclaimed the wife under her breath. "Wasn't that a step in the passage?" She sat bolt upright, her face pale, her eyes very bright. They listened a moment. The night was utterly still about them.

"Rubbish!" cried the cousin loudly. "It was my foot knocking the fender; like this—look!" She repeated the sound vigorously.

"I do believe it was," the other said, only half convinced. "But it is queer. You know I feel exactly as though someone had come into the flat—quite recently, since *you* came, I mean—just before that tinkling began, in fact."

"Come, come," laughed the cousin, "you'll give us both the jumps. At one o'clock in the morning it's easy to imagine anything. You'll be hearing elephants on the stairs next!" She looked sharply about her. "Let's brew our chocolate and get to bed," she added. "We shall sleep like tops."

"One o'clock already! Then Harry's half-way across by now," said the wife, smiling at her friend's language. "But I'm *so* glad, oh, so glad, you're here," she added; "and I think it's most awfully sweet of you to give up a comfy big house . . ." They kissed again and laughed. Soon afterwards, having scalded their throats with hot chocolate, they went to bed.

"It simply can't ring now!" remarked the cousin triumphantly as they passed the receiver dangling in mid-air.

"That's a relief," her friend said. "I feel less nervous. Really, I'm too ashamed of myself for anything."

"Fog's clearing, too," Sybil added, peering for a moment through the narrow window by the front door.

An hour later the little flat was still as the grave. No sound of traffic was heard. Even the tinkling of the telephone seemed a whole twenty-four hours away, when suddenly—it began again: first with

159

little soft tentative noises, very faint, troubled, hurried, buried almost out of hearing inside the box; then louder and louder, with sharp jerks—finally with a challenging and alarming peal. And the wife, who had kept her door open, without pretence of sleep, heard it from the very beginning. In a moment she found herself in the passage, and Sybil, wakened by her cry, was at her heels. They turned up the lights and stood facing one another. The hall smelt—as things only smell at night—cold, musty.

"What's the matter? You frightened me. I heard you scream—"

"The telephone's ringing again—violently," the wife whispered, pale to the lips. "Don't you hear it? This time there's someone there—*really!*"

The cousin stared blankly at her. The laugh choked in her throat. "*I* hear nothing," she said defiantly, yet without confidence in her voice. "Besides, the thing's still disconnected. It *can't* ring—look!" She pointed to the hanging receiver motionless against the wall. "You're white as a ghost, though," she added, coming quickly forward.

Her friend moved suddenly to the instrument and picked up the receiver. "It's someone for me," she said, with terror in "It's someone who wants to talk to me! Oh, hark! hark how it rings!" Her voice shook. She placed the little disc to her ear and waited while her friend stood by and stared in amazement, uncertain what to do. *She* had heard no ringing!

"You, Harry!" whispered the wife into the telephone, with brief intervals of silence for the replies. "*You?* But how in the world so soon?—Yes, I can just hear, but very faintly. Miles and miles away your voice sounds—What?—A wonderful journey? And sooner than you expected—*Not* in Paris? Where, then?—Oh! my darling boy—No, I don't quite hear; I can't catch it—I don't understand. . . . The pain of the sea is nothing—is *what?* . . . You know nothing of *what . . ?*"

The cousin came boldly up. She took her arm. "But, child, there's no one there, bless you! You're dreaming—you're in fever or something—"

"Hush! For God's sake, hush!" She held up a hand. In her face and eyes was an expression indescribable—fear, love, bewilderment. Her body swayed a little, leaning against the wall. "Hush! I hear him still; but, oh! miles and miles away—He says—he's been trying for hours to find me. First, he tried my brain direct, and then—then—oh! he says he may not get back again to me—only he can't understand, can't explain *why*—the cold, the awful cold, keeps his lips from—— Oh!"

She screamed aloud as she flung the receiver down and dropped in a heap upon the floor. "I don't understand—it's death, death!" . . .

And the collision in the Channel that night, as they learned in due course, occurred a few minutes after one o'clock; while Harry himself, who remained unconscious for several hours after the boat picked him up, could only remember that his last desire as the wave caught him was an intense wish to communicate with his wife and tell her what had happened. . .The next thing he knew was opening his eyes in a Dieppe hotel.

And the other curious detail was furnished by the man who came to repair the telephone next day. At the Exchange, he declared, the wire, from midnight till nearly three in the morning, had emitted sparks and flashes of light no one had been able to account for in any usual manner.

"Queer!" said the man to himself, after tinkering and tapping for ten minutes, but there's nothing wrong with it at *this* end. It's the subscriber, most likely. It usually is!"

The South Wind

It is impossible to say through which sense, or combination of senses, I knew that Someone was approaching—was already near; but most probably it was the deep underlying "mother-sense" including them all that conveyed the delicate warning. At any rate, the scene-shifters of my moods knew it too, for very swiftly they prepared the stage; then, ever soft-footed and invisible, stood aside to wait.

As I went down the village street on my way to bed after midnight, the high Alpine valley lay silent in its frozen stillness. For days it had now lain thus, even the mouths of its cataracts stopped with ice; and for days, too, the dry, tight cold had drawn up the nerves of the humans in it to a sharp, thin pitch of exhilaration that at last began to call for the gentler comfort of relaxation. The key has been a little too high, the inner tautness too prolonged. The tension of that implacable north-east wind, the *bise noire*, had drawn its twisted wires too long through our very entrails. We all sighed for some loosening of the bands—the comforting touch of something damp, soft, less penetratingly acute.

And now, as I turned, midway in the little journey from the inn to my room above La Poste, this sudden warning that Someone was approaching repeated its silent wireless message, and I paused to listen and to watch.

Yet at first, I searched in vain. The village street lay empty—a white ribbon between the black walls of the big-roofed chalets; there were no lights in any of the houses; the hotels stood gaunt and ugly with their myriad shuttered windows; and the church, topped by the Crown of Savoy in stone, was so engulfed by the shadows of the mountains that it seemed almost a part of them.

Beyond, reared the immense buttresses of the Dent du Midi, terrible and stalwart against the sky, their feet resting among the crowding pines, their streaked precipices tilting up at violent angles towards the stars. The bands of snow; belting their enormous flanks, stretched for miles, faintly gleaming, like Saturn's rings. To the right I could just make out the pinnacles of the Dents Blanches, cruelly pointed; and, still farther, the Dent de Bonnaveau, as of iron and crystal, running up its gaunt and dreadful pyramid into relentless depths of night. Everywhere in the hard, black, sparkling air was the rigid spell of winter. It seemed as if this valley could never melt again, never know currents of warm wind, never taste the sun, nor yield its million flowers.

And now, dipping down behind me out of the reaches of the darkness, the New Comer moved close, heralded by this subtle yet compelling admonition that had arrested me in my very tracks. For, just as I turned in at the door, kicking the crunched snow from my boots against the granite step, I *knew* that, from the heart of all this tightly frozen winter's night, the "Someone" whose message had travelled so delicately in advance was now, quite suddenly, at my very heels. And while my eyes lifted to sift their way between the darkness and the snow, I became aware that It was already coming down the village street. It ran on feathered feet, pressing close against the enclosing walls, yet at the same time spreading from side to side, brushing the window-panes, rustling against the doors, and even including the shingled roofs in its enveloping advent. It came, too—*against the wind. . . .*

It flew up close and passed me, very faintly singing, running down between the chalets and the church, very swift, very soft, neither man nor animal, neither woman, girl, nor child, turning the corner of the snowy road beyond the *curé's* house with a rushing cantering motion, that made me think of a body of water—something of fluid and generous shape, too mighty to be confined in common forms. And, as it passed, it touched me—touched me through all skin and flesh upon the naked nerves, loosening, relieving, setting free the congealed sources of life which the *bise* so long had mercilessly bound, so that magic currents, flowing and released, washed down all the secret byways of the spirit and flooded again with full tide into a thousand dried-up cisterns of the heart.

The thrill I experienced is quite incommunicable in words. I ran upstairs and opened all my windows wide, knowing that soon the Messenger would return with a million others—only to find that already it had been there before me. Its taste was in the air, fragrant and alive; in my very mouth—and all the currents of the inner life ran sweet again, and full. Nothing in the whole village was quite the same as it had been before. The deeply slumbering peasants, even behind their shuttered windows and barred doors; the *curé*, the servants at the inn, the consumptive man opposite, the children in the house behind the church, the horde of tourists in the *caravanserai*—all knew—more or less, according to the delicacy of their receiving apparatus—that Something charged with fresh and living force had swept on viewless feet down the village street, passed noiselessly between the cracks of doors and windows, touched nerves and eyelids, and—set them free. In response to the great Order of Release that the messenger had left everywhere behind her, even the dreams of the sleepers had shifted into softer and more flowing keys....

And the Valley—the Valley also knew! For, as I watched from my window, something loosened about the trees and stones and boulders; about the massed snows on the great slopes; about the roots of the hanging icicles that fringed and sheeted the dark cliffs; and down in the deepest beds of the killed and silent streams. Far overhead, across those desolate bleak shoulders of the mountains, ran some sudden softness like the rush of awakening life ... and was gone. A touch, lithe yet dewy, as of silk and water mixed, dropped softly over all ... and, silently, without resistance, the *bise noire*, utterly routed, went back to the icy caverns of the north and east, where it sleeps, hated of men, and dreams its keen black dreams of death and desolation....

...And some five hours later, when I woke and looked towards the sunrise, I saw those strips of pearly grey, just tinged with red, the Messenger had been to summon ... charged with the warm moisture that brings relief. On the wings of a rising South Wind they came down hurriedly to cap the mountains and to unbind the captive forces of life; then moved with flying streamers up our own valley, sponging from the thirsty woods their richest perfume....

And farther down, in soft, wet fields, stood the leafless poplars, with little pools of water gemming the grass between and pouring their musical overflow through runnels of dark and sodden leaves to join the rapidly increasing torrents descending from the mountains. For across the entire valley ran magically that sweet and welcome message of relief which Job knew when he put the whole delicious tenderness and passion of it into less than a dozen words: "*He comforteth the earth with the south wind.*"

Special Delivery

Meiklejohn, the curate, was walking through the Jura when this thing happened to him. There is only his word to vouch for it, for the inn and its proprietor are now both of the past, and the local record of the occurrence has long since assumed the proportions of a picturesque but inaccurate legend. As a true story, however, it stands out from those of its kidney by the fact that there seems to have been a deliberate intention in it. It saved a life—a life the world had need of. And this singular rescue of a man of value to the best order of things makes one feel that there was some sense, even logic, in the affair.

Moreover, Meiklejohn asserts that it was the only psychic experience he ever knew. Things of the sort were not a 'habit' with him. His rescue, thus, was not one of those meaningless interventions that puzzle the man in the street while they exhilarate the psychologist. It was a deliberate and very determined affair.

Meiklejohn found himself that hot August night in one of the valleys that slip like blue shadows hidden among pine-woods between the Swiss frontier and France. He had passed Ste. Croix earlier in the day; Les Rasses had been left behind about four o'clock; Buttes, and the Val de Travers, where the cement of many a London street comes from, was his goal. But the light failed long before he reached it, and he stopped at an inn that appeared unexpectedly round a corner of the dusty road, built literally against the great cliffs that formed one wall of the valley. He was so footsore, and his knapsack so heavy, that he turned in without more ado.

Le Guillaume Tell was the name of the inn—dirty white walls, with thin, almost mangy vines scrambling over the door, and the stream brawling beneath shuttered windows with green and white stripes all patched by sun and rain. His room was sevenpence, his dinner of soup, omelette, fruit, cheese, and coffee, a *franc*. The prices suited his pocket and made him feel comfortable and at home. Immediately behind

167

the hotel—the only house visible, except the sawmill across the road, rose the ever-crumbling ridges and precipices that formed the flanks of Chasseront and ran on past La Sagne towards the grey Aiguilles de Baulmes. He was in the Jura fastnesses where tourists rarely penetrate.

Through the low doorway of the inn, he carried with him the strong atmosphere of thoughts that had accompanied him all day— dreams of how he intended to spend his life, plans of sacrifice and effort. For his hopes of great achievement, even then at twenty-five, were a veritable passion in him, and his desire to spend himself for humanity a devouring flame. So occupied, indeed, was his mind with the emotions belonging to this line of thinking, that he hardly noticed the singular, though exceedingly faint, sense of alarm that stirred somewhere in the depths of his being as he passed within that doorway where the drooping vine-leaves clutched at his hat.

He remembered it a little later. The sense of danger had been touched in him. He felt at the moment only a hint of discomfort, too vague to claim definite recognition. Yet it was there the instant he stepped within the threshold and afterwards he distinctly recalled its sudden and unaccountable advent.

His bedroom, though stuffy, as from windows long unopened, was clean; carpetless, of course, and primitive, with white pine floor and walls, and the short bed, smothered under its duvet, very creaky. And very short! For Meiklejohn was well over six feet.

'I shall have to curl up, as usual, in a knot,' was his reflection as he measured the bed with his eye; 'though tonight I think—after my twenty miles in this air—'

The thought refused to complete itself. He was going to add that he was tired enough to have slept on a stone floor, but for some undefined reason the same sense of alarm that had tapped him on the shoulder as he entered the inn returned now when he contemplated the bed. A sharp repugnance for that bed, as sudden and unaccountable as it was curious, swept into him—and was gone again before he had time to seize it wholly. It was in reality so slight that he dismissed it immediately as the merest fancy; yet, at the same time, he was aware that he would rather have slept on another bed, had there been one in the room—and then the queer feeling that, after all, perhaps, he would *not* sleep there in the end at all. How this idea came to him he never knew. He records it, however, as part of the occurrence.

After eight o'clock a few peasants, and workmen from the sawmill, came in to drink their demi-litre of red wine in the common room downstairs, to stare at the unexpected guest, and to smoke their vile tobacco. They were neither picturesque nor amusing—simply dirty and slightly malodorous. At nine o'clock Meiklejohn knocked the ashes from his briar pipe upon the limestone window-ledge, and went upstairs, overpowered with sleep. The sense of alarm had utterly disappeared; his mind was busy once more with his great dreams of the future—dreams that materialised themselves, as all the world knows, in the famous Meiklejohn Institutes. . . .

Berthoud, the proprietor, short and sturdy, with his faded brown coat and no collar, slightly confused with red wine and a 'tourist' guest, showed him the way up. For, of course, there was no *femme de chambre*.

'You have the corridor all to yourself,' the man said; showed him the best corner of the landing to shout from in case he wanted anything—there being no bell—eyed his boots, knapsack, and flask with considerable curiosity, wished him goodnight, and was gone. He went downstairs with a noise like a horse, thought the curate, as he locked the door after him.

The windows had been open now for a couple of hours, and the room smelt sweet with the odours of sawn wood and shavings, the resinous perfume of the surrounding hosts of pines, and the sharp, delicate touch of a lonely mountain valley where civilisation has not yet tainted the air. Whiffs of coarse tobacco, pungent without being offensive, came invisibly through the cracks of the floor. Primitive and simple it all was—a sort of vigorous 'backwoods' atmosphere. Yet, once again, as he turned to examine the room after Berthoud's steps had blundered down below into the passage, something rose faintly within him to set his nerves mysteriously a-quiver.

Out of these perfectly simple conditions, without the least apparent cause, the odd feeling again came over him that he was—in danger.

The curate was not much given to analysis. He was a man of action pure and simple, as a rule. But tonight, in spite of himself, his thoughts went plunging, searching, asking. For this singular message of dread that emanated as it were from the room, or from some article of furniture in the room perhaps—that bed still touched his mind with a peculiar repugnance—demanded somewhat insistently for an explanation.

And the only explanation that suggested itself to his unimaginative mind was that the forces of nature hereabouts were—overpowering; that, after the slum streets and factory chimneys of the last twelve months, these towering cliffs and smothering pine-forests communicated to his soul a word of grandeur that amounted to awe. Inadequate and far fetched as the explanation seems, it was the only one that occurred to him; and its value in this remarkable adventure lies in the fact that he connected his sense of danger partly with the bed and partly with the mountains.

'I felt once or twice,' he said afterwards, 'as though some powerful agency of a spiritual kind were all the time trying to beat into my stupid brain a message of warning.' And this way of expressing it is more true and graphic than many paragraphs of attempted analysis.

Meiklejohn hung his clothes by the open window to air, washed, read his Bible, looked several times over his shoulder without apparent cause, and then knelt down to pray. He was a simple and devout soul; his Self lost in the yearning, young but sincere, to live for humanity. He prayed, as usual, with intense earnestness that his life might be preserved for use in the world, when in the middle of his prayer—there came a knocking at the door.

Hastily rising from his knees, he opened. The sound of rushing water filled the corridor. He heard the voices of the workmen below in the drinking-room. But only darkness stood in the passages, filling the house to the very brim. No one was there. He returned to his interrupted devotions.

'I imagined it,' he said to himself. He continued his prayers, however, longer than usual. At the back of his thoughts, dim, vague, half-defined only, lay this lurking sense of uneasiness—that he was in danger. He prayed earnestly and simply, as a child might pray, for the preservation of his life. . . .

Again, just as he prepared to get into bed, struggling to make the heaped-up duvet spread all over, came that knocking at the bedroom door. It was soft, wonderfully soft, and something within him thrilled curiously in response. He crossed the floor to open—then hesitated. Suddenly he understood that that knocking at the door was connected with the sense of danger in his heart. In the region of subtle intuitions, the two were linked. With this realisation there came over him, he declares, a singular mood in which, as in a revelation, he knew that Nature held forces that might somehow communicate directly and positively with—human beings. This thought rushed upon him out of the night, as it were. It arrested his movements. He stood there upon the bare pine boards, hesitating to open the door.

The delay thus described lasted actually only a few seconds, but in those few seconds these thoughts tore rapidly and like fire through his mind. The beauty of this lost and mysterious valley was certainly in his veins. He felt the strange presence of the encircling forests, soft and splendid, their million branches sighing in the night airs. The crying of the falling water touched him. He longed to transfer their peace and power to the hearts of suffering thousands of men and women and children. The towering precipices that literally dropped their pale walls over the roof of the inn lifted his thoughts to their own wind-swept heights; he longed to convey their message of inflexible strength to the weak-kneed folk in the slums where he worked. He was peculiarly conscious of the presence of these forces of Nature—the irresistible powers that regenerate as easily as they destroy.

All this, and far more, swept his soul like a huge wind as he stood there, waiting to open the door in answer to that mysterious soft knocking.

And there, when at length he opened, stood the figure of a man—staring at him and smiling.

Disappointment seized him instantly. He had expected, almost believed, that he would see something un-ordinary; and instead, there stood a man who had merely mistaken the door of his room, and was now bowing his apology for the interruption. Then, to his amazement, he saw that the man beckoned: the figure was someone who sought to draw him out.

'Come with me,' it seemed to say.

But Meiklejohn only realised this afterwards, he says, when it was too late and he had already shut the door in the stranger's face. For the man had withdrawn into the darkness a little, and the curate had taken the movement for a mere acknowledgment of his mistake instead of—as he afterwards felt—a sign that he should follow.

'And the moment the door was shut,' he says, 'I felt that it would have been better for me to have gone out into the passage to see what he wanted. It came over me that the man had something important to say to me. I had missed it.'

For some seconds, it seemed, he resisted the inclination to go after him. He argued with himself; then turned to his bed, pulled back the sheets and heavy duvet, and was met sharply again with the sense of repugnance, almost of fear, as before. It leaped out upon him—as though the drawing back of the blankets had set free some cold blast of wind that struck him across the face and made him shiver.

At the same moment a shadow fell from behind his shoulder and dropped across the pillow and upper half of the bed. It may, of course, have been the magnified shadow of the moth that buzzed about the pale-yellow electric light in the ceiling. He does not pretend to know. It passed swiftly, however, and was gone; and Meiklejohn, feeling less sure of himself than ever before in his life, crossed the floor quickly, almost running, and opened the door to go after the man who had knocked—twice. For in reality less than half a minute had passed since the shutting of the door and its reopening.

But the corridor was empty. He marched down the pine-board floor for some considerable distance. Below he saw the glimmer of the hall, and heard the voices of the peasants and workmen from the sawmill as they still talked and drank their red wine in the public room. That sound of falling water, as before, filled the air. Darkness reigned. But the person—the *messenger*—who had twice knocked at his door was gone utterly. . . . Presently a door opened downstairs, and the peasants clattered out noisily. He turned and went back to bed. The electric light was switched off below. Silence fell. Conquering his strange repugnance, Meiklejohn, with a prayer on his lips, got into bed, and in less than ten minutes was sound asleep.

'I admit,' he says, in telling the story, 'that what happened afterwards came so swiftly and so confusingly, yet with such a storm of overwhelming conviction of its reality, that its sequence may be somewhat blurred in my memory, while, at the same time, I see it after all these years as though it was a thing of yesterday. But in my sleep, first of all, I again heard that soft, mysterious tapping—not in the course of a dream of any sort, but sudden and alone out of the dark blank of forgetfulness. I tried to wake. At first, however, the bonds of unconsciousness held me tight. I had to struggle in order to return to the waking world.

'There was a distinct effort before I opened my eyes; and in that slight interval I became aware that the person who had knocked at the door had meanwhile opened it and passed into the room. I had left the lock unturned. The person was close beside me in the darkness—not in utter darkness, however, for a rising three-quarter moon shed its faint silver upon the floor in patches, and, as I sprang swiftly from the bed, I noticed something alive moving towards me across the carpetless boards.

'Upon the edges or a patch of moonlight, where the fringe of silver and shadow mingled, it stopped. Three feet away from it I, too, stopped, shaking in every muscle. It lay there crouching at my very

172

feet, staring up at me. But was it man or was it animal? For at first, I took it certainly for a human being on all fours; but the next moment, with a spasm of genuine terror that half stopped my breath, it was borne in upon me that the creature was—nothing human. Only in this way can I describe it. It was identical with the human figure who had knocked before and beckoned to me to follow, but it was another presentation of that figure.

'And it held (or brought, if you will) some tremendous message for me—some message of tremendous importance, I mean. The first time I had argued, resisted, refused to listen. Now it had returned in a form that ensured obedience. Some quite terrific power emanated from it a power that I understood instinctively belonged to the mountains and the forests and the untamed elemental forces of Nature. Amazing as it may sound in cold blood, I can only say that I felt as though the towering precipices outside had sent me a direct warning—that my life was in immediate danger.

'For a space that seemed minutes, but was probably less than a few seconds, I stood there trembling on the bare boards, my eyes riveted upon the dark, uncouth shape that covered all the floor beyond. I saw no limbs or features, no suggestion of outline that I could connect with any living form I know, animate or inanimate. Yet it moved and stirred all the time—*whirled within itself*, describes it best; and into my mind sprang a picture of an immense dark wheel, turning, spinning, whizzing so rapidly that it appears motionless, and uttering that low and ominous thunder that fills a great machinery-room of a factory. Then I thought of Ezekiel's vision of the Living Wheels. . . .

'And it must have been at this instant, I think, that the muttering and deep note that issued from it formed itself into words within me. At any rate, I heard a voice that spoke with unmistakable intelligence: '"Come!" it said. "Come out—at once!" And the sense of power that accompanied the Voice was so splendid that my fear vanished and I obeyed instantly without thinking more. I followed; it led. It altered in shape. The door *was* open. It ran silently in a form that was more like a stream of deep black water than anything else I can think of—out of the room, down the stairs, across the hall, and up to the deep shadows that lay against the door leading into the road. There I lost sight of it.'

Meiklejohn's only desire, he says, then was to rush after it—to escape. This he did. He understood that somehow it had passed through the door into the open air. Ten seconds later, perhaps even less, he, too, was in the open air. He acted almost automatically; reason, reflection, logic all swept away. Nowhere, however, in the soft moonlight about him was any sign of the extraordinary apparition that had succeeded in drawing him out of the inn, out of his bedroom, out of his—bed. He stared in a dazed way at everything—just beginning to get control of his faculties a bit—wondering what in the world it all meant. That huge spinning form, he felt convinced, lay hidden somewhere close beside him, waiting for the end. The danger it had enabled him to avoid was close at hand. . . . He *knew* that, he says. . . .

There lay the meadows, touched here and there with wisps of floating mist; the stream roared and tumbled down its rocky bed to his left; across the road the sawmill lifted its skeleton-like outline, moon-light shining on the dew-covered shingles of the roof, its lower part hidden in shadow. The cold air of the valley was exquisitely scented.

To the right, where his eye next wandered, he saw the thick black woods rising round the base of the precipices that soared into the sky, sheeted with silvery moonlight. His gaze ran up them to the far ridges that seemed to push the very stars farther into the heavens. Then, as he saw those stars crowding the night, he staggered suddenly backwards, seizing the wall of the road for support, and catching his breath. For the top of the cliff, he fancied, moved. A group of stars was for a fraction of a second—hidden. The earth—the scenery of the val-ley, at least—turned about him. Something prodigious was happening to the solid structure of the world. The precipices seemed to bend over upon the valley. The far, uppermost ridge of those beetling cliffs shifted downwards. Meiklejohn declares that the way its movement hid momentarily a group of stars was the most startling—for some reason horrible—thing he had ever witnessed.

Then came the roar and crash and thunder as the mass toppled, slid, and finally—took the frightful plunge. How long the forces of rain and frost had been chiselling out the slow detachment of the gi-ant slabs that fell, or whence came the particular extra little push that drove the entire mass out from the parent rock, no one can know. Only one thing is certain: that it was due to no chance, but to the nicely and exactly calculated results of balanced cause and effect. From the beginning of time, it had been known—it might have been ac-curately calculated, rather—that this particular thousand tons of rock would break away from the crumbling tops of the precipices and crash downwards with the roar of many tempests into the lost and myste-rious mountain valley where Meiklejohn the curate spent such and such a night of such and such a holiday. It was just as sure as the return of Halley's comet.

'I watched it,' he says, 'because I couldn't do anything else. I would far rather have run—I was so frightfully close to it all—but I couldn't move a muscle. And in a few seconds, it was over. A terrific wind knocked me backwards against the stone wall; there was a vast clattering of smaller stones, set rolling down the neighbouring *couloirs*; a steady roll of echoes ran thundering up and down the valley; and then all was still again exactly as it had been before. And the curious thing was—ascertained a little later, as you may imagine, and not at once—that the inn, being so closely built up against the cliffs, had almost entirely escaped. The great mass of rock and trees had taken a leap farther out, and filled the meadows, blocked the road, crushed the sawmill like a matchbox, and dammed up the stream; but the inn itself was almost untouched.

'*Almost*—for a single block of limestone, about the size of a grand piano, had dropped straight upon one corner of the roof and smashed its way through my bedroom, carrying everything it contained down to the level of the cellar, so terrific was the momentum of its crushing journey. Not a stick of the furniture was afterwards discoverable—as such. The bed seems to have been caught by the very middle of the fallen mass.'

The confusion in Meiklejohn's mind may be imagined—the rush of feeling and emotion that swept over him. Berthoud and the peasants mustered in less than a dozen minutes, talking, crying, praying. Then the stream, dammed up by the accumulation of rock, carried off the debris of the broken roof and walls in less than half an hour. The rock, however, that swept the room and the *empty* bed of Meiklejohn the curate into dust, still lies in the valley where it fell.

'The only other thing that I remember,' he says, in telling the story, 'is that, as I stood there, shaking with excitement and the painful terror of it all, before Berthoud and the peasants had come to count over their number and learn that no one was missing—while I stood there, leaning against the wall of the road, something rose out of the white dust at my feet, and, with a noise like the whirring of some immense projectile, passed swiftly and invisibly away up into space—so far as I could judge, towards the distant ridges that reared their motionless outline in moonlight beneath the stars.'

Clairvoyance

In the darkest corner, where the firelight could not reach him, he sat listening to the stories. His young hostess occupied the corner on the other side; she was also screened by shadows; and between them stretched the horse-shoe of eager, frightened faces that seemed all eyes. Behind yawned the blackness of the big room, running as it were without a break into the night.

Someone crossed on tiptoe and drew a blind up with a rattle, and at the sound all started: through the window, opened at the top, came a rustle of the poplar leaves that stirred like footsteps in the wind. 'There's a strange man walking past the shrubberies,' whispered a nervous girl; 'I saw him crouch and hide. I saw his eyes!'

'Nonsense!' came sharply from a male member of the group; 'it's far too dark to see. You heard the wind.' For mist had risen from the river just below the lawn, pressing close against the windows of the old house like a soft grey hand, and through it the stir of leaves was faintly audible.... Then, while several called for lights, others remembered that the hop-pickers were still about in the lanes, and the tramps this autumn overbold and insolent. All, perhaps, wished secretly for the sun.

Only the elderly man in the corner sat quiet and unmoved, contributing nothing. He had told no fearsome story. He had evaded, indeed, many openings expressly made for him, though fully aware that to his well-known interest in psychical things was partly due his presence in the weekend party. 'I never have experiences—that way,' he said shortly when someone asked him point blank for a tale; 'I have no unusual powers.' There was perhaps the merest hint of contempt in his tone, but the hostess from her darkened corner quickly and tactfully covered his retreat. And he wondered. For he knew why she invited him. The haunted room, he was well aware, had been specially allotted to him.

And then, most opportunely, the door opened noisily and the host came in. He sniffed at the darkness, rang at once for lamps, puffed at his big curved pipe, and generally, by his mere presence, made the group feel rather foolish. Light streamed past him from the corridor. His white hair shone like silver. And with him came the atmosphere of common sense, of shooting, agriculture, motors, and the rest. Age entered at that door. And his young wife sprang up instantly to greet him, as though his disapproval of this kind of entertainment might need humouring.

It may have been the light—that witchery of half-lights from the fire and the corridor, or it may have been the abrupt entrance of the Practical upon the soft Imaginative that traced the outline with such pitiless, sharp conviction. At any rate, the contrast—for those who had this inner clairvoyant sight all had been prating of so glibly!—was unmistakably revealed. It was poignantly dramatic, pain somewhere in it—naked pain. For, as she paused a moment there beside him in the light, this childless wife of three years' standing, picture of youth and beauty, there stood upon the threshold of that room the presence of a true ghost story.

And most marvellously she changed—her lineaments, her very figure, her whole presentment. Etched against the gloom, the deli-cate, unmarked face shone suddenly keen and anguished, and a rich maturity, deeper than any mere age, flushed all her little person with its secret grandeur. Lines started into being upon the pale skin of the girlish face, lines of pleading, pity, and love the daylight did not show, and with them an air of magic tenderness that betrayed, though for a second only, the full soft glory of a motherhood denied, yet somehow mysteriously enjoyed. About her slenderness rose all the deep-bos-omed sweetness of maternity, a potential mother of the world, and a mother, though she might know no dear fulfilment, who yet yearned to sweep into her immense embrace all the little helpless things that ever lived.

Light, like emotion, can play strangest tricks. The change pressed almost upon the edge of revelation. . . . Yet, when a moment later lamps were brought, it is doubtful if any but the silent guest who had told no marvellous tale, knew no psychical experience, and disclaimed the smallest clairvoyant faculty, had received and registered the vivid, poignant picture. For an instant it had flashed there, mercilessly clear for all to see who were not blind to subtle spiritual wonder thick with pain. And it was not so much mere picture of youth and age ill-matched, as of youth that yearned with the oldest craving in the world, and of age that had slipped beyond the power of sympathetically divining it. . . . It passed, and all was as before.

The husband laughed with genial good-nature, not one whit annoyed. 'They've been frightening you with stories, child,' he said in his jolly way, and put a protective arm about her.

'Haven't they now? Tell me the truth. Much better,' he added, 'have joined me instead at billiards, or for a game of Patience, eh?' She looked up shyly into his face, and he kissed her on the forehead.

'Perhaps they have—a little, dear,' she said, 'but now that you've come, I feel all right again.'

'Another night of this,' he added in a graver tone, 'and you'd be at your old trick of putting guests to sleep in the haunted room. I was right after all, you see, to make it out of bounds.' He glanced fondly, paternally down upon her. Then he went over and poked the fire into a blaze. Someone struck up a waltz on the piano, and couples danced. All trace of nervousness vanished, and the butler presently brought in the tray with drinks and biscuits. And slowly the group dispersed. Candles were lit. They passed down the passage into the big hall, talking in lowered voices of tomorrow's plans. The laughter died away as they went up the stairs to bed, the silent guest and the young wife lingering a moment over the embers.

'You have not, after all then, put me in your haunted room?' he asked quietly. 'You mentioned, you remember, in your letter—'

'I admit,' she replied at once, her manner gracious beyond her years, her voice quite different, 'that I wanted you to sleep there—someone, I mean, who really knows, and is not merely curious. But—forgive my saying so when I saw you'—she laughed very slowly—'and when you told no marvellous story like the others, I somehow felt—'

'But I never see anything—' he put in hurriedly.

'You feel, though,' she interrupted swiftly, the passionate tenderness in her voice but half suppressed. 'I can tell it from your—'

'Others, then,' he interrupted abruptly, almost bluntly, 'have slept there—sat up, rather?'

'Not recently. My husband stopped it.' She paused a second, then added, 'I had that room—for a year—when first we married.'

The other's anguished look flew back upon her little face like a shadow and was gone, while at the sight of it there rose in himself a sudden deep rush of wonderful amazement beckoning almost towards worship. He did not speak, for his voice would tremble.

'I had to give it up,' she finished, very low.

'Was it so terrible?' after a pause he ventured.

She bowed her head. 'I had to change,' she repeated softly.

'And since then—now—you see nothing?' he asked.

Her reply was singular. 'Because I will not, not because it's gone.'
. . . He followed her in silence to the door, and as they passed along the passage, again that curious great pain of emptiness, of loneliness, of yearning rose upon him, as of a sea that never, never can swim beyond the shore to reach the flowers that it loves . . .

'Hurry up, child, or a ghost will catch you,' cried her husband, leaning over the banisters, as the pair moved slowly up the stairs towards him. There was a moment's silence when they met.

The guest took his lighted candle and went down the corridor. Goodnights were said again.

They moved away, she to her loneliness, he to his un-haunted room. And at his door he turned. At the far end of the passage, silhouetted against the candlelight, he watched them—the fine old man with his silvered hair and heavy shoulders, and the slim young wife with that amazing air as of some great bountiful mother of the world for whom the years yet passed hungry and unharvested.

They turned the corner, and he went in and closed his door.

Sleep took him very quickly, and while the mist rose up and veiled the countryside, something else, veiled equally for all other sleepers in that house but two, drew on towards its climax. . . .

Some hours later he awoke; the world was still, and it seemed the whole house listened; for with that clear vision which some bring out of sleep, he remembered that there had been no direct denial, and of a sudden realised that this big, gaunt chamber where he lay was after all the haunted room. For him, however, the entire world, not merely separate rooms in it, was ever haunted; and he knew no terror to find the space about him charged with thronging life quite other than his own. . . . He rose and lit the candle, crossed over to the window where the mist shone grey, knowing that no barriers of walls or door or ceiling could keep out this host of Presences that poured so thickly everywhere about him.

It was like a wall of being, with peering eyes, small hands stretched out, a thousand pattering wee feet, and tiny voices crying in a chorus very faintly and beseeching. . . . The haunted room! Was it not, rather, a temple vestibule, prepared and sanctified by yearning rites few men might ever guess, for all the childless women of the world? How could she know that he would understand—this woman he had seen but twice in all his life? And how entrust to him so great a mystery that was her secret? Had she so easily divined in him a similar yearning to which, long years ago, death had denied fulfilment? Was she clairvoyant in the true sense, and did all faces bear on them so legibly this great map that sorrow traced? . . . .

And then, with awful suddenness, mere feelings dipped away, and something concrete happened. The handle of the door had faintly rattled. He turned. The round brass knob was slowly moving. And first, at the sight, something of common fear did grip him, as though his heart had missed a beat, but on the instant, he heard the voice of his own mother, now long beyond the stars, calling to him to go softly yet with speed. He watched a moment the feeble efforts to undo the door, yet never afterwards could swear that he saw actual movement, for something in him, tragic as blindness, rose through a mist of tears and darkened vision utterly. . . .

He went towards the door. He took the handle very gently, and very softly then he opened it.

Beyond was darkness. He saw the empty passage, the edge of the banisters where the great hall yawned below, and, dimly, the outline of the Alpine photograph and the stuffed deer's head upon the wall. And then he dropped upon his knees and opened wide his arms to something that came in upon uncertain, viewless feet. All the young winds and flowers and dews of dawn passed with it . . . filling him to the brim . . . covering closely his breast and eyes and lips. There clung to him all the small beginnings of life that cannot stand alone . . . the little helpless hands and arms that have no confidence . . . and when the wealth of tears and love that flooded his heart seemed to break upon the frontiers of some mysterious yet impossible fulfilment, he rose and went with curious small steps towards the window to taste the cooling, misty air of that other dark Emptiness that waited so patiently there above the entire world.

He drew the sash up. The air felt soft and tender as though there were somewhere children in it too—children of stars and flowers, of mists and wings and music, all that the Universe contains unborn and tiny. . . . And when at length he turned again the door was closed. The room was empty of any life but that which lay so wonderfully blessed within himself. And this, he felt, had marvellously increased and multiplied. . . .

Sleep then came back to him, and in the morning, he left the house before the others were astir, pleading some overlooked engagement. For he had seen Ghosts indeed, but yet not ghosts that he could talk about with others round an open fire.

The Golden Fly

It fell upon him out of a clear sky just when existence seemed on its very best behaviour, and he savagely resented the undeserved affliction of it. Involving him in an atrocious scandal that reflected directly upon his honour, it destroyed in a moment the erection his entire life had so laboriously built up—his reputation. In the eyes of the world, he was a broken, discredited man, at the very moment, moreover, when his most cherished ambitions touched fulfilment. And the cruelty of it appalled his sense of justice, for it was impossible to vindicate himself without inculpating others who were dearer to him than life. It seemed more than he could bear; and the grim course he contemplated—decision itself as yet hung darkly waiting in the background—appeared the only way of escape that offered.

He had discussed the matter with friends until his brain whirled. Their sympathy maddened him, with hints of *qui s'excuse s'accuse*, and he turned at last in desperation to something that could not answer back. For the first time in his life, he turned to Nature—to that dead, inanimate Nature he had left to poets and rhapsodising women: 'I must face it alone,' he put it. For the Finger of God was a phrase without meaning to him, and his entire being contained no trace of the religious instinct.

He was a business man, honest, selfish, and ambitious; and the collapse of his worldly position was paramount to the collapse of the universe itself—his universe, at any rate. This 'crumbling of the universe' was the thought he took out with him. He left the house by the path that led into solitude, and reached the heathery expanse that formed one of the breathing-places of the New Forest. There he flung himself down wearily in the shadow of a little pine-copse. And his crumbled universe lay down with him, for he could not escape it.

Taking the pistol from the hip-pocket where it hurt him, he lay upon his back and watched the clouds. Half stunned, half dazed, he stared into the sky. The perfumed wind played softly on his eyes; he smelt the heather-honey; golden flies hung motionless in the air, like coloured pins fastening the sunshine against the blue curtain of the summer, while dragon-flies, like darting shuttles, wove across its pattern their threads of gleaming bronze. He heard the petulant crying of the peewits, and watched their tumbling flight. Below him tinkled a rivulet, its brown water rippling between banks of peaty earth. Everywhere was singing, peace, and careless unconcern.

And this lordly indifference of Nature calmed and soothed him. Neither human pain nor the injustice of man could shift the key of the water, alter the peewits' cry a single tone, nor influence one fraction of an inch those cloudy frigates of vapour that sailed the sky. The earth bulged sunwards as she had bulged for centuries. The power of her steady gait, superbly calm, breathed everywhere with grandeur—undismayed, unhasting, and supremely confident. . . . And, like the flash of those golden flies, there leaped suddenly upon him this vivid thought: that his world of agony lay neatly buttoned up within the tiny space of his own brain. Outside himself it had no existence at all. His mind contained it—the minute interior he called his heart. From this vaster world about him it lay utterly apart, like deeds in the black boxes of japanned tin he kept at the office, shut off from the universe, huddled in an overcrowded space within his skull.

How this commonplace thought reached him, garbed in such startling novelty, was odd enough; for it seemed as though the fierceness of his pain had burned away something. His thoughts it merely enflamed; but this other thing it consumed. Something that had obscured clear vision shrivelled before it as a piece of paper, eaten up by fire, dwindles down into a thimbleful of unimportant ashes. The thicket of his mind grew half transparent. At the farther end he saw, for the first time—light. The perspective of his inner life, hitherto so enormous, telescoped into the proportions of a miniature.

Just as momentous and significant as before, it was somehow abruptly different—seen from another point of view. The suffering had burned up rubbish he himself had piled over the head of a little Fact. Like a point of metal that glows yet will not burn, he discerned in the depths of him the essential shining fact that not all this ruinous conflagration could destroy. And this brilliant, indestructible kernel was—his Innocence. The rest was self-reared rubbish: opinion of the world. He had magnified an atom into a universe. . . .

Pain, as it seemed, had cleared a way for the sublimity of Nature to approach him. The calm old Universe rolled past. The deep, majestic Day gave him a push, as though the shoulder of some star had brushed his own. He had thought his feelings were the world: instead, they were merely his way of looking at it. The actual 'world' was some glorious, unchanging thing he never saw direct. His attitude of mind was but a peephole into it. The choice of his particular peephole, moreover, lay surely within the power of his individual will. The anguish, centred upon so small a point, had seemed to affect the entire spread universe around him, whereas in reality it affected nothing but his attitude of mind towards it.

The truism struck him like a blow between the eyes, that a man is what he thinks or feels himself to be. It leaped the barrier between words and meaning. The intellectual concept became a hard-edged fact, because he realised it—for the first time in his very circumscribed life. And this dreadful pain that had made even suicide seem desirable was entirely a fabrication of his own mind. The universe about him rolled on just the same in the majesty of its eternal purpose. His tiny inner world was clouded, but the glory of this stupendous world about him was undimmed, untroubled, unaffected. Even death itself. . . .

With a swift smash of the hand, he crushed the golden fly that settled on his knee. The murder was done impulsively, utterly without intention. He watched the little point of gold quiver for a moment among the hairs of the rough tweed; then lie still for ever . . . but the scent of heather-honey filled the air as before; the wind passed sighing through the pines; the clouds still sailed their uncharted sea of blue. There lay the whole spread surface of the Forest in the sun. Only the attitude of the golden fly towards it all was gone. A single, tiny point of view had disappeared. Nature passed on calmly and unhasting; she took no note.

Then, with a rush of awe, another thought flashed through him: Nature *had* taken note. There was a difference everywhere. Not a sparrow falleth, he remembered, without God knowing. God was certainly in Nature somewhere. His clumsy senses could not register this difference, yet it was there. His own small world, fed by these senses, was after all the merest little corner of Existence. To the whole of Existence, that included himself, the golden fly, the sun, and all the stars, he must somehow answer for his crime. It was a wanton interference with a sublime and sovereign Purpose that he now divined for the first time.

He looked at the wee point of gold lying still and silent in the forest of hairs. He realised the enormity of his act. It could not have been graver had he put out the sun, or the little, insignificant flame of his own existence. He had done a criminal, evil thing, for he had put an end to a certain point of view; had wiped it out; made it impossible. Had the fly been quicker, less easily overwhelmed, or more tenacious of the scrap of universal life it used, Nature would at this instant be richer for its little contribution to the whole of things—to which he himself also belonged.

And wherein, he asked himself, did he differ from that fly in the importance, the significance of his contribution to the universe? The soul . . . ? He had never given the question a single thought; but if the scrap of life he owned was called a soul, why should that point of golden glory not comprise one too? Its minute size, its trivial purpose, its few hours of apparently futile existence . . . these formed no true criterion . . . !

Similarly, the thought rushed over him, a Hand was being stretched out to crush himself. His pain was the shadow of its approach; anger in his heart, the warning. Unless he were quick enough, adroit and skilled enough, he also would be wiped out, while Nature continued her slow, unhasting way without him. His attitude towards the personal pain was really the test of his ability, of his merit—of his right to survive. Pain teaches, pain develops, pain brings growth: he had heard it since his copybook days. But now he realised it, as again thought leaped the barrier between familiar words and meaning. In his attitude of mind to his catastrophe lay his salvation or his . . . death.

In some such confused and blundering fashion, because along unaccustomed channels, the truth charged into him to overwhelm, yet bringing with it an unwonted sense of joy that seemed to break a crust which long had held back—life. Thus tapped, these sources gushed forth and bubbled over, spread about his being, flooded him with hope and courage, above all with—calmness. Nature held forces just as real and living as human sympathy, and equally able to modify the soul. And Nature was always accessible.

A sense of huge companionship, denied him by the littleness of his fellow-men, stole sweetly over him. It was amazingly uplifting, yet fear came close behind it, as he realised the presumption of his former attitude of cynical indifference. These Powers were aware of his petty insolence, yet had not crushed him. . . . It was, of course, the awakening of the religious instinct in a man who hitherto had worshipped merely a rather low-grade form of intellect.

And, while the enormous confusion of it shook him, this sense of incommunicable sweetness remained. Bright haunting eyes, with love in them, gazed at him from the blue; and this thing that came so close, stood also far away upon the line of the horizon. It was everywhere. It filled the hollows, but towered over him as well towards the pinnacles of cloud. It was in the sharpness of the peewits' cry, and in the water's murmur. It whispered in the pine-boughs, and blazed in every patch of sunlight. And it was glory, pure and simple. It filled him with a sense of strength for which he could find but one description—Triumph.

And so, first, the anger faded from his mind and crept away. Resentment then slunk after it. Revolt and disappointment also melted, and bitterness gave place to the most marvellous peace the man had ever known. Then came resignation to fill the empty places. Pain, as a means and not an end, had cleared the way, though the accomplishment was like a miracle. But Conversion *is* a miracle. No ordinary pain can bring it. This anguish he understood now in a new relation to life—as something to be taken willingly into himself and dealt with, all regardless of public opinion. What people said and thought was in their world, not in his. It was less than nothing. The pain cultivated dormant tracts. The terror also purged. It disclosed. . . .

He watched the wind, and even the wind brought revelation; for without obstacles in its path it would be silent. He watched the sunshine, and the sunshine taught him too; for without obstacles to fling it back against his eye, he could never see it. He would neither hear the tinkling water nor feel the summer heat unless both one and other overcame some reluctant medium in their pathways. And, similarly with his moral being—his pain resulted from the friction of his personal ambitions against the stress of some noble Power that sought to lift him higher. That Power he could not know direct, but he recognised its strain against him by the resistance it generated in the inertia of his selfishness. His attitude of mind had switched completely round. It was what the preachers termed development through suffering.

Moreover, he had acquired this energy of resistance somehow from the wind and sun and the beauty of a common summer's day. Their peace and strength had passed into himself. Unconsciously on his way home he drew upon it steadily. He tossed the pistol into a pool of water. Nature had healed him; and Nature, should he turn weak again, was always there. It was very wonderful. He wanted to sing. . . .

The Temptation of the Clay

1

Some men grow away from places, others grow into them: It is a curious and delicate matter. Before now, a man has been thrown out by his own property, yet his successor made immediately at home there. Once let Imagination dwell upon this psychology of places and it will travel very far. Here lies a great mystery, entangled with the mystery of life itself, delicately baited, too. Only the utterly obtuse, one thinks, can ignore the hint offered by Nature—that there is this very definite relationship existing between places and human beings, and that the aggressive attitude is not always chiefly upon the side of the latter.

So it is that there are spots of country—mere bits of scenery, a valley, plain, or river bank, estate or even garden—that undeniably bid a man stay, and welcome; or for no ascertainable reason reject him, and make him anxious to leave. Campers, looking for a night's resting-place, know this well; and so, may owners of estates and houses—campers on a larger scale, seeking to settle somewhere for the few years of a life-time. Neither one nor other, however, one thinks, unless he be a swift-minded poet with vivid divination, gets quite to the root of the matter.

Very suggestive are the mysterious processes by which such results are sometimes brought about, a certain pathos in them too. For the rejected owner is usually of that hard intellectual type that is utterly insensible to the fairy flails of Beauty, and seeks, therefore, in vain through all his stores of logic for a reasonable cause and effect; whereas the accepted one, exquisitely adjusted though he may be to the seduction of the place that takes him in, yet is unable to tell in words what really happens, or to express a tithe of that sweet marvellous explanation that lies concealed within his heart. The one denies it, the other makes wild, poetic guesses; but neither really knows.

Dick Eliot understood something of the two points of view per-haps, because he experienced both acceptance and rejection; and this story, of how a place first welcomed him, then violently tossed him out again, is as queer a case of such relationship as one may ever hear. But, then, Dick Eliot combined in himself a measure of both types of mind; he was intellectual, and knew that two and two make four, but he was also mystical, and knew that they make five or nothing, or a million—that everything is One, and One is everything. Neither was, perhaps, very strong in him, because life had not provided the op-portunity for one or other's exclusive development; but both existed side by side in his general mental composition. And they resulted in a level so delicately poised that the apparent balance yet had instability at its roots.

★★★★★★★★★★★★

Leaving England at twenty-two or three—there were misunder-standings with his University, where in classics and philosophy he had promised well; with his step-parents who regarded him as well lost; and in a sense, that yet did not affect his honour, with his country's law—he had since met life in difficult, rough places. He had lived. All manner of experiences had been his; he had known starvation in strange cities, and had more than once been close to death—queer kinds of death. But, also, he had been close to earth, and the earth had wonderfully taught him.

The results of this teaching, not recognised at the time, came out later to puzzle and amaze him. For years he dwelt in the wilderness with life reduced to its essentials—the big, crude, thundering facts of it—so that he had come to regard scholarship, once so valued, as over-rated, and action as the sole reality. The poetic, mystical side of him passed into temporary abeyance. Worldly achievement and ambition led him. This, however, was a mood of youth only, a reaction due to the resentment of his exile, and to the grievance he cherished against the academic conventions—so he deemed them—that had cut him off from his inheritance.

At thirty, or thereabouts, he fell in love and married—a vigorous personality of a woman with Red Indian in her blood, picked up in some wild escapade along the frontiers of Arizona and New Mexico; and, within six months of marriage, the death of an aunt had left him unexpected master of this little gem of an estate in the south of Eng-land where the following experience took place.

This impulsive action of an aunt whom he had seen but once, due to her wish to spite the other claimants rather than to any pretended love for himself, resulted in a radical change of life. He came home, ignored by his relations, and ignoring them in turn. The former love of books revived; the imaginative point of view re-asserted itself; he saw life from another angle. Action, after all, was but a part of it, another form of play. The mental life was the reality; he studied, meditated, wrote.

Once more the deep, poetic mystery of things lit all his thoughts with wonder. Corrected by the hard experiences of his early years, the philosopher and dreamer in him assumed the upper hand, though the speculative dreams he indulged were more sanely regulated than before. The imagination was now more finely tempered.

To look at, he was sometimes obviously forty-five, yet at others could easily have passed for thirty:—a tall, lean figure of a man; spare, as though the wilderness had taken that toll of him which no amount of subsequent easy living could efface. To see him was to think of men toiling in a hard, stern land where all things had to be conquered and nothing yielded of itself, where, moreover, human life was cheap and of small account. He was alert, always in training, cheeks thin, neck sinewy, knees ready instantly to turn a horse by grip alone, the reins unnecessary so that both hands were free to fight. The eyes were keen and dark, moustache clipped very short and partly grizzled; deep furrows marked the jaw and forehead; but the muscular hands were young, the fling of the shoulders young, the toss and set of the big head young as well. And he always dressed in riding breeches, with a strap about the waist instead of braces. You might see him hitch them up as he stepped back to leap the stream, or to take the pine knolls with a run downhill.

Indeed, the imaginative side of him seemed almost incongruous; and that such a figure could conceal a mystical, tenderly poetic side not one man in a thousand need have guessed. But, in spite of these severer traits, the character, you felt, was tender enough upon its underside. It was merely that the control of the body and emotions acquired in the wilds had never been unlearned, and that no amount of softer living could let it be forgotten.

About the rather grim and over-silent mouth, for instance, there were marks like the touches of a flower that sometimes made the sternness seem a clumsy mask. An intuitive woman, or a child, must have found him out at once.

After years spent as he had spent them among the conditions of primitive lands, Dick Eliot came back with his 'uncivilised' wife, to find that with the old established values of English 'County' existence they had little or nothing in common. Their ostracism by the neighbourhood has no place in this story, except to show how it threw them back intensely into the little property he had inherited. They lived there a dozen years, isolated, childless, knowing that solitude in a crowd which yet is never loneliness.

The 'Place,' as they always called it, took them, and welcome, to itself. The land, running to several hundred acres, was comparatively worthless, mere jumbled stretch of sand and pines and heathery hills; too remote from any building centre to be easily sold, and of no avail for agricultural purposes. For which, since he had just enough to live on quietly, both were grateful: they could keep it lovely and unspoilt. All round it, however, was an opulent, over-built-upon country that they loathed, since they felt that its quality, once admitted, would cause the Place to wither and die. The gross surfeit of prosperous houses, preserved woods, motoring hotels, and the rest would settle on its virgin face. Builders and business men would commercially appraise it, financiers undress it publicly so that it would know itself naked and ashamed. Deep down its soul would turn weakly and diseased, then disappear, and their own assuredly go with it.

For both had loved the Place at sight. She in particular loved it—with a kind of rude enthusiasm she forced, as it were, upon his gentler character. Its combination of qualities fascinated her—the old-world mellowness with the unkempt, untidy wildness. The way it kept alive that touch of the wilderness she had known from childhood, set in the midst of so much over-civilised country all about, gave her the feeling of having a little, precious secret world entirely to herself. She forced this view with all the vigour of her primitive poetry upon her husband till he accepted it as his own. It became his own; only she realised it more vitally than he did. The contrast laid a spell upon her, and she would not hear of going away. They lived there, in this miniature world, until they knew it with such close intimacy that it became identified with their very selves. She made him see it through her eyes, so that the place was haunted, saturated, invested with their moods of worship, love, and wonder. It became a little mystery-world that their feelings had turned living.

★★★★★★★★★★★★

Thus when, after twelve years' happiness together, she died there, he stayed on, sole guardian as it were of all she had loved so dearly. Too vital a man to permit the slightest morbid growth which comes from brooding, he yet lived among fond memories, aware of her presence in every nook and glade, in every tree, her voice in the tinkle of the stream, new values everywhere. Each ridge and valley, made familiar by her step and perfume, strengthened recollection, and more than ever before the Place seemed interwoven with herself and him, subtle expression of vanished joys.

The Past stayed on in it; it did not move away; it remained the Present. Her death had doubly consecrated the little estate, making it, so to speak, a sacrament of dear communion. The only change, it seemed, was that he identified it with her being more than with himself or with the two of them. He guarded it unspoilt and sweet because of her who held it once so dear—as another man might have kept a flower she had touched, a picture, or a dress that she had worn. Now it was doubly safe from the damage she had feared—commercial spoliation.

'Keep the Place as it is, Dick,' she had so often said with a vehemence that belonged to her vigorous type, 'I'd hate to see it dirtied!' For her the civilised country round had always been 'dirty.' And he did so, almost with the feeling that he was keeping her person clean at the same time; for what a man thinks about is real, and he had come to regard the Place and herself as one.

Throwing himself into definite work to occupy his mind, he kept it as the apple of his eye, living in solitude, and cared for only by a motherly old housekeeper (years ago his mother's maid) whose services he had by fortunate chance secured. He spent his leisure time in writing—studies of obscure periods in forgotten history that, when published, merely added to the clutter of the world's huge mental lumber-room, to judge by the reviews. Once he made a journey to his haunts of youth, *their* youth, in Arizona, but only to return dissatisfied, with added pain. He settled down finally then, throwing himself with commendable energy into his studies, till the hurrying years brought him thus to forty-five.

Rarely he went to London and pored over musty volumes in the British Museum Reading-room, but after a day or two would hear the murmur of the mill-wheel singing round that portentous, dreary dome, and back he would come again, post-haste. And perhaps he chose his line of study, rather than more imaginative work, because it reasonably absorbed him, while yet it stole no single emotion from his past with her, nor trespassed upon the walking of one dear faint ghost.

3

And it was upon this gentle, solitary household that suddenly Mánya Petrovski descended with her presence of wonder and of magic. Out of a clear blue sky she dropped upon him and made herself deliciously at home. Only daughter of his widowed sister, married to a Russian, she was fourteen at the time of her mother's death; and the duty seemed forced upon him with a conviction that admitted of no denial. He had never seen the child in his life, for she was born in the year that he returned to England, family relations simply non-existent; but he had heard of her, partly from Mrs. Coove, his housekeeper, and partly from tentative letters his sister wrote from time to time, aiming at reconciliation.

He only knew that she was backward to the verge of being stupid, that she 'loved Nature and life out of doors,' and that she shared with her strange father a certain sulking moodiness that seemed to have been so strong in his own half-civilised Slav temperament. He also remembered that her mother, a curious mixture of puritanism and weakly dread of living, had brought her up strictly in the manufacturing city of the midlands where they dwelt 'wealthily,' surrounded by an atmosphere of artificiality that he deemed almost criminal.

For his sister, fostering old-fashioned religious tendencies, believed that a visible Satan haunted the frontiers of her narrow orthodoxy, and would devour Mánya as soon as look at her once she strayed outside. She too had claimed, he remembered, to love Nature, though her love of it consisted solely in looking cleverly out of windows at passing scenery she need never bother herself to reach. Her husband's violent tempers she had likewise ascribed to his possession by a devil, if not by *the*—her own personal—devil himself.

And when this letter, written on her death-bed, came begging him, as the only possible relative, to take charge of the child, he accepted it, as his character was, unflinchingly, yet with the greatest possible reluctance. Significant, too, of his character was the detail that, out of many others surely far more important, first haunted him: 'She'll love Nature (by which he meant the Place) in the way her mother did—artificially. We shan't get on a bit!'—thus, instinctively, betraying what lay nearest to his heart.

None the less, he accepted the position without hesitation. There

194

was no money; his sister's property was found to be mortgaged several times above its realisable value, and the child would come to him without a penny. He went headlong at the problem, as at so many other duties that had faced him—puzzling, awkward duties—with a kind of blundering delicacy native to his blood. 'Got to be done, no good dreaming about it,' he said to himself within a few hours of receiving the letter; and when a little later the telegram came announcing his sister's death, he added shortly with a grim expression, 'Here goes, then!' In this plucky, yet not really impulsive decisiveness, the layer of character acquired in Arizona asserted itself. Action ousted dreaming.

And in due course the preparations for the girl's reception were concluded. She would make the journey south alone, and Mrs. Coove would meet her. Moreover, evidence to himself at least of true welcome, Mánya should have the bedroom which had been for years unoccupied—his wife's.

For all that, he dreaded her arrival unspeakably. 'She'll be bored here. She'll dislike the Place—perhaps hate it. And I shall dislike her too.'

<h1 style="text-align:center">4</h1>

Eliot ruled his little household well, because he ruled himself. No one, from the tri-weekly gardener to the rough half-breed Westerner who managed the modest stable, felt the least desire to trifle with him. Even Mrs. Coove, in the brief morning visits to his study, did not care about asking him to repeat some sentence that she had not quite caught or understood. Yet, in a sense, as with all such men, it was the woman who really managed him. 'Mrs.' Coove, big, motherly, spinster, divined the child beneath the grim exterior, and simply played with him. She it was who really 'ran' the household, relieving him of all domestic worries, and she it was, had he fallen ill—which, even for a day, he never did—who would have nursed him into health again with such tactfully concealed devotion that, while loving the nursing, he would never have guessed the devotion.

So, it was largely upon Mrs. Coove that he secretly relied to welcome, manage, and look after his little orphaned niece, while, of course, pretending that he did it all himself.

'She'll want a companion, sir, of sorts—if I may make so bold—someone to play with,' she told him when he had mentioned that later, of course, he would provide a 'governess or something' when he had first 'sized up' the child.

He looked hard at her for a moment. He realised her meaning, that the hostile neighbourhood could be relied on to supply nothing of that kind.

'Of course,' he said, as though he had thought of it himself.

'She'll love the pony, sir, if she ain't one of the booky sort, which I seem to remember she ain't,' added Mrs. Coove, looking as usual as though just about to burst into tears. For her motherly face wore a lachrymose expression that was utterly deceptive. Her contempt for books, too, and writing folk was never quite successfully concealed.

In silence he watched the old woman wipe her moist hands upon a black apron, and the perplexities of his new duties grew visibly before his eyes. She had little notion that secretly her master stood a little in awe of her superior domestic knowledge.

'The pony and the woods,' he suggested briefly.

'A puppy or a kitten, sir, would help a bit—for indoors, if I may make so bold,' the housekeeper ventured, with a passing gulp at her own audacity; 'and out of doors, sir, as you say, maybe she'll be 'appy enough. Her pore mother taught—'

The long breath she had taken for this sentence she meant to use to the last gasp if possible. But her master cut her short.

'Miss Mánya arrives at six,' he said, turning to his books and papers. 'The dog-cart, with you in it, to meet her—please.' The 'please' was added because he knew her vivid dislike of being too high from the ground, while judging correctly that the pleasure would more than compensate her for this risk of elevation. It was also intended to convey that he appreciated her help, but deplored her wordiness. Laconic even to surliness himself, he disliked long phrases. It was a perpetual wonder to him why even lazy people who detested effort would always use a dozen words where two were more effective.

So Mrs. Coove, accustomed to his ways, departed, with a curtsey that more than anything else resembled a sudden collapse of the knees beneath more than they could carry comfortably.

'Thank you, sir; I'll see to it all right,' she said, obedient to his glance, beginning the sentence in the room but finishing it in the passage. She looked as though she would weep hopelessly once outside, whereas really, she felt beaming pleasure. The compliment of being sent to meet Miss Mánya made her forget her dread of the elevated, swaying dog-cart, as also of the silent half-breed groom who drove it. Full of importance she went off to make preparations.

And later, when Mrs. Coove was on her way to the station five miles off, dangerously perched, as it seemed to her, in mid-air, he made his way out slowly into the woods, a vague feeling in him that there was something he must say goodbye to. The Place henceforth, with Mánya in it, would be not quite the same. What change would come he could not say, but something of the secrecy, the long-loved tender privacy and wonder would depart. Another would share it with him, a trespasser, in a sense an outsider.

And, as he roamed the little pine-grown vales, the mossy coverts, and the knee-high bracken, there stole into him this queer sensation that it all was part of a living Something that constituted almost a distinct entity. His wife inspired it, but, also, the Place had a personality of its own, apart from the qualities he had read into it. He realised, for the first time, that it too might take an attitude towards the new arrival. Everywhere, it seemed, there was an air of expectant readiness. It was aware. . . . It might possibly resent it.

And, for moments here and there, as he wandered, rose other ideas in him as well, brought for the first time into existence by the thought of the new arrival. This element, like a sudden shaft of sunlight on a landscape, discovered to him a new aspect of the mental picture. It was vague; yet perplexed him not a little. And it was this: that the thing he loved in all this little property, thinking it always as his own, was in reality what *she* had loved in it, the thing that *she* had made him see through the lens of her own more wild, poetic vision. What he was now saying goodbye to, the thing that the expected intruder might change, or even oust, was after all but a phantom memory—the aspect she had built into it.

This curious, painful doubt assailed him for the first time. Was his love and worship of the Place really an individual possession of his own, or had it been all these years but her interpretation of it that he enjoyed vicariously? The thought of Mánya's presence here etched this possibility in sharp relief. Unwelcome, and instantly dismissed, the thought yet obtruded itself—that his feelings had not been quite genuine, quite sincere, and that it was her memory, her so vital vision of the Place he loved rather than the Place itself at first hand.

For the idea that another was on the way to share it stirred the unconscious query: What precisely was it she would share?

And behind it came a still more subtle questioning that he put away almost before it was clearly born: Was he really *quite* content with this unambitious guardianship of the dream-estate, and was the grievance of his exile so completely dead that he would, under all possible conditions, keep its loveliness inviolate and free from spoliation?

The coming of the child, with the new duties involved, and the probable later claims upon his meagre purse, introduced a worldly element that for so long had slept in him. He wondered. The ghosts all walked. But beside them walked other ghosts as well. And this new, strange pain of uncertainty came with them—sinister though exceedingly faint suggestion that he had been worshipping a phantom fastened into his heart by a mind more vigorous than his own.

Ambition, action, practical achievement stirred a little in their sleep.

★★★★★★★★★★★★

And on his way back he picked some bits of heather and bracken, a few larch twigs with little cones upon them, and several sprays of pine. These he carried into the house and up into the child's bedroom, where he stuck them about in pots and vases. The flowers Mrs. Coove had arranged he tossed away. For flowers in a room, or in a house at all, he never liked; they looked unnatural, artificial. Flowers and food together on a table seemed to him as dreadful as the sickly smelling wreaths people loved to put on coffins. But leaves were different; and earth was best of all. In his own room he had two wide, deep boxes of plain earth, watered daily, renewed from time to time, and more sweetly scented than any flowers in the world.

Opening the windows to let in all the sun and air there was, he glanced round him with critical approval. To most the room must have seemed bare enough, yet he had put extra chairs and tables in it, a sofa too, because he thought the child would like them. Personally, he preferred space about him; his own quarters looked positively unfurnished; rooms were cramped enough as it was, and useless upholstery gave him a feeling of oppression. He still clung to essentials; and an empty room, like earth and sky, was fine and dignified.

But Mánya, he well knew, might feel differently, and he sought to anticipate her wishes as best he might. For Mánya came from a big house where the idea was to conceal every inch of empty space with something valuable and useless; and her playground had been gardens smothered among formal flowerbeds—triangles, crescents, circles, anything that parodied Nature—paths cut cleanly to neat patterns, and plants that acknowledged their shame by growing all exactly alike without a trace of individuality.

He moved to the open window, gazing out across the stretch of hill and heathery valley, thick with stately pines. The wind sighed softly past his ears. He heard the murmur of the droning mill-wheel, the drum and tinkle of falling water mingling with it. And the years that had passed since last he stood and looked forth from this window came up close and peered across his shoulder. The Past rose silently beside him and looked out too. . . . He saw it all through other eyes that once had so large a share in fashioning it.

Again, came this singular impression—that, while he waited, the whole Place waited too. It knew that she was coming. Another pair of feet would run upon its face and surface, another voice wake all its little echoes, another mind seek to read its secret and share the mystery of its being.

'If Mánya doesn't like it—!' struck with real pain across his heart. But the thought did not complete itself. Only, into the strong face came a momentary expression of helplessness that sat strangely there. Whether the child would like himself or not seemed a consideration of quite minor importance.

A sound of wheels upon the gravel at the front of the house disturbed his deep reflections, and, shutting the door carefully behind him, he gave one last look round to see that all was right, and then went downstairs to meet her. The sigh that floated through his mind was not allowed to reach the lips; but another expression came up into his face. His lips became compressed, and resolution passed into his eyes. It was the look—and how he would have laughed, perhaps, could he have divined it!—the look of set determination that years ago he wore when in some lonely encampment among the Bad Lands something of danger was reported near.

With a sinking heart he went downstairs to meet his duty.

But in the hall, scattering his formal phrases to the winds, a boyish figure, yet with loose flying hair, ran up against him, then stepped sharply back. There was a moment's pitiless examination.

'Uncle Dick!' he heard, cried softly. 'Is *that* what you're like? But how wonderful!' And he was aware that a pair of penetrating eyes, set wide apart in a grave but eager face, were mercilessly taking him in. It was he who was being 'sized up.' No redskin ever made a more rapid and thorough examination, nor, probably, a more accurate one.

'Oh! I *never* thought you would look so kind and splendid!'

'Me!' he gasped, forgetting every single thing he had planned to say in front of this swift-moving creature who attacked him.

She came close up to him, her voice breathless still but if possible softer, eyes shining like two little lamps.

'I expected—from what Mother said—you'd be—just Uncle

Richard! And instead it's only Uncle—Uncle Dick!'

Here was unaffected sincerity indeed. He had dreaded—he hardly knew why—some simpering sentence of formality, or even tears at being lonely in a strange house. And, in place of either came this sort of cowboy verdict, straight as a blow from the shoulder. It took his breath away. In his heart something turned very soft and yearning. And yet he—winced.

'Nice drive?' he heard his gruff voice asking. For the life of him he could think of nothing else to say. And the answer came with a little peal of breathless laughter, increasing his amazement and confusion.

'I drove all the way. I made the driver let me. And the mothery person held on behind like a bolster. It was glorious.'

At the same moment two strong, quick arms, thin as a lariat, were round his neck. And he was being kissed—once only, though it felt all over his face. She stood on tiptoe to reach him, pulling his head down towards her lips.

'How are you, Uncle, please?'

'Thanks, Mánya,'. he said shortly, straightening up in an effort to keep his balance, 'all right. Glad you are, too. Mrs. Coove, your "mothery person who held on like a bolster," will take you upstairs and wash you. Then food—soon as you like.'

He had not indulged in such a long sentence for years. It increased his bewilderment to hear it. Something ill-regulated had broken loose.

Mrs. Coove, who had watched the scene from the background and doubtless heard the flattering description of herself, moved forward with a mountainous air of possession. Her face as usual seemed to threaten tears, but there was a gleam in her eyes which could only come from the joy of absolute approval. With a movement of her arm that seemed to gather the child in, she went laboriously upstairs. The back of her alone proved to any seeing eye that she had already passed willingly into the state of abject slavery that all instinctive mothers love.

'We shan't be barely five minutes, sir,' she called respectfully when half-way up; and the way she glanced down upon her grim master, who stood still with feet wide apart watching them, spoke further her opinion—and her joy at it—that he too was caught within her toils. 'She'll manage you, sir, if I may make so bold,' was certainly the thought her words did not express.

They vanished round the corner—the heavy tread and the light, pattering step. And he still stood on there, waiting in the hall. A mist rose just before his eyes; he did not see quite clearly. In his heart a surge of strong, deep feeling struggled upwards, but was instantly suppressed. Mánya had said another thing that moved him far more than her childish appreciation of himself, something that stirred him to the depths most strangely.

For, when he asked her how she enjoyed the drive, the girl had replied with undeniable sincerity, looking straight into his eyes:

'The last bit was like a fairytale. Uncle, *how* awfully this place must love you!'

She did not say, 'How you must love the place!' And—she loathed the 'dirty' country all about.

Then, the first rush of excitement over, a sort of shyness, curiously becoming, had settled down all over her like a cloud. It settled down upon himself as well. But—she had said the perfect thing. And his doubts all vanished. It *was*—yes, surely—the Place she loved.

And yet, when all was over, there passed through him an unpleasant afterthought—as though Mánya had applied a test by which already something in himself was found gravely wanting.

5

With its sharp, pine-grown declivities, its tumbling streams, stretches of open heather, and its miniature forests of bracken, the dream-estate was like a Lilliputian Scotland compressed into a few hundred acres. All was in exquisite proportion.

The old house of rough grey stone, set in one corner, looked out upon a wild, untidy garden that melted unobserved into woods of mystery beyond, and farther off rose sharp against the sky a series of peaked knolls and ridges that in certain lights looked like big hills many miles away. There were diminutive fairy valleys you could cross in twenty minutes; and several rivulets, wandering from the moorlands higher up, formed the single stream that once had worked the Mill.

But the Mill, standing a stone's-throw from the study windows, so that he heard the water singing and gurgling almost among his book-shelves, had for a century ground nothing more substantial than sunshine, air, and shadow. For the gold-dust of the stars is too fine for grinding. But it ground as well the dreams of the lonely occupant of the grey-toned house. And he let it stand there, falling gradually into complete decay, because beneath those crumbling wooden walls—he remembered it as of yesterday—the sudden stroke had come that in a moment, dropping as it seemed out of eternity, had robbed him of his chief possession—fashioner of the greatest dream of all. The splash and murmur of the water, the drone of the creaking wheel in flood time, the white weed that gathered thickly over the pond formed by the ancient dam, and the red-brown tint of walls and rotting roof—all were like the colour of the water's singing, the colour of her memory, and the colour of his thinking too, made sweetly visible.

Indeed, despite his best control, *she* still lurked everywhere, so that he could not recall a single experience of the past years without at the same time some vivid aspect of the scenery, as she saw it, rising up clearly to accompany it. In every corner stood the ghost of a still recoverable mood. Here he had suffered, fought, and prayed; here he had loved and hated; here he had lost and found. All the kaleidoscope aspects of growing older, of hopes and fears and disappointments, were visualised for him in terms of the Place where he had met and dealt with them for his soul's good or ill. But behind them always stood that Figure in Chief; it was she who directed the ghostly band; and she it was who coaxed the romantic scenery thus into the support of all his personal moods, and continued to do so with even greater power after she was gone.

His respect for the Place seemed, therefore, involved with his respect for himself and her. That tumbling stream had an inalienable right of way; that mill of golden-brown claimed ancient lights as truly as any mental palace of thoughts within his mind; and the little dips and rises in the woods were as sacred—so he had always felt—as were those twists and turns of character that he called his views of life and his beliefs. This blending of himself with the Place and her had been very carefully reared. The notion that its foundations were not impregnable for ever was a most disturbing one. That the mere arrival of an intruder could shake it, possibly shatter it, touched sacrilege. And for long he suppressed the outrageous notion so successfully that he almost entirely forgot about it.

★★★★★★★★★★★★

This strip of vivid land whereon he dwelt acquired, moreover, a heightened charm from the character of the odious land surrounding it. For on all sides was that type of country best described as over-fed and over-lived-upon. The scenery was choked and smothered unto death; it breathed, if at all, the breath of a fading life pumped through it artificially and with labour. Heavily beneath the skies it lay—acres of inert soil.

There were, indeed, people who admired it, calling it typical of something or other in the south of England; but for him these people, like the land itself, were *bourgeois*, dull, insipid, and phlegmatic as the back of a sheep. Like rooms in a big club, it was over-furnished with too solid upholstery—thick, fat hedges, formal oak woods, lifeless copses stuck upon slopes from which successful crops had sucked long ago the last vestiges of spontaneous life; and spotted with self-satisfied modern cottages, 'improved' beyond redemption, that made him think with laughter of some scattered group of city aldermen. 'They're pompous City magnates,' he used to tell his wife, 'strayed from the safety of Cornhill, and a little frightened by the wind and rain.'

Everywhere, amid bushy trees that looked so pampered they were almost sham, stood 'country houses,' whole crops of them, dozing after heavy meals among gardens of sleek tulip and geraniums. They plastered themselves, with the atmosphere of small Crystal Palaces, upon every available opening, comfortably settled down and weighted with every conceivable modern appliance, and in 'Parks' all cut to measure like children's wooden toys. They stood there, heavy and respectable, living close to the ground, and in them, almost without exception, dwelt successful business men who owned a 'country seat.' From his uncivilised, wild-country point of view, they epitomised the soul of the entire scenery about them—something gross and sluggish that involved stagnation. They brooded with an air of vulgar luxury that was too stupid even to be active. Here 'resided,' in a word, the wealthy.

When he walked or drove through the five miles of opulent ugliness that lay between Mill House and the station, it seemed like crossing an inert stretch of adipose tissue, then lighting suddenly upon a pulsating nerve-centre. To step back into the fresh and hungry beauty of his pine valley, with its tumbling waters and its fragrance of wild loveliness, was an experience he never ceased to take delight in. The air at once turned keen, the trees gave out sharp perfumes, waters rustled, foliage sang. Oh! here was life, activity, and movement. Vital currents flowed through and over it. The grey house among the fir-trees, beckoning to the Mill beyond, was a place where things might happen and pass swiftly. Here was no stagnation possible. Thrills of beauty, denied by that grosser landscape, returned electrically upon the heart. With every breath he drew in wonder and enchantment.

And all this, for some years now, he had enjoyed alone. Rather than diminishing with his middle age, the spell had increased. Then came this sudden question of another's intrusion upon his dream-estate, and he had dreaded painful alteration. The presence of another, most likely stupid, and certainly unsympathetic, must cause a desolating change. Alteration there was bound to be, or at the best a readjustment of values that would steal away the wild and accustomed flavour. He had dreaded the child's arrival unspeakably. It had turned him abruptly timid, and this timidity betrayed the sweetness of the treasure that he guarded. For it came close to fear—the fear men know when they realise an attack they cannot, by any means within their power, hope to defeat.

And alteration, as he apprehended, came; yet not the alteration he had dreaded. Mánya's arrival had been a surprise that was pure joy. Its wonder almost woke suspicion. And the surprise, he found, grew into a series of surprises that at first took his breath away. The alchemy that her little shining presence brought persisted, grew from day to day, till it operated with such augmenting power that it changed himself as well. No stranger fairytale was ever written.

6

Next day he put his work aside and devoted himself whole-heart-edly to the lonely child. It was not only duty now. She had stirred his love and pity from the first. They would get on together. Uncon-sciously, by saying the very thing to win him—'Uncle, *how* the Place must love you!'—she had struck the fundamental tone that made the three of them in harmony, and set the whole place singing. The sense of an intruding trespasser had vanished. The Place accepted her.

It was only later that he realised this completely and in detail, though on looking back he saw clearly that the verdict had been given instantly. For no revision changed it. 'I'm all right here with Uncle,' was the child's quick intuition, meeting his own halfway:— 'We three are all right here together.' For she leaped upon his beloved dream-estate and made it seem twice as wild and living as before. She delighted in its loneliness and mystery. She clapped her hands and laughed, pointed and asked questions, made her eyes round with won-der, and, in a word, put her own feelings from the start into each nook and corner where he took her. There was no shyness, no confusion; she made herself at home with a little air of possession that, instead of irritating as it might have done, was utterly enchanting. It was like the chorus of approval that increases a man's admiration for the woman he has chosen.

She brought her own interpretations, too, yet without destroy-ing his own. They even differed from his own, yet only by showing him points and aspects he had not realised. The child saw things most oddly from another point of view. From the very first she began to say astonishing things. They piqued and puzzled him to the end, these things she said. He felt they unravelled something. In his own mind the personality of the Place and the memory of his wife had become confused and jumbled, as it were.

Mánya's remarks and questions disentangled something. Her child's divination cleared his perceptions with a singular directness. She had strong in her that divine curiosity of children which is as far removed from mere inquisitiveness as gold-dust from a vulgar finished orna-ment. Wonder in her was vital and insatiable, and some of these ques-tions that he could not answer stirred in him, even on that first day of acquaintance, almost the sense of respect.

Morning and afternoon, they spent together in visiting every cor-ner of the woods and valleys; no inch was left without inspection; they followed the stream from the moorlands to the Mill, plunged through the bracken, leaped the high tufts of heather, and scrambled together down the precipitous sandpits. She did not jump as well as he did, but showed equal recklessness. And the depths of shadowy pinewood made her hushed and silent like himself. In her childish way she *felt* the wild charm of it all deeply. Not once did she cry 'How lovely' or 'How wonderful'; but showed her happiness and pleasure by what she did.

'Better than yesterday, eh?' he suggested once, to see what she would answer, yet sure it would be right.

She darted to his side. 'That was all stuffed,' she said, laconically as himself, and making a wry face. And then she added with a grave expression, half anxious and half solemn, 'Fancy, if *that* got in! Oh, Uncle!'

'Couldn't,' he comforted himself and her, delighted secretly.

But it was on their way home to tea in the dusk, feeling as if they had known one another all their lives, so quickly had friendship been cemented, that she said her first genuinely strange thing. For a long time, she had been silent by his side, apparently tired, when suddenly out popped this little criticism that showed her mind was actively working all the time.

'Uncle, you *have* been busy keeping it so safe. I suppose you did most of it at night.'

He started. His own thoughts had been travelling in several direc-tions at once.

'I don't walk in my sleep,' he laughed.

'I mean when the stars are shining,' she said. She felt it as delicately as that, then! She felt the dream quality in it. 'I mean, it loves you best when the sun has set and it comes out of its hole,' she added, as he said nothing.

'Mánya, it loves you too—already,' he said gently.

Then came the astonishing thing. The voice was curious; the words seemed to come from a long way off, taking time to reach him. They took time to reach her too, as though another had first whispered them. It almost seemed as though she listened while she said them. A sense of the uncanny touched him here in the shadowy dark wood:

'It's a woman, you see, really, and that's why you're so fond of it. That's why it likes me too, and why I can play with it.'

The amazing judgment gave him pause at once, for he felt no child ought to know or say such things. It savoured of precociousness, even of morbidity, both of which his soul loathed. But reflection brought clearer judgment. The sentence revealed something he had already been very quick to divine, namely, that while the ordinary mind in her was undeveloped, backward, almost stunted, by her bringing up, another part of her was vividly aware. And this other part was taught of Nature; it was the fairy thing that children had the right to know. She stood close to the earth. Landscape and scenery brought her vivid impressions that fairytales, rather stupidly, translate into princes and princesses, ogres, giants, dragons.

Mánya, having been denied the fairy books, personified these impressions after her own fashion. What was it after all but the primitive instinct of early races that turned the moods of Nature into beings, calling them gods, or the instinct of a later day that personified the Supreme, calling it God? He himself had 'felt' in very imaginative moments that bits of scenery, as with trees and even the heavenly bodies, could actually express such differences of temperament, seem positive or negative, almost male or female. And perhaps, in her original, child's fashion, she felt it too.

Then Mánya interrupted his reflections with a further observation that scattered his philosophising like an explosion. Something, as he heard it, came up close and brushed him. It made him start.

'In some places, you see, Uncle, I feel shy all over. But here I could run about naked. I could undress.'

He burst out laughing. Instinctively he felt this was the best thing he could do. A sympathetic answer might have meant too much, yet silence would have made her feel foolish. His laughter turned the idea in her little mind all wholesome and natural.

'Play here to your heart's content, for there's no one to disturb you,' he cried. 'And when I'm too busy,' he added, thinking it a happy inspiration, 'Mrs. Coove can—'

'Oh,' she interrupted like a flash, 'but she's too bulgy. She could never jump like you, for one thing.'

'True.'

'Or play hide-and-seek. She couldn't fit in anywhere. She'd never be able to hide, you see.'

And so, they reached the house, like two friends who had found suddenly a new delight in life, and sat down to an enormous tea, with jam, buttered muffins, and a stodgy indigestible cake straight from the oven. His tea hitherto had consisted of one cup and two pieces of thin bread and butter. But the appetite of twenty-five had come back again.

A new joy of life had come back with it. After so many years of brooding, dreaming, solitary working, he had grown over solemn, the sense of fun and humour atrophying. He had erected barriers between himself and all his kind, hedged himself in too much. The arrival of this child brought new impetus into the enclosure.

Without destroying what imagination had prized so long, she shifted the old values into slightly different keys. Already he caught his thoughts running forward to construct her future—what she might become, how he might help her to develop spiritually and materially—yes, materially as well. His thoughts had hitherto run chiefly backwards.

This need not, indeed could not, involve being unfaithful to the past. But it did mean looking ahead instead of always looking back. It was more wholesome.

Yet what dawned upon him—rather, what chiefly struck him out of his singular observations perhaps, was this: not only that the Place had whole-heartedly accepted her, but that she had instantly established some definite relation with it that was different to his own. It was even deeper, truer, more vital than his own; for it was somehow more natural. It had been discovered, though already there; and it was not, like his own, built up by imaginative emotion. Hence came his notion that she disentangled something; hence the respect he felt for her from the start; hence, too, the original, surprising things she sometimes said.

7

For several days he watched and studied her, while she turned the Place into a private playground of her own with that air of sweet possession that had charmed him from the first. Backward and undeveloped she undeniably was, but, in view of her stupid, artificial bringing up, he understood this easily. Of books and facts, of knowledge taught in school, she was shockingly ignorant. The wrong part of her had been 'forced' at the wrong time; the 'play' side had been denied development, and, while gathering force underground, her little brain had learned by heart, but without real comprehension, things that belonged properly to a later stage. For if ever there was one, here was an elemental being, free of the earth, native of open places, called to the wisdom of the woods. It all had been suppressed in her. She now broke out and loose, bewildered, and a little rampant, wild rather, and over joyful. She revelled like an animal in new-found freedom.

In time she sobered. He led her wisely. Yet often she went too fast for him to follow, and slipped beyond his understanding altogether. For there were gaps in her nature, unfilled openings in her mind, loopholes through which she seemed to escape too easily, perhaps too completely, into her playground, certainly too rapidly for him to catch her up. It was then she said these things that so astonished him, making him feel she was somehow an eldritch soul that saw things, Nature especially, from a point of view he had never reached. Her sight of everything was original. A bird's-eye view he could understand; most primitive folk possessed it, and in his wife, it had been vividly illuminating. But Mánya had not got this bird's-eye view, the sweeping vision that takes in everything at a single glance from above. Her angle was another one, peculiar to herself. Laughing, he thought of it rather as seeing everything from below—a fish's point of view!

Brightness described her best—eyes, skin, teeth, and lips all shone. Yet her manner was subdued, not effervescent, and in it this evidence of depth, a depth he could not always plumb. It was a nature that sparkled, but the sparkle was suppressed; and he loved the sparkle, while loving even more its suppression. It gathered till the point of flame was reached, and it was the possible out-rushing of this potential flame that won his deference, and sometimes stirred his awe. His dread had been considerable, anticipation keen; and the relief was in proportion. Here was a child he could both respect and love; and the sense of responsibility for the little being entrusted to his charge grew very strong indeed.

In due course he supplied a governess, Fräulein Bühlke. She came from the neighbouring town, with her broad, flat German face, framed in flaxen hair that was glossy but not oiled, and smoothed down close to the skull across a shining parting. Mechanically devout, rather fussy, literal in mind, exceedingly worthy and conscientious, her formula was, 'You think that would be wise? Then I try it.' And the 'trying,' which the tone suggested would be delicate, was applied with a blundering directness that defeated its own end.

Her method was thumping rather than insinuating, and her notion of delicacy was to state her meaning heavily, add to it, 'Try to believe that I know best, dear child,' and then conscientiously enforce it. Mánya she understood as little as an okapi, but she was kind, affectionate, and patient; and though Eliot always meant to change her, he never did, for the getting of a suitable governess was more than he and Mrs. Coove could really manage. '*Der liebe Gott weisst alles,*' was the phrase with which she ended all their interviews. And if Mánya's obedience showed a slight contempt, it was a contempt he did not think it wise entirely to check.

For he himself could never scold her. It was impossible. It felt as though he stepped upon a baby. Their relations were those of equals almost, each looking up to the other with respect and wonder. Her schoolroom life became a thing apart. So did the hours in his study. Her walks with the governess and his journeys to the British Museum were mere extensions of the schoolroom and the study. It was when they went out together, roaming about the Place at will, exploring, playing, building fires, and the rest, that their true enjoyment came—enjoyment all the keener because each stuck valiantly to duty first.

Her face, though not exactly pretty, had the charm of some wild intelligence he had never seen before. The nose, slightly tilted, wore a tiny platform at its tip. The mouth was firm, lips exquisitely cut, but it was in the dark, shining eyes that the expression of the soul ran into focus; though at times she knew long periods of silence that seemed almost sullen, when her eyes turned dead and coaly, and she seemed almost gone away from behind them. One day she was old as himself, another a mere baby; something was always escaping the leash and slipping off, then coming back with a rush of some astonishing sentence it had gone to fetch. Her physical appearance sometimes was elusive too, now tall, now short, her little body protean as her little soul.

Like running water, she was all over the house, not laughing much, not exactly gay or cheerful either, but somehow charged to the brim with a mysterious spirit of play—grave, earnest play, yet airy with a consummate mischief sometimes that was the despair of Fräulein Bühlke, who wore an expression then as though, after all, there were things God did not know. Yes, like running water through the rooms and corridors, and tumbling down the stairs behind the kitten or round the skirts of 'bulgy' Mother Coove. Swift and gentle always, yet with force enough to hurt you if you got in her way; almost to sting or slap. Soft, and very girlish to look at, she was really hard as a boy, flexible too as a willow branch, and with a rod of steel laced somewhere invisibly through her tenderness, unsuspected till occasion—rarely—betrayed its presence. It shifted its position too; one never knew where that firmness which is character would crop out and refuse to bend. For then the childishness would vanish. She became imperious as a little natural queen. The half-breed groom had a taste of this latter quality more than once, and afterwards worshipped the ground she walked on. To see them together, she in her dark-grey riding-habit, holding a little whip, and he with his sinister, wild face and half malignant manners, called up some picture of a child and a savage animal she had tamed.

★★★★★★★★★★★★

But the thing Mánya chiefly brought into his garden, and so also into the garden of his thoughts, was this new element of Play. She brought with her, not only the child's make-believe, but the child's conviction, earnestness, and sense of reality.

'Tell me *one* thing,' she had a way of saying, sure preface to something of significant import that she had to ask, accompanied always by a darker expression in the eyes, puzzled or searching and not on any account to be evaded or lightly answered; 'Tell me one thing, Uncle: do these outside things come after us into the house as well?'

'Only when we allow them, or invite them in,' he replied, taking up her mood as seriously as herself, yet knowing her question to be a feint. She knew the true answer better than himself. She wished to see what he would say. Her sly laughter of approval told him that.

'They're already there, though, aren't they?' she whispered, and when he nodded agreement, she added, 'Of course; they're everywhere really all the time. They don't move about as we do.'

But she had often this singular way of seeing things, and saying them, from the original point of view whence she regarded them—from beneath, as it were, topsy-turvy some might call it, almost a little mad, judged by the sheep-like vision of the majority, yet for herself entirely true, consistent, not imagined merely.

Her literal use of words, too, was sometimes vividly illuminating—as though she saw language *directly*, and robbed of the cloak with which familiar use has smothered it. She undressed phrases, making them shine out alone.

'Moping, child?' he asked once, when one of her silent fits had been somewhat prolonged. 'Unhappy?'

'No, Uncle. And I'm *not* moping.'

'What is it, then?'

'*Fräulein* told me I was self-ish, rather.'

'That's all right,' he said to comfort her. 'Be yourself—self-ish—or you're nothing.'

She followed her own thought, perhaps not understanding him quite.

'She said I must put my Self out more for others. Mother used to say it too.'

He turned and stared at her. The little face was very grave.

'Eh?' he asked. 'Put your Self out?'

Mánya nodded, fixing her eyes, half dreamy, upon his own. She had been far away. Now she was coming back.

'So, I'm learning,' she said, her voice coming as from a distance. 'It's *so* funny. But it's not really difficult—a bit. I could teach you, I think, if you'd promise faithfully to practise regularly.'

There was a pause before he asked the next question.

'How d'you do it, child?' came a little gruffly, for he felt queer emotion rising in him.

She shrugged her shoulders.

'Oh, I couldn't tell you *like that*. I could only show you.'

There was a touch of weirdness about the child. It stole into him—a faint sense of eeriness, as though she were letting him see through peepholes into that other world she knew so well.

'Well,' he asked, more gently, 'what happens when you *have* put your Self—er—out? Other things come in, eh?'

'How can I tell?' she answered like a flash. 'I'm out.'

He stared at her, waiting for more. But nothing followed, and a minute later she was as usual, laughing, her brilliant eyes flashing with mischief, and presently went upstairs to get tidy for their evening meal that was something between an early dinner and high tea. Only at the door she paused a second to fling him another of her characteristic phrases:

'I wonder, Uncle. Don't you?' For she certainly knew some natural way, born in her, of moving her Self aside and letting the tide of 'bigger things' sweep in and use her. It was her incommunicable secret.

And he did wonder a good deal. Wonder with him had never faded as with most men. It had often puzzled him why this divine curiosity about everything should disappear with the majority after twenty-five, instead, rather, of steadily increasing the more one knows. Familiarity with those few scattered details the world calls knowledge had never dulled its golden edge for him. Only Mánya, and the things she asked and said, gave it a violent new impetus that was like youth returned.

And her notion of putting one's Self out in order to let other things come in filled him with about as much wonder as he could comfortably hold just then. He dozed over the fire, thinking deeply, wishing that for a single moment he could stand where this child stood, see things from her point of view, learn the geography of the world she lived in. The source of her inspiration was Nature of course. Yet he too stood close to Nature and was full of sympathetic understanding for her mystery and beauty. Did Mánya then stand nearer than himself? Did she, perhaps, dwell inside it, while he examined from the outside only, a mere onlooker, though an appreciative and loving onlooker?

It came to him that things yielded up to her their essential meaning because she saw them from another side, and he recalled an illuminating line of Alice Meynell about a daisy, and how wonderful it must be to see from 'God's side,' even of such a simple thing.

Mánya, moreover, saw everything in some amazing fashion as One. The facts of common knowledge men studied so laboriously in isolated groups were but the jewelled facets that hung glittering upon the enormous flanks of this One. The thought flashed through his mind. He remembered another thing she said, and then another; they began to crowd his brain. 'I never dream because I know it all awake,' she told him once; and only that afternoon, when he asked her why she always stopped and stood straight before him—a habit she had—when he spoke seriously with her, she answered, 'Because I want to see you properly. I must be opposite for that! No one can see their own face, or what's next to them, can they?'

Truth, and a philosophical truth! Of no particular importance, maybe, yet strange for a child to have discovered.

Even her ideas of space were singularly original, direct, unhampered by the terms that smother meaning. 'Up' and 'down' perplexed her; 'left' and 'right' perpetually deceived her; even 'inside' and 'outside,' when she tried to express them, landed her in a chaos of confusion that to most could have seemed only sheer stupidity. She stood, as it were, in some attitude of naked knowledge behind thought, perception unfettered, untaught, in which she knew that space was only a way of talking about something that no one ever really understands. She saw space, felt it rather, in some absolute sense, not yet 'educated' to treat it relatively. She saw everything 'round,' as though her spatial perceptions were all circles. And circles are infinite, eternal.

With Time, too, it was somewhat similar. 'It'll come round again,' she said once, when he chided her for having left something undone earlier in the day; or, 'when I get back to it, Uncle,' in reply to his reminding her of a duty for the following day. To the end she was 'stupid' about telling the time, and until he cured her of it her invariable answer to his question, 'what o'clock it was,' would be the literal truth that it was 'just now, Uncle,' or simply 'now,' as though she saw things from an absolute, and not a relative point of view. She was always saying things to prove it in this curious manner.

And, while it made him sometimes feel uncomfortable in a way he could not quite define, it also increased his attitude of respect towards the secret, mysterious thing she hid so well, though without intending to hide it. She seemed in touch with eternal things more than other children—not merely with a transient expression of them filtered down for normal human comprehension. Some giant thing she certainly knew. She lived it. Death, for instance, was a conception her mind failed to grasp. She could not realise it. People had 'left' or 'gone away,' perhaps, but somehow for her were always '*there*.'

Thus started, his thoughts often travelled far, but always came up with a shock against that big black barrier—the army of the dead. The dead, of course, were always somewhere—if there was survival. But though he had encountered strange phases of the spiritualistic movement in America, he had known nothing to justify the theory of interference from the other side of that black barrier. The deliverances of the mediums brought no conviction. He sometimes wondered, that was all. And in particular he wondered about that member of the great army who had been for years his close and dear companion.

This was natural enough. Could it be that his thought, prolonged and concentrated, formed a prison-house from which escape was difficult? And had his own passionate thinking that ever associated her memory with the Place, detained one soul from farther flight elsewhere? Was this an explanation of that hint Mánya so often brought him—that her presence helped to disentangle, liberate, unravel . . .? Was the Place haunted in this literal sense? . . .

8

Yet, perhaps, after all, the chief change she introduced was this vital resurrection of his sense of play. For Play is eternal, older than the stars, older even than dreams. She taught him afresh things he had already known, but long forgotten or laid aside. And all she knew came first direct from Nature, large and undiluted.

He learned, for instance, the secret of that deep quiet she possessed even in her wildest moments; and how it came from a practice in her mother's house, where all was rush and clamour about worldly 'horrid things'—her practice of lying out at night to watch the stars. But not merely to watch them for a minute. She would watch for hours, following the constellations from the moment they loomed above the horizon till they set again at dawn. She saw them move slowly across the entire sky. For 'mother hurried and fussed' her so, and by doing this she instinctively drew into her curious wild heart the deep delight of feeling that there was lots of room really, and no particular hurry about anything.' Her inspiration was profound, from ancient sources, natural.

And her 'play,' for the same reason, was never foolish. It was creative play. It was the faculty by which the poets and dreamers re-create the world, and thus rejuvenate it. Adam knew it when he named the beasts, and Job, when he made rhymes about taking Leviathan with a hook, and sang his little heart-sweet songs about the conies and the hopping hills. In the wise it never dies, for it is most subtly allied to wisdom, and only the dreamless can divorce it quite. It is the natural, untaught poetry of the soul which laughs and weeps with Nature, knowing itself akin, seeing itself in everything and everything in itself. Mánya in some amazing fashion, not yet educated out of her, knew Nature in herself.

She did naughty things too, as he learned from Mrs. Coove, when he felt obliged to lecture her, but they were invariably typical and explanatory of her close-to-Nature little being. And he understood what she felt so well that his lectures ended in laughter, with her grave defence 'Uncle, you'd have done the same yourself.' Once in particular, after a fortnight of parching drought, when the gush of warm rain came with its welcome, drenching soak, and the child ran out upon the balcony in her nightgown to feel it on her body too—how could he prove her wrong, having felt the same delight himself? 'I was thirsty and dry all over. I *had* to do it,' she explained, puzzled, adding that of course she had changed afterwards and used the rough Turkey towel 'just as you do.'

But other things he did not understand so well; and one of these was her singular habit of imitating the sounds of Nature, with an accuracy, too, that often deceived even himself. The true sounds of Nature are only two—water and wind, with their many variations. And Mánya, by some trick of tone and breath, could reproduce them marvellously.

'It's the way to get close,' she told him when he asked her why, 'the way to get inside. If you get the sound exact, you feel the same as they do, and know their things.' And the cryptic, yet deeply suggestive explanation contained a significant truth that yet just evaded his comprehension. They often played it together in the woods, though he never approached her own astonishing excellence. This, again, stirred something like awe in him; it was a little eerie, almost uncanny, to hear her 'doing trees,' or 'playing wind and water.'

But the strangest of all her odd, original tricks was one that he at length dissuaded her from practising because he felt it stimulated her imagination unwisely, and with too great conviction. It is not easy to describe, and to convey the complete success of the achievement is impossible without seeing the actual results. For she drew invisible things. Her designs, so clumsily done with a butt of pencil, or even the point of her stick in the sand, managed to suggest a meaning that somehow just escaped grasping by the mind.

They made him think of puzzle-pictures that intentionally conceal a face or figure. Vague, fluid shapes that never quite achieved an actual form ran through these scattered tracings. She used points in the scenery to indicate an outline of something other than themselves, yet something they contained and clothed. His eye vainly tried to force into view the picture that he felt lay there hiding within these points.

On a large sheet of paper, she would draw roughly details of the landscape—tops of trees, the Mill roof, a boulder or a stretch of the stream, for instance—and persuade these points to gather the blank space of paper between them into the semblance, the suggestion rather, of some vague figure, always vast and always very much alive. They marked, within their boundaries, an outline of some form that remained continually elusive. Yet the outline thus framed, whichever

215

way you looked at it, even holding the paper upside down, still remained a figure; a figure, moreover, that moved. For the child had a
way of turning the paper round so that the figure had an appearance
of moving independently upon itself. The reality of the whole business was more than striking; and it was when she came to giving these
figures names that she decided to put a stop to it.

★★★★★★★★★★★★

One day another curious thing had happened. He had often
thought about it since, and wondered whether its explanation lay in
mere child's mischief, or in some power of discerning these invisible
Presences that she drew.

They were returning together from a scramble in the gravel-pit
which they pretended was a secret entrance to the centre of the world;
and they were tired. Mánya walked a little in front, as her habit was, so
that she could turn and see him 'opposite' at a moment's notice when
he said an interesting thing. Her red tam-o'-shanter, with the top-
knot off, she carried in her hand, swinging it to and fro. From time
to time, she flicked it out sideways, as though to keep flies away. But
there were no flies, for it was chilly and growing dark. The pines were
thickly planted here, with sudden open spaces.

Their footsteps fell soft and dead upon the needles. And sometimes
she flung her arm out with an imperious, sudden gesture of defiance
that made him feel suspicious and look over his shoulder. For it was
like signing to someone who came close, someone he could not see,
but whose presence was very real to her. The unwelcome conviction
grew upon him. Someone, in the world she knew apart from him, accompanied them.

A few minutes before she had been wild and romping, playing at
'mushrooms' with laughter and excitement. She loved doing this—
whirling round on her toes till her skirts were horizontal, then sinking
with them ballooning round her to the ground, the tam-o'-shanter
pulled down over her entire face so that she looked like a giant toad-
stool with a crimson top. But now she had turned suddenly grave and
silent.

'Uncle!' she exclaimed abruptly, turning sharply to face him, and
using the hushed tone that was always prelude to some startling question, 'tell me *one* thing, please. What would *you* do if—'

She broke off suddenly and sprang swiftly to one side.

'Mánya! if what?—' He did not like the movement; it was so obviously done to avoid something that stood in her way—between

216

them—very close. He almost jumped too. 'I can't tell you anything while you're darting about like a deer-fly. What d'you want to know?' he added with involuntary sharpness.

She stood facing him with her legs astride the path. She stared straight into his eyes. The dusk played tricks with her height, always delusive. It magnified her. She seemed to stand over him, towering up.

'If someone kept walking close beside you under an umbrella,' she whispered earnestly, 'so that the face was hidden and you could never see it what would *you* do?'

'Child! But what a question! The carelessness in his tone was not quite natural. A shiver ran down his back.

She moved closer, so that he felt her breath and saw the gleam of her big, wide-opened eyes.

'Would you knock up the umbrella with a bang,' she whispered, as though afraid she might be overheard, 'or just suddenly stoop and look beneath—catching it that way?'

He stepped aside to pass her, but the child stepped with him, barring his movement of escape. She meant to have her answer.

'Take it by surprise like that, I mean. *Would* you, Uncle?'

He stared blankly at her; the conviction in her voice and manner was disquieting.

'Depends what kind of thing,' he said, seeing his mistake. He tried to banter, and yet at the same time seem serious. But to joke with Mánya in this mood was never very successful. She resented it. And above all he did not want to lose her confidence.

'Depends,' he said slowly, 'whether I felt it friendly or unfriendly; but I *think*—er—I should prefer to knock the brolly up.'

For a moment she appeared to weigh the wisdom of his judgment, then instantly rejecting it.

'*I* shouldn't!' she answered like a flash. 'I should suddenly run up and stoop to see. I should catch it that way!'

And, before he could add a word or make a movement to go on, she darted from beside him with a leap like a deer, flew forwards several yards among the trees, stooped suddenly down, then turned her head and face up sideways as though to peer beneath something that spread close to the ground. Her skirts ballooned about her like the mushroom, one hand supporting her on the earth, while the other, holding the tam-o'-shanter, shaded her eyes.

'Oh! oh!' she cried the next instant, standing bolt upright again, 'it's a whole lot! And they've all gone like lightning—gone off there!' She pointed all about her—into the sky, towards the moors, back to the forest, even down into the earth—a curious sweeping gesture; then hid her face behind both hands and came slowly to his side again.

'It wasn't one, Uncle. It was a lot!' she whispered through her fingers. Then she dropped her hands as a new explanation flashed into her. 'But p'raps, after all, it was only one! Oh, Uncle, I do believe it *was* only one. Just fancy—how awfully splendid! I wonder!'

Neither the hour nor the place seemed to him suitable for such a discussion. He put his arm round her and hurried out of the wood. He put the woods behind them, like a protective barrier; for his sake as well as hers; that much he clearly realised. He somehow made a shield of them.

In the garden, with the stars peeping through thin clouds, and the lights of the windows beckoning in front, he turned and said laughing, quickening his pace at the same time:

'Rabbits, Mánya, rabbits! All the rabbits here use brollies, and the bunnies too.' It was the best thing he could think of at the moment. Rather neat he thought it. But her instant answer took the wind out of his sham sails.

'That's just the name for them!' she cried, clapping her hands softly with delight. 'Now they needn't hide like that anymore. We'll just pretend they're bunnies, and they'll feel disguised enough.'

They went into the house, and it was comforting to see the figure of Mother Coove filling the entire hall. At least there was no disguising her. But on the steps Mánya halted a moment and gazed up in his face. She stood in front of him, deaf to Mrs. Coove's statements from the rear about wet boots. Her eyes, though shining with excitement, held a puzzled, wild expression.

'Uncle,' she whispered, with sly laughter, standing on tiptoe to kiss him, 'I wonder—!' then flew upstairs to change before he could find a suitable reply.

But he wondered too, wondered what it was the child had seen. For certainly she had seen something.

Yet the thought that finally stayed with him—as after all the other queer adventures they had together—was this unpleasant one, that his so willing acceptance of the little intruder involved the disapproval, even the resentment, of—another. It haunted him. He never could get quite free of it. Another watched, another listened, another—waited. And Mánya knew.

9

Autumn passed into winter, and spring at last came round. The dream-estate was a garden of delight and loveliness, fresh green upon the larches and heather all abloom. The routine of the little household was established, and seemed as if it could never have been otherwise. The relationship between the elderly uncle and his little charge was perfect now, like that between a father and his only daughter, spoilt daughter, perhaps a little, who, knowing her power, yet never took advantage of it. He loved her as his own child; and that evasive 'something' in her which had won his respect from the first still continued to elude him. He never caught it up. It had increased, too, in the long, dark months.

Now, with the lengthening days, it came still more to the front, grown bolder, as though 'spring's sweet trouble in the ground' summoned it forth. This sympathy between her being and the Place had strengthened underground. The disentangling had gone on apace. With the first warm softness of the April days, he woke abruptly to the fact, and faced it. The older memories had been replaced. It seemed to him almost as though his hold upon the Place had weakened. He loved it still, but loved it in some new way. And his conscience pricked him, for conscience had become identified with the trust of guardianship thus self-imposed. He had let something in, and though it was not the taint of outside country *she* had said would 'dirty' it, it yet was alien. It was somehow hostile to the conditions of his original Deed of Trust.

Then, into this little world, dropping like some stray bullet from a distant battle, came with a bang the person of John C. Murdoch. He came for a self-proposed visit of one day, being too 'rushed' to stay an hour longer. Chance had put him 'on the trail' of his old-time 'pard of a hundred camps,' and he couldn't miss looking him up, not 'for all the money you could shake a stick at.' More like a shell than mere bullet he came—explosively and with a kind of tempestuous energy. For his vitality and speed of action were terrific, and he was making money now 'dead easy' so easy, in fact, that it was 'like picking it up in the street.'

'Then you've done well for yourself since those old days in Arizona,' said Eliot, really pleased to see him, for a truer 'partner' in difficult times he had never known; 'and I'm glad to hear it.'

'That's so, Boss'—he had always called the 'Englisher' thus because of his refined speech and manners—'God ain't forgot me, and I've got grubstakes now all over Yurrup. Just raking it in, and if you want a bit, why, name the figger and it's yours.' He glanced round at the modest old-fashioned establishment, judging it evidence of unsuccess.

'What line?' asked Eliot, dropping into the long-forgotten lingo.

'Why, patents, bless your heart,' was the reply. 'They come to me as easy as mother's milk to baby, and if the heart don't wither in me first, I'll patent everything in sight. I'll patent the earth itself before I'm done.'

And for a whole hour, smoking one strong green cigar upon another, he gave brief and picturesque descriptions of his various enterprises, with such energy and gusto, moreover, that there woke in Eliot something of the lust of battle he had known in the wild, early days, something of his zest for making a fortune, something too of the old bitter grievance—in a word, the spirit of action, eager strife and keen achievement, which never had quite gone to sleep. . . .

'And now,' said Murdoch at length, 'tell me about yerself. You look fit and lively. You've had enough of my chin-music. Made yer pile and retired too? Isn't that it? Only you still like things kind o' modest and camp-like. Is that so?'

But Eliot found it difficult to tell. This side of him that life in England had revived, to the almost complete burial of the other, was one that Murdoch would not understand. For one thing, Murdoch had never seen it in his friend; the Arizona days had kept it deeply hidden. He listened with a kind of tolerant pity, while Eliot found himself giving the desired information almost in a tone of apology.

'Every man to his liking,' the Westerner cut him short when he had heard less than half of the stammering tale, 'and your line ain't mine, I see. I'm no shadow-chaser—never was. You've changed a lot. Why'—looking round at the little pine-clad valley—'I should think you'd rot to death in this place. There's not room to pitch a camp or feed a horse. I'd choke for want of air.' And he lit another cigar and spat neatly across ten feet of lawn.

John Casanova Murdoch—in the West he was called 'John Cass,' or just 'John C.,' but had resurrected the middle name for the benefit of Yurrup—was a man of parts and character, tried courage, and unfailing in his friendship. 'Straight as you make 'em' was the verdict of the primitive country where a man's essential qualities are soon recognised, 'and without no frills.' And Eliot, whatever he may have thought, felt no resentment. He remembered the rough man's kindness to him when he had been a tenderfoot in more than one awkward place. John C. might 'rot to death' in this place, and might think the vulgar country round it 'great stuff,' but for all that his host liked to see and hear him. He remembered his skill as a mining prospector and an engineer; he was not surprised that he had at last 'struck oil.'

They talked of many things, but the visitor always brought the conversations round to his two great healthy ambitions, now on the way to full satisfaction: money and power. Upon some chance mention of religion, he waved his hand impatiently with enough vigour to knock a man down, and said, 'Religion! Hell! I only discuss facts.' And his definition of a 'fact' would no doubt have been a dollar bill, a mining 'proposition,' or a food-problem—some scheme by which John C. could make a bit. Yet though he placed religion among the fantasies, he lived it in his way. He ranked the Pope with Barnum, each of them 'biggest in his own line of goods,' and 'Shakespeare was right enough, but might have made it shorter.'

And Eliot, listening, felt the buried portion of his nature waken and revive. It caused him acute discomfort.

'Now show me round the little hole a bit,' said Murdoch just before he left. 'I'd like to see the damage, just for old times' sake. It won't take above ten minutes if we hustle along.'

They hustled along. Eliot led the way with a curious deep uneasiness he could not quite explain. His heart sank within him. Gladly he would have escaped the painful duty, but Murdoch's vigorous energy constrained him. The whole way he felt ashamed, yet would have felt still more ashamed to have refused. He 'faced the music' as John Casanova Murdoch phrased it, and while doing so, that other music of his visitor's villainous nasal twang cut across the deep-noted murmur of the wind and water like a buzz-saw with a bit of wire trailing against its teeth.

The entire journey occupied but half an hour, for Eliot made short-cuts, instinctively avoiding certain places, and the whole time Murdoch talked. His business, practical soul expanded with good nature. 'The place ain't so bad, if you worked it up a bit,' he said, striking a match on the wall of the mill, and spitting into the clear water, 'but it's not much bigger than a chicken-run at present. If I was you, Boss, I'd have it cleaned up first.' Again, he offered a cheque, thinking the unkempt appearance due to want of means. His uninvited opinions were freely offered, as willingly as he would have given money if his old 'pard' had needed it; given kindly too, without the least desire to wound.

He picked out the prettiest 'building sites,' and explained where an artificial lake could be made 'as easy as rolling off a log.' His patent wire would fence the gardens off 'and no one ever see it'; and his special concrete paving, from waste material that yielded a hundred *per cent* profit, would make paths 'so neat and pretty you could dance to heaven on 'em.' The place might be developed so as to 'knock the stuffing' out of the country round about, and the estate become a 'puffect picture-book.'

'You've got a gold mine here, and God never meant a gold mine to lie unnoticed like a roadside ditch. Only you'll need to gladden it up a bit first. You could make it hum as a picnic or amusement resort for the town people. Take it from me, Boss. It's so.'

And the effect upon Eliot as he listened was curious; it was two-fold. For while at first the chatter wounded him like insults aimed directly at the dead, at the same time, to his deep disgust, it stirred all his former love of practical, energetic action. The old lust and fever to be up and doing, helping the world go round, making money and worldly position, woke more and more, as Murdoch's vigorous, crude personality stung his will, stung also desires he thought for ever dead. It made him angry to find that they were not dead, and yet he felt that he was feeble not to resent the gross invasion, even cowardly not to resist the coarse attack and kick the vulgar intruder out. It was like a breach of trust to take it all so meekly without protesting, or at least without stating forcibly his position, as though he were not sufficiently sure of himself to protect his memories and his dead.

But this was the truth: he was not sure of himself. The blinding light of this simple fellow's mind showed up the hidden inequalities to himself. Another discovered his essential instability to himself. This other side of him had existed all the time; and his attachment to the Place was partly artificial, built up largely by the vigorous assertion of the departed. His love had coloured it wonderfully all these years, but—it was a love that had undergone a change. It had not faded, but grown otherwise. Another kind of love had to some extent replaced and weakened it. He felt mortified, ashamed, but more, he felt uneasy too.

The wrench was pain. 'If only she were here and I could explain it to her,' ran his thought over and over again, followed by the feeling that perhaps she was there, listening to it all—and judging him.

Behind the trees, a little distance away, he saw the flitting figure of Mánya, watching them as they passed noisily along the pathways of her secret playground. Her attitude even at this distance expressed resentment. He imagined her indignant eyes. But, closer than that, another watched and followed, listened and disapproved—that other whom she knew yet never spoke about, who was in league with her, and seemed more and more to him, like a phantom risen from the dead.

With difficulty, and with an uneasiness growing every minute now, he gave his attention to his talkative, well-meaning, though almost offensive guest, at once insufferable yet welcome. One moment he saw him in his camping-kit of twenty years ago, with big sombrero and pistols in his belt, and the next as he was today, reeking of luxury and money, in a London black tail-coat, white Homburg hat, diamonds shining on his fingers and in his gaudy speckled tie, his pointed patent-leather boots gleaming insolently through the bracken and heather.

And through his silence crashed a noise of battle that he thought the entire Place must hear. But clear issue to the battle there was none. The opposing sides were matched with such deadly equality. Which was his real self, lay in the balance, until at the last John Casanova unwittingly turned the scales.

It came about so quickly, with such calculated precision, as it were, that Eliot almost felt it had all been prepared beforehand and Murdoch had come down on purpose. It was like a sudden flank attack that swept him from his last defences. Help that could not reach him in the form of Mánya signalled from the distance with her shining eyes, her red tamo'-shanter the banner of reinforcements that arrived too late. For John C. stood triumphantly before him, a conqueror in his last dismantled fortress. His face alight with enthusiasm that was all excitement, he held his hands out towards him, cup-wise.

'See here,' he said with excitement, but in a hard, dry tone that reminded Eliot of prospecting days in Arizona, 'Boss, will you take a look at this, please?'

He had been rooting about in the heather by the edge of the sand-pits. And he thrust his joined hands beneath the other's nose. Something the size of a hen's egg, something that shone a dirty white, lay in them against the thick gold rings. 'Didn't I tell you the place was a gol-darned gold mine? But what's the use o' talking? Will you look at this, now?' He repeated it with the air of a man who has suddenly discovered the secret of the world. The voice was quiet with intense excitement kept hard under.

And Eliot obeyed and looked. He saw his visitor, his Bond Street trousers turned up high enough to show the great muscles of his calves, the Homburg hat tilted across one eye, coat-sleeves pulled up and smeared with a whitish mud. There was perspiration on his forehead. It only needed the sombrero and the pistols to complete the picture of twenty years ago when Cass Murdoch, after weeks of heavy labour, found the first gold-dust in his pan. For John C. *had* found gold. It lay, a dirty lump of white earth, in his large spread hands. Those hands were the pan. The breeze that murmured through the pine trees came, sweet and keen, from leagues of open plain and virgin mountains far away. . . . Eliot smelt the wood-fire smoke of camp . . . heard the crack of the rifle as someone killed the dinner. . . .

'Well, John C.,' he gasped, as he dropped back likewise into the vanished pocket of the years, 'what's your luck? Out with it, man, out with it!'

'A fortune,' replied his visitor. 'Put yer finger on it right now, an' don't tell mother or burst out crying unless yer forced to!' High pleasure was in his voice.

He stepped closer, transferring the lump of dirt into the hand his host unconsciously stretched open to receive it. It lay there a moment, looking even dirtier than before against the more delicate skin. Eliot felt it with finger and thumb. It was soft and sticky and a little moist. It stained the flesh.

Then he looked up and stared into his companion's eyes—blankly. A horrible excitement worked underground in him. But he did not even yet understand.

'You've got it,' observed John C., with dry finality.

'Got what?' asked Eliot.

'Got it right there in yer westkit pocket,' said the other, with an air of supreme satisfaction. His cigar had gone out. He lit it again in leisurely fashion, spat accurately at a distant frond of bracken, eyed the lump of dirt again with inimitable pride, and added, 'Got it without asking; the working soft and easy too; water-power on the spot, and the sea all close and handy for shipping it away.' He made a gesture to indicate the tumbling stream and the sea-coast a few miles beyond.

Then, seeing that his host still stared with blank incomprehension, holding the little lump at arm's length as though it might bite or burn him, he deigned to explain, but with a note of condescending pity in his voice, as of a man explaining to a stupid child.

'Clay,' he said calmly, 'and good stuff at that.'

'Clay,' repeated Eliot, still a little dazed, though light was breaking on him. 'Bricks . . .?' he asked, with a dull sinking of the heart.

'Bricks, nothing!' snapped the other with impatient scorn, as though his friend were still a tenderfoot in Arizona. 'Good, white pottery clay, and soft as a baby's tongue. The best God ever laid down for man. Worth twice its weight in dust. And all to be had for the trouble of shovelling it out. Old pard, you've struck it good and hot this time; and here's my blessing on yer both.'

Eliot dropped the lump his fingers held so long and took half-heartedly the giant hand that squeezed his own. Across his brain ran visions of slender vases, exquisite white cups and bowls and pitchers, plates and sweet-rimmed basins, all fashioned in delicate-toned shades of glaze—beautifully finished pottery—'worth twice their weight in dust.'

10

And half an hour later, when John Casanova Murdoch had boomed away in his luxurious motorcar like a departing thunderstorm, Eliot, coming back by the pinewood that led from the high road, heard a step behind him, and turned to find Mánya's face looking over his very shoulder.

'Uncle, who was that?' There was a touch of indignation in her voice that was almost contempt.

'Man I knew in America—years ago,' he said shortly. He still felt dazed, bewildered. But shame and uneasiness came creeping up as well.

'He won't come again, will he?'

'Not again, Mánya.'

The child took his arm, apparently only half relieved.

'He was like a bit of the dirty country,' she said, and when he interrupted with 'Not quite so bad as that, Mánya,' she asked abruptly with her usual intuition, 'Did he want to buy, or build, or something horrid like that?'

'We haven't met for twenty years,' he said evasively. 'Used to hunt and camp together in America. He went to the goldfields with me.' He was debating all the while whether he should tell her all. He hardly knew what he thought. Like a powerful undertow there drove through the storm of strange emotions the tide of a decision he had already come to. It swept him from all his moorings, though as yet he would not acknowledge it even to himself.

'Uncle,' she cried suddenly, stepping across the path, and looking anxiously into his face, 'tell me one thing: will anything be different?'

And the simple question, or perhaps the eager, wistful expression in her voice and eyes, showed him the truth that there was no evading. He must tell her sometime. Why not now?

He decided to make a clean sweep of it.

'Mánya,' he began gently, 'this Place one day—when I am gone, you know—will be your own. But there'll be no money with it. You'll have very little to live on.'

She said nothing, just listening with a little air of boredom, as though she knew this already, yet felt no special interest in it. It belonged to the world of things she could not realise much. She nodded. They still stood there, face to face.

'I've been anxious, child, for a long time about your future,' he went on, meeting her dark eyes with a distinct effort, for they seemed to read the shame he felt rising in his heart; 'and wondering what I could do to make you safe——'

'I'm safe enough,' she interrupted, tossing her hair back and raising her chin a little.

'But when I'm gone,' he said gravely, 'and Mrs. Coove has gone, and there's no one to look after you. Money's your only friend then.'

She seemed to reflect. She moved aside, and they walked on slowly towards the house.

'That's a long way off, Uncle. I'm not afraid.'

'But it's my duty to provide for you as well as possible,' he said firmly.

And then he told her bluntly and in as few words as possible of the discovery of the clay.

The excitement at first in the child was so great that nothing would satisfy her but that they should at once turn back and see the place together. They did so, while he explained how 'Mr. Murdoch,' who was learned in *strata*, their depth and dip and outcrop, had declared that this deposit of fine white clay was very large. Its spread below the heather-roots might be tremendous. 'My aunt,' he said, 'your great-aunt Julia, lived all her life upon a gold mine here without knowing it, poor as a church mouse.'

This particularly thrilled her. 'How funny that she never *felt* it!' was her curious verdict. 'Was she *very* deaf?'

'Stone deaf, yes,' he replied, laughing, 'and short-sighted too.'

'Ah!' said the child, as though things were thus explained. 'But she might have digged!'

She ran among the heather when he showed her the place, found lumps of clay, played ball with them and was wildly delighted. She treated the great discovery as a game; then as a splendid secret 'just between us two.' Mr. Murdoch wouldn't tell, would he? That seemed the only danger that she saw—at first.

But her uncle knew quite well that this excitement was all false; and far from reassuring him, it merely delayed the deeper verdict that was bound to come with full comprehension. All the discovery involved had not reached her brain. As yet she realised only the novelty, the mystery, the wonder. The spot, moreover, where the great deposit showed its lip was beside the loveliest part of all the wood, and just where the child most loved to play.

At last, then, as her body grew tired and the excitement brought the natural physical reaction, he saw the change begin. She paused and looked about her half suspiciously, like an animal that suspects a trap. Her glance ran questioningly to where her uncle leaned, watching her, against a tree. She eyed him. He thought she suddenly looked different, though wherein the difference lay escaped him. He felt as if he were watching a wild animal, only half tamed, that distrusts its owner, and would next deny his mastership and wait its opportunity to spring. The simile, he knew, was exaggerated, but the picture rose within him none the less. Misgiving and uneasiness grew apace.

Abruptly Mánya stopped her wild playing and with the movement of a little panther ran towards him. She took up a position, as usual, directly opposite. With the strange air of dignity that sometimes clothed her, the figure of the child stood there among the darkening trees and asked him questions, keen, searching questions. He was grateful for the shadows, though he felt they did not screen his face from her piercing sight; but it was her imperious manner above all that made his defence seem so clumsily insincere, and the questions a veritable inquisition.

Before the flood of them, as before their pitiless scrutiny, he certainly quailed. Their keen directness convicted him almost of treachery, and he was hard put to it to persuade her and himself that it really was a sense of duty he obeyed in this decision to work the clay. 'I'm doing it all for her,' he repeated again and again to himself, and loathed, with a dash of terror, that curious sudden drive, as of a blow from outside, that sent his tongue into his cheek.

But the terror, he dimly divined, was due to another feeling as well, equally vague yet equally persistent. For it seemed that while she listened to his explanations, another listened in the darkness too.

Her resentment and distress he realised vividly; but he felt also the resentment and distress—of another. And more than once, during this strange dialogue in the darkening wood, he knew the horrible sensation that this 'other' had come very close, so close as to slip between himself and the child. Almost—that the child was being used as the instrument to express the vehement protest . . .!

But he faced the music, to use the lingo of John C., and spared himself nothing. He told Mánya, though briefly, that workmen must swarm all through her secret playground, that machinery must grind and boom across the haunted valleys, that the water of her little stream must yield the power to turn great ugly wheels, and that perhaps even a little railway might be built to convey the loads of precious clay down to the sea where steamers would call for them. Acres of trees, too, would be swept away, and heather-land marred and scarred with pits and ditches and quarries. But the benefits in time would all be hers. He put it purposely at its worst, while emphasising as best he could the interest and excitement that must accompany the developments. The dream of many years was nevertheless shattered into bits in half an hour.

The child listened and understood. He was relieved, if puzzled at the same time, that she betrayed no emotion of disappointment or indignation. What she felt she dealt with in her own way—inside. At the stream, however, on her way home, she paused a moment, watching it slip through the darkness underneath the old mill-wheel.

'It won't run any more—for itself,' she said in a low, trembling little voice, that was infinitely pathetic.

'No; but it will run for you, Mánya,' he answered, though the words had not been addressed really to him; 'working away busily for your future.'

And then she burst into tears and hid her face against his coat. He found no further thing to say. He walked beside her, feeling like a criminal found out.

But at the end, as they neared the house side by side, she suddenly turned and asked another question that caused him a thrill of vivid surprise and discomfort—so vivid, in fact, that it was fear.

They were standing just beneath *her* bedroom window then. Memory rushed back upon him with overwhelming force, and he glanced up instinctively at the empty panes of glass. It was almost as though he expected to see a face looking reproachfully down upon him. Through him like spears of ice, as he heard the words, there shot again the atrocious sensation that it was not Mánya, the child, who asked the question, but that Other who had recently moved so close. For behind the tone, with no great effort to conceal it either, trailed a new accent that Mánya never used. Greater than resentment, it was anger, and within the anger lay the touch of a yet stronger note—the note of judgment.

'But, tell me one thing, Uncle,' she asked in a whispering voice: will the Place let you?'

11

Motive, especially in complex natures, is often beyond reach of accurate discovery, and a mixed motive may prove quite impossible of complete disentanglement. But for the sense of shame that Eliot felt, he might never have discerned that with his genuine desire to provide for Mánya's future there was also involved a secret satisfaction that he himself would profit too. The sight of gold demolishes pretence and artifice; and deep within he felt the old lust of possession and acquisition assert itself. All these years it had been buried, not destroyed. His love of the Place, his worship of Memory, his guardianship of the little dream-estate, compared to the prize of worldly treasure, were on the surface. They were artificial.

This little thing had proved it. The child's tears, her significant question above all, had shown him to himself. If not, whence came this sense of ignominy before her own purer passion, the loss of confidence, this inner quailing before Another who gazed reprovingly, resentfully, upon him from the shadows of the past? That note of menace in Mánya's suggestive question was surely not her own. It haunted him. Day and night, he heard it ringing in his brain. This new distrust of himself that he recognised read into it something almost vindictive and revengeful.

But Eliot, for all that, was not the man to give in easily. He resolutely dismissed this birth of morbid fancy. Clinging to the thought that his duty to his niece came first, he resisted the suggestion that imputed a grosser selfishness. Cass Murdoch, too, unwittingly helped; for the side of his character John C.'s visit had revived—the love of fight and energetic action—came valiantly to the rescue. To a great extent he persuaded himself that his motive was—almost entirely—a pure one. Preparations for developing the clay went forward steadily.

Mánya too appeared to help him. She said no more distressing things; she showed keen interest in the coming and going of surveyors, architects, soil experts, and the like.

And Murdoch's discovery was no false alarm; the bed of clay was deep and extensive as he prophesied, its quality very fine. Men came with pick and shovel; sample pits were dug; the stuff was tested and judged excellent; and the verdict of the manufacturers, to whom 'lots' were forwarded on approval, pronounced it admirable for a large and ready market. There was money in it, and the supply would last for years. The papers heralded the fortunate discoverer, and a moderate fortune undeniably was in sight.

The preparations, however, took time, and the finding of the initial capital, which Murdoch readily supplied, also took time, and spring meanwhile slipped into summer before the enterprise was fairly on its feet. Soft winds sighed lazily among the larches, and the scent of flowers pervaded every valley; the pine-trees basked in the sunshine, the pearly water laughed and sang; and at night the moon shot every glade with magic that was like the wings of moths whose flitting scattered everywhere the fine dust of a thousand silvery dreams. The beauty of the little haunted estate leaped into a rich maturity that was utterly enchanting, like wild flowers that are sweetest just before they die.

And over Mánya, too, there passed slowly a mysterious change, for it seemed as if for a time she had been standing still, and now with a sudden leap of beauty passed into the glory of young womanhood. With her short skirts and tumbled hair, her grave and wistful face, swinging idly that red tam-o'shanter from which she was inseparable, he saw her one evening on the lawn outside his study window, and the change flashed into him across the moonlight with a positive shock. The child had suddenly grown up. A barrier stood between them.

But the barrier was not so sudden as it seemed, for, on looking back, he realised the daily, almost imperceptible manner of its growth. Its complete erection he realised now, but he had been aware of it for a long time—ever since his decision to work the clay, in fact. Here was the proof her deceptive silence had concealed. She had felt it too deeply for words, for arguing, for disappointment volubly expressed; but it had struck into the roots of her little being and had changed her from within outwards. It had aged her. Reality had broken in upon her world of play and dream. He had destroyed her childhood at a single blow. She questioned, doubted, and grew old.

But though everyone grows older in identically this way, by sudden leaps, as it were, due to the forcing impulse of some strong emotion, with Mánya it brought no radical alteration. She deepened rather than definitely changed. The sense of wonder did not fade, but ripened. The crude facts of life could never satisfy a nature such as hers, and though she realised them now for the first time, they could not enter to destroy. They drove her more deeply into herself. That is, she dealt with them.

And the change, though he devoted hours of pondering reflection over it, may be summed up briefly enough in so far as it affected himself. There was a difference in their relationship. He stood away from her; while she, on her side, drew nearer to something else that was not himself. With this elusive and mysterious Thing she lived daily. She took sides with it and with the Place, against himself. It went on largely, he felt, behind his back. She grew more and more identified with some active influence that had always been at work in all the wild gardened loveliness of the property, but was now more active than before. Stirred up and roused it was; he could almost imagine it—aggressive. And Mánya, always knowing it at closer quarters than himself, was now in definite league with it. There was opposition in it, though an opposition as yet inactive.

And in the silent watches of the night sometimes, when imagination wove her pictures all unchecked, he again knew the haunting thought close beside his bed: that the mind and hand of the dead were here at work, using the delicate instrument of this rare, sensitive child to convey protest, resentment, warning. Over the little vales, from all the depth of forest, and above the spread of moorland just beyond, there breathed this atmosphere of disapproval.

Mánya, never telling him much, now told him less than before; for he had forfeited the right to know.

If it made him smile a little to notice that she had made Mother Coove lengthen her dresses, it did not make him smile to learn that she still wore her old shorter ones once the darkness fell, or that she now went out to play in her wild corners of the woods chiefly after dusk. For he saw the significance of this simple manoeuvre, and divined its meaning. She felt shy now in the daylight. This new thing in the spirit of the Place had changed it all. She could not be abandoned as before, go naked and undressed as once she graphically put it. The vulgar influence from outside had come in. It stared offensively. It asked questions, leered, turned everything common and unclean.

And she changed from time to time her playground as the workmen drove her out. She moved from place to place, seeking new corners and going farther into the moors and open spots. She followed the stream, for instance, nearer to its source where its waters still ran unstained. And from the neighbourhood of the sample pits that gaped like open sores amid the beauty, she withheld herself completely. Nothing could persuade her to come near them.

Towards himself especially, her attitude was pregnant with suggestion, and though he made full allowance for the phantoms conscience raises, there always remained the certainty that the child, and another with her, watched him sharply from a distance. She was still affectionate and simple, even with a new touch of resigned docility that was very sweet, as though resolved to respect his older worldly wisdom, yet with an air of pity for his great mistake that was half contempt, half condescension. Her silence about the progress of the work made him feel small. It so mercilessly judged him. And, while the dignity he had always recognised in her increased, it seemed now partly borrowed— his imagination leaned more and more towards this unwelcome explanation—from this invisible Companion who overshadowed her.

He felt as though this silence temporarily blocked channels along which something would presently break out with violence and scorn to overwhelm him; till at last he came to regard her as a prisoner regards the foreman of the jury who has formed his verdict and is merely waiting to pronounce it—Guilty. Behind her, as behind the foreman, gathered the composite decision of more than one, and the decision was hostile. It urged her on against him. Opposition accumulated towards positive attack. He dreaded some revelation through the child; and piling guess on guess he felt certain who was this active Influence that sought to use her as its instrument. The dead now, day and night, stood very close beside him.

And meanwhile, things ran far from smoothly with the work itself. Unforeseen difficulties everywhere arose to baffle him. Even Murdoch made oppressive, troublesome conditions about the money that seemed unnecessary, insisting upon details of management with a touch of domineering interference that exasperated. Obstacles rose up automatically, involving, as it were, the very processes of Nature itself. There was a strike that delayed the railway builders for a month, and when they returned the heavy summer rains had washed yards of embankment down again.

Soon afterwards a falling tree killed a workman, and there ensued compensation worries that threatened a law-suit. The clay itself, too, played them sudden tricks, proving faulty the maps the surveyors had drawn; its depths and direction were not as supposed, its angle to the lie of the slope deceptive, so that an extra branch of single line for the trucks became essential. And the money was insufficient; further advances became imperative, and, though readily forthcoming, involved more delay. The spirit of lonely peace and beauty departed from the Place, hiding its injured face among the moorland reaches further up. Obstruction, with turmoil and confusion at its back, rose up on every side to baffle him.

Though the advance was steady enough on the whole, and the difficulties were only such as most similar enterprises encounter, Eliot was conscious more and more of this sense of obstacles deliberately interposed. It all seemed so nicely calculated to cause the maximum of trouble and delay. The interference was so cunningly manoeuvred. He brought all his old energy and force to meet them, but there was ever this curious sense of advised and determined opposition that began to sap his confidence.

'More trouble, sir,' the foreman said one morning, when Eliot went down to view the work, unaccompanied as usual by Mánya. 'There seems no end to it.'

'What is it this time?' He abhorred these conversations now. It always seemed that Another stood behind his shoulder, listening.

'The clay has gone,' was the curious answer. He said it as though it had gone purposely to spite them like a living thing.

'Gone!' he exclaimed incredulously.

'Sunk away, gone deeper than we expected,' was the answer. The man shrugged his shoulders as though something puzzled him. 'A kind of subsidence come in the night,' he added gloomily.

They stared at one another for a full minute with eyes that screened other meanings. Eliot felt a sort of fury rise within him. Somehow the idea of foul play crossed his mind, though instantly rejected as absurd.

'With this loose sandy bottom, and a steep slope that ain't drained properly, you're never very sure of where you are,' said the man at length, feeling his position made some explanation necessary. He seemed to regard the clay as something ever on the move.

'I see,' said Eliot, grateful for a solution that he could apparently accept. They talked of ways and means to circumvent it.

'Queerest job I ever come across, sir,' the foreman muttered, as at length Eliot turned away, pretending not to hear it.

And scenes like this were frequent. Another time it was the white weed—with the pretty little flower Mánya loved to twine about her tam-o'shanter—that had gathered so thickly on the artificial ponds where the water was stored, that it clogged the machinery till the wheels refused to turn; and next, a group of men that quit working without any reasonable excuse—open symptom of a hidden dissatisfaction that had been running underground for weeks. There was something about the job they didn't like. Rumours for a long time had been current—queer, unsubstantiated rumours that those in authority chose to disregard. Superstition hereabouts was rife enough without encouraging it.

Taken altogether, as products of a single hostile influence at work, these difficulties easily assumed in his imaginative mind the importance of a consciously directed opposition. He remembered often now those words of Mánya, the last time she had opened her lips upon the subject. For she had credited the Place with the power of resisting him; only by 'the Place' she now meant this mysterious personal influence that she knew behind it.

Yet he persisted in his consciousness of doing right. His duty to the child was clear; her future was in his charge; and the fact that he meant to leave her everything proved that his motive, or part of it at least, was above suspicion. From John C. he also gathered comfort and support. He had only to imagine him standing by his side, repeating that remark about religion, to feel strong again in his determination. Cass Murdoch recognised no mystery or subtlety anywhere. He discussed only facts.

The consciousness that he was partly traitor none the less remained, and with it the feeling that the very Tradition he had nursed and worshipped all these years was up in arms against him. Mánya, standing closer to Nature than himself, had divined this Tradition and, in some fashion curiously her own, had personified it. And this personification linked on with the dead. His love of the Beauty, and his love of a particular memory he had read into the Place, she had most marvellously disentangled. Both were genuine in him; yet he had suffered them in combination to produce a false and artificial Image existing only in his own imagination. There was conflict in his being. His motive was impure.

Behind them stood the giant, naked thing the child divined that was—Reality. She knew it face to face. What was it? The mere definite question which he permitted himself made him sometimes hesitate and wait, not unwilling to call a halt. He was aware that the child stood ever in the background, waiting her time with that sly laughter of superior knowledge. These obstacles and difficulties were sent as warnings; and while he disregarded them of set purpose, something deep within him paused to question—and while it questioned, trembled. For protest, he seemed to discern, had become resentment, resentment grown into resistance; resistance into hostile opposition, and opposition now, with something horribly like anger at its back, was hinting already at a blank refusal that involved almost—revenge.

Hitherto he had been hindered, impeded, thwarted merely; soon he could be deliberately overruled and stopped. Nature, ever defeating an impure motive, would rise up against him and cry finally No.

'But, Uncle, tell me one thing: will the Place let you?' rang now often through his daily thoughts. He heard it more especially at night. At night, too, when sleep refused him, he surprised himself more than once framing sentences of explanation and defence. They rose automatically. They followed him even into his dreams. 'My duty to the child is plain. How can I help it? If you were here beside me now, would you not also approve?'

For the idea that *she* was beside him grew curiously persuasive, so that he almost expected to see her in the corridors or on the stairs, standing among the trees or waiting for him by the Mill itself where last she drew the breath of life.

And by way of a climax came then Mánya's request to change her room, and his own decision to move himself into the one she vacated. The reason she gave was that the 'trees made such a noise at night' she could not sleep, and since it had three windows, two of which were almost brushed by pine branches, the excuse, though discovered late, seemed natural enough. At any rate he did not press her further. She occupied a room now at the back where a single window gave a view far up into the moors. And, turning out the unnecessary furniture to suit his taste, he moved into the one she had vacated—his wife's.

12

Summer passed in the leisurely, gorgeous way that sometimes marks its passage into autumn, and the work ploughed forward through the sea of difficulties. The conspiracy of obstacles continued. There was progress on the whole, but a progress that seemed to bring success no nearer. The beds of clay, however, were definitely determined now, and their extent and depth fulfilled the most sanguine expectations. The troubles lay with the railway, the men, water, weather, and a dozen things no one could have foreseen. These seemed far-fetched, and yet were natural enough. And they continued—until Eliot, never a man who yielded easily, began to feel he had undertaken more than he could manage. He weakened. The idea came to him that he would sell his interest and leave the development to others.

To retire from the fight and acknowledge himself defeated was a step he could not lightly take. There was a bitterness in the thought that stung his pride and vanity. There was also the fact that if he held on and first established a paying business, he could obtain far more money—for Mánya. Yet he felt somehow that it was from Mánya herself that the suggestion first had come. For the child gave hints in a hundred different ways that he could not possibly misunderstand. They were indirect, unconsciously given, and they followed invariably upon curious little personal accidents that about this time seemed almost a daily occurrence.

And these little accidents, though perfectly natural taken one by one as they occurred, when regarded all together seemed to compose a formidable whole. They pointed an attack almost. The menace he had imagined was becoming aggressive. Someone who knew his habits was playing him tricks. Someone with intimate knowledge of the way he walked and ran and moved laid traps for him. And at each little 'accident' Mánya laughed her strange, sly laughter—precisely as a child who says 'I told you so! You brought it on yourself!' She had expected it, perhaps had seen it coming. And now, to avoid more grave disasters, she wanted him—elsewhere. Her deep affection for him, sinner though he was in her eyes, sought to coax him out of the danger zone.

When he slipped in jumping the stream—he, who was sure-footed as a mountain goat! and turned his ankle; and when the heavy earth, loosened by the rains, rolled down upon him as he climbed the embankment, or when the splinter that entered his hand as he vaulted the fencing near the wharf, led to festering that made him carry his arm in a sling for days—in every case it was the same: the child looked up at him and smiled her curious little smile of one who knew. She was in safety, but he stood in the line of fire. She knew who it was that laid the traps. She saw them being laid. It was always wood, earth, water thus that hurt him and never once an artificial contrivance of man.

'Uncle, it wouldn't happen if you stayed away,' was what she said each time, though never phrased the same. And the obvious statement only just covered another meaning that her words contained. She knew worse things would come, and feared for him. 'There's no good hiding, Uncle Dick, because it's in the house as well.'

He grew to feel unwelcome in his own woods and garden, an intruder in his own moors and valleys, an element the Place rejected and wished elsewhere. The Place had begun to turn him out. And Mánya, this queer mysterious child, in league with the secret Influence at work against him, was being used to point the warnings and convey the messages. Her silent attitude, more even than her actual words, was the messenger. The hints thus brought, moreover, now troubled themselves less and less with disguise. He realised them at last for what they were: and they were beyond equivocation threatening.

And it was at this point that Eliot made the journey up to London to see Cass Murdoch, and feel his way towards escape. Retirement was the word he used, and the sentence John C. heard in the bar of the big hotel as they discussed clay and cocktails was 'sell my interest to more competent hands who will get quicker and bigger results than I can. The work and worry affect my health.'

The interview may be easily imagined, for John Casanova Murdoch was more than willing to buy him out, though the conditions, with one exception, have no special interest in this queer history: Eliot was to lease the Place for a period of years. And this meant leaving it.

In the train on his way back his emotions fought one another in a regular pitched battle. He stood in front of himself suddenly revealed—a traitor. It seemed as if for a moment he saw things a little from his niece's inverted point of view, standing outside of Self and looking up. It provided him with unwelcome sensations that escaped analysis. Love and hate are one and the same force, according to the point in the current where one stands; repulsion becomes, from the opposite end, attraction; and a great love may be reversed into a great hate.

There is no exact dividing line between heat and cold, no neat frontier where pleasure becomes pain, just as there is really no such absolute thing as left and right, uphill and downhill, above and below. Mánya stood outside these relative distinctions men have invented for the common purposes of description. He understood at last that the power which had drawn his life into the Place as by a kind of absorption, was now inverted into a process of turning him out again as by a kind of determined elimination.

It was being accomplished, moreover, as he felt and phrased it to himself, from outside; by which perhaps he meant from beyond that fence which men presumptuously assume to contain all the life there is. But the dead stand also beyond that fence. And Mánya, being so obviously in league with this hostile, eliminating Influence stood hand in hand, therefore, with—the dead.

But for him The Dead meant only one.

13

He walked home from the station, which he reached at nine o'clock. Crossing the zone of the 'dirty' country, now successful invader of the dream-estate, he entered his property at length by the upper end of the Piney Valley. A passionate wind was searching the trees for music, and handfuls of rain were flung against the trunks like stones; but, on leaving the road the tempest seemed to pass out towards the sea, leaving an unexpected, sudden hush about his footsteps. The moon peered down through high, scudding clouds.

It was partly that the storm was breaking up, and partly that the valley provided shelter; but it gave him the feeling that he had entered a little world prepared for his reception. He was expected, the principal figure in it. Attention everywhere focussed on himself. He felt like a prisoner who comes out of streets indifferent to his presence and enters a Court of Law. This ominous silence preceded the arrival of the Judge.

The path at once dipped downwards into a world of shadows where the splashes of moonlight peered up at him like faces on the ground. He heard the water murmuring out of sight; and it came about his ears like whispering from the body of the Court. There reigned, indeed, the same gentle peace and stillness he had known for years, but somewhere in it a brooding unaccustomed element that was certainly neither peace nor stillness. Something unwonted stirred slowly, very grandly, through the darkness.

He paused a moment to listen; he looked about him; he pushed aside the bracken with his stick, and his eyes glanced up among the lower branches of the trees. And everywhere, it seemed, he encountered other eyes—eyes usually veiled, but now with lifted lids. Then he went on again, faster a little than before. A touch of childhood's terror chilled his blood. And it took at first a childhood's form. He thought of some big, savage animal that lurked in hiding, its presence turning the once friendly wood all otherwise and dreadful. A giant paw filled the little valley to the brim. The stir of the wind was the opening and shutting of its claws. The lips were drawn back to show the gums and teeth. Something opened; there came a rush of air. The awful spring would follow in a moment. . . .

Another hood of memory lifted then and showed him Mánya, as

238

she played about the sand-pits—then paused when the full discovery dawned upon her mind. She had eyed him. She had given him this similar impression of an animal waiting its opportunity to spring. But now it was the Place that waited to spring. . . .

He banished the bizarre, exaggerated picture his imagination conjured up, but could not banish the emotion that produced it. The Place *was* different. Change spread all over it. Potential attack hummed through the very air. Thus, might a man feel walking through a hostile crowd. But thus, also might he feel in the presence of a friend to whom in a time of confidence he had betrayed himself too lavishly—a friend now turned against him with this added power of knowing all his secrets. His own imagination leaped upon him, calling him coward, traitor, unfaithful steward.

Fear made him bitterly regret the familiarity that years of unguarded dreaming had established between himself and—and— His mind hesitated horribly between the choice of pronouns; and when he finally chose the neuter, it seemed that a curious running laughter passed within the sounds of wind and water. It almost was like the mockery of Mánya's laughter taken over by the dying storm.

While he evaded the direct attack, his mind, however, continued searching for the word that should describe accurately, and so limit all this vague, distressing feeling of hostility. But for long he could not find it. The new element that breathed through the sombre intricacies of the glen played with him as it pleased until he could catch it in the proper word, and so imprison it. Branches seemed no longer soft and feathery: they bristled, pointed, stood rigid for a blow. The stream no longer murmured: it laughed and cried aloud. The shadows did not cover smoothly: they concealed; and the whole atmosphere of the Place, instead of welcoming, repelled.

And then, quite suddenly, the word emerged and stood before his face: Disturbance.

Less than disorder, yet more than mere disquietude, this word described the attitude he was conscious of. In its aggressive, threatening, sinister meaning, he accepted it as true.

There was Disturbance. Somewhere in those chains of iron that bind the operations of Nature within invariable, unyielding laws, a link had weakened. Disturbance was the result—but a disturbance that somehow let in purpose. Urging everywhere through the manifestations of Nature in his dream-estate was the drive and stress of purposiveness.

The discovery of the word, moreover, announced the approach, though not yet the actual entrance, of the Judge. There were steps, and the steps were in himself. Someone walked upon his life.

★★★★★★★★★★★★

He quickened his pace like a terrified child. With genuine relief at last he reached the house. But even in the friendly building he was aware of this keen discomfort at his heels. It penetrated easily. The Disturbance came in after him into the house itself. Hanging up coat and hat, he then passed into the Study, and the prosaic business of drinking milk and munching water-biscuits scattered the strange illusion for a time. It weakened, at any rate, for it never wholly disappeared. It waited.

The house was silent, everyone in bed. He locked the front door carefully, stared at his face a moment in the hat-stand mirror—wondering at a certain change in the expression of the features, though he could not name it—and with his lighted candle went on tiptoe up to bed. But the instant he entered the room he was aware that the feeling of distress had already preceded him. He was forestalled. There was this dark disquiet in the very atmosphere of his bedroom. The Disturbance had established itself in these most private, intimate quarters that once had been his wife's. It was strongest here.

Dismissing a sharp desire to sleep in another room—anywhere but in the place made sacred by long-worshipped memories—he began to undress. He said to himself with a certain vehemence, 'I'll ignore the thing.' But it was fear that said it. A frightened child without a light might as well determine to ignore the darkness. For this thing was urgent everywhere about him, inside and outside, like the air he breathed. And the next minute, instead of ignoring it, he made an attempt to face it. He would drag the secret out. The fact was, both will and emotions were already in disorder. He knew not how or where to take the thing.

The attempt then showed him another thing. It was no secret. The terror in his heart and conscience made pretence of screening something that he really knew quite well. This aggressive, hostile Presence was a Presence that he recognised, and had recognised all along.

And instinctively he turned to this side and to that, examining the room; for space in this room, he realised, was no longer quite as usual: there was a change in its conditions. Everything contained within it—the very objects between the four walls—were affected. He felt them altered; they had become otherwise. He himself was changed as

240

well, become otherwise. And if anything alive—another person or an animal even—came in, they also, in some undetermined, startling way, would look otherwise than usual. They would look different.

Hurriedly he sought a concrete simile to steady his shaking mind on, and his mind provided this: That, if the temperature were suddenly lowered, the invisible moisture would at once appear, otherwise—frost-crystals on the windowpanes, snow, and so forth. The change would not be untrue or even distorted, no falseness in it anywhere, nor exaggeration—only otherwise. And if the presence of the dead, whom he felt so close now in this room, turned visible owing to the changed conditions of the space about him, he would see—but the thought remained unfinished in his mind . . .

He thrust the terror down into the depths. Yet the idea must have been very insistent in him, for he crossed the floor on tiptoe to lock the door securely, and stood already within easy reach of it, one hand actually stretched out, when there came a faint knocking on the panelling within a few inches of his very face. He saw the handle turn. With suggestive, dreadful stealthiness the door then opened, the merest crack at first, then gradually wider and wider. And the slowness was exasperating. The seconds dragged like hours. Had he not been spellbound he would have violently slammed it to again or torn it instead wide open.

There was just time in his bewildered mind to wonder what form this Presence from the dead would take, when he realised that the figure stood already by his side. She had crossed the threshold. With amazement he saw that it was Mánya.

She came in swiftly. She was on the carpet close against him before he could speak a word or move. And she looked, as he had expected, otherwise: she looked extraordinary. The word came to him in the way she might herself have used it, getting its first meaning out—extra-ordinary.

And her appearance was—might well have been, at least—ludicrous. For she was dressed to go out, but in a fashion that at any other time must have been cause for laughter. Now it stood at the very opposite pole, however. It was superb. Her red tam-o'-shanter was perched carelessly, almost gaily, on her hair, which was already fashioned into plaits for the night, and underneath the garden jacket that he knew so well, he saw white drapery that plainly was her little nightgown. She had pulled her stockings on, but had not fastened them. They hung down, partly showing her skin below the knee. The boots flapped open, with no attempt to button them. Her hurry had been evidently great, and she looked at the first glance like someone surprised by a midnight call of fire.

Yet these details, which he took in at a single glance, stirred no faintest touch of amusement in him, for about her whole presentment was this other nameless quality that showed her to him—utterly otherwise than usual. It made him wince and shudder, yet pause in a wondering amazement too—amazement that barely held back awe. He stared like a man struck suddenly dumb. The phrase the child so often used came back upon him with the force of a shock. The girl had put her Self out. This being that stood just opposite to his face was not Mánya. It was another. It was *the* other!

And both doubt and knowledge dropped down upon him in that fearful moment: knowledge, that it was the Influence she had been so long in league with, and that sought to use her as its instrument of protest; and doubt, as to exactly what—or who—this Influence really was.

For it came to him as being so enormously bigger and vaster than anything his mind could label 'the dead.' He felt in the presence of a multitude. He had once felt thus when seeing a single Redskin steal like a shadow round the camp, knowing that the night concealed a host of others. About her actual form and body, too, this sense of multitude also spread and trembled, only just concealed: and indescribable utterly.

For the edges of the child were ill-defined and misty, so that he could not see exactly where her outline ceased. The candle-light played round and over her as though she filled the room. She might have been all through the air above him, behind as well as opposite, close in front as well. In a sense he felt that she had come to him through the open windows and from the night itself, and not merely along the passage and through the narrow door. She came from the entire Place.

He made a feverish struggling effort to concentrate his mind upon common words. He wanted to move backwards, but his feet refused to stir. The familiar sound of her name he uttered close into her face:—

'Mánya! And at this hour of the night!' he stammered.

His voice was thick and without resonance in his mouth, smothered like a sound in a closed box. And as he heard the name a kind of silent laughter reached him inaudible really, as though inside him—sly laughter like her own. For the name had lost its known familiarity. It, too, was different and otherwise, though for the life of him he could not seize at first wherein the alteration lay.

She smiled, and her eyes, wide opened, were like stars. The breath came soft and windily between her lips, but no words with it. It was regular, deep, unhurried. There was something in her face that petrified him—something, as it were, non-human. He began to forget who and where he was. Identity slipped from him like a dream.

With another effort, this time a more violent one, he strove to fasten upon things that were close and real in life. He felt the buttons down his coat, fingering them desperately till they hurt his hands and escaped from his slippery moist skin.

'Mánya!' he repeated in a louder voice, while his mind plunged out to seek the child he had always known behind the familiar name.

And this time she answered; but to his horror, the whole room, and even space beyond the actual room, seemed to answer with her. The name was repeated by her lips, yet came from the night beyond the open window too. He had made a question of it. The answer, repeating it, was assent.

'Man y-a . . .' he heard all round him, while the head bent gently down and forward.

The shock of it restored to him some power of movement, and he stumbled back a step or two further from her side. It might well have been whimsical and cheap, this artificial play upon a name, but instead of either it was abominably significant. This motionless figure, so close that he could feel her breath upon his face, was positively in some astonishing way more than one. She *was* many. The laughter that lay behind the trivial little thing was a laughter both grand and terrible. It was the laughter of the sea, of the woods, of sand—a host that no man counteth—the laughter of a multitude.

And he thrust out both his hands automatically lest she should touch him. He shook from head to toe. Contact with her person would break up his being into millions. The sensation of terror was both immense and acute, sweeping him beyond himself. Like her, he was becoming many—becoming hundreds and thousands—sand that none can number.

'Child!' he heard his voice repeating faintly, yet with an emphasis that spaced the words apart with slow distinctness, 'what does this mean?' In vain he tried to smother the beseeching note in it that was like a cry for help.

He stepped back another pace. She did not move. Composure then began to come back slowly to him, a little and a little. He remembered who he was, and where he was. He said to himself the commonplace thing: 'This is Mánya, my little niece, and she ought to be asleep in bed.' It sounded ridiculous even in his mind, but he tried deliberately to think of ordinary things.

And then he said it aloud: 'Do you realise where you are and what you are doing, child?' And then he added, gaining courage, a question of authority: 'Do you realise what time it is?'

Her answer came again without hesitation, as from a long way off. A smile lit up the entire face, gleaming from her skin like moonlight. There were tears, he saw, upon the cheeks. But the face itself was radiant, wonderful.

'The time,' she said, peering very softly into his eyes, 'is *now*.' And she took a slow-gliding step towards him, with a movement that frightened him beyond belief.

But by this time, he had himself better in hand. He understood that the child was walking in her sleep. It was her little frame that was being worked and driven by—Another. She was possessed. Something was speaking through the entranced physical body. Her answer regarding time was the answer absolute, not relative, the only true answer that could be given. Other answers would be similar. He understood that here was the long-expected revelation, and that he must question her if he wished to hear it. He resolved to do so, but with a cold awe in his heart as though he were about to question—Death.

They both retained their first positions, three feet apart, standing. The candle behind him on the table shed its flickering light across her altered features. Outside he heard the trees shaking and tossing in the gusts of rainy wind.

'Who are you then?' he asked hesitatingly, in a low tone.

There was no reply. But effort, showing that she heard and tried to answer, traced a little frown above the eyebrows; and the eyes looked puzzled for a moment.

'You mean,' he whispered, 'you cannot tell me?' The head bowed slowly once by way of assent.

'You cannot find the word, the language?' he helped her. 'Is that it?' He still whispered, afraid of his own voice.

'Yes,' was the answer, spoken below the breath. Then instantly afterwards, straightening herself up with a vigorous movement that startled him horribly, she made a curious, rushing gesture of the whole body, spreading her arms out through the air about her. 'I am—*like that!*' the voice sprang out loud and clear.

She seemed by the gesture to gather space and the night into her wide embrace. She repeated it. The face smiled marvellously. Through this slim body, he realised, there rolled something ancient as the stars. It poured through space against him like a sea. It turned his little ideas of space all—otherwise.

'Tell me where you come from,' he asked quickly, eager yet dreading to hear.

'From everywhere,' came the answer like a wind.

He paused, breathless with astonishment. He felt himself dwindling. Here was a vaster thing than he had contemplated. It was surely no single discarnate influence that possessed the child!

'And for whom?' It was whispered as before. The figure stepped with a single gliding stride towards him, coming so close that he held his ground only by a tremendous effort of the will.

'For you!' The voice came like a clap of wind again, at once soft yet thundering, filling the entire room.

'For me,' he faltered. 'Your message is for me?'

He felt the assault of strange, violent sensations he had never known before and could not name. A boyhood's dream rushed back upon him for an instant. He recalled his misery and awe when he stood before the Judgment Throne for some unforgivable breach of trust which he could not explain because the dream concealed its nature. Only this was ten times greater, and his guilt beyond redemption.

'And I,' he stammered, 'who am I?'

Her eyes looked him all over like a stare of the big moon.

'*You*,' she answered, without pause or hesitation.

'You do not know my name?' he insisted, still clinging to the clue that her he spoke with must be from the dead.

The little frown came back between the eyes. She nodded darkly.

'*You*,' she repeated, giving the answer absolute again, the only really true one.

The girl stood like a statue, serene and solemn. She stared through and beyond him, motionless but for a scarcely perceptible swaying, and calm as a meadow in the dawn. Enormous meanings passed from her eyes across the air, and sank down into him like meanings from a forest or a sea.

From these, he realised, came her stupendous inspiration, and, so realising, he knew at last his deep mistake. For not so do the Dead return. They never, indeed, return, because from the heart that loved them, they have never gone away, but only changed their magic intercourse in kind. And, had *she* known, she would have approved the wisdom of his great decision, while clearing his motive of all insincerity at the same time.

It was not *she* who brought the protest and the menace. It was something bigger by far, something awful and untamed. It was the Place itself. And behind the Place stood Nature. It was Nature that possessed the child and used her little lips and hands and body for its thundering message of disapproval.

Mánya was possessed by Nature.

★★★★★★★★★★★★

And the shock of the discovery first turned him into stone. His body did not stir the fraction of an inch. In that moment of vivid realisation these two little human figures stood facing one another, motionless as columns; and, while so standing, the One who brought the Message for himself drew closer.

For several minutes he saw absolutely nothing. The approach was too big for any sensory perceptions he could recognise. And then, mercilessly, pitilessly, the power of sight returned.

He knew the touch of a giant, earthy hand was upon his arm. Beside him, in the flickering candle light, stood Nature. He looked into a host of mighty eyes that yet his imagination translated into merely two—eyes set wide apart beneath enormous brows. He met the gaze of the Gigantic, the Patient, the Inexorable that saw him as he was, and judged him where he stood. And a melting ran through his body, as though the bones slipped from their accustomed places, leaving him utterly without support. He swayed, but did not fall. His physical frame stood upright to receive like a blow the revelation that was coming.

And then, with a curious, deep sense of shame, he realised abruptly that his position in regard to her was inappropriate. He, at any rate, had no right to stand. His proper attitude must be a very different one.

He took her by the hand and, bending his head with an air of humble worship, led her slowly across the room. The touch of her was wonderful—like touching wind—all over him. With a reverence he guided her, all unresisting, to a highbacked chair beside the open window. She lowered herself upon it, and sat upright. She stared fixedly before her into space. No clothing in the world could have stolen from her childish face and figure the nameless air of grandeur that she wore. She was august.

And he knelt before her. He raised his folded hands. A moment his eyes rested on the dispassionate little face, then looked beyond her into the night of wind and rain. His gaze returning then sought the eyes again.

And the child, sweet little human interpreter of so vast a Mystery, bent her head downwards and looked into his heart. Wind stirred the hair upon her neck. He saw the bosom gently rise and fall.

'What is it that you have to say to me?' he whispered, like a prayer for mercy. 'What is the message that you bring?'

Her lips moved very slightly. The smile broke out again like moonlight across the lowered face. The words dropped through the sky. Very slowly, very distinctly, they fell into his open heart: simple as wind or rain.

'Leave—me—as—I—am—and—as—you—found—me. Leave—us—together—as—we—are—and—as—we—were.'

14

There came then a sudden blast that swept with a shout across the night; and through his mind passed also a tumult like a roaring wind. Both winds, it seemed to him, were in the room at once. He had the sensation of being lifted from the earth. The candle was extinguished. And then the sound and terror dipped away again into silence and into distance whence it came. . . .

★★★★★★★★★★★★

He found himself standing stiffly upright, though he had no recollection of rising from his knees. With an abruptness utterly disconcerting he was himself again. No item of memory had faded; he remembered the entire series of events. Only, he was in possession of his normal mind and powers, fear, awe, and wonder all departed. Mánya, who had been walking in her sleep, was sitting close before him in the darkness. He could just distinguish her outline against the open window.

But he was master of himself again. Even the wild improbability, the extravagance of his own actions, the very lunacy of the picture that the night now smothered, left him unbewildered. And the calmness that thus followed the complete transition proved to him that all he had witnessed, all that had happened, had been—true. In no single detail was there falseness or distortion due to the excitement of a hysterical mood. It had been right and inevitable.

He lit the candle again quietly, with a hand that did not tremble.

He saw Mánya sitting on the highbacked chair with her head sunk forward on her breast. Gently he raised the face. The eyes were now closed, and the regular, deep breathing showed that the girl was sound asleep—but with the normal sleep of tired childhood.

The Immensity to which he had knelt and prayed in her was gone, gone from the room, gone out into the open darkness of the Place. It had visited her, it had used her, it had left her. But at the same time, he understood, as by some infallible intuition, that the warning to depart she brought him was not yet complete. It had reached his mind, but not as yet his soul. In its fulness the Notice to Quit could not be delivered between close, narrow walls. Its delivery must be outside.

He looked at the sleeping child in silence for several minutes. She sat there in a semi-collapsed position and in momentary danger of falling from her chair. The lips were parted, the eyes tight shut, the red tam-o'-shanter dropping over one side of the face. Both hands were folded in her lap. By the light of two candles now he watched her, while the perspiration he had not been as yet aware of, dried upon his skin and made him shiver with the cold. And, after long hesitation, he woke her.

With difficulty the girl came to, stared up into his face with a blank expression, rubbed her eyes, and then, with returning consciousness of who and where she was, looked mightily astonished.

'Mánya, child,' he began gently, 'don't be frightened.'

'I'm not,' she said at once. 'But, where am I? Is that you, Uncle?'

'Been walking in your sleep. It's all right. Nothing's happened. Come, I'll see you back to bed again.' And he made a gesture as though to take her hand.

But she avoided him. Still looking bewildered and perplexed, she said:

'Oh—I remember now—I wanted to go out and see things. I want to go out still.' Then she added quickly as the thought struck her, 'But does *Fräulein* know? You haven't told *Fräulein*, Uncle, have you? I mean, you won't?'

He shook his head. This was no time for chiding.

'I often go out like this—at night, when you're all asleep. It's the only time now, since——'

He stopped her instantly at that. 'You fell asleep while dreaming! Was that it?' He tried to laugh a little, but the laughter would not come.

' I suppose so.' She glanced down at her extraordinary garments.

But no smile came to the eyes or lips. Then she looked round her, and gazed for a minute through the open window. The rain had ceased, the wind had died away. Moist, fragrant air stole in with many perfumes. 'I don't remember quite. I was in bed. I had been asleep already, I think. Then—something woke me.' She paused. 'There was something crying in the night.'

'Something crying in the night?' he repeated quickly, half to himself.

She nodded. 'Crying for me,' she explained in a tone that sent a shudder all through him before he could prevent it. 'So, I thought I'd go out and see. Uncle, I *had* to go out,' she added earnestly, still whispering, 'because they were crying—to get at you. And unless *I* brought them—unless they came through me,' she stopped abruptly, her eyes grew moist, she was on the verge of tears—'it would have been so terrible for you, I mean——'

He stiffened as he heard it. He made a violent effort at control, stopping her further explanation.

'And you weren't afraid—to go out like this into the dark?' he asked, more to cover retreat than because he wanted to hear the reply.

'I put myself out for you,' she answered simply. 'I let them come in. That way you couldn't get hurt. In me they had to come gently. They were an army. Only, nothing out of me could hurt you, Uncle.' She suddenly put her arms about his neck and kissed him. 'Oh, Uncle Dick, it was lucky I was there and ready, wasn't it?'

And Eliot, remembering that great Disturbance in the woods, pressed the child tenderly to himself, praying that she might not understand his heart too well, nor feel the cold that made his entire body tremble like a leaf. He had thought of an angry animal Presence lurking in the darkness. It had been bigger than that, and a thousand times more dangerous!

'You see,' she added with a little gasp for breath when he released her, 'they waked me up on purpose. I dressed at an awful rate. I got to the door—I remember that perfectly well—and then——' An expression of bewilderment came into her face again.

'Yes,' he helped her, 'and then—what?'

'Well, I forget exactly; but something stopped me. Something came all round me and took me in their arms. It was like arms of wind. I was lifted up and carried in the air. And after that I forget the rest, forget everything—till now.'

She stopped. She took off her tam-o'-shanter and smoothed her untidy hair back from the forehead. And as he looked a moment at her—this little human organism still vibrating with the passage of a universal Power that had obsessed her, making her far more than merely child, yet still leaving in her the sweetness of her simple love he came to a sudden, bold decision. He would face the thing complete. He would go outside.

'Mánya,' he whispered, looking hard at her, 'would you like to go out—now—with me? Come, child! Suppose we go together!'

She stared at him, then darted about the room with little springs of excitement. She clapped her hands softly, her eyes alight and shining.

'Uncle Dick! You really mean it? Wouldn't it be grand!'

'Of course, I mean it. See! I'm dressed and ready!' And he pointed to his boots and clothes.

'It's the very best thing we can do, really,' she said, trying to speak gravely, but the mischievous element uppermost at the idea of the secret nocturnal journey. 'They'll see that you're not afraid, and you'll be safe then for ever and ever and ever! Hooray!'

She twirled the tam-o'-shanter in the air above her head, skipping in her childish joy.

'And we'll go past *Fräulein's* door,' she insisted mischievously, as he took her outstretched hand and led the way on tiptoe down the dark front stairs.

'Hush!' he whispered gruffly. 'Don't talk so loud.' She fastened up her garments, and they moved like shadows through the sleeping house.

15

That journey he made with this 'child of Nature' among the dripping trees and along soaked paths was one that Eliot never forgot. For him its meaning was unmistakable. His early life again supplied a parallel. He had once seen a wretched man marched out of camp with two days' rations to shift for himself in the wilderness as best he might—a prisoner convicted of treachery, but whose life was spared on the chance that he might redeem it, or die in the attempt. He had seen it done by redskins, he had seen it done by white. And hanging had been better. Yet the crime—stealing a horse, or sneaking another's 'grub -stakes'—was one that civilisation punishes with a paltry fine, or condones daily as permissible 'business acumen.'

In primitive conditions it was a crime against the higher law. It was sinning against Nature. And Nature never is deceived.

Richard Eliot was now being drummed out of camp. And the child who led him, mischief in her eyes and the joy of forbidden pleasure in her heart, was all unconscious of the awful role she played. Yet it was she who as well had pleaded for his life and saved him.

Nature turned him out; the Place rejected him; and Mánya saw him safely to the confines of that wilderness of houses, ugliness, commercial desolation where he must wander, till he re-made his soul or lost it altogether.

They cautiously opened the front door, and the damp air rushed to meet them.

'Hush!' he repeated, closing it carefully behind him. But the child was already upon the lawn. Beyond her, dark blots against the sky, rose the massed outline of the little pointed hills. There were no stars anywhere, though the clouds were breaking into thinning troops; but it was not too dark to see, for a moon watched them somewhere from her place of hiding. The air was warm and very sweet, left breathing by the storm.

'Hush, Mánya!' he whispered again, ill at ease to see her go. She ran back, her feet inaudible upon the thick, wet lawn, and took his hand. 'We'll go by the Piney Valley,' she said, assuming leadership. And he made no objection, though this was the direction of the sample pits. It led also, he remembered, to the Mill—the spot where she who had left him in charge had gone upon her long, long journey.

They went forward side by side. The wind below them hummed gently in the tree-tops, but it did not reach their faces. The whole wet world lay breathing softly about them, exhausted by the tempest. It was very still. It watched them pass. There was no effort to detain them. And in Dick Eliot's heart was a pain that searched him like a pain of death itself.

But his companion, he now clearly realised, was merely the child again—eerie, wonderful, eldritch, but still the little Mánya that he knew so well. Mischief was in her heart, and the excitement of unlawful adventure in her blood; but nothing more. The vast obsessing Entity that had constituted her judge and executioner was now entirely gone. He was spared the added shame of knowing that she realised what she did.

Sometimes she left his side, to come back presently with a little rush of pleasurable alarm. He was uncertain whether he liked best her going from him or her sudden return. Their tread was now muffled by the needles as they went slowly down the pathways of the Piney

Valley. The occasional snapping of small twigs alone betrayed their movements. Heavy branches, soaked like sponges, splashed showers on the ground when their shoulders brushed them in passing, and drops fell of their own weight with mysterious little thuds like footsteps everywhere about them in the woods.

Mánya dived away from his side. She came back sometimes in front of him and sometimes behind. He never quite knew where she was. His mind, indeed, neglected her, for his thoughts were concentrated within himself. Her movements were the movements of a block of shadow, shifting here and there like shadows of trees and clouds in faint moonlight.

'Uncle, tell me one thing,' he heard with a start, as she suddenly stood in front of him across the narrow pathway, and so close that he nearly bumped against her. 'Isn't there something here that's angry with you? Something you've done wrong to?'

'Hush, child! Don't say such things!' He felt the shiver run through him. He pushed her forward with his hands.

'But they're being said—all round us. Uncle, don't you hear them?' she insisted.

'I've always loved the Place. We've always been happy here together.' He whispered it, as though a terror was in him lest it should be overheard and—contradicted.

Her answer flabbergasted him. Her intuitions were so uncannily direct and piercing.

'That's what I meant. You've been unkind. You've hurt it.'

'Mánya,' he repeated severely, 'you must not say such things. And you must not think them.'

'I'm so awfully sorry, Uncle Dick,' she said softly in the dark, and promptly kissed him. The kiss went like a stab into his heart.

Then she was gone again, and he caught her light footstep several yards in front, as though a shower of drops had fallen on the needles.

'Uncle,' came her voice again close beside him. She stood on tiptoe and pulled his ear down to the level of her lips. 'Hold my hand tight. We're coming near now.' She was curiously excited.

'To the Mill?' he asked, knowing quite well she meant another thing.

'No, to the pits the men dug,' she answered, nestling in against him, while his own voice echoed faintly, 'Yes, the sample pits.' He felt like passing the hostile outposts of the Camp who would shoot him but for the presence of the appointed escort.

A sigh of lonely wind went past them with its shower of drops. And these little hands of wind with their fingers of sweet rain helped forward his expulsion. The empty wilderness beyond lay waiting for his soul. It heard him coming.

And a curious, deep revelation of the child's state of mind then rushed suddenly upon him. He knew that she expected something. And her answer to the question he put explained his own thought to himself.

'What is it you expect, Mánya?' he had asked unwisely.

'Not *expect* exactly, Uncle, for that would be the wrong way. But I *know*.'

And several kinds of fear shot through him as he heard it, for the words lifted a veil and let him see into her mind a moment. She had said another of her profoundly mystical truths. Expectation, anticipation, he divined, would provide a mould for what was coming, would give it shape, but yet not quite its natural shape. To anticipate keenly meant to attract too quickly: to force. The expectant desire would coax what was coming into an unnatural form that might be dreadful because not quite true. Let the thing approach in its own way, uninvited by imaginative dread. Let it come upon them as it would, deciding its own shape of arrival. To expect was to invite distortion. This flashed across him behind her simple words.

'You fearful child!' he whispered, forcing an unnatural little laugh.

'The soft, wet, sticky things, half yellow and half white,' she began, resenting his laughter,' always moving, and never looking twice the same—'

Then, before he could stop her, she stopped of her own accord.

She clutched his arm. He understood that it was the closeness of the thing that had inspired the atrocious words. She held his arm so tightly that it hurt. They stood in the presence of others than themselves.

Yet these Others had not *come* to them. The movement of approach was not really movement at all. It was a condition in himself had altered so that he knew. Out here the veil had thinned a little, as it had thinned in the room an hour ago. And he saw space otherwise. This Power that in humanity lies normally inarticulate was breaking through. In the room its language had been a stammer; it was a stammer now. Or, in the terms of sight, it was a little fragment utterly inexplicable by itself, since the entire universe is necessary for its complete expression.

Yet Eliot did perceive the enormous thing behind—the thing to which he had been unfaithful by prostituting his first original love. And the fact that it was interwoven with his ordinary little human feelings at the same time only added to the bewilderment of its stupendous reality.

He saw for a fleeting moment just as Mánya saw—from her immediate point of view.

'It's here,' she whispered, in a voice that sounded most oddly everywhere; 'it's here, the angry thing you've hurt.'

On either side of the path, where the heatherland came close, he saw the openings the men had dug—pale, luminous patches of whitish yellow. Between the bushy tufts they shone faintly gleaming against the night. Perspective, in that instant, became the merest trick of sight, a trivial mental jugglery. That slope of coal-black moor actually was extraordinarily near. The tree-tops were just as well beneath his feet, or he stood among their roots. Either was true. There was neither up nor down. The sky was in his hands, a little thing; or the stars and moon hid washed within the current of his blood. Size was illusion, as relative as time. No object in itself had any 'size' at all. He saw her universe, all true, as ever, but from another point of view. And the entire Place ran down here to a concentrated point. The sample pits pressed close against his face.

'The pits,' she whispered, with a sound of wind and water in her breath.

So, for a moment, he saw from the point of view whence Mánya always saw. He and the child and the Spirit of the Place stood side by side on that narrow shelf of darkness, sharing a joint and absolute comprehension. Her elemental aspect became his own, for his inner eye was against the peep-hole through which her Behind -the -Scenes was visible. He realised a new thing, grand as a field of stars.

For the Place here focussed almost into sentiency. Those slow-moving forces that stir to growth in crystals, waken and breathe in plants, and first in the animal world know consciousness, here moved vast and inchoate, through the structure of the dream-estate he owned. Yet moved not blind and inarticulate. For the stress of some impulse, normally undivined by men, urged them towards articulate expression. Here was reaction approximate to those reactions of the nervous cells which in their ultimate result men call emotions. And this irresistible correspondence between the two appalled him.

The raw material of definite sensation here poured loose and terrible about him from the ground. In them, moreover, was anger, protest, warning, and a menacing resentment—all directed against his mean, insignificant being. From these sample pits issued the menace and the warning, just as literally as there issued from them also the soft, white clay that would degrade the immemorial beauty he had once thought he loved with a clean, pure love. The pits were wounds. They drew all the feelings of the injured Place into the tenderness of sentient organs.

But behind the threatening anger he recognised a softer passion too. There was a sadness, a deep yearning, and a searching melancholy as well, that seemed to bear witness to his rejection with a sighing as of the sea and wood and hills.

And here, doubtless, came in the interweaving of his own little human emotions. For an overpowering sorrow soaked his heart and mind. The judgment that found him wanting woke all his stores of infinite regret. It would have been better for him had he found that millstone which can save the soul, because it removes temptation.

'It is too late,' breathed round him in three weeping voices that passed out between his lips as a single cry together. 'It is too late.'

Yet nothing happened; that is, he saw nothing—nothing translatable by any words that he could find. Time dwindled and expanded curiously. The past ran on before him, and the future grouped itself behind his back. The seconds and minutes which men tick off from the apparent movement of the sun gave place to some condition within himself where they lay gathered for ever into the circle of the Present. He remembers no actual sequence of acts or movements. Duration drew its horns back into a single point. . . . It is sure, however, that these two human beings marched presently on. They steadily became disentangled from the spot, and somehow or other moved away from the staring pits.

For Eliot, looking back, recalls that it felt like walking past the mouths of loaded cannon; also, that the pits watched them out of sight as portraits follow a moving figure with their expressionless stare. He thinks that he looked straight before him as he went. He is sure no single word was spoken—until they left the trees behind and emerged into the open. The Mill, the old, familiar building, was the thing that first restored him to a normal world again. He saw its outline, humped and black, shouldering its way against the sky. He heard the water running under the wheel. But even the Mill, like a hooded figure, turned its face away. It expressed the melancholy of a multitude. And the woods were everywhere full of tears.

Mánya, he realised then beside him, was making the humming sound of the water that flowed beneath that motionless wheel. Her voice became the voice of the Place—the undifferentiated sound of Nature. It was the voice of dismissal and farewell. Here was the Gateway through which his soul passed out into the Wilderness.

He involuntarily stooped down to feel her, and she lifted her face up in the darkness and kissed him. But it was across a barrier that she kissed him. He already stood outside.

★★★★★★★★★★★★

And half an hour later they were indoors again and the house was still. Mánya slept as soundly as the placid Fräulein Bühlke or the motherly Mrs. Coove doubtless also slept.

But he lay battling with strange thoughts for hours. Night and the wind were oddly mingled with them; water, hills, and masses of strong landscape too. They rose before his mind's eye in a giant panorama, endlessly moving past beneath huge skies, and visible against a pale background of luminous, yellowish white.

It had strange movements of its own, this yellowish background, like the swaying of a curtain on the stage; and sometimes it surged forwards with a smothering sweep that enveloped everything of beauty he had ever known. It then obliterated the world. Stars were extinguished; scenery turned to soil. The Spectre of the Clay he had invoked possessed the Place.

He lay there frightened in his sleepless bed and saw the dawn—a helpless little mortal, destroyed by his faithlessness and breach of trust. And all night long there lay outside, yet watching him, something else that equally never slept—agile, alert, unconquerable. Only it was no longer *disturbed*. For its purpose was accomplished. It had turned him out.

And it is not necessary to tell how John Casanova Murdoch soon thereafter took the work in hand and developed the Place, as he expressed it, 'without a hitch.' For John C. had made no promises of love; nor had he pretended to establish with Nature that intimate relationship of trust and worship which invokes the spiritual laws. Nature took no note of him, for he worked frankly with her, and his motive, if not exalted, was at least a pure one. And the clay, as he phrased it a little later in his expressive Western lingo, soon was 'paying hand over fist. The money was pouring in—more money than you could shake a stick at!'

ALSO FROM LEONAUR
AVAILABLE IN SOFTCOVER OR HARDCOVER WITH DUST JACKET

MR MUKERJI'S GHOSTS *by S. Mukerji*—Supernatural tales from the British Raj period by India's Ghost story collector.

KIPLINGS GHOSTS *by Rudyard Kipling*—Twelve stories of Ghosts, Hauntings, Curses, Werewolves & Magic.

THE COLLECTED SUPERNATURAL AND WEIRD FICTION OF WASHINGTON IRVING: VOLUME 1 *by Washington Irving*—Including one novel 'A History of New York', and nine short stories of the Strange and Unusual.

THE COLLECTED SUPERNATURAL AND WEIRD FICTION OF WASHINGTON IRVING: VOLUME 2 *by Washington Irving*—Including three novelettes 'The Legend of the Sleepy Hollow', 'Dolph Heyliger', 'The Adventure of the Black Fisherman' and thirty-two short stories of the Strange and Unusual.

THE COLLECTED SUPERNATURAL AND WEIRD FICTION OF JOHN KENDRICK BANGS: VOLUME 1 *by John Kendrick Bangs*—Including one novel 'Toppleton's Client or A Spirit in Exile', and ten short stories of the Strange and Unusual.

THE COLLECTED SUPERNATURAL AND WEIRD FICTION OF JOHN KENDRICK BANGS: VOLUME 2 *by John Kendrick Bangs*—Including four novellas 'A House-Boat on the Styx', 'The Pursuit of the House-Boat', 'The Enchanted Typewriter' and 'Mr. Munchausen' of the Strange and Unusual.

THE COLLECTED SUPERNATURAL AND WEIRD FICTION OF JOHN KENDRICK BANGS: VOLUME 3 *by John Kendrick Bangs*—Including twor novellas 'Olympian Nights', 'Roger Camerden: A Strange Story', and ten short stories of the Strange and Unusual.

THE COLLECTED SUPERNATURAL AND WEIRD FICTION OF MARY SHELLEY: VOLUME 1 *by Mary Shelley*—Including one novel 'Frankenstein or the Modern Prometheus', and fourteen short stories of the Strange and Unusual.

THE COLLECTED SUPERNATURAL AND WEIRD FICTION OF MARY SHELLEY: VOLUME 2 *by Mary Shelley*—Including one novel 'The Last Man', and three short stories of the Strange and Unusual.

THE COLLECTED SUPERNATURAL AND WEIRD FICTION OF AMELIA B. EDWARDS *by Amelia B. Edwards*—Contains two novelettes 'Monsieur Maurice', and 'The Discovery of the Treasure Isles', one ballad 'A Legend of Boisguilbert' and seventeen short stories to cill the blood.